House *of* Secrets

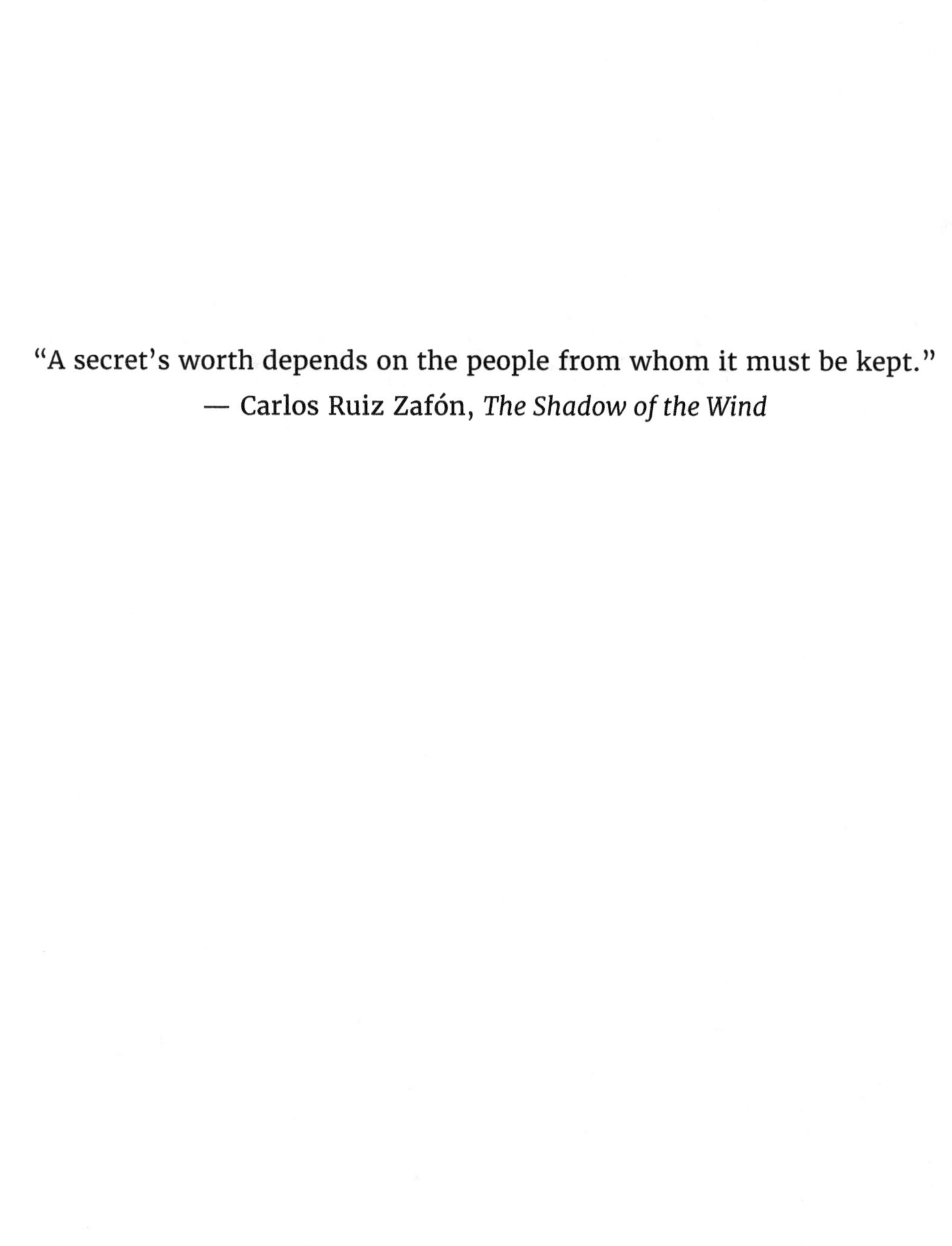
"A secret's worth depends on the people from whom it must be kept."
— Carlos Ruiz Zafón, The Shadow of the Wind

House *of* Secrets

Every Room Holds a Story

Presented by

The Ohio Writers' Association

House *of* Secrets

Every Room Holds a Story

Published by:
Ohio Writers' Group
DBA Ohio Writers' Association
838 Campbell Avenue
Columbus, OH 43223 USA

Made possible in part by a grant from the Ohio Arts Council

Typesetting: George Pallas

Cover Design: Joseph Graves

Editors: George Pallas, Jim Hodnett, Brian Luke, Christina Moore

Print ISBN-13: 979-8-9870174-3-2

eBook ISBN-13: 979-8-9870174-4-9

Audiobook ISBN-13: 979-8-9870174-5-6

Printed in USA

Contents

Introduction

Secrets. They are an integral part of the human experience. They are hidden compartments within each of us where we store our deepest hopes, fears, desires, and vulnerabilities. Secrets also give us a measure of control, allowing us to decide what we reveal to the world and what we reserve for ourselves.

If keeping secrets is integral to the human soul, so is the desire to uncover the secrets of others. Our often insatiable curiosity leads us to uncover buried truths, to unravel the mysteries others try to keep to themselves.

The delicate balance between preserving, revealing, and discovering secrets is part of our humanity. From these related but conflicting impulses, we develop trust and discretion and learn to cherish the power of knowledge.

House of Secrets is a collection of twenty-six short stories related in some manner to guarding or uncovering secrets, written by emerging writers who have significant connections to the State of Ohio. You are sure to find enjoyment within these pages.

"A secret remains a secret until you make someone promise never to reveal it"

— Fausto Cercignani

The Parlor

It's All About Relationships

"I never understood why Clark Kent was so hell bent on keeping Lois Lane in the dark."
— Audrey Niffenegger, *The Time Traveler's Wife*

Art House

Martin Vian

"*I paint what I see hiding.*" — Emilia Essig, *One Possible Future*

Dak has a new empty place.

Unpacking the box marked *Bathroom*, I can't help looking at my tooth—the half on the counter next to my toothbrush, razor, and car keys. The chunk of molar has lain there for a couple of days, and I miss it. Miss having it in my mouth. The place where it'd been now feels craggy and empty and foreign, and the new topography is unsettling. I force myself to put a few more items from the box into my new medicine cabinet hidden behind the vanity mirror. These things I take or use or apply daily are part of my routine, and any routine feels important right now. But they *are* just things I remind myself, not really part of me.

The part of me on the counter looks ugly. Not the bright white enamel a tooth ought to be, but dishwater white, coffee-stained. I'll need to brush more. Will they all begin to break apart? Is something weakening my hard bits? Will my bones come next? I've never broken a bone. Not one. This, despite the childhood of climbing trees and buildings, hopping fences and even trains. *Reckless*, my father might have said. *Curious*, my mother might say.

I imagine the other parts I've lost as the tip of my tongue traces this new gap over and over. I know I'll get used to it as time goes by, but right now, I feel Dak's crater and look at Dak's tooth, and I feel broken. It makes me want to put the thing in my pocket so that I won't lose this, too, on top of it all. I don't. It isn't that I feel unbreakable. Those days are long gone. But to be brought down—dentally—by a popcorn kernel is a stark reminder of my disintegrating reality. Its fragility. Things weren't always so fragile.

♦

Some things go unmentioned (decades back).

The new movie, *Brazil*, was absurd but artful, with a sort of surreal romance, so it made for a perfect first date. First *official* date. I knew Siggy pretty well. Really well, in some ways. In art classes together all through high school, we were always on the same wavelength, it seemed. She was a natural–pretty, very smart, and quiet. Quiet, that is, next to my boisterousness—usually clownish attempts at sarcasm and counter-culture commentary. My edgier teachers had appreciated this in me, I imagined. In one parent-teacher conference, my mother was consoled, *"Yes, Dak's a pain in our butts, but—he'll make a really great adult."*

Siggy seemed adult already. And now, a year out of high school, I'd finally found the nerve to ask her to do something that would *mean* something. Now we'd be more than classmates, comrades, fellow artists.

"Alrighty then. Pretty wild ride," I said when we hit the sidewalk in front of the theater. We both squinted hard at the assault of daylight after the dark in there. A couple walking ahead of us was muttering about similarities to 1984's Big Brother, and I couldn't help but shake my head. "Oh God no. So different," I said quietly. "I mean, this is a satire or whatever, and Orwell is scary as shit. Menacing, you know. Way more calculating or plotting or—"

"Machiavellian," Siggy offered.

"Yeah. Yeah, exactly. 1984's Big Brother is super Machiavellian. But the Ministry of Information in *Brazil* is just sort of bumbling through with big iron boots. Sure, it's futuristic and dystopian and all that, but it's just layers and layers of this kind of Frankensteined techno-bureaucracy built up and bolted together. The whole machinery of it is—"

"Kind of Rube Goldberg," she said, "I totally agree," with a sort of puff. Not a full giggle or laugh, but playful. And she smiled her quiet smile.

She was so smart. So exactly right. So out of my league. "Yes. Totally," I added lamely.

We were quiet for another two blocks, and I felt the importance of this or at least the novelty of it. Giving each other space to process what we'd just seen, neither of us felt the need to fill the silence. My dates with other girls—other *women*—almost always slipped into conversational mutual masturbation: I ask you something (because I'm interested in you), and you tell me something poignant or amusing (but not too revealing, to make me feel like I asked a good question), then I say how cool or funny or amazing that is (to make you feel good about sharing) and I say how it reminds me of a story of mine (going only skin deep), and on it would go—never getting anywhere near a climax (at least conversationally). But it was different with Siggy. Or it might be if I could just keep being myself, whatever *that* was. *Chancy*, I thought.

In the next block was The Bexley. It was unusual to have two theaters within blocks of each other, but The Bexley Art Theater wasn't a normal theater. It was a house of unmentionable things. *"Art"* was, in this case, code for *pornography*.

And the fact that it was in Bexley made it a contradiction. Bexley was mostly old-money mansions and always seemed to me a stuffy highbrow neighborhood. Porn was rarely highbrow, but there the place was, tucked in among the other, more *upstanding* storefronts. Those shop owners all hated having the art theater as a neighbor. The city, too, was reportedly trying to run the place out, but apparently, pornography was doing well enough to pay the presumably highbrow rent. In a few years, the internet would make The Bexley a relic, but for now, the "art house"—its category co-mingled with truly experimental cinema—was alive and well.

I wanted to make movies. Regular movies. Siggy and I had started college that year, and she was studying fine art—painting specifically. She'd tested out of most of her freshman Gen-Ed requirements and actually had some in-major classes already: painting, figure drawing, anatomy. I wanted to study film, but they shuttered the program that very year. So I would try theater. No, psychology. No, broadcast journalism. I hadn't tested out of math or English or basic chemistry, but there would be time for those later. Instead, I just took classes that sparked my imagination. Then after a year of dipping in toes, I opted out instead—for a while—to look around.

Walking past The Bexley, we both stayed quiet. Now, *this* quiet was an awkward one, at least for me. Posters in the blacked-out windows, with their titles provoking and images titillating, felt risky to comment on. Siggy and I had not been intimate. *Not just yet*, I thought, as if I could decide. And so I only managed a smirk at the graphic window dressing.

I dared a glance at her face and imagined I saw the gentle tug of a smile. I felt a tiny thing quiver—two tiny things—tiny and warm and electric. One in my head, right behind my mind's eye, and another somewhere deep in my pelvic region. And they reached up and down at once, rooting through or around things inside me, meeting in the middle of my chest where they blossomed into a deep breath.

She looked at me looking at her. "You okay?"

"Yeah," I said. "All good." *Perfect*, I thought.

Siggy was every inch who I imagined spending my creative life beside. Exactly who I'd cast in the story of my bohemian future. I pictured her paintings in every room of our place. Canvases everywhere, freshly stretched and gessoed and waiting on her spattered easel. Works-in-progress drying against the walls. A whispering tinge of turpentine and oil paint and maybe sandalwood in the air. Reels of film would be stacked on my makeshift door-desk around a second-hand 16mm film editor, scraps of celluloid, and splicing tape littering the desktop. And there'd be a wildly eclectic collection of records—vinyl LPs—spanning wooden plank shelves across cinderblocks. It was so clear. I'd visited this place so many times in my head.

"So, what's our sequel?" I asked.

"I'm thinking Saturday. My place. If you want."

◆

Saturday night unfolds.

Siggy's apartment was in an old brick row house that'd been partitioned—up and down—to make two rentable spaces. Hers was down. Small, artfully simple, and tidy. Comfortable, I thought as I surveyed the spare furnishings and browsed her collection of offbeat curios perched here and there next to a book or plant or photo frame. Vintage troll doll. Velvet kaleidoscope. Balsa wood butterfly with real wings affixed. When I lifted it, the delicate blue wings beat softly until its rubber band unwound. I laid it down again, spent and nearly weightless.

"Wine?" Siggy asked, stepping half out of the small kitchen, holding a bottle and two tumblers.

"Sure." I grinned. "Thanks," I added as my finger lightly traced the edge of a simple wooden mantle above the bricked-over fireplace. "Norwegian?"

Siggy poked her head back around the corner, brows arched in a question. Then a smile crept in as my reference dawned, and her brows arched again—this time not as a question. "Put on some music if you want." She nodded to the album collection and turntable. "They're organized by when they came out—so don't give me shit about *Let it Be* and *Abbey Road*," she added, preemptive. There had always been music playing in Mr. McGill's art classes, so we knew each other's musical weaknesses well.

"This isn't the normal cover art," I noted as we nursed our wine to the strains of U2's *Boy* filling the room.

"It's an early British release," Siggy said. "Isn't the photo beautiful?" It was. The grainy black & white image of a young boy—blown out to mostly white—shirtless, arms behind his head with an indecipherable stare was stark and beautiful. "They changed it for the American release. The record company worried about the public reaction to a bare-chested little boy."

"What—like *pedophilia*-kind of worried?"

"Prigs," Siggy said.

"Total prigs!" And we both laughed.

We reached the bottom of the bottle with the fade of the final track, "Shadows and Tall Trees." So when another cut started—just raw guitar swimming in reverb, like bagpipes in a gymnasium—I scanned the album jacket. "Wait, what is this?"

"Unlisted track. Only on some early releases," Siggy said and emptied her glass. "Called 'Saturday Night' or 'Saturday Matinee,' depending on who you ask."

"Seems fitting." I finished my last sip too. "Well, we missed the matinee, but it's still not too late for a movie."

"Never."

And with that, we set out on High Street to find a film—strolling, talking, not talking—in the perfect cool summer twilight.

"Fucking Sig and Dak!" It was jarring, and we both swiveled, then took a second to recognize our high school friend. "Shit, what are the chances?" Jenna said, hugging us both. "Good to see you. Both. Together!"

Blushing, smiling, but with nothing to say to that, we traded looks. Then Siggy, seeming not entirely sure what we'd just agreed to, invited Jenna back to the apartment. "Just to hang out for...a bit," Siggy said, emphasizing "a bit." Then added, "Sorry to say, we finished the wine."

At this, Jenna lifted a paper bag conspicuously shaped like a bottle. "No worries, I'll share!"

It was good to catch up back at Siggy's place. It might be *our* place, I thought, then dismissed it, then thought it again as we traded stories of the old days. The notion of *old days* would be a stretch for such newly-minted adults, but Jenna'd known me since elementary school—so, *lots* to mine. She dominated the reminiscing, though much of it featured/embarrassed me.

Siggy grinned and occasionally shook her head at the exploits, only some of which she'd heard before. Tales of climbing trees, exploding model airplanes, and making Super 8 movies as tweens wandered into the Home Ec mishap, cream pies for our Nazi librarian, and the Medusa-like sculpture—sanctioned by Mr. McGill and spray painted in front of the high school. And there was the apparent mismatch of athletics with rock & roll and psychedelics, where I dabbled.

"If the track team even counts as athletics," Jenna added with her signature snark.

All of it was evidence of my attention splintering as my interests crept out in every direction—like roots or branches getting thinner and thinner as they sought out water or the sun. Curious. Reckless.

I watched Siggy, mostly laughing at all this. At my wandering. It seemed she knew where she was headed and was drawing a straight line to it. I wondered at this, appreciated it, even envied it.

I appreciated Jenna's energy too, and her unfiltered humor, but as she talked, I realized how much I wanted my date back. I'd had some brief, nearly meaningless carnal history with Jenna and knew I didn't want to repeat that...*configuration* tonight. The realization surprised me—a moment I noted with clarity. That I wanted something else. Wanted something that *was* meaningful. I kept catching Siggy's eye, pretty sure she was on the same page. Then, just as it felt like one of us might need to force the issue, Jenna stood abruptly and declared, as was her way, "This was fucking amazing, but I need to go. Leave you guys to it." Hugs, kisses, and she was gone.

"Well, okay then," Siggy said, watching our party crasher head off down the walk and up the street in the now starlit evening.

"Well, okay then," I agreed and reached for her hand, not tentatively, but gently, weaving my fingers with hers. And I waited for her, hoping we were in sync.

She turned, that smile tugging again at her cheek, and she led me to the couch. I started to sit, but she just shook her head a little. She pulled up one of the cushions, and I caught on. The couch unfolded into something like a cloud—soft white linens, tousled from being folded away, inviting, dreamy. It may have been the wine, but the whole scene felt dreamy as I kissed her, then pulled her close—for the first time.

The feeling of newness stirred me. The arch of her back, the curve of her slight hips, the feel of her skin as my hand traced a line up her back under the loose cotton of her shirt, all so new. Her lips were full and soft, pressed against mine—warm and sweet with the lingering trace of wine. This treasure had been right here, and I'd only ever grazed the surface—and only from a distance. As we maneuvered onto the bed and shed our layers, it all seemed so breezy and so quiet. So impossibly tender.

Something unfamiliar poured into what'd held a mere friendship only moments earlier and now billowed out like rich cream in coffee, filling this redrawn *us* with a new lightness. The suppleness of it all—the sheets, the pillows, her hair, lips, skin—everything, frictionless. Ethereal. Tangled pathways that normally busied my imagination, leading off in every direction—places I'd go, things I'd make, worlds I'd explore—they all fell away. I was left here, only in this moment, with Siggy. Around and surrounded by Siggy.

My lips traced the folds of her ear, down the curve of her neck, over the tiny well where her collarbones met, down over her breasts and belly. I ranged over her exquisite outer terrain and then her inner landscape—a secret miracle of a place—and I lost myself in her. Altogether lost our boundary. One moment I could feel where I ended and she began, and then, surrendering, I simply couldn't. I imagined, from how she moved and from the breathless sounds she made and from the touch she offered me, that she might be there too. With me. In me too.

The love we made there was actual and shimmering and, as it would turn out, momentary.

~~But Still~~ *And* it would remain a touchstone of sublime and delicate pleasure for the rest of my life—an intimacy I'd try to recreate, without luck, likely forever. But it drew out something, or more accurately, it laid open something in me that I wasn't ready to have out there—planted in the world.

With men (and maybe women) on the verge of being consumed, the fear of losing oneself inevitably sets in. And like most fears, it's a mess of things: doubting our map, misreading our compass, trading pencil for ink. Disbelieving our worthiness. Warring pictures strained my imagination—between the artist's life and all the other lives one might lead. So when she invited me to go out to celebrate her birthday, there was a reason I couldn't go. A reason, when looking back, I wouldn't recall. More occasions, more calls wondering where my head was, what I was thinking, why I couldn't make it work. Some dignified exasperation on Siggy's part.

A year went by, and the conversation faded. Our connection sputtered, and I just couldn't see my hand in it. I didn't hear the hurt in her. Not then. But there were times I would imagine myself in some glorious future, being interviewed for something I'd (finally) achieved, and I'd be asked the question, "If you could talk to your younger self now, what advice would you give?" My imagined answer was always something nauseating: "Keep trying things" or "Never stop believing in yourself." But then I'd get the question, "Any regrets?" And as the years piled on, the answer to that one got clearer. It gnawed at my conscience. Remorse turned to scar tissue, the ache of it subsumed.

◆

There's a floor below the cutting room.

As will happen in a life of experimentation, a lot doesn't pan out. Maybe most of it. Five years of swirling that pan and no real glints of anything. Needing a job and hoping for something—really *anything*—related to film, I looked for work as a projectionist. Half a dozen job interviews left me still panning. Without actual projectionist experience, no respectable cinema or theater chain would hire me. But The Bexley Art Theater had no such standards. Or rather, basic mechanical competence and walking upright seemed to be the bar.

The projection job itself was technical and something I could get my head around. My hands, too, since it was still a very physical job in those days. Reels of film lay flat on their sides on big circular platters three feet wide. Film spooled from one of the feed platters, sprocketed past the projection light and lens, then wound back onto a take-up platter below. These rigs were meant to eliminate reel changes, make the viewing experience seamless, and theoretically free up the projectionist during the film. In practice, what I ended up doing surprisingly often was splicing the film back together when it broke. These films were not well cared for.

Almost without fail—comically, in retrospect—the film would break right at a climax. Literally. On screen: legs in the air, mid-thrust, mid-wail, mid-shudder. Screen fluttering to bright white, I would race to pause the spinning platters, cut the film at the break so ends would match up (sometimes sacrificing a frame or two), apply splicing tape at the new seam, and re-engage the platter. Then, as the new jump cut coiled onto the take-up platter, I'd slip a little square of sponge in where the splice was to mark it amidst the windings. Presumably so it could be repaired more expertly later by some proper porn-film repair team—including re-inserting any removed frames. But the box in the corner of the projection booth brimming with discarded celluloid scraps suggested, for this sort of film, those frames just wouldn't be missed.

Fifty-two seconds for a splice was my fastest—actually, a very long time in this context. Groans from the theater below were full of exasperation from patrons trying to keep up with the action. At least, that's what I imagined when I allowed myself to imagine any detail of that nether space. Thankfully, as the projectionist, I never had to actually enter the theater proper. A cleaning person or crew—I never laid eyes on them—must've done their work overnight. But other employees, like Lucas, who worked the ticket counter and concessions, might be asked to go in there between showings and screw the lightbulbs back into their sockets in the sconces along each wall. Patrons would unscrew them to get some imagined privacy in their little corner of the theater.

When I wasn't splicing breaks in the films, I wrote. Working on a screenplay, making scant progress during stretches of "plot development" happening on screen between splices. My story was trying hard to be a love story against a backdrop of political intrigue. I scribbled out scenes longhand on a legal pad with AMPAD stamped in the blue binding strip at the top and nearly as many doodles in the margins as words on the page. I tried to ignore the attempts at acting and laughable lines delivered on screen between the real action. Then I tried to block out those sounds of escalating intercourse: moaning, squishing, sucking, throaty obscenities, and truly rotten jazz. I thought, wrote, scratched out my own shitty dialogue or scene direction while listening for the snap, clack and flap of a break in the film.

Some days I might produce a few pages, but the environment was seeping in and pulling my plot in directions I hated myself for. It wasn't the raw acrobatics that soured but the lie of it all. The emptiness, in light of what I had known, made a mess of me. When I was done most days and headed back to my crappy apartment, I felt covered in a miserable residue—a confusing mixture of degradation and arousal. Often I'd need a long shower to let it out and wash it away. Then *Casablanca* or *The Adventures of Buckaroo Banzai Across the Eighth Dimension* would go in the VHS machine, and the world would almost right itself. Almost.

"I need you to work the ticket counter, Dak," Ritchie said when I showed up one Wednesday. Ritchie ran The Bexley. The other projectionist would stay late to cover me. "Just until Lucas gets here." It would be fine, Ritchie assured me.

Down there in the lobby were concessions and posters adorning the walls, almost like a real theater—a mainstream theater, a family theater, with block-busters—but decidedly off. Our decor reeked of tacky Vegas burlesque. And the patrons were a mixed lot. Surprising, really. From run-down middle-aged men to young bankers or lawyers or accountants to one couple who must've been in their eighties. The old man looked downright gentlemanly in his wheelchair: heather cardigan, elegant cashmere scarf, silver hair, neat and trim. His wife (I assumed) wore a very fine plaid suit of Scottish wool—rich red, white, and black, somehow both conservative and bold. They bought their tickets, quiet and straight-faced and utterly unashamed.

"Enjoy the show," I heard myself say.

The man nodded, just barely, looking unaccustomed to any actual interaction in this place. Then his wife maneuvered to open the door to the theater proper in a well-practiced move and wheeled her man into the dark.

An hour in, the phone rang. "Bexley Art Thea—" I started.

"Jesus hates child molesters!" Click.

Lucas, who had just arrived, must've read the look on my face because he lowered his voice and said, "Been getting a lot of those since the story broke on the news." He looked apologetic and then sympathetic when my blank face made it clear I wasn't aware of *the story*. "Ritchie was accused by a...*prostitute*—" his voice hushing even more, "—of some pretty crazy stuff." Lucas scanned my face, maybe assessing what I could handle. "The guy makes us all look depraved." Ritchie had allegedly spent a long weekend with a young man, who was not legally an adult—a long weekend the young man apparently decided went too far.

I realized I was still holding the phone and set it quietly back on its hook.

"Or he might be after Ritchie's money," Lucas added.

"Ritchie has a lot of money?" I asked, my voice now a whisper too.

"Pretty nice car," Lucas said. "I don't know. Maybe."

"How does this place...doesn't it get to you?" I asked. "I mean, how do you fit *this*—" my eyes scanning the lobby, "—into the rest of your life?"

Lucas considered me and my question. Then he took a moment to fold his jacket and stow it under the ticket counter. "Sometimes, I go straight from here to the library."

"The bar?" There was a campus bar called The Library. I had never been.

"No, the *actual* library. The main branch downtown. And I just wander the stacks. Sit and read a little. Let that place be the place I remember before going home to Tommy."

I took Lucas's idea. But instead of the library, I went to the museum, hoping the beauty there might displace all that was staining my imagination. Admission was free on Sundays, and that was when I ran into her. Siggy had started using her given name, Emilia. I thought it sounded more serious. More *artistically* serious. And she looked amazing. Tougher, somehow, and even leaner in a stark white tee, jeans, black leather jacket, and Converse high-tops. She was painting a lot, showing her work, and getting some recognition—not a phenomenon, but, well, a painter.

When it was my turn, I talked about the screenplay. About the premise, the progress I was making, and how good I felt about this being *the* thing I needed to take it up a notch. My career in cinema that is. I wouldn't, of course, tell her about The Bexley. Unmentionable.

"I owe you an apology," she said once we'd covered the pleasantries.

Brows knitted. I'm sure I looked confused. *She* was apologizing to *me*. It didn't make any sense, and I readied myself for the rebuke I was owed instead.

"For making such a big deal about—our...time together," she said. Her tone was sincere, and the thought was well-considered. "I shouldn't have made the assumptions I did. And I'm sorry about that. About the fuss."

So few words, but each syllable crumpled me and cemented my sense of self-loathing. I was the one who'd made assumptions—imagined a whole life with her, or maybe with the *idea* of her—a whole *way* of life. And then I couldn't stay there. Couldn't be that person—or at least not *only* that person.

"No, you shouldn't...I was—" I sputtered, grasping at words.

"It's okay, Dak," she said quietly, holding my gaze for a long moment. This disarmed me and shushed me, and we walked, wordless, through the museum lobby and out into the dull gray Sunday.

"I'm glad I ran into you." She said it with an almost Siggy-esque smile. "Goodbye, Dak. Take care of yourself." We hugged, and as she turned back toward the museum doors, she explained, "I'm actually meeting someone."

"Oh," I managed.

"Great to see you," she said and walked back through the doors.

I turned and descended the marble steps, then crossed the pitted asphalt to my car in the visitor's lot.

"You stuck around longer than I thought you would," Ritchie said without much emotion.

I said goodbye to Lucas with a hug, and I left The Bexley, tucking the whole fact of it away. Just a few frames no one would miss.

◆

Secrets aren't kept, only outrun.

That life I'd imagined broke up and fell away with the passing months and years. The place it had been filled up with "reality," as my father might have quipped if he'd lived to offer quips. Like incessant waves against the rocks, five thousand days wore the rough landscape down to a smooth living. I spent those years finding a way to turn my general charm and enthusiasm into a career of sorts. Selling workplace training, of all things.

I'm making people smarter, I told myself. In the beginning, it was actual class-es with instructors where people could learn how to do whatever it was they did better. Then with the computer revolution came *virtual learning*—a wave of digital...everything. Somewhere in there, I married, and my marriage was good for a long time, or at least fruitful. We had a son who was a hellion, like me. Smart. And a smart ass, too, just as I had been. And we turned all our passions to raising that boy.

I took a job in management and got sucked into the jet stream. The living I made there was actual and substantial and, as it would turn out, addicting. At work, they called me David because that was my real name. My given name. Dak was a nickname coined somewhere in my childhood, and it faded. Promotions and commendations and raises came year after year. And yet, the better the suits, the more ill-fitting the part I needed to play wearing them. And no film or pages or art of any kind anywhere in sight. But, but, *but*, my new title was pretty darn good—vice president. The day I got it, I brought it home proudly and was about to tell my wife when she said she needed to go. As in, for good.

"It's not real anymore, David." Just like that.

"What? What about Dak?" I said. When the boy hit his teen years, my son took my nickname since I wasn't using it anymore. My wife explained how we'd share custody, though *custody* of that boy was a bit ironic. Not one to be *contained* by anybody. The younger Dak wasn't surprised when we told him. We all saw it coming, really. I could never quite manage to give my wife the happiness she was hoping for—my own. And so we'd divvy up our lives and our things, and we'd split the boy.

What I didn't see coming was the downsizing at work. "This isn't about you, David," my boss said, alongside the woman from HR nodding sympathetically. "The board needed us to cut 20%. It was an exceptionally hard decision." The man's tone was flat, having delivered this same speech a dozen times already. Though it wasn't about me specifically, I was nevertheless one of the cast-offs. Expendable. Dead weight.

I would keep the boxes I used to clear out my office, the contents of which mostly went into the dumpster. A nearly dead philodendron, folders filled with papers of great import just one day prior, the newly printed business cards proving I was a vice president for a minute and a half. But I needed more boxes to move my personal possessions out of the house, so I forced myself to be brutally unsentimental.

My brain hurt as I cleared my basement shelves, packing up books, old CDs, DVDs, and the even older VHS fossils, including *Casablanca* and *Buckaroo Banzai*. Sorting and sifting had always sapped my energy—narrowing of any kind. There were boxes for items I would move, a bin for trash, and one box for things the used book store might buy. I didn't need the money—not yet—but there were some things I couldn't quite bring myself to throw away.

The books on the highest shelf were my film books. Wedged between Eisenstein's Film Form and *Round up the Usual Suspects* was a legal pad stamped with the AMPAD emblem, doodles in the margins. I fingered the pages and the old ink, skimming what I'd once upon a time dreamed up, scratched out, and rewrote. Dialogue. Scene direction. Notes-to-self. I didn't really absorb the scrawled content. I was using too much mental energy trying to maintain my mantra of "no sentimentality." Still, it tugged at my will, daring me to smile or get misty. I sniffed the pages for some reason—stale paper and dust. A solemn deep breath, and then it left my fingers, seemingly in slow motion, flipping end-over-end, pages curling and flapping and landing, sheets tousled, in the trash bin. Unsentimental.

At the bookstore, there was a buying counter where they assessed the condition of books, records, CDs, and movies and assigned a value, and it was busy when I got there. So I stood in line, scrolling numbly through condolences on my phone—for my variety of recent losses. I used my foot to nudge the box of old media forward as the queue advanced bit by bit. When it was my turn, and I lifted my box to the counter, it took a moment to process her face. And judging by her narrowed eyes, it took Siggy a moment too.

"Hello, Dak." Her voice was the same, but her smile was different. Where there'd once been a connection between her smile and the future—*one possible future*—there was now just politeness.

"Oh my god, hi—" and I suddenly realized I didn't know what name I should use. Was she still *Siggy*, at least for some who knew her *before?* Or was she officially *Emilia*, through and through? Would using *Siggy* disrespect her professional name, her persona as an artist, her choices as an adult? "—it's so good to see you," I said, dodging it altogether. "How are you? Still painting?"

"I'm good," she said. "Yes, some. And working here."

"I love this place." I was a little too exuberant, but I was sincere—as in, *this would be a great place to work.*

"Just a couple of days a week."

"That's great."

"How about you? How are you doing?"

"Well—" I started and laughed a little, "—right now, I happen to be between things." I thought about the accomplishments (such as they were), the beautiful wife (soon to be not mine), the big house (soon to be not mine), the job title (only fleetingly mine), but I mentioned none of these. *Between things* sounded like something that might be chronic, like I couldn't hold a job, and that was not the impression I wanted her to have of me. Then I realized none of it would interest her anyway. Both because she likely wouldn't care about those things as tokens of a good life and, more painfully, because my life wasn't of consequence to her now in any way.

"I'm okay," I said. "Trying to clear out some stuff I don't need anymore." Indicating the books and CDs and movies she was removing from the box and stacking in their respective piles: *will buy* and *won't buy.*

She smiled politely, and then, when she pulled *Brazil* from the box, she paused. There wasn't so much a smile as a softening in the set of her jaw and just an extra blink or two of her eyes, lashes fluttering slowly as only butterfly wings can. Of course, I had no idea she'd be going through this box. I had been using my *no-sentimentality* filter, and there it was. "Sure you want to get rid of this?" she asked, brows arched.

I had no words—was for a moment suspended *between* words.

"At any rate, we have ten copies already," she added. "Meaning, we wouldn't buy it anyway. So I guess you'll hang on to that one."

I just smiled and nodded and then realized I should say *something*. Should *try* to say *something*. "Oh yeah, well, I needed a good one to watch with my son for movie night tonight."

"Oh," she said. "How old is your son? I mean—that's a pretty weird movie." And there was a real grin.

"Ha, he's fourteen, but Dak loves movies. The weirder, the better."

She looked confused.

"Sorry. He's Dak too. I mean, he's Dak *also*—not Dak the second. Little Dak. Though not so little anymore, I guess."

"Huh, novel move," she said. "So *Dak* gets another go at it," and she slid the *won't buy* pile back to me. "Well, I hope you have a great—weird movie night." Then she smiled in a way Siggy might have. "Take care, Dak. Good seeing you." And that was that.

My son had fallen asleep about the time Sam, *Brazil*'s hero, was apprehended by the Ministry of Information. So when I bit the popcorn kernel that busted my tooth, I had no one to share my astonishment with. I took the molar fragment into the bathroom and peered into my mouth, marveling at the place it'd been. There was no pain, just this new gap. I set the thing down next to my toothbrush with a pang of loss and a trace of reverence. Then I went back out and gently spun my son around to lie on the couch. The boy drew his knees up, and I covered him with a blanket, then stood there watching him dream while the credits rolled and the music played to its end.

◆

Now, just two days out, the tooth looks grayer. The space where it'd been will become part of a new landscape. And I've little doubt the broken edges will smooth a bit each year that passes. The new apartment is a small space, and the landscape here is still littered with moving boxes, including a few my son brought over. Stuff I guess the boy wants to have here when staying with me, which he isn't at the moment. On top of one of those boxes, written in black marker, are the words:

Dad's

WTF???

That's new, I think. Not curiosity, but curiosity about *me*. I wonder about all I've left out, and about how much is left to pass along—or even especially ~~important relevant~~ right to pass along—for posterity. Entire passages of this life belong in parentheses, but which ones?

I can't help myself. Inside the box is my old David Lee Roth tee shirt with a devil prancing behind bold block letters spelling PURE FUCKING ROCK. It's really more like a costume. I never really listen to David Lee Roth *or* Van Halen, so I understand why my son has a question about that. There are other items in the box, too, that probably do need some explaining when time allows. Near the bottom, some rumpled pages are sticking out, and I uncover the old legal pad. I flatten some of its creased pages, and a sigh escapes as something inside me flutters. The younger Dak must've rescued it from the trash bin back at the house—the house where I had been living until everything began to disintegrate. Not the art house, but the other one.

Martin Vian is an aspiring writer living in the Midwest. His many years as an experience designer, songwriter, and dogged family man have provoked his work in fiction—both short and long. Martin is an active member of multiple writing groups and is currently hard at work on his second novel.

Secret o' Life

Ed Davis

"**C**raig needs somebody full-time," I say while Vivienne serves up post-dinner lemongrass tea with gluten-free gingersnaps in her kitchen. Her place is like a monastery with statues, glass-beaded wall hangings, and quilted tapestries everywhere. "That woman from health care only comes in for a while every morning, then a few minutes in the evening. I've been walking Mahler while she's there, but I can do more, a lot more."

"Then perhaps the three of us should share responsibilities equally," she says, trying to head me off at the pass. But I'm ready for her.

"His house is tiny. The last thing a man recovering from his second brain surgery needs is a crowd."

She places her delicate china cup back on its saucer. "I think we both know who it is you don't want over there."

I try to look innocent, but you can't hide from her.

"Marla McIntyre is living among us for a reason," she says. "A being with her immense losses has great power."

I pet Persephone, the only one of my friend's three felines who likes me.

"What power?" I say.

"To pierce others' bubbles."

I snort. "She sure pierced mine when I tried to welcome her to the 'hood by leaving my best gazpacho on her doorstep. She gave it right back to me the next day without a bite eaten. Folks in Katy used to be so eager to eat my food they'd get into fights trying to jump line on Tex-Mex night."

"As for you, dear Beatrice, I've observed that your love for Craig seems more eros than philia."

Zappo. For a few seconds, I feel like a deer looking down the barrel of a thirty ought six. She's right. Brotherly love is not what I've felt since his first surgery a year ago. When he came to in recovery, I was the first person he saw. Then he did something he never does. He smiled. At me.

"Surely," my friend continues, "you don't perceive Marla as your rival for his affections? She's not his type."

I glance around at statues of Buddha, Kwan Yin, Krishna and Vishnu, Hera and Athena. Viv cherry-picks religions the same way she does the herbs and remedies she recommends to clients. Still, she can be full of crap sometimes.

"Well," I say, "she's not so much a rival for his affections as...."

"His interest," she says.

"I'm not sure he's that interested. He mostly just answers her questions at our get-togethers."

Viv shakes her head, but she's smiling.

"Bea, honey, you've got to let her in. Like he has."

"Why? I've known him ten years. She's known him less than one."

"You know why."

"Maybe I do, maybe I don't."

"Bea, she's thirteen years younger than he is."

"And I'm fifteen years older, but, hey, older women are good for men. Even Oprah says so."

"Just because Marla is schooled in the classical music he plays on his radio show doesn't mean he prefers her company. Shall we see what the universe thinks of your caretaking project?"

Project. I stifle another snort. "What do you have in mind?"

She rises, leaves the room for a moment, and comes back carrying the teakwood box holding her Tarot deck. I relax a little. With a ceremonious uplifting fluff of her silk sleeves, she sits down and looks at me. I stare right back. A lot of her New Age crap sticks in my craw, but I can handle Ouija Board stuff, no problem.

"We'll just do one card tonight."

I nod and cross my arms.

"Your question, dear?"

How can I rescue Craig from the clutches of that evil woman? Instead, I say, "How can I best help Craig to heal?"

She closes her eyes for a long moment. "So, you mean, 'What can I do to enhance healing in our community?'"

I nod. Whatever. She shuffles and holds the deck, cards fanned out, toward me. It feels a little like the first time Daddy passed me the tequila bottle and told me to take a snort. Eyes locked on hers, I pluck one from the middle and lay it down.

The death card. She lets me absorb it for a few seconds. Then:

"Don't take it literally, hon. Just enter the card and see what it's telling you."

Because Viv is my best friend, I humor her and study the five figures on it. Death, in black armor, sits astride a white horse with just his skeleton face and hands showing. A dude wearing robes and a pope hat faces the Grim Reaper. Then there's a man sprawled on the ground with a crown near his head. A child holds up flowers while an older girl behind her leans away, eyes closed. I fancy I'm the innocent toddler with flowers, but I know I'm the one turning away with her nose in the air. The skeptic. I inhale as deeply as I can before somebody with my voice speaks.

"Okay, something's going to die, should die. Is that what it means?"

Viv has the teensiest smile on her lips when she says, "Your take is the only one that really matters."

She picks up the card, puts it back inside the deck, the deck in the box, and looks at me with her best ball-is-in-your-court stare.

"I'd better let Handy out for a pee and poop," I mutter.

Standing, she lays a hand on my shoulder. I see myself out into the sweet night air of Ambrosia Drive, feeling like I just had hands laid on me and was prayed and prophesied over. I'm glad I have a dog to keep me tethered to the earth.

♦

The next day is Sunday, and I rise at dawn to hear the robin chorus while Handsome and Mahler do their thing. Passing by Marla's, I see the spot beside the door where I'd left my bowl of gazpacho right after she moved in. The next day when I came to get my bowl back, she told me to put it where the sun don't shine. I know she calls me Bootsie behind my back because of my Laredos. That's okay. I call her Stewpot when I see how many wine bottles are in her recycling bin.

As Viv reminded me a thousand times, she's mourning the deaths of her husband and teenage boy, which turned her into a monster. Viv found her son's obituary online and decided we'd leave it at her door to let her know we knew her secret grief and "give her the space to process it before doing more." But Craig, bless his sweet soul, said we couldn't just put the obit clipping in a dish by itself and suggested we add a sprig of Artemisia annua, the cinnamon-smelling plant most folks call Sweet Annie.

"It's the secret o' life," he said. "Makes a dying man stand, a dead man walk."

And, by God, it worked. Marla came over to Viv's, we coaxed her inside, and she wound up adopting both stray kitties we'd been fostering. But we never saw them again, since she never invited us inside. Viv claimed those kittens were helping to heal Marla's grief behind her closed door. Maybe so, but the woman didn't stop at taking our kitties; she stole Craig, too.

And she must be still downing a bottle or two every night after work.

I force myself not to look down the street toward Craig's. All I really ever wanted to do was cuddle with him, maybe spoon some. "Constant caretaker" is what Vivienne's called me ever since she weaseled my story out of me years ago. After Daddy died of cirrhosis, I gave up my plans to go to college and stayed in Katy to take care of Mama, who had colon cancer by then. By the time she died eight years later, I knew college would be wasted on me. Viv looked so sad after I said that, I'd had to cheer her up.

"But hey, Mama paid me back by teaching me to cook. When I first went to work at High Steaks, I waitressed. Then when the cook quit, I tried a shift, then just went on cooking the next day and the next till Floyd Stanley quit looking for anybody, and I became full-time. When Floyd passed four years later, I bought the place, changed the name to Bea's Nest, and the rest is history."

Viv's face had lost a lot of that sadness, making me cocky enough to add, "I ain't good for much else, but I can cook."

She leaned forward so fast I almost expected a slap like Daddy used to give me when I sassed back.

"Don't ever say that again," she said in the quiet tone I've learned is her healer voice. "You can do absolutely anything you want."

So I decide right now, as the bird choir sings the street to life, that I'm the one that's best qualified to take care of Craig when he comes home.

It's been a good day already, and the sun ain't even up.

◆

Viv called Monday morning to say she'd "consulted with" Marla, and they both agreed that I'd make the best live-in caretaker for "our dear Craig." Huh. Viv just doesn't want me and Marla coming to blows over a man. I kept my voice calm, then did a happy dance with Handsome when the call was over.

Prematurely, as it turned out.

There's a big difference between taking care of someone with slowly progressing cancer and a man recovering from brain surgery. It was easy the first twenty-four hours when he mostly slept, but when he finally woke up, he'd gotten both his affect and his ego back. Nothing—not food or drink or raising or lowering the hospital bed they brought for him—made him happy. He didn't have a TV and didn't want to listen to the radio, wouldn't even read. His bird-watching binoculars lay abandoned on the nightstand.

Though I gave him his pain pills on time, he wanted more. I wouldn't budge, so he began acting hateful, shaking his head side to side till I thought he'd rip off his bandages. I considered leaving the grouch to the professional home health care worker. But his insurance doesn't cover more than the twice-daily check-ins, and we all think he needs more than that.

◆

The third day, my nemesis walks right in without knocking, carrying a dish. I smell oregano.

"He can only eat bland food right now," I tell her.

Her mouth is tight when she says, "Then take care of it for later."

She places the dish on the arm of the couch where I'm sitting. By the time I put it in the fridge, I hear the bedroom door close and lock. Damn her! Like a flash, I race down the hall to Craig's bedroom and stand listening with all my might but hear only my own heart pounding like a fracking drill.

Then I hear a strange sound coming from inside.

At first, I figure it's Mahler whining, proof positive Marla's doing something less than therapeutic. My hand is an inch from the doorknob when the whine rises higher, louder until it becomes weeping. Hell's bells. Marla, the boozehound, is in there crying at the bedside of a man recovering from a brain tumor. Not for him, oh no, for herself. She's the kind that brings their troubles to someone's sickbed so they can feel better. My mama, in her last days, had comforted many a soul about to get a divorce, get thrown out of their home, or lose their kids. She'd pat their hands and let them cry till I wanted to scream, "Who's crying for you, Mama?" She'd see me getting mad and shake her head.

While rage pours through me like a hundred twenty volts of house current, I somehow keep my hand off that knob. Who can I blame? The woman wants an intimate moment, same as me, with this good man who will probably die sooner rather than later. Maybe she's finally learning how to mourn. I know all this, but I still hate her guts for being in there with him, leaving me to put away food and empty bedpans. But I hear Viv saying, "Let her in," so I let my pounding forehead fall against the door and breathe in and out. Finally, the weeping stops, Mahler quits whining, and I go away. At least the witch wasn't obviously drunk. Maybe her tears are even real.

◆

When she comes out, I'm hiding in the kitchen, and she heads straight for the front door and throws it open. I hold my breath and will her to go through it fast. She pauses. Then she tosses behind her:

"Thank you for all you're doing for him. Your skills are perfectly suited to this kind of work."

She shuts the door fast before she can appreciate my raised middle finger.

◆

It's been a month of Sundays since I last stood on the bridge over Shawnee Springs Creek in Glenora Wood. Even though the late afternoon sun makes the water gleam like sheets of fire and the April air smells mud-delicious, I'm still mad as a stepped-on rattler at the wicked witch. While Handsome and Mahler, best of pals, sit on the boards behind me, I put my elbows on the rail and lean. It's mighty hot and humid for April.

I look at my phone. I have about ten minutes before I should get back and relieve Mrs. Bailes, who is with Craig now. I need this break. As bad a boy as Craig has been, it's Marla that has me on the ropes. Skills perfectly suited for the job. It wasn't enough that she'd breezed right past me to steal time alone with him and treated me like her slave. She'd had the gall to cry at a sick man's bedside when he was the one who should be crying!

"I ain't doing it for you!" I holler. Behind me, Mahler stands up and barks. I sure wish I'd hollered it at the witch, but she made her escape too fast. Turning, I bend down and pet the little dog's head till she sits back down with her older buddy. I obviously need to get a grip. The whole point of being here is to surrender to the power of this place. Power, Viv had called Marla's grief. Well, she can stick it as far as I'm concerned.

When I stand up straight, my head seems clearer. Dogs and sacred ground'll do that. Ah, Ohio, my adopted country! Thought I'd be in Texas forever till Clyde Conyers came and swept me off my feet. And because he'd been reassigned to Wright–Patterson Air Force Base in Dayton, we landed in Ohio. Lasted for a whole year we did, but the end came as we both knew it would, me just kindling for his fire. He had rages, even got into fights at work. I was next. I couldn't face slinking back to Katy with my tail between my legs. Plus, I found out I actually liked snow and the Ohio State Buckeyes. But I lost base housing. When I wondered out loud to one of Clyde's drinking buddies where I'd live, the guy said the only place for me was "that hippie village where they don't give a damn what you do or look like."

Shawnee Springs, he meant: the town that time forgot.

The first time I sauntered into the village coffee shop, I met a tall, pretty woman with heavy makeup wearing a micro-mini-skirt like I hadn't seen since 1965. We chatted in line for a minute till I realized she was a man, and really nice. And if that didn't clinch the deal, on my second visit, I saw signs for some place called Glenora Wood. A thousand-acre preserve right beside the town! After Clyde, I thought I'd never believe in love at first sight again, but when I made it to the bottom of those 121 stone steps, and my soles landed on the ground where Tecumseh might've walked, I was home.

Now that I'm more centered, I let Mahler lead me and Handy on across the bridge, drawn by rivulets trickling down the bank from the spring above, the ground rusty from the iron-rich water. When we reach the steps, I look down to make sure my old boy can navigate them all right, and when I look up, there's a man standing in front of the little waterfall only ten yards away.

I pull both leashes tight. Why hadn't I seen the guy sooner? He's wearing an old ratty canvas coat with a sheepskin collar on one of the warmest days we've had all spring. I might've turned left and traipsed on up the bank to the spring, except for the two braids flowing down his back, blacker than Texas crude. I stare at his back, trying to think of something to say, usually not a problem for an ex-waitress, but today it is. There is something coming off him, like heat off a radiator. Everything's really quiet, not even a bird chirping.

While water hisses, streaming down into the rock pool, I'm wondering what he's thinking. Then it comes to me that he's yearning for something lost. Well, hell's bells, if he's as Native American as he looks, he and his people have lost their whole way of life! Looking at his noble profile is almost like looking at the history of this place before whites. I want to ask him how can you live after you've lost everything.

Quiet as I can, I guide Handy down the steps till the three of us are standing right beside him. He stinks to high heaven. Thank God the water's motion dilutes it some. When his head swings my way, I see he's young. I grin up at him, he's so much taller.

"Haven't I seen you somewhere?"

It's a stock opening I use to make folks talk to me, but his face is serious while he ponders it.

"No," he finally says. "But I've seen you."

I tighten the leash on Handsome as if he alone is keeping me grounded. Mahler is looking all around like an oblivious teenage girl. Is the boy a stalker? But I don't think so. I just pretend he didn't say that.

"Well, it's good to see you enjoying yourself on one of God's gorgeous days."

With the barest lifting of his eyebrows, he silently corrects me. Not enjoying so much as just being here, belonging to this place like the sun in the sky, the sycamores up on the bank. I try to think of what to say next, but he speaks first.

"This living water"—he reaches and fills his palm, letting it run between big squarish fingers—"is good for us."

Handsome sits down, listening attentively.

"It's rich in iron," I say. "That's why it turns the rocks and ground gold."

He nods like I said something profound. Then he leans forward, head to the side, two braids dangling like twin black snakes, and drinks. At last, he pulls back and smacks his lips before wiping his face on his filthy sleeve. Then he turns to me with those serious dark eyes.

"You will drink?"

And even though I never have in my fourteen years in Ohio tasted these waters—no doubt tainted with runoff from farmers' fields—I lean forward, close my eyes and let the cold stream wash over my face and fill my mouth. When I swallow, the cold runs through me like a blade. I gasp. Beside me, he laughs in slow syllables, ah-ha-ha-ha. I laugh, too. Handy joins in, yip-whimpering as he coils around my knees. It's the most pleasant thing that's happened to me in a long time out here, and that's saying a lot.

I'm about to ask him where he came from and what he's doing out here. But before I can, there's barking, and off to my left comes a girl in cut-offs and flip-flops leading two Rottweilers. Handsome backs up while Mahler springs forward, barking, till I pull her back. The girl rushes past me and somehow gets her dogs up onto the bridge.

By the time I look back to where the boy was, he's gone. The trail to the right is empty. Before I can decide whether I've seen a ghost or not, I hear Methodist Church's bell. It's past time I was heading back. Both dogs seem more than ready when I begin leading them back the way we came. Drying water chills my face. What happened was almost like baptism. Which is a kind of death. The card was not wrong. Death can give life.

◆

As soon as Craig's meds knock him out, my euphoria over what happened with the braided boy has mostly worn off, and I'm ready for a second opinion. I call Vivienne and describe my experience with the kid. I don't tell her about Marla's home invasion; I know she'll take the witch's side, say she's still healing, and I should overlook such behavior, blah blah blah.

There's silence for a while. I imagine Viv sitting at the table where I drew the death card, eyes closed, her beautiful brown hands on top of the box holding the deck. But then again, maybe she's unloading the dishwasher. With her, you never know which you're going to get, shaman, naturopath, or ex-paralegal. Finally, she exhales.

"He embodies the spirit of the Shawnee who inhabited Glenora long before Europeans."

Her words excite me, but before I can ask more questions, she butts in.

"Sweetie, I gotta run. It's almost time for adjudication."

My guilty pleasure is Ben and Jerry's Chocolate Fudge Brownie. Hers is Judge Judy. She's off to court, leaving me to fret. The spirit of a Shawnee sharing sacred water with me is a lot to swallow. Still, something's changed, and it makes me less worried about Craig. But I'm not completely willing to consider that Marla's "power" can help him recover better than I can.

◆

When I startle awake, my neck seizes into sudden pain. Glancing at the clock, I see it's after six. Hell's bells, I slept through the night and didn't hear a peep out of Craig—both our bedroom doors are open—or from either dog. Now that's rare. I look down at the foot of the bed where Handy should be sitting up, trying to stare me awake. No dog.

I'm up in a flash, still fully clothed. At the door to Craig's room, I stop. Mahler sits at the head of the bed, forelegs crossed before him, looking at me mournfully. At the bottom, Handsome lies, head on paws, as if thinking *where've you been?*

Then I gaze back up. Something's different, and I don't know what it is at first. My heart quieted down enough for me to listen. Nothing. Looks to me like Craig's not only not snoring, he doesn't seem to be breathing.

I panic and retreat to the living room, cell phone in hand. I can't take it if he's dead. I need to know before calling the squad who'll just desecrate his body. Trying to breathe slowly, I call Vivienne, but her phone goes to message. She's probably meditating or doing Qigong. My ticker feels like it's pounding in ten-penny nails. There's only one other choice. The witch answers on the second ring.

"Can you come over to Craig's fast? I need your opinion."

"Look, Bea, if he's—"

"Hurry."

◆

I pace the living room, flying back to the bedroom every thirty seconds or so. Even with the overhead light on, sometimes I think he's breathing, sometimes not. I'm afraid if I touch him and he's as cold as Mama was when I found her, my heart will explode. I'm back in the living room, when Marla busts through the front door in a fruity cloud of soap and shampoo. She looks like a million bucks in a green-skirted suit with creases that could cut glass.

"What's wrong?" she says.

"I'm not sure Craig's breathing."

"Did you call 911?"

"Will you just go see?"

The Corporate Director of Communication stands there thinking. It's like files are being accessed and discarded at lightning speed. Come on, Marla, I'm holding out my flowers to you up there on your high, white horse. After a few seconds, she grabs my arm.

"Come on, then."

Back in the bedroom, she cuts on the overhead, and Mahler blinks to attention beside the nightstand with its million pill bottles. The little Shih Tzu's master lies under a striped sheet with his head wrapped in a bandage. Our king is fallen, and it's my fault. Handsome knows what I'm thinking and licks my fingers supportively. Then Marla's hand is on my shoulder.

"Look, Bea. He's breathing."

She's right; I see the sheet rise and fall. His face is bathed in light, sunken stubbled cheeks, open mouth, the lips I hoped one day to kiss. He needs this take-charge director, not a total fruitcake like me. I jump when a voice speaks behind us:

"Is everything okay here?"

We turn to see Viv in the doorway, decked out in silky scarves and a robe. Even more dramatic is her scent, which takes my breath away. Then I glimpse the dried sprig of Artemisia in the crook of her arm. Craig's superpower.

"Sorry, Bea," she says, "I just got your voicemail after my shower and came as soon as I could."

Truth be told, I'm not all that glad to see Viv. I want to say that me and Marla got things under control. Instead, I manage to squeak, "I overslept and thought he might've died. I guess I panicked."

The hand on my shoulder is now pressing life back into me. When I look at her, my former nemesis is shaking her head sternly.

"Then she called me."

Vivienne is nodding. Is that a mischievous smile?

"Great teamwork," she pronounces at last. "Thanks for coming right over, Marla. And thank you, dear Bea, for your constant care." She spreads her arms, her wide sleeves becoming wings. "For taking care of all of us."

Horseshit. But then I remember the way I'd feel on those Tex-Mex nights when it seemed like the whole goddamn town was in line outside the diner. I can feed you, I'd think, all of you. And the sweat poured while we chopped onions, stirred the chili sauce and sang country hits along with Country Legends 91.7 FM out of Houston.

"Would one of you ladies get me a glass of water?"

We all turn toward the man in the bed. We'd nearly forgotten him for a minute.

"I'll get it," Viv says. Stepping forward, she places the Artemisia on the nightstand with the pill bottles before leaving the room. Marla's the first to speak.

"I know I was cruel to you at first. But—"

"I let you do it," I say. Then I barely squeeze her forearm the way you would a banana to see if it's over-ripe. "Never again."

Before she can reply, Craig begins to whistle a complicated tune, probably classical. The more I listen, the more I like it, especially since it gets all mixed up with the Artemisia scent. "Secret o' life," he'd called it when he suggested sending some Sweet Annie to this woman beside me. No wonder she cried at his bedside. She's grateful to him. Maybe gratitude's the real secret, that and sharing your pain and not keeping it all to yourself. Like I've been doing since Mama died.

"Jesu, Joy of Man's Desiring," Marla whispers, then louder: "Johann Sebastian Bach."

I like the name Yo-hann. And Bach is a bubble bursting on the lips. When Craig stops, I look behind me, and there's Vivienne carrying four crystal goblets on a silver tray.

"I thought we would all benefit from the soothing properties of the elixir of life, source and symbol of the unconscious."

"Better than Chardonnay, now that I quit," Marla mutters.

Hell's bells, Marla McIntyre's sober as a judge! I marvel while we all take a glass and raise them high.

"I'd like to make a toast," I say.

Now they're all looking at me, which would usually make me uncomfortable, but today I don't care. I lift my glass.

"To the living water that defeats death."

I don't care if they think I'm crazy. I'm seeing a boy with his head in the falls, black braids shining.

"And to your health," Viv says, standing beside Craig, who's sitting up now, his pillow fluffed behind him, thanks to her. She clinks his glass. Marla and I do the same to each other's, then drink. The patient is grinning like a kid eating chocolate pancakes with whipped cream. Tilting his head, he cocks his ear.

"Awaking, I thought I heard a murmuration. But now I look around and see... exaltation, a flight of larks!"

"More like a murder of old crows," quips Viv.

Our laughter rises then falls like starlings turning together in a wave. Craig, the birdwatcher, is back, and I'm getting misty. Sure, he'll die soon—so will I—but not today. I'm seeing, in my mind's eye, like a Tarot card, two women standing on a bridge under towering old trees with red and gold leaves, looking down into the creek. One holds flowers toward the other, who looks like she's crying. The dark comes down fast, but a sliver of moon is on the rise. Two dogs sit patiently on the boards behind, waiting for what comes next.

Ed Davis has immersed himself in writing and contemplative practices since retiring from college teaching. *Time of the Light*, a poetry collection, was released by Main Street Rag Press in 2013. His latest novel, *The Psalms of Israel Jones* (West Virginia University Press 2014), won the Hackney Award for an unpublished novel in 2010. Many of his stories, essays, and poems have appeared in anthologies and journals such as *Multiplicity Review*, *The Plenitudes*, *Leaping Clear*, *Slippery Elm*, *Hawaii Pacific Review*, and *Bacopa Literary Review*.

Ed lives with his wife in the bucolic village of Yellow Springs, Ohio.

In Memoriam

Jim Hodnett

Preston was the first to arrive and regretted it. It was not easy being alone in this house so full of memories, many of them the kind that hit his gut like a stab wound before carving a path to his brain. The kitchen, where he stood now, had been the beating heart of Uncle Jack's house. Wasn't it the same with most homes? He pushed a stool into place under the island, where the three of them had sat to eat the ice cream Jack would serve them whenever they stayed with him. Preston could hear Jack's baritone voice, both warm and authoritative, as he placed individual toppings on their ice cream: M&M's for Asher, sprinkles for Susannah, and a cascade of chocolate syrup for Preston.

"Here you go, kiddos," he'd say as he placed their distinctive bowls of ice cream in front of them. His deep voice and hairy forearms did not seem to contrast at all with the sweet delights he served or his kind demeanor. "There's nothing wrong with being individuals. It's good to be yourselves." He wouldn't tolerate any of them putting down others for their tastes.

Beyond the island and down the hall, Preston could see the door to the guest room, where the three of them had slept together as children in that gigantic—or so it seemed then—queen-sized bed. Sometimes Jack would lie on the bed with them, reading them stories or singing songs until they fell asleep. The guest room, with its shelves full of books and games and photos of the three of them, was also the room Preston had stayed in during breaks from college after Mom died. Her death from breast cancer—agonizing and ironic after years of working as a nurse on an oncology ward—had been mercifully quick. And it had reaffirmed for Preston and his siblings their reliance on Uncle Jack, now their last remaining parental figure. Their dad had died eighteen years earlier.

Asher and Susannah were already on their own when Preston was in college, and he could have stayed with one of them, but they were preoccupied with new careers and new spouses. Besides, it had just seemed natural to drop his things at Jack's house and allow himself to be pampered, as each of them always had been, by their mother's older brother.

They were small when Dad left for Afghanistan and still small when—after his Jeep rolled over an IED—he returned in a flag-draped coffin. Jack had taken over as the male nurturer, babysitting while Mom attended night classes, hosting them for entire weekends, taking them to Disney movies and science museums, attending their concerts and games, and always, always encouraging them to do their best, try their hardest. He never failed to express pride in them, no matter how many notes were played out of tune or how many balls were fumbled or dropped or kicked out of bounds. And there were plenty of miscues where sports were concerned. Susannah was the only real athlete. Asher lacked the focus to succeed in sports. Preston lacked the passion.

Jack could be stern, too, of course. Once, the three of them, feeling bored and petulant, taunted the neighbor's dog with sticks and water pistols until it began to lunge and growl at them from the other side of the chain-link fence. Hearing the ruckus, Jack burst through the back door and confronted them. "That dog wasn't doing anything to you! He's a good dog, a friendly one, but you riled him up! Animals deserve respect—just like humans. That was pure meanness." He made them go into the house and sit in separate corners until they calmed down. But later, as always, he followed up by reminding them, "I'm doing this because I love you. I want you to grow up to be good people, people who make the world better, not worse." Preston and Susannah, at least, had taken his words to heart.

Preston was stirred from his memories by an assortment of bangs and scuffles that announced Susannah's arrival. She appeared in the kitchen, carrying a precariously balanced load of trash bags, cardboard boxes, tape, and felt-tip pens. "And there's more in the car," she said as she emptied the contents of her arms onto the countertop. The commotion of her entrance was a relief. It allowed Preston to push the memories away, keep them at arm's length.

He and his sister hugged, holding and rocking longer than was typical of them. Preston could feel in Susannah's embrace the same sagging weight of grief that had been harboring in his body since Jack's memorial service the day before. Their uncle had died suddenly of a heart attack at the age of sixty-eight. They had expected to have him around another decade or more. Weren't they entitled after losing both parents so early? Jack was already a beloved figure to their children, whom they often brought for visits. And they had also made certain he knew he need not fear old age. Of that, they would've made sure.

Susannah and Preston, along with Asher, the eldest, had agreed to meet at Jack's house this Saturday morning to begin the process of sorting through their uncle's belongings, deciding what to keep, what to donate, and what to throw away. As his sole adult heirs, they had long possessed copies of his will and, a day or two after his death, had gone through his files to find financial records. Asher, the eldest and an attorney, had calculated that they would each receive around two hundred thousand dollars plus one-third of whatever the house sold for, probably an additional seventy-five thousand each. Jack had died with no debts, except for some recent incidental purchases on a credit card. His mortgage and car were paid off. He had lived a tidy life.

It would just be the three of them at the house today. Susannah and Preston's husbands were at home with their respective children, and Asher's wife, a devout, conservative evangelical Christian, didn't like being around Susannah and Preston. This was never said out loud, but Preston knew it to be true. Rebecca didn't come to his and Michael's wedding, claiming a migraine, and several years before, had seemed reluctant to include Susannah in her own wedding party. She had passive-aggressively—or so it appeared to Susannah and Preston—chosen a horrendous, cream and gray, ruffled-and-puffed-sleeve bridesmaid dress that she knew tall, broad-shouldered, former collegiate swimmer Susannah would look awful in. It was flattering on Rebecca's petite best friend and her similarly diminutive sister/maid of honor, but Susannah said it made her look like an ostrich doing a spread-winged mating dance. As much as he wanted to spare his sister's feelings, Preston had to agree.

Preston and Susannah had just poured themselves coffee when they heard the front door open and close, then loud footsteps heading in their direction. Asher bounded into the kitchen with a clap of his hands and a take-charge attitude. "So, how much have you gotten done yet?" he asked, not even bothering to say *hello* first. Asher was the only one with curly hair, just starting to gray at the temples, and he was the shortest, though stocky and muscular. He had started lifting weights when Susannah and Preston began to surpass him in height—compensating, Preston had always thought. Preston was the tallest—angular and ectomorphic. He tended to contain his movements as though he feared his long and gangly limbs were offensive. But Susannah wore her height gracefully, without apology. In truth, Preston suspected, she privately gloated when she grew taller than Asher. Gloated even more when his late growth spurt proved inadequate to overtake her.

So there they stood in the kitchen: oldest to youngest, shortest to tallest.

Before answering Asher, the two younger siblings—deliberately, it seemed, and almost in unison—took leisurely sips of coffee. "We just got here," said Preston.

"And it's only five after nine," added Susannah.

"Well, you've had time to make coffee," challenged Asher.

"Not make, just pour." Susannah pointed to a cardboard carafe on the counter. "You know Jack didn't like coffee, didn't even own a coffeemaker." She nodded toward a bakery box by the carafe. "And there are muffins, too."

"Well, still, we haven't got all day."

"As a matter of fact, we do," retorted Preston. "It's Saturday, and we agreed we would spend the day doing this, as long as it takes."

"Okay, okay. But there's no sense wasting time."

Preston and Susannah looked at each other but said nothing. Asher grabbed one of the cardboard cups and filled it with coffee from the carafe. Preston had brought the coffee and muffins, of course. That had not been planned, but it was expected. He was the nurturer. Asher was too alpha to think about such things, and Susannah was too feminist. She was a social worker and had worked for several years at a Planned Parenthood clinic. But after her own first child was born seven years ago, she decided to do something less controversial, something that came with fewer death threats and profane voicemails.

Preston taught elementary school, like their Uncle Jack, and thought he might be a principal someday, also like Uncle Jack. Jack was the first person in the family Preston told he was gay, even before Susannah and certainly before Asher. He had half-expected Jack to reciprocate with a coming-out speech of his own. After all, genetically speaking, having a maternal gay uncle increases a boy's chances of being gay. But his never-married uncle, who, so far as his niece and nephews knew, had never dated anyone, did not respond in kind. He just hugged his nephew, said he didn't care, and that Preston and whoever he loved would always be welcome in his home.

Asher grabbed a blueberry muffin and took a bite. Preston watched as his eye caught a yellowed card stuck to the refrigerator with a magnet. He already knew about the card. It was a thank-you note with a maudlin, printed Hallmark sentiment. But in clumsy cursive, a line had been added. *The flars was lovely. Your friend, Edna.* "What's this?" Asher asked, removing it from the stainless-steel surface and holding it in front of his siblings.

"He never told you about that?" asked Susannah in a tone it seemed to Preston, meant to be point-scoring. "His first year as principal, the son of one of the cafeteria ladies died in a hit-and-run. Just a little tyke, about seven or eight. Jack sent flowers to the funeral home, went to the visitation, and attended the service. He said Edna's card was the nicest note anyone had ever written him."

"Wow! And he kept it all these years." marveled Asher. "The man was too good to be true."

Preston and Susannah glanced at each other. For once, Asher had hit the mark on something in the realm of humanity.

Preston set down his coffee cup. "Well, shall we start here in the kitchen? I think we can box up most of the utensils and dishes and take them to Salvation Army unless something looks vintage or antique. We can set stuff like that aside, might get some money for it, or maybe one of us could keep it for sentimental value."

"Okay," said Asher, "you two can work on that. I'm going to go to the bedroom and start sorting through his clothes. Most of them will probably go to charity. I don't think anyone in the family is his size. Besides, I've never seen him wear anything new since he retired. Which was what? Three years ago? So probably nothing is in style."

Preston could see Susannah bristling at being assigned kitchen duty by Asher, but she said nothing. They had both learned to be choosy about their battles with their older brother, and today was not the time to argue about gender stereotyping. They got to work opening cabinets and drawers and filling up boxes and trash bags. They'd been occupied fewer than fifteen minutes when Asher—dear, distractible Asher (*how had he gotten through law school?*)—strode into the room holding a T-shirt in front of him. "Hey, look at this!" he said with a smile. The shirt was bright red and printed on the front in white comic book font with *I'm not one of those hootchie-cootchie boys!* Preston and Susannah chuckled when they read it but laughed out loud when Asher flipped it around to show them the back, on which was printed in smaller font, *Oh yes, he is!* as though a note had been taped to its back.

"Where did that come from?" asked Preston.

"His closet," answered Asher. "There are dozens of them in there. It's crazy! I don't think I ever saw him wear a T-shirt with lettering on it in his life."

"Me neither," said Susannah. They walked to Jack's closet and examined shelves full of tees. *Jazz Fest '87*, one read. *Keep on Truckin'!* read another. The shirts seemed a chronicle of experiences and attitudes they would never have associated with their uncle: *Flower Power Reunion, I Climbed Pike's Peak! Whip It Good! I'm Bad!* and many others.

"Wow, it's like he had a whole secret other life we didn't know about," said Susannah.

Preston scrunched his face. "Or maybe they were gifts that he just didn't know what to do with," he suggested as he sorted through them. "None of them look like they were ever worn. Some even still have store tags on them." Yet he found the stash of T-shirts unsettling, as though Jack had lived not just a tidy life but an unrequited one. It was as if he had spent his nearly seven decades standing and looking from the edges of existence, with excitement and passion just out of his reach. But then, "Oh my gosh! Look at this!" he exclaimed, holding up a baby-blue shirt on which was printed, *World's Greatest Uncle.* "I gave this to him." He blinked back tears. "I'm going to keep it."

Susannah rubbed his shoulder. "Well, I'm going to keep a couple of them, too," she said. "If nothing else, I can sleep in them and think of Jack when I do. Remember how he used to lie in bed with us until we fell asleep? We'd cuddle up to him like puppies. And when we woke up the next morning, we'd all be tucked in and warm, and he'd be in the kitchen cooking scrambled eggs and toasting Pop-Tarts."

Preston smiled at the memory, but Asher said, "Yeah, I bet seeing you in one of these shirts will be quite a turn-on for Roger."

"Asher," replied Susannah, "I appreciate your concern for my sex life, but believe me, Roger has no difficulties with his turn-on switch, thank you very much."

Asher smirked. "Doesn't surprise me. I always figured him for a hound."

Susannah rolled her eyes. "Jealous!" she said. "I'm going back to the kitchen." Preston followed her, clutching his baby-blue tee. They had barely been working another fifteen minutes when Asher once again approached them, this time carrying a box.

"You guys have to see this," he said, a sober expression lengthening his face. Preston looked up, then froze when he eyed his brother.

But Susannah, who had her back turned to him, snapped a reply. "Oh, Ash, for god's sake, we can't look at everything you find. We'll never finish. Whatever it is, just put it in a trash bag or the donation pile."

"No, you need to see," repeated Asher. He set the box on the island countertop.

Hearing the muted alarm in his brother's voice, Preston approached the cardboard container. He gasped when he looked inside. "Oh, my god!" he said.

Susannah, still looking impatient, walked over to stand behind him and peered past his shoulder. "Oh, shit!" she said, covering her mouth.

The box was full of photos of children, almost all under the age of four or five—and almost all of them naked. The three siblings were silent as they examined the pictures, other than to emit occasional exclamations of disbelief.

"Crazy, just crazy," said Asher.

"Jesus," said Preston.

Susannah cried over one of a small, blonde girl holding a garden hose and wearing nothing but pigtails. She dropped it on the counter and flicked her shaking hands up to her shoulders as though the photo was toxic to the touch.

To their relief, there were no photos of children being abused or even in provocative poses. But genitals were often visible. The children seldom looked at the camera. They pored over picture books, drank from sippy cups, or frolicked through flowers. It was as though their images had been stolen from them.

"I just don't understand. Why would he have these?" asked Susannah.

"Well, isn't it obvious?" Asher said after a long pause. "He really did have a secret life. Our uncle was a pedophile."

"Don't you dare say that!" said Preston, his cheeks flashing red. "Jack wasn't creepy. He was just—asexual. There's no way he would ever hurt another human, let alone a child."

"How can you be so sure?" Asher assumed his attorney voice as though conducting a deposition. "We have evidence to the contrary in front of us."

"Oh, for god's sake!" said Susannah. "Like Preston said, Jack was asexual. He never dated anyone, didn't show any interest in sex at all."

Asher sighed. "I have known men who *appeared* to be asexual. I have known men who *said* they were asexual. But I have never known anyone I believed actually *was* asexual. They always have something: a porn collection or sex vacations—a secret life of some sort."

"Oh, you're just a cynic!" said Preston. "That's not who Jack was. I know it."

"Like I said, we have evidence to the contrary. Maybe *this* was his porn collection."

"Oh, come on!" argued Preston. "Lots of people love photos of children. Just because you think they're adorable doesn't mean you're attracted to them. Parents take photos of their children in the bathtub all the time or lying bare-assed on a diaper. It's innocent. It doesn't mean a thing. And lots of great art has been of naked children. What's that statue in Belgium? The Peeing Boy of Brussels? It's a fountain! It's cute! Nobody thinks it's sexual."

"Not us, anyway," said Asher.

Susannah gasped. "Oh, my God! I just thought..." She placed her fingers over her lips. "I mean, none of these photos are of us, are they?"

"That occurred to me, too," said Asher. "I don't think so, but who remembers what they looked like at four or five?"

"We have pictures of ourselves at those ages. That's how we know," said Preston, impatience in his voice. "And there aren't any of us in this box. Anyway, I can't believe you two are talking this way. You seriously think Jack would do anything like that to one of us? He loved us! Other than Mom, he was the best thing about our childhoods."

"We're not making any accusations," said Susannah. She paused and closed her eyes. "I don't have any memory of him doing anything to me..."

Asher shrugged. "Me neither."

"But you've got to admit," Susannah continued, "these photos make you wonder what he might have done, if not to us, then to someone."

"Oh, please!" said Preston, his voice rising in volume. "He was a teacher and a principal for over forty years. There's never been a single complaint about him. Someone would have come forward by now, wouldn't they? After all this time?" He looked back and forth between their faces, searching for confirmation, for reassurance. "I talk to people all the time who were in his class or went to his school. They all adored the man—just like all those people he taught with or worked with who spoke at the service yesterday—they thought he was the greatest."

They were all quiet for a few moments. Then Asher asked, "Pres, are you sure he never did anything to you?"

"Of course, I'm sure. Why would you even ask?"

Asher made a gesture of futility with his hands. "I don't know. You were so young when Dad died, and you turned out gay..."

"Oh, no! You are not going there, are you? Conflating pedophilia and homo-sexuality? I didn't 'turn out gay'! I was born gay! Jack had nothing to do with it."

"Okay, okay. It's just...you have to wonder."

Preston gritted his teeth and spat his words out. "You've been hanging out too much with that fundamentalist wife of yours..."

"Okay, okay!" Susannah interrupted. "Let's just stay on topic here! Both of you! Now, we've got all these pictures. What are we going to do with them?"

Preston simmered for a few moments as they contemplated her question. "Let's just throw them away," he said.

"But what if somebody—some homeless person—rummages through the trash and finds them?" asked Asher.

"Then we burn them."

"You can't burn trash in this neighborhood," said Asher. "It's against city ordinances. Someone might report us, and then what'll we do when the police show up? Besides, I'm an attorney. It's unethical—and illegal—to destroy potential evidence."

"Evidence of what?" demanded Preston.

"Oh, here we go! Are you just going to stay in denial? These photos are child abuse, potentially, at least! Yeah, I know. Maybe if he had only one or two, you could explain it away. But a collection? Dozens of them?"

"So, what are you suggesting we do?" asked Susannah.

"We have to turn them over to the authorities—child protective services or the police..."

"And drag our uncle's name through the mud when there is no reason to believe he did anything to anyone?" asked Preston. He lifted his hands, palms up in front of him. "What would be the point?"

"Someone took these photos," said Asher. "Someone sold them, disseminated them, put them on the internet probably, and without the kids' permission—or their parents'. They should be caught and punished. Would you want strangers to have photos like these of your kids? I mean, even if no one ever touched them in a bad way, it's wrong. It's abuse."

Preston plopped onto one of the kitchen stools, placed his elbows on the countertop, and hid his face behind his hands. Again, the memories made the journey from his gut to his brain. The ice cream, the songs, the smiles, the kisses, and hugs—all of them innocent, all of them pure love, pure Jack.

Susannah put her hands on his humped shoulders. "Asher's right..." she began.

"They'll confiscate his computer, you know," said Preston without looking up. "The police will come. They'll search every inch of the house. Their cars will be parked out front. The whole neighborhood will know something's up. Word will get out, just like it did with that doctor at the children's hospital. He lived down the street from Michael and me. It was awful. And just because he had some stuff on his computer. No one ever said he hurt a kid. He helped them, healed them. But he'll never practice again."

Susannah continued to rub Preston's shoulders and angled her head as though to catch his eyes. "But we have to think about the children in these photos, Preston. Other people may have harmed them—even if Jack didn't, even if the doctor never directly harmed anyone either—and other children may have been hurt, too, by the people who took these photos and put them out there."

"And it won't just be Jack," Preston continued, a somber, faraway look in his eyes. "They'll make assumptions about us, too, just like Asher did about me. They'll think he abused us. They'll think we abuse our children. It's bad enough already how people look at Michael and me when we're out with Carter and Phoebe. The stares we get! And the frowns! Sometimes even snide remarks! People can be cruel—really cruel."

Preston could see Susannah look at Asher, a plea for help, it seemed. "Look, Pres," he said. "I'm sorry for what I said about you and Jack and being gay. It was stupid. I shouldn't have said it. But like Suze said, we have to think about those kids..."

"I always knew I was different," said Preston. "I knew I wouldn't ever have a girlfriend or a wife. At first, I didn't know why, but I knew. I just knew. So I thought I would always be alone. But seeing Jack—what a good man he was, how much people loved him, admired him—I thought, 'Well, I can be happy anyway, even if I am alone—like Uncle Jack. And I'll be a good uncle to Asher and Susannah's kids. And I'll be happy.'" Preston lifted his head and looked at his siblings.

"Oh, Pres." He felt Susannah's cheek on top of his head. "I'm so sorry. We never knew..."

Asher moved to Preston's other side and sat on the stool next to him. He put his arm on his younger sibling's shoulder. "Look, man, I know I can be an ass. I'm sorry, really. I loved Jack, too, and I appreciate everything he did for us. But..."

"I know, I know," said Preston. He stood and walked the few steps to the box and looked inside. He picked up one or two of the pictures and examined them. They felt heavy on his fingers as though laden with years of anguish. He dropped them back into the pile, then looked at his siblings. "Before we call the police and they come ransack the house, I'd like some time to walk around, to make sure I can remember it the way it's always been, the way Jack kept it."

"Sure," said Susannah. "I'll walk with you if you like."

Preston nodded.

"I'll come, too," said Asher.

They started in the backyard, Preston remembering games of hide-and-seek and tag they played while Jack cooked hot dogs on the patio grill or just sat and watched them in their play or maybe joined in to teach them how to hold a bat or pitch a ball. Then they proceeded to the guest room—"their" room—where they slept, played board games, or wrestled on the floor. In the den, he remembered hours the three of them had played with crafts or sat on the couch watching movies on DVDs—often with Jack by their side.

As they walked from room to room, they were hushed. Preston could hear their feet make scraping sounds on the hardwood floors. He would sometimes reach out to touch a table, a chair back, a shelf. Or sometimes they would all linger to look at something that seemed intrinsically Jack: a pastoral painting, the bust of Beethoven on the baby grand, or a classic book on a shelf. Preston noticed Hawthorne's *The Scarlet Letter* on an end table by Jack's favorite chair. It was bookmarked about two-thirds from the end.

The last room they visited was Jack's bedroom. Like the rest of the house, it was clean and spare but also comfortable and inviting, like Jack himself. As he looked at the light gray comforter covering the firm futon mattress resting on a low platform frame, Preston recalled a stormy night he had lain with Jack in that bed. Thunder had vibrated the walls and rattled the windows. Asher and Susannah did not wake up, but Preston did. Only four or five, he grabbed his teddy and toddled hurriedly into Jack's room. "Uncle Jack, I'm scared," he said as he poked his uncle's shoulder.

Jack rousted and blinked. "Oh, well, what are you scared of, buddy—the thunder?"

"Uh-huh."

"You want to sleep with me?"

Preston nodded and climbed into Jack's bed. He nestled himself between Jack's arm and torso and laid his head on his uncle's comfortable but firm chest—Jack had always stayed fit. Preston remembered the soft texture of his uncle's cotton tee and boxers, the tickly scruff on his chin, and the soothing scent of menthol on his face. Jack kissed him on the head and rubbed his arm, and told him not to worry, that thunder was just the sound clouds make when they bump into each other.

Years later, Preston would think of that night as an awakening, a moment when he had realized in some not fully formed way that he craved the love and embrace of a man, that it was core to who he was. But that night, as he lay cradled by his uncle, he could feel Jack's heart beating—fast, it seemed to him. And as he drifted off to sleep, he heard what sounded like quiet sobs. He remembered thinking that Jack could not be crying because grown-ups don't cry, at least not grown-up men.

When he woke in the morning, the sun was streaming columns of light between gaps in the curtains. He could hear Jack in the kitchen, and all seemed well. But during breakfast, Asher made fun of him for being afraid of thunder. Preston got so angry that he threw a fork at him, barely missing his eye.

"Whoa, whoa, whoa!" yelled Jack. "What the hell? We don't do things like that! You could have put his eye out! Then how would you feel?" Preston remembered noting that his uncle was angry and that that was unusual. He rarely lost his temper with them, and Preston had never heard him curse. His uncle's voice rose in volume. "And Asher, you shouldn't make fun. It's bullying! Both of you are wrong! We all have feelings that are bad or mean, but that doesn't mean we act on them. We have to learn to control ourselves when we want to do something bad. You can't always act on your feelings!" His face was red, and beads of sweat shone on his forehead.

When he finished, they were all silent and motionless, each of them, including Jack himself, appearing stunned by this kind and loving man's loss of composure. After a few moments, Jack turned his back to them and braced himself on the stove, breathing heavily. "Just eat your breakfasts," he said. And they did, without another word.

Preston felt a gnarl in the pit of his stomach as he remembered that stormy night and the angry morning after, a gnarl as taut and rigid as his grief. Wiping tears from his eyes, he looked at his siblings. "It's not fair," he said, "it's not fair. He was a good man—the best." Yet as he turned and left the room, he added, "But let's do it. We have to. Let's call the police."

Susannah hurried to catch up with him. Asher pulled a phone from his pocket.

Jim Hodnett is a retired educator and psychologist. Though an Arkansas native and a former resident of both Texas and New York, he has lived in Columbus, Ohio for over thirty years. He shares life with his partner/husband of twenty-eight years, Joe Heimlich. He has been writing short stories and memoirs since 2011.

The Distance Between Us

Terri Sutton

We were in my father's pickup truck, a beater held together by jury-rigged repairs fashioned by shade tree mechanics. I sat next to him, still grinning because my father had chosen me to go with him over my brother, who was eleven and the only boy in the family. At eight, I already understood the unwritten rule that my father would spend more time with my brother, that when my mother, the chief enforcer of this rule, ordered, "Take your son with you," with an equal measure of reminder and reprimand, my father would stretch out his arm and beckon my brother to follow him. I was also old enough to realize I barely knew my father and, more importantly, he barely knew me, a reality that birthed a lingering sadness whenever I thought about my dad.

It was a sunny day in Toledo, a Sunday morning, and my father's only free day from both his second-shift factory job and his side job painting for Whites who lived in neighborhoods where we couldn't live. As his truck sputtered down potholed streets, I braced myself against the smells of cigarettes, paint thinner, and something I couldn't name. For relief, I leaned forward, careful to avoid brushing against the cracks in the leather seats, split open like wounds, hung my head out the window, and welcomed the warm air that rushed in, pinning my braids back like dog ears.

Our outing was to Mr. Lee's, a two-pump service station, for gas and Pall Mall cigarettes. Before my father could turn off the truck, the owner, a short man with smiling eyes and pants that puddled over his shoes, rushed out to us. "Fill it up," my father said, and it occurred to me that I was witnessing something my brother was not—a shared scene with my father. I smiled triumphantly.

As my father got out of the truck, he said, "You want chips or something?" his tone as promising as the roll of the dice.

"Fritos," I said. Another dagger in my brother's heart.

Because my father had grown up in the Jim Crow South, our drive home was at a guarded pace. Though it was the sixties, he passed cars when necessary and slowed even more if he spied the police slyly hidden on a side street.

I wasn't an outgoing child, but at that moment, I searched for something to say to him even though I believed we had nothing in common. Many times I'd watched my father at family gatherings, surrounded by his brothers and cousins, tell stories about cars he wanted to buy or talk about the money he'd earned on a paint job. At home, I'd listened to his conversations with my mother about paying the bills and with my brother about his being on the track team, but he never talked to me.

That day, the silence settled between us, and I accepted the limits of our relationship. I stared out the window watching the houses slide by, and quietly munched my Fritos, determined to devour the whole bag and avoid sharing them with my brother.

Minutes later, my father turned into the alley behind our house and stopped in front of the garage he rented from our neighbor. He lifted its old-fashioned door and pulled the truck in. Before that day, I hadn't been in the garage. Now I could see it was a dark, narrow tunnel.

As I scooted off the seat, I heard the garage door make a low groaning noise before it slammed shut. Everything went dark. I stood still and listened for a voice to tell me I wasn't alone.

"Daddy," I called, inching toward the garage door. With one hand on the still-warm truck and the other patting at the empty space around me, I took tiny, scared steps until I reached the end of the truck and could touch the closed garage door. Without ventilation, the darkness felt warm and heavy. It gripped my throat; its mouth brushed my neck; it whispered, "You'll never leave the garage. Your father has forgotten you."

I couldn't judge how much time passed, whether it was five or fifty minutes, but I know after I began to sweat, and after I began to cry, and after I became convinced my father's love was so paltry that he could forget me, the garage door whined open and there he stood, silhouetted in a rectangle of sunlight.

I stared in his direction, expecting an explanation or an apology or a comforting hug. Instead, he smiled at me and said, "Come on."

I swiped at the tears on my cheeks and followed after him. Outside the garage, the crumpled Fritos bag in my pocket, I slowed my pace and watched him disappear through the side door, letting the distance between us widen.

◆

In the six years remaining until my father's death from a heart attack, we never spoke about this. I never told my mother about being forgotten in the garage, and I never rode in my father's pickup truck again.

In the early days, I tested theories about what might have happened that day. My father was a notorious jokester, so I wondered if this was a joke that misfired, that he expected when he returned for me, we'd share a laugh about it. Or maybe he was preoccupied with some weighty problem about illness or money, and it had momentarily made him forget about me. Then there was the theory that he was expecting an important telephone call—perhaps from a White client to arrange for his painting services—and in his haste to earn money to support his family, he'd rushed from the garage and left me.

As time passed and I saw no evidence that any of these theories were true, I settled on what seemed the simplest interpretation: that his leaving me in the garage was an undeniable confirmation that he didn't love me. I buried my dream of building a relationship with him, and in time the tender bruise of longing hardened into a shell of indifference.

◆

Many years later when I began to forget things I needed; things I wanted; things I treasured; things I thought were safely tucked in my purse or in a drawer or on a shelf; things that were valuable; things that were irreplaceable; things that were loved; I thought about my father, and that day he forgot me in the garage.

Terri Sutton lives in Toledo, Ohio. She has an MFA from Vermont College. Her work can be found in the anthology *Age Ain't Nothin' But a Number* and the online journals *Under the Sun, HowWeAre,* and *bioStories.*

A Thousand Words Denied

Jerry W. Vandal

The sun was beginning to rise as Greg Hilliard walked into the school building with a box filled with binders, books, a Harry Potter Funko, and a variety of wall décor. He was eager to set up his room and imagined how he could make it a place his students wanted to be. He was also anxious to make adjustments from his first year, which was a long and strenuous nine months of learning to create assignments, grade papers, maneuver through the field of mines that were parents' expectations and entitlements, and administrative oversight that at no point made him feel like a better teacher.

Walking through the newly waxed hallways, he was comforted by the silence. Soon loud and motley adolescents would fill them. As he made his way to the end of the hall, he saw Tiana Harlowe, one of the few teachers he had gotten to know the previous year, in her room getting organized. He balanced the box in one arm and knocked outside her open door.

"Greg, glad to see you came back," said Tiana as she removed a variety of items from several large bags with various mathematical formulas printed on them. She waved him in. He couldn't help but notice the framed picture of Tiana and her now husband Mikhail and a new rectangular sign with her name: Mrs. Kozlov.

He rested his box on the edge of Tiana's desk. "Last year was tough, but I owe it to myself to give it another go."

She smiled. "Well, the kids need good people in their lives. And this field needs more good men in it."

Greg looked around the room. He held in his laughter at the clock on the wall—math formulas represented each hour, and he couldn't interpret any of them. "So, how was the wedding?"

Tiana's eyes almost widened, and she excitedly flashed her hands. "It was amazing," she said, a sparkle in her eyes that Greg hadn't seen in a long while. "Everything I ever wanted. And then we were able to go to Punta Cana for the honeymoon before I had to get back here and start prepping."

"That's great. Very happy for you," he said, meaning it but feeling a slight ping in his gut as he glanced at the framed photo.

"Thanks. What about you? How was your break?"

"Did some reading. Some thinking."

"Hopefully, more than just that."

He smiled and shrugged his shoulders. "Had something planned, but it went by quicker than I imagined." Greg looked at his watch and picked up his box. "But that's how it goes, I guess. Better get to setting my room up. You've already got a leg up on most of us."

"I'll see you," she said with a welcoming smile as Greg waved and left the room.

Greg set up his room that day and then sat down to finalize things for his first lesson. He looked forward to teaching *Romeo and Juliet* but knew that Shakespeare wasn't the best way to lead teenagers into the year. He settled on Ray Bradbury's, *The Sound of Thunder*. He was sure it was a good way to get them engaged—time travel and dinosaurs seemed like a solid combo. He got his board ready, sat through an all-staff meeting filled with information that was as useful as staring at a wall, and then went home.

The next day, he stood in front of his desk and waited for his class to make their way in. He was ready to explain the foundations of storytelling. He was ready to introduce his students to various writers and writing styles and to make them think. However, he was less ready to meet new students and quickly learn who they were and the best way to interact with them. It wasn't that he didn't want to; it was just the part he knew he had the most difficulty with, being a person who was never sociable in school.

The bell rang, and Greg opened the door to his room and said hi to each student as they entered. "Go ahead and find yourselves a seat and we'll get started," he said as they filed in. After everyone was seated, he wrote his name on the board and said as enthusiastically as he could, "Welcome to high school ELA, specifically, ELA 9. I'm Mr. Hilliard." There was little surprise at almost all the students' lack of enthusiasm. Sitting in a classroom and being forced to be educated could never top sitting in one's bedroom and staring at one screen or another.

Greg started the class by having each student say the first thing that came to mind when they heard a word. "School," he said as he scanned the room for a hand to get things going. He noted that at least two students were eager as their hands shot up and gesticulated for his attention. Then, there were eight who avoided eye contact with him. One student drew, and another had already begun to nod off. The remainder of the class stared blankly at him.

The first student he called on, a girl whose name was Tricia, turned towards the class behind her and said, "Boring," and got the laugh she wanted. He waved his hand and motioned for everyone to quiet down, reiterating the last word, boring. The next student called out "reading," followed by "Harry Potter," "wizard," "magic," "pagan," "weirdos," and then "gay."

Again, the class laughed—except for a boy who sat in the back of the class-room. His name was Nathan.

Greg wanted to address the comment and the laughter. On the one hand, he knew it was kids being kids—they'd laugh at anything they knew was over that line of appropriateness. For most of them, it was nothing but laughing at a kid for being a jackass. On the other hand, he also knew that one or two felt being gay was more than weird. It was obscene. But he couldn't have that conversa-tion, so he didn't.

"All right, settle down. And let's make sure we're keeping things appropri-ate." He felt his thoughts knotting up at the thought. *Appropriate. What the hell am I saying?* "Let's just move on." He walked around the room and handed out copies of *The Sound of Thunder*. He then wrote the word 'plot' on the board and accompanied it with Freytag's Pyramid. He knew he had to work on how the plot works and the essential elements of literature; he also knew most of the kids didn't care. But one or two of them might.

After getting through the first page, Greg asked questions and filled out the pyramid. "So, let me ask you this. Where would you go if you had a chance to time travel?"

Greg waved his hand toward the girl named Tricia.

"I'd like to go back to the 60s," she said.

Greg nodded his head in support. "Why?"

"I'd like to see the Civil Rights Movement firsthand. See how different it is from what the books say or what we're told." There was defiance in her voice that threw him off. He knew it shouldn't, though. If there was one big difference between when he was growing up and today, everyone asked more questions.

"Interesting," he said as he shifted to sit against his desk. For a moment, he looked down to make sure he wouldn't knock anything over, but he only had his turn-in bin there. "What do you think you might see?"

"Well, we're kind of just told that Martin Luther King led us through the movement preaching peace, and Malcolm X pushed violence. So, we're left to assume that everyone who followed Martin Luther King was just fine being hosed and beaten and everyone following Malcolm X hated white people."

"Excellent points Tricia. The great thing about the age you're growing up in is that you don't have to settle for what you're taught. You have to be careful with your sources, especially those secondary sources...which are what?" he asked. As important as some conversations were, he always tried to tie things to ELA.

Tricia didn't miss a beat. "That's when information is obtained through a secondhand person."

He smiled. "Good. Now, someone else." He looked to the back of the room. "Nathan."

The boy's head popped up, and he looked like the proverbial deer in headlights. Greg felt terrible for a moment but continued. "Where would you travel to?"

"Um…" Nathan stuttered. "It's Nate, please. And well, um…"

"It's okay, Nate," Greg said, acknowledging the request. One of the things he learned the previous year was that making small gestures of acknowledgment helped in so many ways, the most obvious being that it built trust with him. "First thing that pops into your head." He nodded and smiled.

"Well, I guess I'd go into the future."

Greg looked toward the ceiling in thought for a moment and then nodded in approval. "Fair enough. I didn't lay out any parameters. But, if we did have access to a time machine, it's entirely plausible that you could move forward in time. So, Nate, why go into the future? What do you think you'd find?"

Nate swallowed and pushed himself up in his seat. His gaunt features were highlighted by the paleness that had come over his face. "Well, um…I guess I'd just like to see what's changed. See how different things are…or if they're not different."

"What do you hope you'd find?" Greg asked.

Nate looked around the classroom. Greg could tell there was a thought bouncing around in Nate's head, trying to find a way out, needing to find its way out. "I…I don't know. Something cool. Giant robots or something."

Greg extended his hand, the gesture suggesting it was an okay answer. "Giant robots would certainly be cool." He glanced at the clock in the back of the room—intentionally placed there so that he could see the time during lessons, but the students couldn't stare at it easily. He had a minute before class would end, and he'd have his next set of students to work with. "So, let's stop here for today. Keep your copies easily accessible; we'll finish reading tomorrow. Give some more thought to that question. And more importantly," he said as the bell rang and the students began to pick up their books, binders, and book bags. "Have a good rest of your day."

"Nate," Greg said.

Nate looked timidly at him. "Yes, Mr. Hilliard?"

"I noticed you were a bit distracted in class. I know it's the first day back, but it was more than just readjusting to being in school. Is there anything you want to talk about?"

Greg knew Nate wouldn't give him a candid answer. Getting kids to open up was one of the more challenging parts of the job. One of his professors had said, 'Teenagers are like playing a game of chess. You must be patient. You have to play the long game.' So, the most significant move he could make right now was to let Nate know he was someone he could speak to when he was ready.

Nate looked away. "No. I just didn't sleep much last night. First day back jitters, I guess."

"Well," Greg said as his next class began to file in and take their seats. "If you ever need to talk, door's always open. Always."

Nate hoisted his bookbag onto his shoulders and smiled—more out of obligation than appreciation. *The long game.* "Thanks, Mr. Hilliard."

"See you tomorrow," he said.

The rest of the day was reasonably calm. A lot smoother in most regards than his first day the previous year. Still, something gnawed at him as he looked at the corner of his desk—where a picture would look nice. He took a deep breath.

His phone vibrated.

He turned his phone over and opened the text message. It was from Paulo. It read: How was the first day back?

He responded: Not too bad. I only counted three students who fell asleep.

Paulo's next message read: Well, it's only the first day. I'm sure those numbers will increase. :) Seriously though, don't stay too late. I'm starting dinner now. The storm is coming soon. Get home. Be safe. You deserve a warm meal. Love you.

Greg smiled and sent back: Thanks, Luv. See you soon. <3

He opened the drawer on the side of his desk, pulled out a framed picture, and placed it on the corner of his desk. It was Paulo and him on their first vacation together a year and a half ago. They'd traveled to Seattle. The picture was from inside of the Space Needle. He loved the picture. There was something as they sat at the table and just talking that felt right—even as they knew that the dinner cost so much they'd have to settle for fast food on their last day. He stared at it for a long while, thinking about what to do about Nate.

A knock at his doorway.

"One day down. One-hundred-seventy-nine more to go," said Tiana.

"Already counting down?"

"It's always good to be back. But it's a marathon, not a race. So, sometimes it is good to know how far we have to go so we pace ourselves. I worked with a man five or six years ago, an older gentleman. First month or two, he was a ball of fire. But after those first two months, he was spent. He struggled to get to Christmas break."

"Point taken."

She looked at the frame on his desk, and Greg noticed her cheery disposition faded. "I'm sorry."

Greg nodded. "It's not your fault."

"I know. Just pretty shitty that I can leave my picture up with my husband. No one bats an eye. If you had yours up," she threw her hands up and tossed her head around, mimicking the Joker in *The Dark Knight*. "Everyone loses their mind." Her arms fell flatly to her side in defeat.

Greg stared at the picture on his desk. He never planned to make it a topic of conversation. He was sure none of the other teachers did that, and even if they did, no one would ever question them about it. He just wanted it there so that when he was having a hard day and didn't have a moment to send a text, he could glance at the picture and try to recenter himself. It was draining trying to work through a lesson with twenty-plus students who didn't all learn the same way, at the same speed, or have the same attention span. And it was even more difficult navigating through the personalities. Some needed to be pushed, and others hid if you pushed. "Well, the district thinks it'll just bring chaos into the classroom. So, rules are rules, I guess," he said.

"You're an ELA teacher. You've read enough to know that's not always an acceptable answer." Her face tightened. "Well, I have to go. Mikhail is making dinner tonight. Looking forward to it."

Greg smiled. "Enjoy." Then they exchanged salutations, and Tiana left Greg to sit at his desk. He picked the picture up and smiled. Dinner would be waiting for him, too, when he got home. After placing the framed photo back into his drawer, he wondered why he didn't share that with Tiana. He pushed the papers of his lesson plan back together and placed them in his laptop bag. He made sure to turn the lights off before heading home.

He was on autopilot as he drove home. His mind drifted in and out of the talk radio that played. There was more to this than just a picture. He felt like he had to hide this thing about himself. There was a student lost in all of this who was probably as confused as he was at that age and trying to figure himself out. He tried to remember when he was able to come to terms with being attracted to men and that he couldn't make himself be attracted to a woman.

His head began to throb as the thoughts swirled around in his head, a cocktail of confusion about what he should do; what was right didn't mix well with what was allowed. Nathan--Nate-- needed his help, but it would only take a single complaint, and he'd be gone without a job. Paulo made good money, but a single income would only get them so far, especially if he got sick. He took another deep breath and refocused on the drive.

"Nate," he said aloud. "Shit. I'm sorry, kid. I don't know what to do. I wanted to be a teacher to help kids figure themselves out. Always felt stories were the best way to do that. For me, it was. And now I'm going to work tomorrow; know you just need someone to tell you you don't have to hide or apologize for who you are. But who am I kidding? That's not as true as it needs to be."

He pulled into the driveway of their home, parked the car, gathered his things, and went inside. Paolo had dinner ready—Country Fried Steak, garlic-whipped mashed potatoes, and fresh, not canned baked beans. They sat and ate, and Greg told the man he loved about his day, leaving out the part about Nate. Paolo could tell something was wrong. Greg was never very good at hiding his emotions. The glances into the distance were his telltale sign. But he didn't want to talk about it. Greg was still learning how to open up. Paolo pressed more before placing his hand over Greg's, offering a smile, and said, "It's okay. You don't want to talk about it right now. I'll be here when you're ready. Or until my patience runs out, then I will make you tell me." They both laughed.

Greg went to bed that night much like the night before, comforted in Paolo's arms but still struggling to sleep.

When class started the next day, he had the students take out their copies of *The Sound of Thunder*. He glanced at Nate. "When we think about the possibility of time travel, it's very natural to think about what the world was like or what it might be like one day. It's not unnatural to fill the vision with the things we want the world to be. So, as we move forward this year, I'd like you to consider this: what do you want the future to look like? And then, what can you do to make that happen? It starts with accepting yourself. Then it becomes pushing yourself. And then it's about standing up for yourself." He held up his copy. "And read. There's still a lot to be learned from stories. In the case of *The Sound of Thunder*, we are going to learn…" he sighed as his thoughts escaped him. "I'm sorry. Lost myself there for a moment." He wanted to tie the text into a message, but it just wasn't there at that moment. "Um, you know what, let's just get back into the story. We can dissect it after we have a foundation to speak on."

Greg called students out at random. He'd read the story enough times that he could weave in and out, asking questions and leaving it to the students to do the heavy lifting. It struck him during that class period that that's what adults do to kids far too often: they create the questions and leave it to the kids to figure out the answer. And he thought the answer was just to bury it and keep it inside and not let anyone know because it's easier for everyone else.

He glanced at Nate and then opened his drawer. He pulled out the frame of him and Paolo and glanced at it momentarily. They'd met in college and have been together since. He was the first person he'd opened up to about his struggles with his parents, about having no idea what he was doing in college. He was the first person he talked to about being gay. He picked the framed picture from his drawer and placed it in the corner of his desk. He smiled.

And then he continued teaching.

Jerry W. Vandal was born and raised in Cleveland, Ohio. He grew up on a diet of Ninja Turtles, X-Men, and Final Fantasy. He began focusing on telling stories while obtaining degrees in English and Psychology from Cleveland State University. Jerry has seen publication with Gray Haven Comics, in Irish Imbas' *2018 Celtic Mythology Anthology*, and with *Literary Cleveland*. He is an avid reader of comic books, a lover of mythology and make-believe worlds. He resides in Parma Heights with his wife, Emily, and their two dogs, Jenelle and Axel.

Your Other Life

Peter Gorman

Amidst empty pizza boxes, a guitar with broken strings, unopened mail, and bookshelves full of vintage alarm clocks, Theo Goss gives birth to people who have already died. For a fee. Admittedly business has declined over the past year, and there are never repeat customers. But why should there be? If you only get one life, you should only get one other life too.

Julia calls and asks what he's doing. "Your Other Life," he says. She is an auditor who paints on the side. He is unemployed.

"And how long are you going to do this?" she asks, meaning how long is he going to maintain this online game, but perhaps also how long before he gets a job.

"I'll keep at it until no one wants to play anymore."

There is some tension, he thinks, in their differing incomes (he survives mostly on alimony). But there is some tension in every relationship. Perhaps he will get a job soon if it matters to her. He is happy with Julia, and that's something worth preserving.

Back to work.

He begins the first email the same way to every customer: This person was alive once, and this is what happened to them. This person is you.

Subject: Your Other Life
Dear Stefan Sedlak:

In 1871 you are born a boy into the Austrian Empire, in the town of Brno, Czechia. Your father is a laborer, a builder of houses. Your mother takes care of you and your slightly older brother. The family will welcome another son and a daughter in a couple of years. Whether your family is thriving is not something you ponder. You are fed each day, and you sleep with your brother on a bed of rough cotton. You go to school and learn to read. Your family celebrates your birthday every January 18. It seems you are happy.

Your Other Life is the creation of Theo Goss (American, born 19--), a site where customers get a series of emails about a random life. Theo has online census information from 1790–1910 for North America and most of Europe and generates random numbers to select a person from his vast database. Then he does further research to find out anything he can about that person's life.

Yes, he makes up some things. He doesn't make up the known facts: the dates of birth and death, the family information, marriage, if any, and career if found. He does slightly change the person's name and addresses the customer by this name in his emails. Then he tells that person's story. The customer has no say in the selection of a life. He does let them draw out certain parts, fills in details when they want to know more, and skips ahead many years if requested. What he doesn't do is let them live forever.

Subject: Your Other Life
Dear Stefan Sedlak:

You are a good student, but school bores you. By the age of thirteen, you drop out to join your father on a construction crew, building brick houses and an occasional store. At first, you do basic tasks, such as sweeping up and pushing a wheelbarrow; later, you learn bricklaying skills. By the age of 17, you are on a separate crew from your father, and you wonder if this is deliberate, perhaps your father's attempt to give you independence. You also become rather proficient on the violin.

So, a limited education for Stefan Sedlak. This is where customers can get a bit antsy, realizing that they aren't going to continue their schooling, now likely to fade into working–class gray and perpetual obscurity. That's why Theo added that bit about the violin. Let the customer think his life will be more interesting, that maybe he'll become a traveling musician. That won't happen, though. In truth, Stefan Sedlak will never leave Brno until they come to take him away.

This customer has emailed to ask if Stefan Sedlak will marry. He will find out soon enough. The facts are what they are. Many customers believe they will get somebody famous, but the odds of that are infinitesimal. And even if they get a historical figure, it could just as easily be John Wilkes Booth as Lincoln. (No one really wants to be Lincoln anyway, with that assassination looming in their future). The reality is that they get someone obscure, forgotten by history, just like their real life.

◆

An early morning walk in Golden Gate Park with Julia and almost no one else around. They've been dating for five months now. While Theo knows it's delusional to believe he's never been happier (that's just the present tense talking), it feels that way all the same. Julia doesn't care that he's unemployed, that he lives in a modest apartment. He sees the world in a similar way, the way of an artist. "That's more important than income or status," she'd told him. "One of the benefits of being older is realizing that."

Though she did ask him about his job prospects last week.

They walk around the park on a cool spring day, though every day in San Francisco is a cool spring day. Julia favors bold colors for her clothes; today, a long red coat over bright yellow pants. They say little on their walk. They don't have to. It seems as if no one else is around, as if San Francisco has left the stage just for the two of them.

Never been happier.

> Subject: Your Other Life
> Dear Stefan Sedlak:
>
> You first see Kamila behind the counter of a bakery. You are there to get a cake for your mother's birthday. Kamila is blond and looks to be a teenager, though you will soon find out that she's 20, like you. The next time you see her, she's feeding stale bread to the pigeons in the town square. You talk to her for a few minutes, and then some more, until you are late returning home. The next day you find her in the bakery and ask her to walk with you when she is free from work. It is a brisk March afternoon when you propose to her in the park, birds in the trees singing of their return, and no one else in sight as if the city has left the stage to just the two of you.
>
> The marriage takes place at a synagogue in 1892, with both families in full attendance. After two days at a countryside inn, you begin living with your new wife in an attic room at her parents' house. The two of you know nothing of the world beyond Brno, but now you're getting to know each other.

"Things are getting weird with my current customer," Theo tells Julia. "He's emailing me, asking not just for details about his wife, but even suggesting some things, such as that she laugh at his jokes, and maybe she could let her hair down to her shoulders."

"So why not just give him that? The customer's always right."

"Because it violates the code of the game. You can't change the past."

"Theo, it's your game. You can change it all you want."

No, he can't. The great thing about this game is that it has endless possibilities, so long as he leaves it all up to chance. You could be born a merchant or a slave, grow up in a big family or as an orphan, rise up in the world, or never get anywhere at all. You could live to an old age and experience the death of so many others. You could die young yourself. That happens far too often. Theo no longer tells them of their children dying and removes those poor souls from history instead, so there's something he does change. Still lets the customer's character die young, though, if that's what happened.

♦

That night he plays guitar for Julia, having recently replaced the broken strings. He doesn't sing well, but he has a heartfelt vocal style. She has told him so.

Subject: Your Other Life
Dear Stefan Sedlak:

Your days are uncomplicated. You go to work and build houses. You come home to dinner with your in-laws. Kamila still works at the bakery, and though you insist she stay home, she replies that she will only do so once she becomes a mother. The happiest times are when you play the violin for her in the attic room. She paints her toenails, which women don't do in this time and place, but she does it for you. There are arguments, too, mostly about money. And Kamila stops working at the bakery not because she is pregnant but because she is ill, coughing, and at times struggling to breathe.

The customer is unsatisfied. He wants to know more about his life with Kamila "and the joys of going through this world together." No doubt he romanticizes marriage so much because he's never been married. Theo writes him another email with some positive details about Stefan Sedlak's life, such as a romantic outing on the city river and their mutual caring for a red prayer plant (which dies that winter). Also included are details of his wife's illness, now diagnosed as tuberculosis.

Then the customer complains that the game is rigged, and after he receives an email about sending his wife to a sanatorium for treatment, responds with a message that says in its entirety, "Don't do this to me."

This bothers Theo because he knows what happens next. But as he tells himself, you can't change the past.

Subject: Your Other Life
Dear Stefan Sedlak:

Your wife is at the sanatorium with an infectious disease for which there is no known cure. However, she could recover with the aid of doctors and nurses, who seek to keep her rested and nourished. It is her first time outside Brno, and she is not allowed visitors. It is for the safety of her loved ones that she must remain isolated until she recovers. You receive an encouraging letter from her, though a subsequent one expresses her loneliness. In another letter, she admits to feeling worse and regrets having taken so long to write. Then her letters stop altogether until a messenger delivers the news that Kamila died on an unseasonably warm December day in the year of our Lord 1894.

For two days, Theo gets no response. Usually, he gets nothing from customers, but this one had been emailing him every day, so the silence is a bit surprising. Then he gets a reply that says, "Fuck you, Theo Goss." And then nothing more.

Fine. That will end the correspondence. They were at six emails anyway, the contract fulfilled, though he could have gone on for many more if requested, offered at a special rate. Stefan Sedlak has a lot more life to go, though, in 1940, it will end so horribly. Maybe best for the customer that his story ends here. Forget about him. There are other past lives that Theo is now researching and sending a series of emails to customers who won't be any happier with how their lives turn out. They won't lash out, though, most of them. And if anyone does, that person will be a man because it's always a man who wants to let you know what a jerk you are for telling the truth.

◆

He is at Julia's apartment, the evidence of a painter-in-residence in every room. Even the kitchen has a still life of fruit painted on a wall. He wants to talk about art, but Julia doesn't. She is concerned about her son, who is in-between colleges, but Theo can't tell her he knows what she's going through. He knows nothing of being a parent.

When he asks if her son's education costs worry her, she admits that his father is paying for all that. This is news to him. It means they are both essentially receiving alimony. He mentions this and soon regrets it.

Later that night, he calls her and offers to sing and play guitar for her over Zoom. She says she's tired and declines. Two days later, she cancels a dinner date, too, for the same reason.

◆

A week passes. A customer has gotten a soldier in the American Civil War and writes that he is excited about this. It will be fun to write emails about this man's war experiences, but his story will be over soon enough (killed at Chickamauga in 1863). Better than the woman who just died at the age of five in some French village. Or maybe not better. Maybe nothing's better.

He is busy researching the Battle of Shiloh when an email arrives with a subject line that catches his attention. He knows he should ignore it but reads it anyway.

Subject: The Forgettable Life of Theo Goss (a Work in Progress)
Dear Theo Goss:

You are born a boy in a suburb of Oklahoma City. Your father works in advertising, which must have been slim pickings in Oklahoma. Your mother takes care of you and your two sisters. You do not ponder whether your family is thriving (it isn't). You get picked on at school until you're a teenager when they ignore you instead. Your mother dies when you are 16, leaving just dear old Dad, with whom you never get along. You finally go off to college, the University of Tulsa, where you expect to fit in socially for the first time, but you don't. You go to school year-round, so you don't have to go home. Congratulations on graduating college in just three years. It seems there's a bright future ahead!

The email is signed, "Stefan Sedlak."

Fair enough, Theo thinks. There's a lot of information out there about everyone, and almost everything this guy wrote about him is true. No doubt that was just a guess about his relationship with his father, but he got it right. The only wrong detail was going to school year-round—Theo only wishes he'd done that. Instead, he went home for the summers and dealt with his father's bitterness. "Stefan" must have figured that he went to college each summer because he graduated in three years, but he just took extra courses to get out of there early and then get the hell out of Oklahoma.

> Subject: Your Other Life
> Dear Stefan Sedlak:
>
> You continue living in Brno, the only place you've ever known. Sometimes you play the violin at your wife's graveside unless it's too cold or you're too miserable to play. In 1901 your parents die within three months of each other. You take care of the funeral arrangements because, alone among your siblings, you have experience in this area. People are optimistic about the new century, but not you. Your back is often ailing from a lifetime of physical labor. If only you'd stayed in school! But it's too late now. It's too late for everything.

The facts are the facts. Stefan Sedlak never remarries, never becomes more than a laborer, never leaves Brno until the very end, and not by choice. Theo supposes he could give Stefan a romance, a brief affair that could have happened, but back then, if a relationship didn't end in marriage, then it probably ended badly (this is still true). The customer should be thankful that he's given him solitude. He lets Stefan know that these additional emails are "on the house." If he wants to take it to the bitter end, then Theo will bring him there.

Julia is no longer returning his calls. The only person he seems to hear from anymore is Stefan Sedlak.

> Subject: The Forgettable Life of Theo Goss (a Work in Progress)
> Dear Theo Goss:
>
> St. Louis, Atlanta, Chicago.... You spend no more than a year in any of those places, finding out that moving to a new city doesn't change who you are (and how much you'd like to do that!). You do finally meet someone, a woman named Joanne, and you marry her in the year of our Lord 2002. Together you move to the San Francisco Bay Area. You are optimistic about your future in the new century. You've never been happier, though that's not saying much. As the years pass, you wonder why Joanne often works late and takes so many business trips. You want to trust her, you really do, but ultimately you don't. You listen to slow music at half speed, Sinatra singing about loneliness and taking twice as long to do it.

One benefit of having lived long ago, or even in the last century, was that your past stayed past except for some census details. They couldn't find your ex-wife and ask her about your personal issues. Your failings. The revelation that he played music at half speed isn't embarrassing, but that someone could find it out bothers him. True, he was optimistic about his marriage in its early years—who wouldn't be? His story will only get worse, and he doesn't need some stranger to tell him that.

He could write Stefan Sedlak an email about Thomas Edison coming to Brno in 1911 to see the electrical lighting system he designed for a local theatre and let Stefan be there, too, with a woman at his side. She could also be fascinated by the new technology and somewhat in awe of him. True, he will have little money, but he will be in love. He could write all this; maybe Stefan Sedlak will consider it a peace offering. The story about Thomas Edison in Brno is true. The rest, of course, is speculation. But perhaps it really did happen?

And yet he still can't write it.

> Subject: The Forgettable Life of Theo Goss (a Work in Progress)
> Dear Theo Goss:
>
> Did she start seeing him while you were still married, or was it soon after the divorce? You ponder this because your divorce went through in 2013, and she remarried a mere ten months later. Someone she met at work, perhaps? Nothing you dwell on, or at least you try not to. Her new husband works as a programmer in Silicon Valley, and she now has a spouse earning a significant salary, one equal to her own. If only your pride had allowed you to ask for alimony from your ex, you'd be doing all right now and not trying to earn a living by writing about past lives and wrecking them for your customers. If only you weren't so proud. But the facts are what they are.

She'd met her second husband through work, and yes, while still married to her first husband. Not that he's going to clear this up for anyone. And as for being too proud to ask for alimony, he isn't. The alimony—which will only last another year—allows him to spend his days working on Your Other Life. This site alone would never pay the bills. It is a public service. It makes people appreciate what they have, to be glad they're alive in this time and place, and not wish they were back in some past that never was.

He texts Julia. "Are you O.K.?" A day later, she replies, "Yes."

◆

The emails come in the middle of the night. Even though he knows what happens next, it still hurts him to wake up and read a stranger's email about the next chapter in his life story. Once he gets up around 4 a.m. and sees an email with that regrettable subject line, and he doesn't open it, thinking he'll go back to sleep, but sleep doesn't come, and at dawn, he reads about his father's death and how he finds it bittersweet.

His ex-wife had called him when his father died, which was nice, and she was the one who said that his death must be "bittersweet for you." And had he agreed or made any response at all? And how do you get any sleep after a stranger has reminded you of that?

You don't sleep, he finds out. He does so little of it these days. He plays slow music at half speed when he's unhappy because when Sinatra sings for the lonely, and it still doesn't sound lonely enough, he needs to make it even slower. Joanne knew this. Perhaps she shared it with his biographer. Perhaps the guy already figured it out anyway.

He keeps thinking of a recent surprise visit Julia made to his apartment, during which she realized that her portrait of him was missing. Theo pulled it out of the closet, explaining that he'd taken a break from looking at himself, finding the portrait too revealing. She asked what he meant by that, to which he replied that he didn't know, which was true. He regrets ever taking the portrait off his wall, but he's not putting it back.

♦

He finally hears back from Julia, a text that says, "I've met someone else. Do you want to talk about it?"

He doesn't.

For a full day, he stops checking his email since there's no good news that could be out there waiting for him. And then he checks it.

> Subject: The Forgettable Life of Theo Goss (a Work in Progress)
> Dear Theo Goss:
>
> You move twice while in the San Francisco Bay area, thinking a change of location will do you good, but it does no such thing, as you are arrested in 2015 after attempting to buy drugs from an undercover cop. You "do time," as they say, which is a nice way to put it. Not a lot of time, but it is disconcerting. You find the community service somewhat degrading, but you complete it. And what do you do to turn your life around? You start an online game from which players are assigned people from the past, and then you take them through that life and break their fucking hearts. You justify this by telling yourself that if your life is bad, then maybe you can make others think their lives are bad too—and it works! At least for a while, it works. All those gaps on your resume, though. What will you tell potential employers? Do you really want to talk about your website? You could always lie. You're good at that.
>
> Hope you're happy now.

Give him credit. Stefan Sedlak got most of the facts right, except why he started the site and that he's a good liar. Theo never intended to make people unhappy. And if he were good at lying, Stefan Sedlak would have lived happily ever after.

Theo no longer thinks this guy contacted his ex-wife. All the information is out there about him, all his message board comments and social media life. And after finding out those things, one could make reasonable guesses about the rest. But he'd been clean and sober for almost six years now, and he doubted you could find that on the internet.

Out for a walk. He wears a light jacket while listening to his iPod, then shuts it off. There's nowhere to go. He walks to the water and sits on the grass, almost under the Bay Bridge. To his left is Cupid's Span, a massive bow and arrow structure, there to remind him how alone he is, as if he needs reminding. He's tried online dating but found his unemployment status quite the deal-breaker. Maybe he'll try again once he has a real job. Maybe it just isn't meant to be.

◆

Much later, with his computer screen the only light in the darkness, Theo generates a randomly selected person for himself. And then another. And then five more. But he keeps dying young or ends up alone or living in poverty, where life is both too brief and too long. He gets an American soldier who fought in World War I and is forever missing in action and a 19th-century British woman who dies giving birth to her fifth child.

He tries again. He wants to be married with at least three children. He wants to live to see all his children grow. He wants at least mild prosperity. More than anything, he wants to matter and will keep trying until he does.

Peter D. Gorman grew up in Youngstown, Ohio, and graduated from Miami University. He has published short stories in various magazines, including *Hayden's Ferry Review*, *The Pinch*, *Raleigh Review*, and *Sycamore Review*.

Home

Timothy Doyle

My suitcase has changed. Hard-shelled, oblong, and rounded at the corners, it seems oddly shaped now, but that's not what's different. It feels more solid than I remember. Maybe because I never paid much attention to it before. I leave it lying open on the bed and stare at my short row of tightly rolled shirts and pants, at my small clear plastic case of shampoo and toothpaste tucked into the corner. I pay attention to everything now: every object I use; every movement I make; every minute that passes. The world seems more real than it used to. I wonder if that's because I'll be leaving it soon. With no time stretched out in front of me, my ghosts have left, and I'm alone.

I'll never be a ghost. I have no one to haunt. Certainly not my partner, Sean, who was with me for twenty years before he finally left "to pursue other experiences." He wouldn't be worth haunting, even if I could find him. I will not haunt my family. I haven't seen them since I was young, and I will not see them again, with one exception. They are Pentecostals and too sure of themselves to be haunted by me. I've been dead to them for years anyway.

I am leaving this morning, taking my first plane trip in years to go to the place where I was born. I won't see any ghosts along the way.

♦

I feel aggravated on the plane. Almost every person annoys me: the bored, irritable passengers in their rumpled clothes; the flight attendants with their businesslike instructions; the captain when he makes his garbled messages on the intercom. My seat is even more tight and uncomfortable than usual because my body is aching. I am feeling the pain now, as the doctors warned me.

My entire trip is laid out in stages in my mind. I don't have a full count of the stages, but I mark each one off as it passes: the trip to the airport, the boarding, the flight, the landing. I feel a slight relief as each stage passes until I can come home again.

When I feel the familiar bump of the front wheel of the plane hitting the tarmac, I let go of some tension. The wheel bounces like a ball several times, and the plane goes up in the air again before the final bump comes; the rear wheels follow, and the roar of the brakes fills my ears. It is oddly comforting to me that everyone leans slightly forward against their seatbelts as the brakes take hold, all of us immobile for just those few moments, a group united.

"Welcome to Pittsburgh," comes the voice of the flight attendant over the intercom. I don't listen to the blurb that follows. As the plane taxis, I worry that I will not recognize my sister. She started writing to me many years earlier when she married Danny, the brother of my childhood friend, Charlie. Their marriage was outside the Pentecostal church, and she has been an outcast, like me, although my brothers and mother still speak to her.

My hips hurt and my body aches as I follow the slow unwinding of people out of the plane and up the connecting corridor. The long walk past the other gates is as bleak as any airport. But I recognize my sister immediately as I step into the terminal. She is a flood of beige: pants, top and slip-on shoes. Her thin blonde hair is parted at the side and hangs down to her chin in what looks like a haircut she did herself. Maybe part of our childhood that she retains. She is very thin, and her arms and legs are long and very white. She wears glasses now. They are narrow, and the rims are beige.

She recognizes me, too. I can't tell if there is a momentary pause as she looks at me because I have become so thin, even more than she is. But she surprises me by opening her arms without hesitation to hug me.

"I never thought I would see you again," she says in my ear.

She steps back to give me another look.

"How have you been?" she asks, and I know that a part of her would like to bluntly ask other questions, as my parents would have when I was a child. But she has spent too much time being a part of the world, and she knows when to hold back.

"I'm tired," I say, deliberately focusing on the present moment. "I just want to get out of here."

"I understand. It's about an hour and a half drive."

We start to walk.

"Do you have luggage?"

"Just what I'm carrying."

"The car is this way."

At the parking meter machine, I try to pay, but she waves my hand away. She leads me to an older Toyota Corolla that is still in good shape. As we pull out of the garage onto the road, I am grateful that another stage has been completed.

We are driving west into Ohio. I have been worried that we won't have anything to talk about since we haven't seen each other in decades. As children, we weren't friends, but we were closer to each other than to anyone else in our family. Our parents and two brothers, Owen and James, were religious and filled with anger.

Sarah and I were the only children who would sneak out of the house to play, but only when we were absolutely sure we wouldn't get caught. Danny and Charlie, who lived on the farm that bordered ours at the back, were our only playmates.

We were a mismatched crew. Danny always wanted to play some sort of sport, and the rest of us didn't. We didn't have enough people for it anyway. Charlie and I liked to play at the edge of the creek that divided our properties. We were the same age and natural playmates. Sarah played with us, always complaining that she felt left out. Danny played with us reluctantly, but I knew he itched to have some sort of ball in his hand.

◆

As the car moves along the back roads, I am glad that Sarah makes conversation easily. She talks about the IGA store where she has been a manager for over fifteen years. Business is still good. They have no competitors.

"The problem is finding good staff," Sarah says. "When I do hire people, they don't want to work. That's the problem in an area where everybody knows everybody. When they're at work, they act like they're sitting in their living room."

The beige upholstery in Sarah's car is lightly faded, and there is a slight rattling sound coming from the front tire on the driver's side whenever she turns the car to the right. The ride is another stage, and I have already checked it off in my mind. I know I am being superstitious, but I hope that I haven't checked it off prematurely; this trip has been carefully timed, and if the car breaks down, I may not be able to finish my last pilgrimage.

We pass very old farmhouses set close to the road and other houses made out of brick or stone or covered with vinyl, built at various times within the last sixty years, set farther back. Many of the newer houses have large, solitary rocks set at the corners where their driveways meet the road. These are homes of leaden casseroles made with cans of cream of mushroom soup, baked in glass pans with edges permanently blackened from use. I know that deer carcasses often hang in many of the garages I see. A couple of times, we pass a faded wooden stand selling produce along the side of the road.

When she has finished talking about work, Sarah talks about the people who have moved and the people who have stopped farming. Sarah stopped farming when Danny died. She is about to say something else, but the car turns a corner, and what little there is of the town where we grew up comes into view. There is a bank, the courthouse, a few shops, the IGA, the school. We pass through it on the way to the only motel.

"I don't understand why you don't just stay with me," Sarah says. "I'm alone in that big house. It would be nice to have some company, even just for a couple of nights."

"I'm already causing you enough trouble," I say, and she shakes her head, but I'm thankful she doesn't say anything else. I don't want to go near her house, the house where Charlie grew up. I don't want to go near the barn behind it.

A few minutes later, we pull up in front of the motel. It is called 'The Homestead,' and the sign in front of it is very old and reads 'Cable Television, ESPN, CNN.' The sign hasn't changed since I was a teenager.

The young man behind the desk looks too young to have the job.

"I have a reservation," I say. "Hagerty. Two nights." The young man lifts the sole piece of paper on the desk.

"I have it here," he says.

The motel has one story, and its long, single row of rooms is bent in the middle, making an arrow sign if we were to see it from the sky. We drive along, looking at the numbers of the rooms, and Sarah stops in front of mine, not bothering to pull into a spot. There is no one else around. When I get out and start to pull my suitcase from the back seat, Sarah tries to help me.

"I can handle it," I say. "It's not heavy."

She follows me to the door of the room.

"You should at least have agreed to come to my house for dinner."

"I don't want to be any more trouble than I already am."

"What trouble? You keep saying that. It's only two nights after forty years."

"I want to see that restaurant again."

The restaurant is the T–Bar, an odd kind of family restaurant and steak place with a bar on one side. I always wanted to work there when I was a teenager.

Sarah is standing with her hands on her thin hips, and I can't read her mood. It has been too long since I've seen her.

"Is there anything else I can help with?" she asks.

"I'll be fine. I just want to lie down for a little while."

Sarah nods.

"I'll be here at 5:00 to take you to dinner."

The doorknob to the room wobbles a little, and the lock fights the key, but I shield it from Sarah as she gets back into the car. I finally get the door open as she starts the engine. The room smells stale, and when I turn on the overhead light in the front hallway, the bulb seems too dim for its purpose. I remember warnings about bedbugs and pull out the luggage stand for my suitcase. I am very tired now, and it takes some effort to get my suitcase in place. I can hear my medications rattle inside as I thump it down.

The room is dated, but I can't tell from which decade. The wallpaper is a little dingy, and the carpet a little bare. I walk across to the window. The border of grass between the back of the motel and the woods is a dry strip that needs mowing. I watch a robin as it flies to its nest; it looks at me, an unlikely stranger in the room, before it tends to its business.

Sarah is there promptly to take me to dinner at the T–Bar.

"Is the room all right?"

"It's fine."

"Not as good as what you're used to."

"Oh, I wouldn't say that."

I wonder what she thinks about my life and the places I have been. Places that she will never see. She doesn't seem envious, just a little curious. But she doesn't ask any more questions.

The T–Bar is as I remember it. Frozen in time. Big trapezoid–shaped sign with rounded corners out front. The booths are huge, and as we sit down, the only noise is the slight sound of clinking glasses from the kitchen. The waiter acts frightened, as if we are important people. I order a salad. Sarah orders a chicken breast. It comes with mushy vegetables and looks to be covered with cream of mushroom soup.

"Thank you for doing all of this for me," I say.

The conversation comes less easily at dinner. Sarah has already said everything there is to say about her work and has nothing to say about her farm. I don't want to talk about my life because there's really nothing to tell except for the obvious, which I'm sure she has been guessing about. The waiter keeps nervously filling our water glasses whenever we take a sip.

"I know you want to ask," I say. "It's all right. Please do. It'll be easier for me than having to just say it myself."

Sarah puts her worn silverware down and collects herself.

"Is it AIDS?"

I shake my head.

"No, it isn't AIDS. It's just lymphoma. Well, not 'just.' If I'd caught it sooner, then they could have cured it, probably. But it was so late that they were going to have to cut too much out, and the prognosis wouldn't have been good anyway."

Sarah takes a drink of her water.

"I'm sorry," she says.

"Thanks. But there's no need to be."

"I can come if you need help. I can come to where you live."

"That's kind of you. Really, it is. But I have a friend, Tiggy, who lives a few doors down from me, and we have this pact. We always promised that we would help each other out if something like this happened. I'm getting the good end of the deal."

I watch her shiver a little when I say that.

"It's all right," I say. "Really, it is."

Sarah nods, and she looks like a child again. Overall, there is still something childlike about her. She and Danny never had children. I don't know if that was planned or not, and I don't know her well enough to ask about it. Sarah hasn't suffered the added aging that comes with parenting; she hasn't been through the extra work and worrying, as I haven't.

Sarah wants to ask something else, and I watch her struggle with it. I would help her, but I can't tell what she is thinking.

"Do you know...do you have any idea..."

As I study her face, it suddenly occurs to me.

"Where I'll be buried?" It seemed so inconsequential to me that I didn't think about explaining it to her.

"I won't. I'll be cremated, and the ashes will be scattered."

"But you'll have a gravestone?"

"No. I don't want a gravestone."

Even for her, this is an alien idea. I can tell she doesn't know what to say about it. What will there be left of me when the second coming arrives?

"I don't want to leave anything behind."

I watch her thinking as she pushes her vegetables around on her plate. Then she slowly leans toward me.

"Do you hate yourself?" she whispers as she looks into my eyes.

"No. Well, not really."

◆

She drops me off at the motel after dinner. It is still early, and the light is shining through the window, but I pull the drapes shut and get into bed. I pull the cover off, then lift the sheets and slide in, staying close to the edge.

Bedtime doesn't frighten me anymore. The bad dreams are gone. I sleep peacefully every night without medication. I fall asleep easily and don't wake until the sun is up. But on this particular night, being so close now to the house where I was born leaves me lying awake, thinking.

Sarah will take me to our old house the next day. We have planned my visit to coincide with the one day each year when my entire family leaves to visit my father's relatives. It would have been so much easier to do what I want to do if I'd just gone to Sarah's farm, but that was where Charlie grew up. And Sarah has told me that my brother James still walks to the edges of the grounds of the family farm occasionally and might see me. I'm not afraid of what he might say, but being shunned this late in the game is something I'd rather avoid.

I can still picture the house where I grew up so clearly: bare white walls with a cross here and there. My memories of my time in that house are as bare as the place itself, but one memory is clear in my mind. At one point, my mother decided that she was going to homeschool us, Sarah and I, the younger ones. In middle school, my mother pulled us out of the public system, and for three years, we didn't see any other children. But the state intervened. The law came down on her and told her that we had to go back to school. My mother wasn't giving us the proper education.

"The government," my mother said under her breath. "Tool of Satan." Mother invoked the wrath of God on them, but Sarah and I went back to public school again.

When we returned, I was in my sophomore year in high school. I had to work hard to catch up. Sarah and I sat alone together at lunch, the two religious freaks, or at least the children of religious freaks, with stiff, somewhat strange clothing. I can imagine how we looked. We spoke to almost no one.

I saw Charlie right away, but we only nodded at each other. In those few years, he had changed so much; he was taller, and his body was more lanky and fuller, but he wore the same kind of glasses and had the same haircut. He still seemed quiet. He didn't appear to have many friends. For some time, we nodded at each other as we passed in the hallways.

Charlie fascinated me in a way that he never had before. After a while, I found myself gawking at him whenever I saw him. At first, he must have thought it was because of old times, but then he realized it was something more. He started holding my gaze whenever I looked at him. This went on for a while, but we still didn't talk to each other.

Finally, one day he stopped suddenly at my locker.

"It's been a long time," he said.

"Yes."

I wondered if the other kids nearby were looking at us, but I didn't turn around to check. The way he was standing looked more like a challenge than a friendly conversation.

"Do you want to catch up sometime?" he asked.

I just stared into my locker for what seemed to be a very long time.

"Is it hard to get away from home?" he asked, leaning toward me.

I shut my locker and finally glanced around. A couple of kids were looking at us.

"I haven't done it in a while."

"We can go to a movie," he said. "Over in Plainville. I'm driving now. I don't have my license, but I have the truck."

I didn't move.

"Do you ever see movies?" he asked.

"I can," I said.

"How about Friday?"

I nodded.

"Can you meet me by the creek? Seven o'clock?"

Sneaking out the window was as easy as it had been when I was younger. Charlie met me where we had arranged and walked me to his house, and I got in his truck.

The silence in the truck was painful.

"Is it hard being back at school?" he finally asked.

"I'm getting used to it. Is anyone talking about us?"

Charlie shrugged.

"I don't know. I don't talk to many people."

At the theatre, he paid for my ticket. I had never seen a movie in a theatre before, and the bright colors and loud noise almost overwhelmed me. Charlie kept glancing over at me, watching my reactions.

Afterward, we got ice cream and sat in his truck.

"Sometimes, I wondered if I'd ever see you again," he said. "We were pretty tight when we were kids. I never had a friend like you."

"You didn't mind the church stuff?"

"That's not your fault."

Charlie and I started seeing movies most Friday nights. My parents were so used to my docility that they never thought that I would be sneaking out. That was the one real gift that my parents ever gave me. It was so comfortable being with Charlie again; he seemed to be as much of an outcast as I was, although I didn't know why.

One Friday, when we were eating ice cream, he made a comment about feeling like an outsider. He told me he thought he understood how it felt to be me. I was so relieved that I knocked my ice cream off my cone. Charlie laughed, picked up the scoop, and threw it out the window. As he rubbed my face with a napkin, his fingers touched my skin.

The feel of him was like nothing I could have imagined. It was like another universe. He was just cleaning me up, but I closed my eyes, and when I opened them, he was staring at me. I reached over and put my hand on his arm in a way that seemed almost religious, but we both knew it was something else. The ice cream was gone, but he kept wiping my face. Then he let go of the napkin and touched my face with his hand.

"I always liked you," Charlie said.

"I always liked you, too."

He stared at me for the longest time and then leaned forward. He was wondering if I would let him kiss me. I did.

We saw more movies together, but afterward, he would park somewhere, and we would kiss. It was so much better than the ice cream. When summer came and we were free from school, most days, we would meet at the stream. We would lie on the grass, holding each other—fully clothed at first. When we finally got enough courage, we took our clothes off and swam in the stream. And then eventually we took our clothes off and lay together on the bank. Charlie was so gentle. There was nothing but sweetness in him, in the way he always was with me, in the warmth of his lips, in the feel of his skin.

◆

My relationship with Charlie made school easier. He asked me once if I was worried about the church, and I answered him honestly that I had never been concerned about hellfire. I didn't have that kind of personality and had never fit in with my family. At home, I was as quiet as I had always been, and my parents never seemed to consider that anything could be going on. They never checked up on me.

I had always been a good student, and I excelled in high school. Those few years passed quickly. My senior year, I was offered a full-ride scholarship to Vanderbilt University, and I accepted it. My parents weren't sure about it, but I told them I could learn something that might help the farm.

Charlie didn't want me to leave. I told him that if I stayed, our relationship would be found out eventually. He was sullen that entire last summer, but at least he was still willing to see me. After I left for school, I wrote to him, but he never wrote back. I stopped when I thought that someone might take notice of my constant, unreturned letters.

I was relieved when I came home after the first year to find that Charlie was glad to see me. We spent the summer like we did in high school. Being back with him felt normal again, and I could tell he felt the same. I told him that there were places near the university where he could get a job and places where he could stay. He still didn't want to leave the family farm. But I talked to him about it all summer. By the time school was ready to start, I had convinced him. I would go away to school, and he would follow about a month later. It seemed as if I was going to get everything I wanted.

◆

The next morning, I was sitting down to breakfast with my parents, my two brothers, and my sister when my father said, "There was some news last night."

My mother had just put a bowl of oatmeal in front of me, and I was reaching for some sugar. She watched me as I took spoonful after spoonful.

"Charlie Bellam died," my father said.

Everyone looked up from the table, but I was the only person who stopped moving. I looked over at my father, and he was gazing at me, churning oatmeal in his mouth like an animal.

"Died?" I asked. My brothers continued eating. My sister was looking at me from the seat next to my father.

"Yes," my father said. "He was not acting like himself, his brother said. He was jumping up and down from the hayloft. During one of those jumps, he twisted around and fell backward. Broke his neck."

My mother shook her head with such vehemence that it almost made a noise.

"People are so reckless with the gift that God gave them," my mother said. "They refuse to understand it, and then it's gone."

"And they'll be shorthanded over on the farm now," my father said.

I stared at my oatmeal. I couldn't seem to tell what it was. That was the only other time in my life when the objects around me seemed unnaturally real. I could hear the clock ticking on the wall behind me, and I felt as if I was inside it. There was nothing in that room but the bowls of oatmeal, the sugar, the milk. The table. I could feel the weight of my body and the weight of every member of my family. It was so oppressive. After a few moments, I became aware that I must have appeared to be acting strangely. And then, automatically, I did what I had done when I was a child. I let a kind of deadening overwhelm me. A feeling of nothing. I let it fill every inch of me, and then I started to go through the motions of eating my meal.

"We used to see Charlie at school sometimes," my sister said, and I looked up at her. Her voice brought me back, at least from the deepest depths.

My family was looking at me.

"Yeah, I saw him sometimes," I said. "In the cafeteria."

For a moment, I wondered if anyone in my family knew anything. But I realized that they would have said something long before now. My brothers and father started eating again. My sister wasn't eating; she was still looking at me.

"I wonder where his body is," I said suddenly, without being able to stop myself. My family all looked at me again.

"In the morgue," James said, and by the look on his face, he seemed to think I was an idiot.

"Or maybe they just left his dead body in the middle of the barn floor," Owen said, and both he and James laughed.

"Have respect," my mother said.

I spent the rest of my time before I left for school the way I did at that breakfast. I knew that I was acting strangely. I have often thought that their observations of me during that time made my parents finally suspect that something had been going on between me and Charlie. They asked no questions. But I wondered if they seemed to hold themselves differently when they were around me.

I left at the end of that summer and never went back to the farm. I had a friend in college who understood 'my situation' and let me come home with him on holidays and summers. Once I was on my own, I tried to leave Ohio in the past.

I can still never be sure if my parents ever knew anything about me and Charlie. But after college, they easily figured out that I wasn't living my life according to what they considered to be God's plan. They had always told me that my body was a vessel and shouldn't be treated like a material possession, but they treated their own bodies more materialistically than I ever could have withstood.

After my sister married Danny, and she and I started writing to each other, she made overtures to my parents about me, but they wouldn't hear of seeing me again. I wasn't a part of their life anymore. They never wanted me to come back.

♦

The next day, Sarah comes to get me just before eleven o'clock. She takes me to a restaurant farther out in the country. It is a place that serves Amish food, but nothing about it seems very Amish. It's a large, popular place for city people looking to take a drive in the country.

We have time to kill before it will be safe to go to the farm, so Sarah takes me to country places to go shopping. We go to a quilt shop and to a farmer's market. One place is a huge building with rows of every kind of cheese you could think of. Sarah gets lost in it for a while, delving deep into every row before she checks the time and sees that we need to leave.

Sarah drives back through town and turns left on Parkhill Lane, going slowly until the house comes into view. It looks the same. All white and very weathered in places. An old farmhouse, two stories with a long front porch and long windows that never let in enough light. There is a silo to the side and a slightly decaying barn at the back. The ground around the buildings is a mixture of mud and gravel. The place has the air of something makeshift, like an army camp. The house looks like something an army unit has taken over. It feels like enemy territory.

It is an appropriately covert operation. My sister is smuggling me in on the one afternoon when no one is around. My brother, Owen, owns the hardware store in the next town over and comes by frequently to check on my mother. Since my other brother James runs the farm, he rarely leaves it. Sarah tells me that almost no one ever sees my mother.

"She stays in her room most of the time."

We both stare at the middle second-floor window, which belongs to my mother's bedroom. Although Sarah has assured me that the place is empty, we are nervous. But if Mother had heard Sarah's Toyota, we would have seen the curtains move.

"The car is gone. I'm sure the house is deserted. Do you want to go inside?" Sarah asks. "You have at least a few hours."

"No. I don't want to go inside the house."

I continue to stare at my mother's bedroom window.

"What do you want to do?" she asks. I glance over at her, and the late afternoon sun is reflected in her glasses. I don't say anything immediately.

As we sit there wasting precious time, I can sense that my sister has something on her mind. I wonder why she is reluctant to tell me what it is.

"You want to go to the creek," she finally says. "To that bank on the side of it near the oak tree, where we used to play."

"Why would you say that?" I ask.

She watches her finger as she runs it along the edge of the steering wheel.

"I saw you there once," she says. "With Charlie."

Immediately, I can picture her watching us lying together on the bank, and I feel suddenly embarrassed, as if the years haven't passed and Charlie and I are at that moment lying by the stream, and she is watching us.

"It's all right," she says. "I always liked Charlie so much, but he only wanted to be my friend. I always wondered who my competition was. I never thought it could be you."

"There was never any competition."

"No, there wasn't. I figured that out a long time ago."

I know now that Sarah thinks that I am going to a certain spot where I can remember my dead lover, but I'm not. I can't tell her the real reason I'm there. She wouldn't understand.

"Do you mind if I go alone?" I ask.

"Of course not," she says. "I was expecting it."

"But I don't want to leave you here by yourself."

She looks toward the barn.

"I'll be fine. I haven't been here in a while. I can check on the animals."

We both get out of the car. The gravel is thin under our feet, and my shoes squeak as I walk. Sarah watches me as I start to make my way around the house.

"Take your time," she calls after me.

I walk across the empty farmland, leaving the house behind me, and suddenly, I feel very alone. The soil is bare and looks dry and used. There is a line of trees in the distance. I walk toward it, and it takes a while, but as I come near, I can hear the stream. I slip through the trees and easily find the spot where Charlie and I used to lie together. It is smaller because the bushes have grown in, and the branches overhead are sagging. But it feels the same.

I watch the babbling stream. As I stand there, I can still feel Charlie's skin against my fingers. I can see his wet hair and the sweetness of his smile. I feel the pressure of his lips against mine. But he isn't a ghost anymore. This is nothing but a memory.

"You haunted me for so many years, my love, but not anymore," I say quietly to the place that we shared together.

I hear a bird squawk as if urging me on, and I look up into the sky. With the sound of the creek in my ears, I turn and start walking again onto Sarah's property, which Charlie's family owned. I cross more open farmland, which has begun to turn into a meadow. In the distance is another line of trees, but this one is broken in the middle, leaving an open space that faces the sun. It is an older meadow, the farthest piece of land from Charlie's old house.

I start to walk more slowly. Although I have waited so long for this moment, I feel hesitant now. I worry that it will not be the same. Short stalks of Queen Anne's lace drag against my legs as I move. Then, through the break in the line of trees, I can see the warm glow of the sun lying low in the sky.

The hesitation leaves me, and I quicken my pace, as if, after all this time, I will somehow be deprived of what I have come to see. I reach the break in the line of trees and step out into the meadow.

It is exactly the way I remember it. When I was young, no one seemed to pay any attention to this little corner of land. It was my private place on the rare occasion that I had the courage to leave the house and venture out alone. Throughout the years, I always begged Sarah to leave it the way it is, to cut it down just often enough to keep the woods from slowly coming back. She always asked me why.

The meadow is small, oddly shaped, and not suitable for farming. It is filled with a mass of flowers, mostly goldenrod, that extend in all directions. One day when I was young, wandering there alone, on just such a late summer afternoon as this, I saw it: the sunlight hit the goldenrod at a certain angle, setting it aglow and then turning back on itself, filling the air with an almost ethereal light. Here and there, swallowtail butterflies lazily rested on flowers, and there was the slight buzzing of bees as they collected their nectar. The wind lifted loose bits of petals and seedlings, filling the air with them in a golden haze.

A few times, I shared this meadow with Charlie. I don't know if he ever understood how I felt about the place, but I walked with him here, his warm hand tightly clasped in mine, when we were so many years, it felt, away from tears.

Grace has finally blessed me, and I am grateful for it. I am here, one last time, on a late summer afternoon, and the light is as warm and glowing as I remember. The light, feathery bits of flowers and seedlings are once again drifting through the air in a sea of disintegration. I feel as if I am dissolving into them. The horizon is blurred. I am melting with everything around me, floating in pieces up into the sky. I am not afraid. Here, the weight of everything seems as light as the breeze. Throughout every moment of my life, the truest part of myself has always been here in this field, taking in that radiant sunlight, which, really, I have only seen a handful of times, but that has always felt like home to me.

Timothy Doyle studied Russian and creative writing at Ohio State University. He lives in Columbus, Ohio, and spends most of his time trying to remember brilliant story ideas that he forgot to write down.

The Basement

Where Nefarious Things Happen

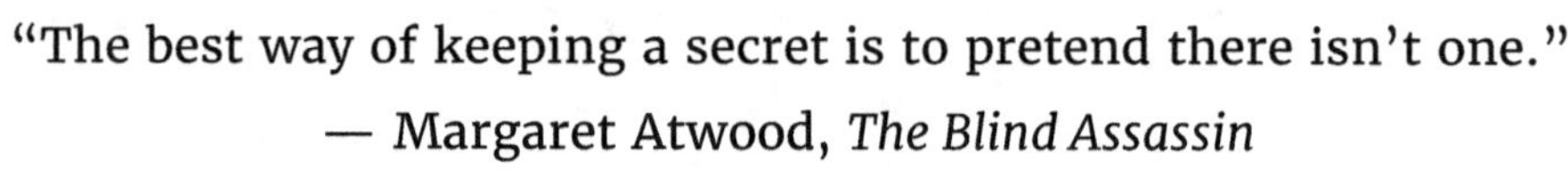

"The best way of keeping a secret is to pretend there isn't one."
— Margaret Atwood, *The Blind Assassin*

The Evil Twin

George Pallas

Norma Fulton treasured solitude. She lived by herself in an isolated cabin at the edge of Little Bear Lake. Shallow water kept boaters and fishermen at a distance, and the cottages and houses sparsely dotted around her property made the woods unsuitable for hunting. Weeks might go by without her seeing another human being, and that was fine with Norma. She was a self-sufficient woman. She raised chickens and grew most of her own food in a large, well-tended garden. Surplus vegetables and eggs she sold at the local farmer's market and used the money to buy staples like salt, sugar, and coffee. Especially coffee.

On a morning like any other, Norma finished breakfast and started to wash her dishes. The sink only held a few: a small plate, a pot she boiled the eggs in, a fork, and a coffee cup. The cup was almost dry when a persistent rapping sounded at the cabin door. She thought for a moment that she might have imagined it since visitors were such a rarity. But the rapping continued.

Norma didn't open the door immediately. She lived alone with no neighbors nearby, after all. Instead, she peeked through the peephole and decided her visitor was unlikely to be a threat. Opening the door revealed a bedraggled woman in her early or mid-thirties shivering in the doorway. Her dark brown hair was askew, looking like she'd showered and not bothered to dry or comb it out. Mud smeared her clothes, covering her shoes and blue jeans. Brown eyes stared at Norma with an emptiness indicating a recent trauma.

The stranger worked her mouth, trying to say something, but no sounds came out. After a few more tries, she managed to utter, "Accident. I've...been... accident."

Norma led the woman inside and sat her at the kitchen table. Rummaging in a tiny closet, she found a blanket to wrap around her shoulders. Next, she put a kettle on the stove. Hot tea would work wonders for a person who appeared to be half frozen.

While the water heated, she phoned the sheriff. There'd been an accident, she told the deputy who answered. No, she didn't know exactly where. The victim was in her cabin and probably needed medical attention. The deputy promised to send someone right away and hung up.

The teakettle was boiling furiously by now, steam shooting from its spout in a forceful and steady stream. Norma took it off the stove and poured steaming water into the cups she'd placed on the kitchen table while talking with the sheriff's deputy.

The tea worked its magic. Once the drink started to warm her, the woman was able to begin speaking coherently. "My sister and I had a terrible accident. She was driving, and all of a sudden, water was everywhere, and we were sinking. It took all my strength to shove the door open and work my way out. Somehow, I found my way to land in the dark. I must have passed out because I didn't remember anything until the sun was up this morning. And I didn't see Wanda anywhere."

Norma was about to ask the woman her name when a sheriff's cruiser crunched gravel in the driveway. She stood up, crossed to the door, and opened it before the deputy could knock. "Good morning, ma'am," he said. "I'm Deputy Mark Collins. Are you the one who called about an accident?"

"Yes. I have a woman inside here who seems to have been in one. Come on in."

"Yes, ma'am," he said, following her into the cabin, removing his hat as he did.

Not having many visitors, Norma's table only had two chairs. Collins sat in the one she vacated. Seeing that the teacups were almost empty, she took the kettle from the stove and refilled the cups. "Would you like some tea?" she asked.

"No, thank you, ma'am. But I would take a glass of ice water if it isn't too much trouble."

"No trouble at all." She took a tall glass from a cupboard, dropped in ice cubes, and filled it with water. After handing the glass to the deputy, she leaned against the sink to listen because both chairs were occupied.

Deputy Collins took a pen and notebook from his shirt pocket and prepared to start his investigation. Addressing the woman still wrapped in Norma's blanket, he began by asking her name.

"Wendy," she said. "Wendy Morris."

"Walk me through what happened."

Now, the words tumbled out when she spoke. "My sister Wanda and I had a girls' day out. We'd been shopping, to the movies, and to a late dinner. We were on our way home when Wanda—she was driving—decided to take a shortcut. It was so dark that I had no idea where we were, but Wanda said she knew where she was going. But then she started screaming her head off, and the car plunged into the water—I guess it was a lake or something. We went under. It looked like that submarine ride at Disneyland. When the water began coming in, I got my door open and got out. I don't remember how I got to land, but I did. I told this woman here—" she gestured toward Norma, "gosh, I don't know your name, dear."

"Norma. Norma Fulton."

"Anyway, I told Norma I must've passed out. The next thing I remember was waking up with the sun shining in my face."

Collins had been scribbling notes while she talked. When she paused, he asked, "Did your sister make it out of the car?"

"Honestly, I don't know. I didn't see her, so maybe she didn't." A sob escaped, and her shoulders shook with an involuntary shudder.

"Okay, this is important. Where did this happen?"

"I'm not sure. I followed the lake's shoreline until I stumbled across this cabin, so it's back that way somewhere." She pointed to indicate where she thought she'd come from.

"Ms. Morris, what's your sister's name?"

"Wanda Patterson."

Collins spoke into a walkie-talkie he took from his belt, giving his location and where he thought the accident might have occurred. He also requested an ambulance for Wendy. Norma couldn't understand the squawks that came in response, but apparently, the deputy did.

Turning to Wendy, Collins said, "I want to get a few things straight. What time was this?"

"It must have been around 11:00 or 11:30. We left the restaurant before they closed at 11:00, but not too long before."

"Who was driving?"

"Wanda was. She picked me up earlier in the afternoon, and we drove in her car."

"What movie did you see?"

"*Chantilly Bridge*." Collins raised his eyebrows in a silent question. "I doubt you've heard of it. It's a chick flick."

The deputy's quizzical look turned into a grin. "Now, you said you ate a late dinner. Where did you go?"

"Spinnoli's. It's a small family-run place about a mile from the mall. We decided to eat there because we both love their lasagna."

"Is that what you had?"

"Yes. Wanda, too. You see, we're twins, so we almost always order the same thing when we go out to eat."

"Did you have drinks, too?"

"Yes. We shared a bottle of Chianti. I guess it worked out to about two glasses apiece. But Wanda wasn't anywhere near drunk, if that's what you're getting at."

Collins said nothing. Before he could continue questioning, an ambulance swung into Norma's drive. The next few minutes were a blur of activity as the EMTs checked Wendy's vital signs and prepared her for transport. They loaded her into the ambulance in minutes, which roared out of the driveway, slinging gravel and leaving a contrail of dust until it reached the paved road.

Norma watched from the doorway as the ambulance disappeared. She was still standing there when Collins started to leave. The slight frown on her face caused him to stop.

"Something wrong?"

Norma's gaze remained fixed on the driveway. "I don't know...maybe," she said. Her voice sounded detached, as though her thoughts were far away.

Collins waited. If this woman had something to tell him, she'd do it when she was ready. A full minute passed before she turned to the deputy and said, "Something isn't right. I can't put my finger on it, but something's off about that woman."

"You think she's lying?"

"I don't know, deputy. It's hard to say. Her story was plausible enough, but...well, it sounded to me like it was a little bit rehearsed. You know, like she'd practiced it. Did you catch that?"

Collins frowned. "Can't say I did. But I'll let the detectives know. They may want to talk to you later."

"You can almost always find me here, and if I'm not home, I won't be gone long."

Deputy Collins stepped out onto the tiny stoop and donned his hat. "Thank you, ma'am," he said before walking to his patrol car.

◆

Wendy Morris waited with obvious impatience for the interview to begin. Pacing in the police station's small lobby, she looked at her watch every few minutes. Back and forth, back and forth, back and forth. If her edginess bothered the young officer sitting at a reception desk, the officer didn't show it. Now and then, Wendy took a drink from the can of Diet Sprite she'd bought from a break room vending machine.

Almost half an hour passed before Deputy Collins appeared and indicated he was ready. Wendy slammed the now-empty soda can into a trash can and followed Collins into an interview room. Another man was already in the room, seated at a small table. He introduced himself as Detective Steve Hunter. Hunter was devoid of hair. Naturally bald, he shaved the fringe of hair he did have. A large nose and oversized ears gave him the appearance of a buzzard. Collins, by contrast, had a full head of thick dark hair matching his chocolate-brown eyes.

Hunter had a reputation for solving complex cases. A master of detail, little escaped his investigative eye. It was said he decided to be a detective when he read his first Encyclopedia Brown stories in grade school. Nobody knew if that was true, but most people who knew him assumed it was.

Before he asked Collins to bring Wendy into the interview room, Hunter told him they would keep the atmosphere cordial but formal.

Detective Hunter spoke first. "Mrs. Morris—it is *Mrs.* Morris, isn't it?"

"Yes...for now."

"You *are* married, but I understand you and your husband are divorcing."

"That's true," Wendy said, her manner guarded.

"First, I want to offer my—our—condolences on your sister's death."

"Thank you."

"We appreciate you talking with us today at what must be a most difficult time."

"It is."

Hunter moved into questioning. "Now, about your divorce. I understand you'll receive a large sum of money as part of the settlement."

"It's no secret that my husband has been quite successful in business. His company is worth millions, perhaps as much as a billion dollars. Why the hell *shouldn't* I have a share of it? And come to think of it, what business is it of yours?"

"I didn't say you don't deserve to share your husband's success, Mrs. Morris. As for why I'm interested, I'll come to that in a bit. But before we go there, why don't you tell me about your sister and your relationship with her?"

Wendy relaxed, but only a little. "Wanda and I are—were—twins. I'm sure you know this, but twins share a unique bond, way more than being siblings. In short, we were close, quite close.

"Like many sets of twins, our mother dressed us alike when we were kids. We wore the same clothes, hairstyles, and makeup, even as we got older. We did it all through high school because it kept the other kids at school guessing. Nobody could tell which sister was which, and we liked that—a lot. We were so close that Wanda would finish my sentences, and I'd finish hers. Sometimes we knew what the other was thinking without saying anything."

"How about after high school?"

"After we graduated, I went to college. While we were in high school, we planned to go to the same college and be roommates. But Wanda was something of a wild child at heart. When the time came to pack up and head off to school, she took off across the country on a motorcycle with some guy she'd just met instead. Mom and Dad were furious, but she was eighteen, and they couldn't do anything about it."

"So, despite your twinness, you were quite different in many ways."

"Yes. Wanda's been married and divorced three times, and we're not even thirty-five yet! I suppose I shouldn't talk since I'm about to be divorced, too, but—well, you get the picture."

"I think so. Was Wanda into drugs?"

"No. Considering her lifestyle, it's rather remarkable, but drugs never appealed to her. Alcohol, though, was a different story. Wanda could pound down drinks with the best of them. She held her liquor better than most guys I know, too." Wendy's voice held a note of what the two officers took as pride.

"Walk me through the day of the accident."

"Wanda picked me up around 11:30, and we had lunch at that new French bistro, Le Chat Noir. After lunch, we went to Woodmont Mall and had our nails done. We spent the afternoon shopping, killing time until the movie started."

"They watched *Chantilly Bridge*," Collins said. "I checked with the theater. It started at 8:00 and finished about 9:30."

"That's right," Wendy said. "After the movie let out, we went to Spinnoli's for dinner."

"And you said you had some wine, didn't you?" Collins asked.

"We shared some Chianti."

"How much?"

"We each had two glasses, maybe a little more. We split a bottle.

"Tell me how you ended up in Little Bear Lake," Hunter said.

"I don't know. Wanda was driving and said something about a shortcut. One minute, we were riding along, and the next, she was screaming, and the car was in the water."

A subtle tension filled the room, nothing tangible but present, nonetheless. Hunter straightened up in his chair, and his eyes bored into Wendy's. His expression, inscrutable, filled her with a sense of foreboding. "Let me tell you," he said, "about some things we've learned." "You're aware we performed an autopsy on your sister?"

She nodded.

"Autopsies," Hunter said, "can be quite revealing. We learned something quite interesting from your sister's autopsy." He paused to let his words sink in.

He had Wendy's full attention now. Tightening her shoulders, she fixed her eyes on her interrogator, mesmerized, like a rabbit confronted by a rattlesnake. Unable to stand the silence, she blurted out, "What?"

"We learned," he said, drawing out every word, "that your sister drowned."

Wendy relaxed and slumped back in her chair. "Of course, she drowned! She drove into a lake, for God's sake."

"Yes, but the water they found in her lungs wasn't from the lake." Wendy stiffened again. "No, the water in her lungs was chlorinated. It was tap water. So, we have a dilemma. We have a dead woman trapped in a car in a lake who drowned not in lake water but in city water. Would you care to explain that?" Wendy's face went white. "No," he continued, "I didn't think you would.

"Let's consider something else for a moment. This department likes to be thorough with every investigation we conduct. We wanted to be sure the woman we fished out of the lake was who you said she was. In most cases, we'd use DNA to make an identification, but DNA couldn't help us in this case."

"Wanda's and my DNA would be the same, wouldn't it?"

"Maybe, but perhaps not. Studies show that about fifteen percent of identical twins have some differences in their DNA profiles. But the bigger problem is that we don't have a known sample of your sister's DNA to compare. So, we had to use another method.

"Remember that motorcycle trip you said your sister took years ago?"

A look of apprehension spread across Wendy's face. "What about it?"

"Wanda got into a little scrape in Phoenix. The cops out there arrested her for shoplifting."

"Yes," she said, "she told me about it. But she paid the store, and they decided not to prosecute. There was no trial, no conviction, no record."

"She had no *criminal* record, that's true. But she does have an *arrest* record. That record included a set of fingerprints. And I'll bet you can guess what we found. Those fingerprints match yours. *You* are Wanda Patterson. The woman who drowned in Little Bear Lake wasn't you. It was your sister, Wendy Morris."

For a moment, Wanda swayed in her chair, and it looked as if she would faint. "Nonsense!" she croaked. "Every word I told you was the truth! You didn't take my fingerprints! How can you say they match Wanda's?"

"We got your fingerprints from the Sprite can you tossed in the trash can before you walked into this room. One of our evidence techs retrieved the can and dusted it for prints. While you waited for this interview to start, he compared those prints to those taken by the medical examiner and prints we found at the Morris house."

Hunter relaxed a bit. "Here's how I think all this came about. Wendy told you she was getting a divorce from her wealthy husband and that she'd receive a wad of cash as part of the divorce. You, on the other hand, are flat broke. Then you had a brainstorm. You figured that if you did away with Wendy and took over her identity, the money that was supposed to go to *her* would go to *you.*

"I've had detectives following your back trail. The story you told us was close to the truth, at least as far as it went. You had dinner at the Italian restaurant like you said. The staff remembers you and your sister leaving closer to 10:00 than 11:00. You both went to Wendy's house. Somehow, you contrived to entice Wendy into the bathtub. While she was in the water, you suddenly yanked her legs toward you, pulling her face underwater. She drowned in her own bathtub."

"That...that's preposterous!"

"I'm afraid it isn't. We examined the bathrooms in the Morris home. It's an old Victorian-era mansion. Morris spent some significant coin renovating and upgrading it. And in the master bathroom, we found an old-fashioned clawfoot bathtub. It isn't set into the wall, so it would be easy to grab the feet of a person sitting in the tub. It shouldn't surprise you that we found several of your fingerprints on the faucets and the tub.

"Once you knew your sister was dead, you took your car to the lake, strapped her into the driver's seat, and drove it into the water. You waited several hours to report the so-called 'accident,' no doubt trying to confuse us about the time of death."

The woman now outed as Wanda deflated like a tire going flat. She said, "I want a lawyer," and clammed up.

"How do you figure that bit with the bathtub?" Collins asked.

The detective cracked a smile. "In the early 1900s, there was a famous case in England called the Brides in the Bath Murders. The guy used the technique I described to murder three of his wives. *After* taking out life insurance on them, of course. They hanged him in 1915. Knowing something about old crimes comes in handy now and again."

The deputy stared open-mouthed at Detective Hunter. "How do you *know* this stuff?"

Hunter grinned. "I minored in history in college. Plus, I read a lot of true crime books. This was a famous early case for Sir Bernard Spilsbury, one of England's most respected forensic pathologists.

Deputy Collins shook his head and resolved to read more true crime.

Wanda Patterson slumped in her chair and said nothing during this exchange. Then she put her head in her hands to hide the tears she was determined not to show.

Hunter allowed her a few minutes to collect herself before asking her to stand and snapping on the handcuffs.

George Pallas was born in Chattanooga, Tennessee, and grew up in the Nashville area. He studied computer science at Vanderbilt University and moved to Ohio after graduating.

As a writer, George has short stories in two previous anthologies from the Ohio Writers' Association. "Number 845712" appeared in *Outcasts: An Anthology* (2021) and "The Sheriff" in *Metamorphosis: An Anthology* (2022). His first book, *Stalking Horse*, is a mystery novel. He also writes about historical true crime In his blog, Old Crime is New Again, at georgepallas.com.

George now lives in Chicago with his wife, Sharon, and their dog, Sheldon Cooper.

Reaper's Return

Christina Moore

The day starts with a red circle on a road map—a simple warning.

Jerome discovers it when he heads out for his newspaper. The map is neatly folded in a manila envelope.

The map was slipped under his door around three a.m. by a shadow, a blur of gray down a dark hall. The figure was barely captured by the security camera mounted in the hallway. *So much for gated communities*, he thinks.

Jerome doesn't need to examine the map closely to know what's circled. He doesn't understand specifically what the circle refers to, but he knows it refers to something...or any number of somethings. It hardly matters. When the time comes, there's plenty of dirt out there to bury him in a prison cell for the rest of his life or earn him a needle in the arm.

He regrets doing business in a death penalty state.

By afternoon, he's tearing down Route 6 towards what he remembers to be a cornfield. Already October, the corn will be unharvested, seemingly abandoned by an indifferent farmer. *Agricultural subsidies are bad business*, the occasional motorist will think while driving past rows of wasted corn.

Jerome knows why the field is planted but never reaped.

Lives are harvested there, not crops.

When the stalks are mature, it makes for excellent hunting grounds. Jerome should know. He's killed there many times, especially in autumn when the corn is tall and the moonlight is dampened by a curtain of rain.

The further he travels, the more he notices how patchwork fields have given way to gridded streets. Landscapes once saturated with organophosphates are now manicured lawns boasting of low crime rates and good schools.

He passes a small hospital with an empty parking lot. The surrounding grounds are churned bare from recent construction. *You can't even call this the country anymore. This is almost the suburbs. In another five, six years, this area will have its own post office...if it doesn't have one already.*

Jerome pulls off at the last rest stop before his exit, ordering two burgers and a pop at a drive-thru where there was once only a gas station. The vacant face in the window hands out a greasy bag of food in exchange for a few grubby bills. For a second, their reflections intermingle. Two men performing jobs neither of them like.

Jerome doesn't wait for his change.

After more than a decade of conventional life, he was beginning to think he'd outpaced his sins. But time is as much an enemy as it is a friend.

Why were his former employers calling on him now?

Perhaps he sees his answer on either side of the interstate.

Developers intent on lining country roads with blocks of *à la carte* housing must be eyeing that useless field by now. They'll assume they can get the land cheap from whichever farmer can no longer manage to bring in his crop. If they're out-of-towners, they'll be unaware of the narratives which once kept speculators at bay.

Jerome chuckles as he imagines skeletons churning up from graves and into backyard swimming pools like they do in the movies. But there are no skeletons in that field, at least none that he knows of. Nothing but fragments remain of those swallowed by that cursed patch of earth.

The farmer would've seen to it over the years.

The farmer is another factor to be reckoned with. He and the farmer didn't exactly part on good terms.

Jerome doesn't know how much the old guy got paid to keep his mouth shut and his shovel handy, but it must've been substantial. What else could explain a life spent picking through the remains of the dead like some ghoul?

Jerome wonders whether the guy's still alive.

There's a fifty-fifty chance he's dead. Like Schrödinger's cat.

He was past sixty back in the day, his face hardened by too many years in the sun, his bulbous nose ruddy with alcohol. That would place him somewhere past seventy now. Country folk often work into their eighties, weathered hands operating the controls on a combine as proficiently as young ones.

Jerome likes to imagine the farmer in some rocking chair somewhere and not moldering in his own field, but retirement is rare in this line of work. His former employer tended to get rid of anyone nearing a deathbed confession. No reason to believe things have changed in that regard.

The farmer was responsible for plowing and planting, each spring preparing the field for a new crop of reparations. The bodies would be gone come spring, fed to pigs, or reduced to ash. You never know if all parts are accounted for after a hit. Plowing ensured they'd start the season off with a blank slate.

Back in the bad old eighties, such measures were enough to guarantee they'd get away with it.

No body equals no crime.

Times have changed. Once houses start going in, anyone with a shovel and some hostas to plant might come up with a human molar attached to a bit of jawbone. Before DNA, such fragments would be sent to the coroner's office, where they'd be forgotten in a box in the storeroom, nothing but human detritus. Investigators would express concern and might poke around the property for a week or two, but in the end, what was left to find wouldn't be worth the cost of labor.

With a DNA match, a fragment of bone can whisper its name directly into the ear of a cold case detective. Once a dead man has a name, it doesn't take long for him to turn around and name his killer.

Would Jerome's former employer sell him down the river Styx for the sake of some real estate deal? If so, whose names would the soil reveal when interrogated by a backhoe?

If they planned on getting rid of him, they would've done so last night when he was sleeping. He'd treated himself to a bottle of Weller's Reserve. Whatever shadow lurked in the hallway could've made its way through Jerome's front door and into his bedroom, where he lay passed out from drinking three-quarters of a bottle of bourbon.

The assassin could've used Jerome's own gun, or at least that's how Jerome would've done it had it been his job to do.

A bullet to the head and that almost empty bottle on his nightstand would've been all the suicide note needed.

A paper trail would've suddenly appeared for some detective to follow, linking Jerome (and only Jerome) to a long history of vigilante justice and a short history of remorse.

Jerome keeps reassuring himself that his former employers have as much of an interest in keeping people off that land as he does, no matter how much money is on offer or how much they might want to rid themselves of the thing. But he can't seem to shake the thought that no matter what he does or where he goes, he's a marked man—marked with a red circle on a map.

A circle—not an "X."

A meeting rather than a hit?

Perhaps his former employer wants to make sure Jerome's held up his end of the bargain all these years...or maybe they have a few new threats to issue. They did this from time to time—usually by telephone.

Maybe they want to give me back my old job. Jerome chuckles at the thought.

Whatever the case, he resents the summons as much as he fears it. He's moved on, hasn't spoken a word in all this time. He's not wracked with guilt, waiting for just the right confessional or some sympathetic mistress in whom to confide.

Every person he killed deserved to die.

Exonerated murderers.

Those released on parole—a mere slap on the wrist for taking a life.

Anyone who managed to slink through the cracks of a flawed system was fair game. If a victim had the cash to pay for retributive justice, that is.

Back in the day, he'd been hired meat employed by the final Firm—the one hired after all others had failed.

On the face of it, it was just another law firm specializing in appeals, with the standard array of lawyers and investigators vetting every case for merit, whether it was to be fought out in court or in the killing fields.

If it's a simple hitman you want, you'd best go elsewhere.

Jerome likes to think his job was to give people closure...one way or another.

Pulling into a parking space under the shade of a towering oak, he removes the Beretta from its wooden case. After attaching the silencer, he holsters the weapon beneath his trench coat. The coat is heavy, leather lined with Kevlar, but not wearing it would place him at a disadvantage.

He removes the old Stetson from the hatbox in the trunk, restoring it to its rightful place on the front passenger seat. The hat is leather...matching his boots, matching his coat.

He won't wear it while driving. It's too conspicuous. But he likes to keep it near when he's on a job. The hat is his one quirk.

On longer drives, he used to talk to it, pretend it was alive, its upturned brim answering with a silent smirk. The hat used to do the sorts of jobs that Jerome doesn't like to think about on the nights he lays awake waiting for sunrise.

Everyone he killed deserved to die. Except for the ones who didn't.

The hat's been lurking on the shelf in his closet for more than a decade—his own personal boogie man.

"You're free now," Jerome tells it as he settles back down at the wheel, opening the bag of food he'd placed on the console.

Had I wanted to walk away, I would've thrown the hat into a fire, he thinks, taking one of the burgers from its wrapper, the shimmer of grease on paper turning his stomach. He's gratified to find his senses heightened, just as they would've been in the old days.

The hat is by far the most dangerous thing Jerome owns, more dangerous than the gun. The gun contains only bullets. The hat contains the mindset.

Deep down, he knew the day would come when he'd wear it again.

I haven't changed at all. I've switched uniforms, temporarily trading in my Reaper duds for a suit and tie. Yet death is my true calling.

He chews his food slowly, waiting for the light to wane. The burgers lack vitality, flavorless except for the salt. He throws the second one into the grass for the rats to find.

As he pulls back out onto the road, he heads directly west, the horizon the color of spilled wine as the sun settles below the tree line.

"I wish I were back at the apartment," he tells the hat. Its upturned brim smirks its reply.

By the time he arrives at his destination, dusk has fallen.

He acknowledges his arrogance, coming here without knowing what he might face. He's consciously allowed himself to be lured. But he's also confident he'll be able to outmatch whatever trap is set for him—if it's indeed a trap and not an opportunity.

He's not the physical specimen he was in his youth, but he's still in his prime. He's kept himself sharp and in shape, frequenting the gym daily and the shooting range at least once a week.

The one thing he hasn't done in well over a decade is put a bullet in a man.

Jerome turns down the service drive which runs alongside the field. He'll find a red metal barn at the end of this drive.

Part of him hoped to find everything replaced by a strip mall. That being the case, he would've simply turned around and driven away, not stopping until he was beyond the Mexican border.

Mexico is the direction I ought to be driving in right now, regardless, he thinks.

Instead, he puts the car in park.

He'd worked himself up to expect an altered landscape, yet nothing has changed. He's driven directly into his past.

He parks in front of the rolling door fronting the barn. When he worked here, he would've pulled completely in, hiding his vehicle in its dark interior, but the door no longer yields when he pulls the handle. Instead, he leaves the car where it is, inspecting for footprints and tire tracks, signs of others hiding in the night. He can detect nothing in the dusty soil, which has been milled over by paw prints, both cat and rat.

He half expects to find someone here waiting for him. But he's greeted by nothing but the jagged branches of a naked tree.

An apple tree, he remembers. Dead now.

Placing the Stetson on his balding head, he transforms into the Reaper. Years flake away as the field stirs in a bitter wind, welcoming him home...or so he imagines.

It doesn't take long to find the corridor, scythed into the dense wall of cornstalks and out into the field. He used these sorts of corridors himself back in the day, leading those marked for death to slaughter. Sometimes, they used props to make sure the perp knew exactly why he was scheduled to die that day.

The condemned should always know why they're being killed. That was an important rule.

Someone is going through a lot of trouble to impress me, the Reaper thinks, but he's not impressed. The jack-o-lanterns lining the path are needlessly theatrical. He'd be intimidated if it were not for the absurd vision he can't quite shake of the farmer carving each and lighting it with a candle.

He feels like he's heading to a harvest dance and not to what will likely turn out to be a murder, his or someone else's.

Beretta raised, he walks through stalks of corn. The full moon hovers above, its red tinge staining the brown stalks crimson. His gut warns him to turn back, but his nerves remain steady.

Always be in control of yourself is his first motto.

Always control your circumstances is his second—the motto he's now breaking.

As moonlight flickers through the gently swaying field, the Reaper spots a man standing tall amongst the stalks.

He's brought back to the days when he actively hunted, sometimes giving his quarry a running start, the illusion of hope. Experimentally, he puts a bullet into the figure's back. Despite hitting his target, he fails to hear the distinctly percussive sound that a bullet makes when passing through flesh. The figure remains standing.

As soon as Jerome pulls the trigger, he regrets shooting a man in the back—just in case it was a man.

But it turns out to be of no consequence. He's shooting at a scarecrow. Yet more amateur theatrics.

As he continues down the corridor, the scarecrow reveals itself to be a corpse mounted on a post, face picked clean by crows. The thing that was once a man has been here just long enough for maggots to give way to flies. Less than a week but more than a few days.

What a stupid risk, the Reaper thinks.

He doesn't know what risk he's referring to, the risk he's taking by coming out here in the first place, or the risk this other assassin is taking, leaving one of the condemned out in the open, with vultures circling overhead to point the way.

The image of vultures triggers recognition.

Is this the farmer, the Reaper wonders? *Is he part of the narrative which lured me here?*

It looks like him, or a version of him, with his red baseball cap and green coveralls. It's impossible to tell, given the current state of his face, but it doesn't matter. The message is clear. A makeshift sign draped around the neck of the corpse sends the message home with the single word—"snitch."

Okay, Jerome reasons, *I'm out here because the farmer finally "snitched." But to whom did he snitch? To those who'll force me to talk? Or to those who'll force my silence? My presence here tonight suggests the latter, but either way, if I want to live, I'm going to have to shoot my way out of this.*

He wonders what the farmer could have revealed, considering his own culpability in the hundreds of deaths that occurred here. What did he gain besides a shower of crows?

He must have wanted to die with a clear conscience.

Seven decades is high time to save one's soul.

The Reaper walks on as the corridor leads him toward the abandoned house at the back of the field, a house shadowed by trees. The house was the original residence belonging to this field when horses pulled carts down packed dirt roads. Back in 1984, it belonged to no one, or so the Reaper had thought.

The house was just a bit of discarded geometry in an otherwise flat landscape.

He's since come to understand that no house is truly abandoned, no matter how derelict it may appear. Despite listing walls battered by years of westerly winds, he cannot be sure there are no eyes hiding deep within even now.

Blue eyes gazing out at falling snow. A memory. Nothing more.

"Only a fool would live in such a place," Jerome has told himself over the years. He'd underestimated the number of fools willing to take one risk to avoid another.

It was possible some hunter had encroached into the field, mistaking a flicker in the darkness for a fleeing deer, as was reported in the paper. The newspaper article generously suggested that with the night as dark as it was, the hunter might not yet realize he'd killed a young woman. The perpetrator was encouraged to come forward, to accept justice like a man, but he remained a shadow.

Strange, the police never recovered the bullet, even with the use of metal detectors.

The Reaper is certain of one thing. He's completely innocent. This was not his kill.

It was nearly impossible for him to have made that shot at long range with the Beretta.

Except one shot had gone wide. Both he and the farmer knew it. Jerome was an expert marksman, and such things rarely happened. But one round was missing, and it was up to the farmer to account for it. After reading about the death of the woman, Jerome knew where the missing round would be "discovered." The farmer would see to it just as he saw to everything else the Firm asked him to do.

"How well do you shoot?" the Reaper asked less than a week later as the farmer held out the bullet in one palsied hand.

An Amish couple had been living in the house for over a month. They'd committed the oldest sin in the Holy Book, running off to do their thing without permission from God or church. Expelled from their community, they'd been forced to find the nearest structure with a fireplace and chimney just to survive. They lived quietly, fearing discovery and eviction.

The Reaper missed the clues which would've told him he was not alone.

He was focused on his quarry, a serial killer who'd raped and strangled a senator's daughter. Jerome hadn't expected the man to be a match for him, yet his target was fast and tough, nearly escaping with his life intact. He'd crashed blindly through the cornstalks until he reached the house at the edge of the field. Jerome gave chase but was encumbered by the heavy leather coat.

It was difficult to get a bead on his target through the falling snow, but Jerome had no choice but to make the shot. In the end, he managed to take the man down with three bullets, minus the one that went wide.

Even as the police investigated the death of the woman the next morning, they failed to find Jerome's actual mark, a newly initiated corpse laying a mere fifty feet out in the corn, belonging to a man recently acquitted on charges of capital murder.

Had one cop followed those drag marks...

Had one wanted a smoke...

Had one wondered about the coppery scent of blood wafting on the breeze... The entire Firm could've been compromised.

As a precaution, the field was abandoned for the remainder of a season despite the Amish woman's death being ruled an accident.

"My guns could've never done that," he'd maintained when questioned by the Firm, "That's not how I shoot." Even as he said it aloud, he could hear the hat whispering doubts into his ear, doubts about that missing bullet.

Whoever was at fault, the Firm began separating themselves from Jerome from that point forward. When work in the killing field resumed, he was called fewer times to do less important jobs. He began finding traces of other assassins at work in what he'd established as his territory.

He was the Reaper. This was supposed to be *his* field.

Eventually, valuing his life over his will, he walked away, leaving before any real trouble began– before he ended up as soil chemistry himself.

But now he's back, and if he wants to own this field again, he'll have to take it from whoever is now hunting here.

When the Reaper approaches to within a hundred feet of the house, the world explodes, sending a pillar of fire into the clear dark night, scattering flaming debris into dry rows of corn. Jerome is hit by the percussive wave, knocking him to the ground. The rustle of wind through cornstalks is replaced by a pervasive metallic ring.

Blood runs from his left ear down the side of his cheek.

When he looks up, his own shadow emerges from the thick smoke, a giant standing at the end of the corridor backlit by fire. The Reaper staggers to his feet, his equilibrium disrupted by a ruptured eardrum.

The figure stands motionless, a devil surrounded by billowing smoke. He is waiting for Jerome to make the first move.

Despite his disorientation, Jerome quickly realizes he's looking at the most recent incarnation of the Reaper, seeing himself as he must have appeared to his quarry so many years ago.

I invented you, Jerome thinks, training the Beretta on this interloper.

The other is standing slightly out of range, but Jerome is betting his life on being a better shot than this adversary. Like a wounded cat, he works to disguise his injuries as he walks toward the fire.

"What is it you want?" Jerome shouts, but if the figure answers, he can't hear above the ringing in his damaged ears.

I only need to put one bullet in this guy, and I'll leave this place alive.

But the other Reaper isn't moving, not even to unholster whatever gun is concealed beneath that trench coat. The lack of response rattles Jerome, who doesn't want to fire until the other man draws.

No more low tactics.

Let this be a contest of peers. Two gunslingers, equally matched, Reaper to Reaper.

He stands at the threshold of a fiery wind as the bitter chill of approaching winter fingers across his back. The breath of owl wings escaping into the night plays across his face for an instant, a mild reprieve from the inferno erupting in front of him. His fate rests on the tip of a bullet.

It's the shovel that gets him in the end. From behind, as he stands waiting for his adversary to draw. The sharpened edge slices clear through the leather of the hat and into his skull. Apparently, the rules of engagement have changed.

A third reaper has entered the killing field...or is this the new farmer? From Jerome's perspective, labels hardly matter anymore.

The instant Jerome's skull cracks, his vision goes dark, but he recognizes his fate. He'd walked into his past rather than driving off toward the future and was now paying for that mistake with his life. With his senses dulled by the explosion, he didn't hear so much as a footfall behind him.

"I wanted to do this myself," a voice says directly above him. The man speaks with an accent. His Dutch lilt betrays the voice of a man who was once Amish but who now lives amongst the English.

"I'm doing this for her."

The blow grants Jerome clarity. He remembers her now, can see the ghost of her shimmering through his damaged brain...*standing in the window, veiled by snow.*

I felt bad about that bullet, Jerome thinks as a heavy boot pushes his face into the cold, dark soil.

Christina Moore lives in Columbus, Ohio, and works at the Ohio State University Libraries cataloging Greek and Slavic Language materials. She bikes to work every day—a twelve-mile round trip. She enjoys music and photography and is a member of the Magpie Consort. Writing has always interested her, but she began writing in earnest during the pandemic.

Christina shares her home with two marvelous mutts and a magnificent tuxedo cat.

Leakproof

Charles O'Donnell

Diapers have come a long way since Apollo.

The prosaically named Fecal Containment Device served the moon missions well enough, providing the astronaut sealed it properly, but leaks were common, one of the many risks of space flight. When women joined the corps in '78, NASA tasked their top scientists with the development of Disposable Absorption Containment Trunks to address the needs of feminine anatomy. When the DACTs were replaced by the disposable-diaper-inspired Maximum Absorbency Garment, the men thought so much of them that they doffed their FCDs and pulled on the MAGs, and both men and women have flown in MAGs ever since.

When flight engineer Katy Twomey pondered her situation, she didn't start with the history of astronaut hygiene. That thought arose spontaneously when a situation similar to hers came to mind. Some years back, an astronaut equipped with a collection of semi-lethal weapons drove a thousand miles to confront her rival for the affections of a fellow astronaut. The two situations weren't *exactly* the same—the cross-country astronaut's love interest was a man, and Katy's was a woman, and Katy had no plans to challenge her rival with a hammer, knife, and pellet gun—but what made the headlines was that the driver wore an absorbent adult undergarment to avoid bathroom stops en route. The public thought that amusing; the astronaut corps thought it eminently practical. They'd been wearing diapers for decades.

In fact, Katy had no desire to confront *her* rival, Commander Marco Hayes. Marco was married to Claudia Dixon, a mission specialist, and Katy's lover. Katy's and Claudia's secret trysts were limited to times when Marco was on a mission when they could luxuriate in each other's company, secure in the knowledge that Marco was orbiting 250 miles overhead. They were more cautious when assigned to the same mission, sneaking moments of relative isolation in some far corner of the International Space Station for a kiss or an embrace, ideally by a window looking down on the gem-like view of the Earth. Lovemaking in space was out of the question, though they whispered and giggled at the naughtiness of it as if they were in the restroom of a girls' school. The "250-Mile High" club, so said NASA lore, was highly exclusive.

This was due (at least in part) to the fact that NASA prohibited married couples from flying the same mission. Marco and Claudia had never flown together. Marco and Katy had never shared a mission, either, but that was about to change.

◆

"Claudia thinks the world of you," Marco said.

The mission briefing had just broken up. Marco followed Katy out the door.

"Nice of you to say," Katy answered, eyes down. *That was dumb.* "I mean, I think a lot of Claudia, too."

"How many missions have you two flown together?"

"Only two. I mean, two, I think." Katy bit her lip.

"I'll bet they were memorable. Claudia has a way of making an impression. And in the ISS, in close quarters, well... But, of course, I'll never know what that's like—unless we get divorced!" He laughed a breathy laugh as if he were trying to make a bad joke seem funnier than it was.

Memorable? Katy thought. *Memorable? Alone in the dark, gazing out on the spinning earth, no gravity, no up, no down? Two souls striking a perfect chord resonating in infinite space? Memorable?*

"She's a good specialist," Katy said.

"And you're a good flight engineer, Claudia says."

"Thanks. I mean, nice of her to say."

Marco touched Katy's shoulder. "I'm looking forward to flying with you."

Katy put out an awkward hand. "Me, too," she said.

◆

"Don't," Claudia said.

Katy had taken her aside, out of Marco's earshot, though they both could see Marco smiling blandly at the two of them. It was their last chance to talk, to touch, before Katy entered quarantine with the mission crew.

"Do you like this?" Katy asked. "All this sneaking around?"

Claudia turned away so Marco couldn't see her flushed face and shining cheeks. Katy's face burned as well, as it did whenever Claudia was upset.

"I'm sorry," Katy said. "I'm being selfish."

"No, no, no. It's hard for you. I know that. But it's hard for *me*, too."

"I know." *I know. I know. I love you, and what I love is that you are loving. You love me; you love Marco; there's no limit to your love. How could I hope to have it all to myself?*

But she did want it to herself—all of it. She wanted to be the center of Claudia's life, the way Claudia was the center of hers, two bodies captured by mutual attraction orbiting a common center. But mostly, she wanted the secrecy to end: the coming and going in the night when Marco was aloft, the furtive moments in the ISS when they flew together, the pretended coolness all other times.

"Will you do something for me?" Claudia asked.

"Oh, of course. Anything."

Claudia put a faltering hand on Katy's arm. "Spend time with Marco." She laughed. "Oh, what am I saying? You'll have months together crammed into that can. You'll have no choice. But I'm asking you, just get to know him."

Katy nodded. She hugged Claudia one last time, then caught up with Marco as he entered the crew quarters. She gave in to the urge to take one final look at Claudia, small and helpless, so unlike the funny, smart, super-competent mission specialist she loved.

♦

A flight engineer knows every technical detail of the International Space Station, the spacecraft that service it, and all systems on board. Katy Twomey had a rep—an engineer's engineer, her knowledge encyclopedic. She was obsessed: if she ever failed to call to mind any fact or datum instantly and accurately, she'd drill until she could recall the hazy information like a computer from a hard drive. During quarantine and on the long flight to the Baikonur Cosmodrome in Kazakhstan, Katy studied the manuals, drawings, and specifications for the Extravehicular Mobility Unit, or EMU, the suit worn by astronauts during Extra-Vehicular Activities—EVAs, or "space walks." She paid particular attention to the glove lock, a meticulously engineered mechanism whose function had been tested and refined over decades of space flight. The gloves, critical to performing exacting tasks in hard vacuum and microgravity, were of particular interest to NASA engineers, so much so that NASA had challenged multiple contractors to improve the design. Among the objectives of this mission was to test the finalist. Katy, as flight engineer, was the mission lead for the test. She perused its specs, immersing herself so completely that she forgot Marco was sitting beside her on the plane.

"The new gloves," Marco said, glancing at the tablet computer in Katy's lap. Katy looked up with a start.

"What do you think?" Marco asked. "Better? Worse? Same difference?"

"I guess we'll find out," Katy mumbled, then cleared her throat and sat up. "Flexibility, ease of use, reliability should all be improved."

He reached for the tablet. "Can I see?" Katy handed it over.

"Flexibility would be nice," Marco said, flipping through diagrams. "After four hours in those damn things, my hands are a mess." He handed the tablet back. "I'll study it later."

"It's a tricky problem: make a glove that moves with your hand while it's pumped up like a balloon."

"I guess it's tricky. But is it rocket science?"

Katy blurted out a laugh. She looked sideways at Marco. He was grinning, and the corners of his eyes crinkled. She was closer to Marco than she had ever been. He had a big head, and curly black hair, a few gray strands, with just a slightly receding hairline, enough to emphasize his broad forehead. His nose, wide with flaring nostrils, dominated a face with round cheeks and full lips. His skin was tanned, with large pores. He was not a handsome man, but his face was kind and inquisitive. Katy looked at Marco's face steadily, almost staring, before she looked away.

"That's lame," she said.

"But you laughed. Didn't Claudia tell you? I'm a comedian."

"No, she didn't mention it," Katy said, and it was true. Marco was rarely talked about when she and Claudia were together, usually in pronouns only.

"Oh, yes. You'll see. I'll keep you in stitches."

Katy turned back to the tablet. She zoomed in on one detail of the glove lock. She rotated the drawing through three dimensions, imagining how it would function in use. The design had been modified from the flight-tested version NASA had been using since Apollo, a seemingly minor detail, but Katy recognized its significance.

"I can't wait," Katy said. She shut off the tablet and stowed it for landing.

The EVA to install the roll-out solar array on the P6 truss was scheduled for seven hours and fifteen minutes on the twentieth day of Katy's and Marco's stay. A secondary objective would be to flight-test the new gloves. Katy and Marco had already completed the initial phase of EVA preparation, ninety minutes of light exercise in a pure oxygen environment designed to flush nitrogen from blood and body tissues before donning the low-pressure EMU. Now fully suited, they continued the prescribed in-suit light exercise routine, referred to by ISS veterans as the "slo-mo hokey-pokey."

"Have you been avoiding me?" Marco asked. He twisted left, then right, then bent forward as far as the EMU suit would allow.

"I don't think so," Katy answered. But she *had* avoided him, reluctant to keep her promise to Claudia. She twisted in unison with Marco, looking left when he looked left and right when he looked right, avoiding eye contact through their clear bubble helmets.

But Marco wouldn't have it. He did a double take and caught Katy looking.

"I'm glad to hear it," Marco said, smiling his broad smile. "There's not a lot of room in this orbiting double-wide, but I only see you at mealtime."

"We're all busy," Katy said, bending forward. Marco bent with her.

"Uh-huh," he said.

Katy's mind wandered back over the past three weeks, particularly the first week, when astronauts acclimated to microgravity and work assignments were light. During her free time, she pored over the specifications of the prototype gloves, pondered her complicated relationship with Claudia, and refreshed her knowledge of how the human body responds when exposed to hard vacuum.

"You and Claudia," Marco said, snapping Katy out of her reverie.

"What?"

"You met in AsCan training. In systems class, right?"

Katy straightened out and twisted left. Marco mirrored her movements.

"You know, I'm going to get you to talk to me. I promised Claudia."

"Promised?"

"She made me promise that I'd get to know you."

Katy paused her routine. "Orbital mechanics."

"That's right. I remember. She came home that night all excited. Told me four women were in the class, but only two got it."

Katy smiled in spite of herself. "Claudia got it."

"And you. You were the other one."

The instructor, a Ph.D. from Caltech and a veteran of four missions was visibly frustrated.

"Kepler's second law states that a body in orbit around a massive object sweeps out equal areas in equal times. This is a consequence of what fundamental principle of physics?"

Katy knew the answer but, having dominated class discussion up to that point, decided to hold back. The woman next to her in the front row, a petite brunette with large, liquid eyes and hair in an angular bob cut, had also actively participated, to the exclusion of the other women in the class and most of the men. She, too, seemed reluctant to respond to a question to which she obviously knew the answer. The rest of the class remained mute.

"Very well. Ms. Dixon, to what principle am I referring?"

The woman looked down and then, briefly, discreetly, glanced at Katy. "That would be the conservation of angular momentum."

"That is correct. And Ms. Twomey, can you state that principle in formal terms?"

Katy glanced back at the bob-haired woman, who smiled. "The cross product of the radial vector *r* and the linear momentum vector, *mv*, is constant."

"Again, correct. And Ms. Dixon, how does that relate to Kepler's law?"

Katy gazed at the woman as she answered. "Another way to state Kepler's law is that the time derivative of area, equal to the cross product of the radial vector and the velocity, is constant."

"Close, but not quite."

The woman frowned. Katy raised her hand.

"Ms. Twomey?"

"Ms. Dixon has assumed that the mass *m* of the orbiting body is constant."

"That is correct. In *my* class, you will state *all* assumptions." The instructor gathered his materials. "That's all for today. I'll see you here tomorrow, ten a.m. And class..." He swept the room with steely eyes. "...I expect *all* of you to contribute, or I will dismiss you and continue the class just with Candidates Twomey and Dixon."

Katy and her classmate hung back as the room emptied.

"I don't think I made any friends today," the woman said, keeping her eyes on her desk.

"The day's not over." Katy held out her hand. "I'm Katy Twomey."

The woman smiled a tight smile as she put her small, pale hand in Katy's. "I'm Claudia Dixon."

Katy looked straight into Claudia's eyes. She saw a sadness there as if she regretted her own brilliance. Katy stared a moment too long.

"Is something wrong?" Claudia asked.

Katy broke her gaze. "You're afraid to do your best."

Claudia's eyes widened. "How did you know?"

"We're all afraid. You, me, the other women in the class—even some of the men. Just not as many."

Claudia's tight smile broke into a grin. Katy felt her chest tighten.

"Maybe you can teach me," Claudia said.

Claudia squeezed her hand. Katy squeezed back. "I think we can teach each other."

◆

"What about you and Claudia?" Katy asked. "Where did you meet?"

Marco twisted and bent. "She didn't tell you?"

"No. It never came up."

"Huh. Well, we were in college."

"Purdue."

"Yep. Boilermakers, just like Neil Armstrong. Claudia was in aeronautical engineering, and I was in engineering science. We met in physics class."

"So, you're both brilliant."

Marco chuckled. "She keeps me on my toes for sure."

"Yeah. Me, too."

◆

The ostensible reason for the invitation was a study session. After the last class of the day, Katy rushed to her apartment, cleaned and straightened, sprayed air freshener, and put a bottle of chardonnay in the refrigerator. She changed the bedsheets and fluffed and arranged the pillows. She changed into a knit lounge-wear outfit, looked in the mirror, decided it was too obvious, and changed into jeans and a tee. A half-hour before Claudia arrived, she fussed nervously with magazines on the coffee table, books on the end table, and mementos on the shelf. She reacted with a start when the doorbell rang, ran into the bathroom to check her lipstick, then brushed back her hair before answering the door.

Claudia came in with an armload of books and a bag over her shoulder. "Nice place," she said, dropping the books on the couch. "I don't know if we'll get to all this tonight, but I wanted to have it just in case. Where do you want to start?"

Claudia was as casually dressed as Katy, in cargo pants and a tank top. She felt a pang of disappointment—until she noticed that Claudia wore makeup. She *never* wore makeup.

"Um, physiology?" Katy said. "It's my weakest subject."

"Physiology," Claudia said, "the effects of space flight on the human body." The two stood silently for a moment, awkward half-smiles on their faces.

"Want some wine?" Katy asked.

Claudia nodded. "Wine. Sure."

◆

"You must really love her."

Marco paused his routine. "What's not to love?"

Katy bent and twisted. "Nothing, I guess."

Marco let his arms fall to his sides, as far as the EMU suit allowed. "We have the same problems as any married couple, I think."

Katy twisted left, then right. "I'm sure," she said.

"She's emotional, you know? Not over the top or anything, not most of the time. Not about most things. But like..." He resumed his routine. "Like, when her mom died. She was a mess. I get that. Your mom dies, and you're going to react. But it was more than that. They weren't even that close, and she went into mourning. I put up with it as long as I could, but after two months of her playing the tragic figure, I told her to snap out of it. That only made it worse. It almost ended our marriage. God only knows what'd happen if someone really close to her died. Like if *I* died. That'd be the end of her."

Katy stared at the ceiling, sheets pulled to her chin, while Claudia sat on the edge of the bed, her pale, damp skin glowing in yellow light from Katy's bedside lamp.

"Married," Katy said flatly.

"Uh-huh."

"And you were going to tell me this when?"

Claudia faced Katy, eyes red, face flushed. "I wanted to tell you a couple of months ago."

"A couple. Two. Two months ago. When two months ago?"

Claudia turned away.

"Oh. Okay." She got up on one elbow. "Were you going to tell me this before or after the first time we fucked?"

Claudia bent forward. Her body heaved with silent sobs.

Oh, god, Katy thought. *Not now.* She'd endured crying jags for weeks, brought on by all manner of setbacks—a bad quiz score, a failed physical challenge, the stress of a field survival exercise. And yet, Katy's had been the shoulder Claudia cried on. And Claudia propped up Katy on her bad days. To need another and to be needed: Katy didn't want to lose that.

She put her hand tentatively on Claudia's back. "What's his name?" she asked.

"I don't want to tell you," Claudia rasped. She stood up and pulled on her panties. "If I tell you his name, he'll be real to you. Then he'll come between us."

Katy watched Claudia dress. "You probably should shower first so that what's-his-name won't suspect."

Claudia looked at her with her jaw set and her eyes narrowed. "Don't," she said.

"Don't what?"

"Don't that. That snarky thing you do. I hate that."

"I don't know what you're talking about. I just thought you wouldn't want what's-his-name—"

"Marco. His name is Marco. Fuck you."

Katy sat straight up. "Marco...Hayes?"

Claudia silently fastened her bra and slipped on her shirt.

"You're married to an astronaut?"

"Three years. Since he was a candidate." She sat on the bed and pulled on her pants. "He doesn't deserve this."

Katy swung her legs over the side of the bed. She pulled Claudia to her. Claudia hesitated, then hugged Katy tight.

"I'm sorry," Katy said. "I won't let Marco or anyone else come between us."

Marco raised his arms and balled his hands into fists. "They feel pretty good."

Katy flexed her hands. "A little better than standard issue," she said. "The real test is how they feel five hours from now."

The day before the EVA, Katy inspected the EMUs. She found the new gloves in a specially designed case inside the equipment locker labeled HAYES M. The glove mod that had caught Katy's eye was the interface to the locking ring, a flexible bellows secured with eight screws. Making sure that she was unobserved, she took a T6 Torx driver from her pocket and backed out one of the screws on the right-hand glove.

She examined the fastener up close. It looked like something anyone could pick up at a home store for a few pennies. This one, however, was a precision fastener costing hundreds of times more, with machined threads and a micro-texture finish. NASA tests confirmed they met the 99.99% mission reliability goal in all foreseeable applications when installed in clean room conditions and torqued to specification.

She released the screw, letting it float nearly motionless before her eyes. She ran a finger along her nose, coating her fingertip with a thin film of oil. Plucking the screw from the air, she rolled it between her fingers. After re-installing the screw, she repeated the process for the remaining fasteners.

A smear of oil on the threads—that was enough. The movement of the glove during the EVA would do the rest.

Seven years, Katy thought. *I'm through.*

◆

"Depress pump power on," Marco droned, ticking off the final steps of the EVA checklist.

"Check," Katy answered. "Startup complete."

"Depress pump man ISOV open."

"Check. P gage ten...eight...six...five."

"Depress pump man ISOV closed. Power off."

"Check." Katy eyed the EMU pressure gauge. "Leak check...negative."

"EV hatch MPEV open."

"Check. Suit pressure steady."

"Attach tethers."

"Check. P delta zero point two."

Marco opened the airlock hatch. "Showtime!"

◆

A human being can survive for a little more than a minute in hard vacuum. Gas bubbles in the bloodstream block circulation; the victim loses consciousness in fifteen seconds. Seizures follow. Death occurs at 90 seconds, perhaps longer. Three Soviet cosmonauts, the first to die in space, survived for 110 seconds when their capsule lost pressure on re-entry.

Ninety seconds, perhaps longer. Two minutes, tops.

Katy re-read the symptoms in her space physiology text before leaving for the mission. She was interested in the times to unconsciousness and death, considering most of the effects dispassionately.

But not all.

In animal experiments, the subjects suffered involuntary vomiting and defecation. Katy closed her eyes and shivered as she read it. Death was one thing; untidiness was another. She suppressed the thought, reminding herself that the Maximum Absorbency Garments astronauts wore during an EVA were leakproof.

◆

"What's it going to take to get this damn thing to unroll?" Marco complained. At hour five, the EVA was already a half-hour behind schedule due to the roll-out solar array's stubborn refusal to unfurl.

"I've done one of these before," Katy's voice crackled in Marco's headphones. "They can be a bit balky. Give it some encouragement."

"Sure. I'll show it who's boss." Marco tugged at the edge of the coiled array, gripping tightly with his right hand.

Katy's eyes stayed riveted to Marco's glove. "Give it a twist. Right there."

"C'mon, you stupid machine, roll!"

The array shuddered, then jerked as the port boom snapped open.

"That's got it," Marco said. The starboard boom opened, then stalled.

"Shit," Marco cursed. "Katy, what's the time?"

Katy glanced at the display on her EMU. It was blank.

"DCM malfunction," she said. She flipped the display switch, then adjusted the contrast knob. "Nope. Still dead."

"I got it. Five hours, twenty minutes. Should've had this thing deployed an hour ago." He tugged again. "You better head back to the airlock and plug in."

"On my way."

Katy inched along the exterior of the station toward the airlock, more than fifty meters away. Reconnecting to the station umbilical was standard procedure to restart a cranky Display Control Module, but it was not always successful. If Katy couldn't restart her DCM, the EVA would end. Halfway there, she stopped, one glove gripping a handhold, and turned back to Marco.

A voice came over Katy's headphones. "Team, we're getting a suit pressure alarm in here. What's going on?"

"What? Damn!" Marco responded. "Katy, are you..."

Katy held her breath, counting down from fifteen. From twenty meters away, she saw Marco's eyes wide with terror.

Oh, Claudia, I'm so sorry. I'd have done anything for you.

♦

"Fuck me," said Jackson Healy, the station commander. "First death on the ISS, and it happens on my watch."

The two huddled in the Destiny module, outside the airlock where Marco had secured Katy Twomey's body to the bulkhead with bungee cords.

"Marco, you good?" Jackson asked.

Marco nodded. "Yeah. Good."

"Well, I guess we can report that these new gloves are a fucking failure. Fuck me."

"What now?"

"Soyuz capsule will be here day after tomorrow. You'll ride it down, you and..." He tipped his head toward the airlock.

"Yep."

"Yep," Jackson repeated. He pulled himself through the hatch. "Fuck me," he muttered.

Marco stared through the port at Katy, still in her EMU, minus her right glove. Her face, what he could see of it through the vomit-spattered helmet, was marked with purple splotches, evidence of capillaries bursting in the vacuum of space.

He'd given the news to Claudia as soon as he'd secured the body, even before getting out of his suit. As Marco expected, she was devastated, having lost her lover of seven years. *She'll get over it eventually*, Marco thought, *or else she won't*. It didn't matter. Either way, his marriage to Claudia had been fatally wounded. By the end of the year, it would be over.

But, really, the marriage was all but over eight months ago, on the day that Marco discovered Claudia's secret affair—a week before he requested a change to the flight order, landing a spot on the same mission with Katy.

Katy Twomey. He respected her, even liked her. She first came to his attention when he read her report on a failed satellite launch more than two years before. Her investigation was exhaustive, her analysis brilliant, her conclusion stunning: A careless technician had installed a fastener after having contaminated it with skin oil. The screw backed out during ascent, releasing pressure in the fuel tank, causing the launch computer to miscalculate the burn duration. A geosynchronous satellite settled into a useless low orbit, costing the underwriters hundreds of millions of dollars. Katy, the engineer's engineer, was a hero. When he spotted Katy by the equipment lockers the day before, that report came to mind, as well as the imagined trysts between his wife and her lover, the same images with which he'd tortured himself for the last eight months.

Marco sat silently for a few minutes. Then he floated through the Destiny module hatch back to his quarters, stopping briefly at the equipment locker to return the T6 Torx driver he'd borrowed the night before.

Charles O'Donnell writes thrillers with high-tech themes in international and futuristic settings. His works include the espionage thriller, *The Girlfriend Experience*, the political thriller *Moment of Conception*, and the *Shredded* dystopian sci-fi trilogy. His short stories have appeared online and in print journals and anthologies, including *Fall Fiction Anthology* (Dark Ink Press), *Year 1 Anthology* (Dreamers Creative Writing), *Lost and Found* (CSCC GEM-C Writers), and *Metamorphosis* (Ohio Writers' Association).

Charles lives with Helen, his wife and life partner, in Westerville, Ohio.

Redemption

Darin Miller

Millicent Van Puce woke precisely at 7:00 AM, just as she had every morning of every day of every week of every year. Routines were necessary to discipline the human spirit, her mother had always said. Her mother died of cervical cancer fifteen years ago. The doctors gave her six months to live, and she died six months later to the day, a lesson in punctuality.

Millicent was sixty-nine years old. She retained her youthful, slender figure as much as time would allow, lending her a spry posture. Her long, strawberry blond hair had transitioned to a brilliant silver sometime during her forties. Although it was very elegant—not at all tinged with the urine-yellow afflicting so many of her church friends—Millicent faithfully colored it every six weeks, sullying the silver with colors ranging from muddy water to Grey Poupon mustard—whichever was least expensive. Clues to her age were found in her skin which was no longer smooth and supple but leathery and wrinkled.

As was her morning routine, Millicent washed her face in the bathroom sink and styled her hair into a tidy bun on the top of her head, seamlessly integrating the coil of hair with bobby pins so none of the hardware showed. She exited the bathroom and crossed her adjoining bedroom to her closet. She stood there for several minutes, carefully selecting a bright yellow dress with frills along the neckline and sleeves. It was the style of dress mothers forced kindergarten daughters to wear when having a family portrait made. Millicent loved the dress. She bought it fifteen years ago, and it fit as well today as when she purchased it.

"What would you like for breakfast, Hal?" she called out. She didn't expect an answer, although she asked the same question every morning. Hal Van Puce had been her husband for thirty-four years. As was customary at the time, Millicent left school at the age of 15 to marry her 18-year-old war-bound fiancé. He had only been overseas for a few months before he was sent back to the States with a medical discharge.

Hal and his brother, Carter, owned a successful real estate agency. They specialized in buying buildings crippled by time and neglect, refurbishing and selling them for a tidy profit. His robust earnings paid for this elegant old townhouse and had sent all five of their boys through college. Several particularly spectacular dealings had allowed him to retire at the tender age of fifty. This was shortly after Carter, fully inebriated from the agency's Christmas party, had driven his Corvette over the steep edge of the hairpin curve at Pilsner's Bluff. The real estate agency had been snapped up by a nameless, faceless corporation whose business philosophy was all numbers and no humanity.

Hal was no stranger to booze, either. He was not the sloppy, jovial type, however. He was a mean drunk. He frequently took vicious delight in pointing out Millicent's many, many flaws. Once she reached the point of total humiliation, he would stand over her, laughing and laughing, his eyes blazing with hatred. He cheated on Millicent, too. Every chance he got.

Twenty years ago, they had divorced, and those who knew Millicent well knew she had never fully recovered from the experience. She enjoyed the role of martyr.

Millicent fixed the customary bacon, egg, and toast breakfast she had prepared for Hal most mornings when they were married. Procedure was important, and just because Hal was gone, it didn't mean she should alter the routine more than set one place instead of two at the table. At precisely 7:45 AM, Millicent offered up grace and enjoyed her meal.

◆

Today was to be a big day.

Prissy Altwater, Millicent's next-door neighbor and best friend since grade school, had informed her there would be new neighbors moving into the old Jenkins house across the street. Millicent and Prissy were enjoying their twice-weekly luncheon in Prissy's kitchen.

"I hear they're coming all the way from Chicago!" Prissy gushed breathlessly, her ruddy jowls flapping as she spoke. Prissy was a frumpy, round woman with frizzy, unkempt orange hair. She had a nervous habit of continually clasping her hands against her extra-large sundress, turning its front into a sea of wrinkles.

"Really? It doesn't surprise me that they're settling in Port Monte. The Good Lord has less trouble watching a small community like ours since the traffic ain't so thick." Port Monte, Millicent's lifelong hometown, had changed little in the last hundred years. Most of the young people went upstate to find work once they had graduated. Those who remained did so because of the simpler life they could enjoy in a place virtually unchanged by the booming technological advances achieved by Bill Gates and his peers. "Have you heard their names yet?"

"Myra Adams said that all of the utilities were registered to one *Ms.* Abigail Reinhart," Prissy replied. Myra Adams was another former classmate who had worked the last thirty years for Port Monte Gas & Electric. Confidentiality was a foreign concept for Myra. She felt her seniority excused her from the occasional breach. She had semi-retired after her sixty-fifth birthday, and she now spent most of her four-hour work shifts perpetuating gossip with whoever remained alive from her school years.

"Hmm," Millicent said thoughtfully, turning this information over in her mind. "*Ms?* Isn't she married?"

Prissy made a wheezing sound and sneezed. "Excuse me. You know, I'm not sure about that. Myra didn't know any *real* details. I have *heard* she's got three kids, but I haven't heard a word about the mister." Prissy needed to wipe her nose, which Millicent signified with a flick of her fingertip.

"A Christian woman's work is never fully done," Millicent said. "I'll bake them a batch of my special oatmeal raisin cookies, and we'll go welcome them to the neighborhood. The Ladies' Church League can *always* use a new member. Do you think she's Methodist?"

"She will be when you're through," Prissy said with not so much a laugh as a whinny. Millicent had been meaning to speak to her about that, as well.

"She's probably a widow woman, poor thing, trying to feed all those babies."

"Maybe her husband was a drinker like..." Prissy trailed off and made another of her pensive wheezy noises. She had violated a cardinal rule. *Never* speak of Hal. He had moved to Italy shortly after the divorce all those years ago, yet the mere mention of his name seemed to pull the scab from Millicent's most ancient and unhealed wound. Somehow, stories had evolved over time, the bad times becoming worse with each iteration. Maybe because she hadn't actually spoken his *name....*

"*Nobody* drank like Hal. I think the man drank in his sleep. I cannot understand why he would give up the wonderful life we had built. Did you know he had carried on with that hussy Theresa Baker at Holmstead's Wig Shoppe? *Theresa Baker!* She drank like a sailor. Didn't know where she was half the time. I hear a lot of that time was spent in the free clinic, *if* you know what I mean," said Millicent, tapping her forehead with her finger. "I can't believe Hal would leave *me* for the likes of her."

Millicent was gaining momentum, and although Prissy desperately looked for a way to derail this runaway train, her brain and mouth rarely worked in tandem. Before she knew it, her mouth flew open, and out came, "Oh, now, Millie. Hal didn't leave you for Theresa. They had a fling, but it was over before the divorce." Who said that? "Um, but that's neither here nor there," she added with a high-pitched nervous giggle.

Prissy could have exacerbated the condition further by reminding Millicent that Hal had not left her at all. In fact, Millicent had been the one to serve Hal with divorce papers. No one could have blamed her. Hal really *was* a nasty fellow. His own children, all fully grown by then, had severed all ties with him. Millicent had been fully prepared to make them choose daddy or mommy, but it never came to that. Apparently, Hal's devotion to friends and family was as empty as his vows to Millicent. Millicent's and Hal's roles in the divorce had changed in the years that passed, at least according to Millicent. Prissy suspected that by now, Millicent truly believed Hal had left her. It made for a better story.

"Are you implying that Hal was *correct* in his actions?" Millicent said stiffly, snapping Prissy back into the moment. She fixed Prissy with her patented stare, her lips pressed into a tight line, which pulled all the wrinkles forward in her face. Her unblinking eyes burned holes through Prissy, her head slightly bobbing up and down as if to defy Prissy to see any other point of view than her own.

"Oh, lands, no!" Prissy gasped. "Lands, no. Oh, my dear, sweet Millicent. Your burden has been so great." This was the only way Prissy knew to diffuse the situation. It was just as well to agree with everything Millicent said, offer appropriate sympathy, and acknowledge that her former domestic situation, now twenty years old, was as contemptible as anything anyone has ever been forced to endure.

◆

Millicent watched the moving vans come and go throughout the afternoon. The Jenkins place had been on the market for some time and required more than a little repair. White paint had been peeling from the two-story dwelling for the past decade, giving the entire structure a gray and mottled appearance. Most of the houses on Primrose Avenue had well-manicured landscaping with tidy green lawns and twin trees in the front corners of their small suburban lots.

The Jenkins yard needed some serious help.

The grass was primarily crab, and, in many areas, bare patches of earth were clearly visible. One of the twin trees had been cut almost entirely down, leaving behind a blackening stump, and the other had died and was beginning to take on a petrified look, all gnarly and leafless. Millicent made a mental note to offer suggestions for renovation of the property. One of her sons, Bill, was a contractor, and another, Brian, was a landscaper. She would get this unsightly mess straightened out in no time.

An athletic woman in her mid-thirties was moving boxes stacked on the covered porch into the house. She must be Abigail Reinhart. Her long chestnut hair was fastened in a thick ponytail. A blue-and-white bandanna was wrapped around her forehead to keep perspiration from dripping into her eyes. She wore a simple, sleeveless white summer blouse and faded blue jeans. As she stooped to collect the next box, it became apparent that the woman was in good physical condition. Her arms rippled with definition as she flexed and hoisted.

Millicent waited until Abigail had moved most of the boxes into the house, then went over to Prissy's to collect her. Under the guise of neighborly goodwill, they would bring fresh lemonade and a platter of oatmeal raisin cookies. The true purpose of the visit was to extract as much information as possible about this new family and their history. Millicent had already made mental notes of the various church committees and fundraising activities in which Abigail would participate. Any good Christian woman would.

Millicent entered through Prissy's kitchen door carrying the platter of oven-fresh cookies. She called out, "Miss Priss?" This was her custom. No deviation from the routine. "Welcome wagon's pullin' out!"

Prissy flustered into the kitchen, breathless as usual, with frizzy orange wisps of hair trailing behind her like a comet tail and her bright blue sundress billowing in and out with her rapid footsteps. Upon seeing Millicent, she had to quickly convert a hearty laugh to a sneezy cough. Prissy *hated* the yellow dress Millicent seemed insistent upon wearing on so many occasions. Millicent thought it accentuated her slender waistline. Prissy thought it only accentuated her advancing age, and no amount of little girl bows and frills could reverse the wrinkling hands of time.

"I'm ready," Prissy managed. "The lemonade is on the counter."

And so they went, armed with food, beverage, and smiles as big as Cadillacs. Abigail, or Abby as she preferred to be called, was exiting through her front door when she noticed Millicent and Prissy coming up the concrete walk that rolled out like a tongue from the covered porch. She plucked the bandanna from around her forehead and wiped beads of sweat from her brow with the back of her hand. She put on a forced smile. Abby was unaccustomed to uninvited company. Wasn't it visibly clear she was knee-deep in boxes and was obviously very busy? It was so inconsiderate, like when the dentist asks if you've seen any good movies while he is up to his elbows in your mouth.

"Hallelujah, praise Jesus, and welcome to the neighborhood!" Millicent showed all of her teeth in what she believed to be her very best smile. Abby groaned inwardly.

"Afternoon. I'm Abby Reinhart." Was this old, yellow woman some sort of missionary? "Please excuse the mess. Our stuff just arrived a little bit ago, and I'm trying to get it off the front lawn."

"Oh, pish. Don't you worry! We thought we'd bring you some refreshment, seein' as how you been working yourself so hard. I'm Millicent Van Puce, and this here's my best friend since we were skinny little things, Prissy Altwater," Millicent said, placing the pitcher of lemonade on the porch and gesturing toward Prissy, who hung back like a tentative puppy, waiting to see if this stranger was a friend or foe.

"Hi. How very nice of you. Thanks." Abby wondered if she sounded bitchy. She didn't mean it to, but she was too busy for this interruption. The kids were only in school for two more hours, and nothing much would get done for the rest of the day. "I suppose I can spare a quick minute." Eww, that one *did* come out bitchy.

It did not escape Millicent's attention, either. Almost imperceptibly, one of her pencil-sketched eyebrows rose. "If it's not a good time, we could come back."

"I'm so sorry. I didn't mean to be rude. There's just so much to do and so little time before the kids get home," said Abby. "And so little help."

Aha! thought Millicent. *A point of entry!*

"So little help? Has your husband...?" Millicent let the sentence drag out, knowing it would elicit information.

Abby snorted. "Husband? No husband."

"Poor dear. Divorce, or are you a widow woman?" Millicent always used the term 'widow woman.' Prissy giggled inwardly because, to her, it had become the name of a new comic book superhero—the New Adventures of Widow Woman.

"Never been married," Abby replied, a mischievous grin playing on her lips.

Prissy and Millicent gasped in unison. Abby leveled a glare at them. "Is there some problem?"

"Why, no, no," Millicent stammered, pouring glasses of lemonade while avoiding Abby's gaze. "Just a little surprised, that's all."

"Now, why would that be?" Abby asked smugly, preparing to receive the inevitable lecture on morality from this withering old sunflower.

Millicent forced a smile, but she knew then that all her carefully constructed plans for Abby would have to be retooled. Abby could not help in any way with the church youth group; that was for certain. That teenaged lot was so impressionable, and the less they knew of Abby's free-spirited and heathenistic ways, the better they would all be. She said, "You're such a pretty thing. I figured you wouldn't have any trouble landing a man."

"Maybe I just don't apply myself," said Abby, matching Millicent's sugary smile. "Ah, but with three kids, who has time?"

At this point, the conversation became mechanical. Abby felt Chicago was no place to raise her children and was looking for a slice of Americana. She hoped Port Monte could be the pie from which that slice was taken. Millicent made appropriate "*oh's*" and "*hmm's*," all the while surveying with visible distaste all that lay beyond the open front door to the living room. Children's toys were scattered amongst the furniture, haphazardly filling the room. Prissy twisted her sundress into helpless wrinkled submission, frequently clearing her throat and laughing a bit too loudly.

"The Ladies' Church League is organizing a raffle for children's charities," said Millicent as the conversation was drawing to a close. "Your help would be...."

"I'm sorry, Ms. Van Puce," interjected Abby. "I'm up to my eyeballs in alligators, and besides, I don't believe in organized religion."

Another strangely co-joined gasp from Millicent and Prissy. It was as if they were sharing the same set of lungs.

"Are you telling me you don't believe in *God?*" Millicent demanded, her hands planted on her hips.

"No, nothing quite so serious," Abby said. "I just don't trust the motives of men who act in the name of God."

Millicent's eyes narrowed. This was a damned soul standing in front of her. It was time to retreat. She collected the serving platter and lemonade pitcher while Prissy retrieved the glasses. "This has been very enlightening," she said in a clipped voice.

"Hasn't it, though?" Abby retrieved her sugary smile and reapplied it to her face.

"If you change your mind, you can always volunteer at our First Methodist Church. It's on Rogers Boulevard."

"I don't see that happening but thank you. And thanks for the goodies. It will be a wonder if I don't gain ten pounds," said Abby, patting her stomach.

"*I* never had to worry about that," said Millicent, running her hands down her sides. "I just eat and eat and can never gain a pound." Fat old Prissy bristled at this. Millicent was always telling people how she couldn't gain weight if she tried. She usually reserved this for her overweight church friends, seemingly oblivious to the fact that she was pouring salt in their big fat wounds.

Taking their leave, Millicent and Prissy marched across the street, Millicent muttering to herself the entire way. "Oh, Miss Priss, this one's a live wire. Did she say she had *three* children and has *never* been married? Thank goodness Hal isn't around. He'd be 'helping' her with every little thing that broke or didn't flush right."

"Maybe she just needs guidance," Prissy suggested.

"Oh, yes, she needs guidance. I just don't think she *wants* it. I wonder if she even knows who the children's father is. Or fathers are."

"Oooooh! What a thing to say!" Prissy exclaimed, her pudgy cheeks tinting red.

Millicent looked back toward Abby, who had resumed carrying boxes into the house. "Jezebel," she muttered.

◆

Abby glanced up at the clock on the mantel. It was almost six o'clock, and Garrett would be home at any time. Her children, Jessica, Troy, and Molly, were delivered by the school bus three hours ago and had gone upstairs to their respective rooms to do their homework. Jessica was the oldest at ten years of age, Troy was nine, and Molly was six. Abby hadn't planned to have three children, but sometimes things don't work out as planned. Now, she wouldn't trade motherhood for anything, not even when Jessica had one of her frequent 'earth–shattering' crises or when Troy was up to the mischief that came so naturally to a boy his age. Molly was an absolute angel. She had scored very high marks in her preschool testing, and Abby knew the girl was above average. She also was the spitting image of her mother, only on a smaller scale.

The front door opened, and Garrett came into the room, all smiles. He wore a pair of tan khakis and a light green golf shirt. After he had served his duty in the Armed Forces, he had kept his black hair cropped close to the scalp. "Hey, babe! Are you a sight for sore eyes," he said, his eyes twinkling merrily. He pulled Abby into his muscular arms and kissed her with the intensity only a long absence can inspire. He pulled back and gently touched a purplish bruise blooming on Abby's cheek. "What happened to you?"

"Oh, it's so stupid. I know it sounds cliché, but I walked smack dab into the edge of the door when I was moving boxes. It'll be fine," she said.

Then, a choir of delighted voices filled the room, punctuated with hard footfalls as the children tromped down the stairs. "*Daddy!*"

The children swarmed Garrett, and he wrapped his long arms around all three of them, kissing and nuzzling the tops of their heads. "My little grunts! How's your new school? Have you made new friends?"

Abby leaned against the mantle and watched with satisfaction as the children babbled on about everything from the three weeks since they had last seen their father. He was so good with them, laughing and asking silly questions. Abby wondered to herself how she had gotten so lucky.

"All right, little monkeys, don't you think it's my turn?" Abby asked, hooking an arm around Garrett's elbow. "You three go on back upstairs. Dinner will be ready soon, and I *will* be checking homework." She patted each of them lightly on the bottom and sent them skittering up the stairs.

Abby turned her attention back to Garrett and tucked herself to his chest, wrapping her arms around his waist. She kissed him warmly. "God, it's good to see you. Longest damn three weeks of my life," she said.

Garrett smiled down at her. "I wish I could've been more help. I couldn't get the parties to find common ground to save my skin." Garrett was an arbitrator, usually the last hope for settling lawsuits before they went to trial. "But finally, we ironed it out. Nobody was happy, but they could all live with it."

"Yay! Our man Reinhart!" Abby simulated a cheering crowd.

"I'd ask you what you've been doing, but it's pretty obvious you've been working your cute little butt off," he said, still grinning. "Have you met any of our esteemed neighbors?"

"As a matter of fact, yes. A couple of hours before the kids got home from school, some ladies from across the street came over with lemonade and cookies," she replied.

"Well, that sounds promising. I don't think I ever once spoke to our neighbors in Chicago."

"Yeah, well, don't get your hopes too high. One of the ladies was a crackpot."

Garrett laughed. "A little crackpot or a great big one?"

"Hard to say. I'm leaning towards a great big one. She's running around using the Holy Spirit as a weapon. She was looking down her nose at me through her living room window all morning until she finally came over, dragging along the lady who lives beside her. I don't think she approves of women who wear pants. Oh, and you should have *seen* them. In all fairness, I shall refrain from picking on the neighbor lady whose name is Prissy. That's right. *Prissy.* She's a big old girl, but she had all the presence of a little mouse. She was pinned under the thumb of this other one named Millicent. I swear, she must be one hundred and ten years old. Millicent was wearing this yellow thing I would find offensively young for our six-year-old Molly. She looked like Bo-Peep's great-great-grand-mother, and I might be off by a generation or two, if you know what I mean. I don't think she said two words before she started prying, trying to lead me into revealing some juicy family gossip. Yeah, like our family has any big secrets." Abby extracted herself from Garrett's embrace and crossed to the stove, where she stirred a creamy concoction bubbling in a saucepan. She added, "Isn't there a happy medium? Why do people either disassociate completely or stick their noses so far into your business that you feel like you've just been sneezed on?"

Garrett stepped up behind Abby, wrapped his arms around her, and pressed the side of his face into her soft hair. "Bad, hunh? What did you do?"

Abby turned around to face Garrett, a mischievous smile playing on her lips. "What makes you think I did anything?" she asked innocently.

"History," he said. "Out with it."

"I just had a little fun with her. Pretty early on, it became all too obvious that she had gotten the idea that it was just me and the kids moving in, probably since I've been doing all the legwork while you've been away. She needed jus-tification for this arrangement. I cannot believe that in this day and age, single parenthood is still viewed the way it is by people like her. Well, when she started fishing for information, I just kind of started making it up. Just so you'll know, you don't exist. Millicent probably doesn't even think I *know* who the father of my children is," she giggled.

"You are so bad. Well, she's gonna see me soon enough," Garrett said. "What will you say when she confronts you?"

"Oh, she won't confront me. Maybe it will teach her a lesson. Trust me. I don't want this lady coming to our back door asking to borrow cups of sugar," Abby said, returning her attention to the saucepan. She twisted the knob to ex-tinguish the flame and called, "Kids! Dinner!"

◆

Millicent stared through the lace curtain in her front parlor. She stood back just far enough so no one could see her. She had been standing motionless since the late afternoon sun had trailed off in the west, and darkness had nestled the quiet neighborhood to its bosom. She watched the Reinhart house intently.

Shortly after six, a broad-shouldered man arrived across the street in a non-descript brown sedan. He had gone to the door and, without knocking, went right in. The lights in the Reinhart living room illuminated the scene as if Abby and this man were on a stage. Millicent saw Abby and the man exchanging affection.

Harlot, thought Millicent. *Why, the children are* right there!

Millicent broke away from her vigil when Abby pulled the curtains a little while later. It had been some time since she had been to the bathroom, and her bladder was surprisingly full. She relieved herself, then went into the kitchen to make a cold-cut sandwich. Once it was prepared, she pulled a straight-backed Victorian chair to the window in the parlor and resumed her surveillance, nibbling on the sandwich distractedly until it was gone.

The brown sedan remained in the driveway hour after long hour. Millicent knew there wasn't anything proper about this relationship, so she didn't expect to see the car leave. She wasn't disappointed.

At five o'clock the next morning, the man emerged with a briefcase under his arm. He reversed out of the driveway and quietly drove off toward town. *Probably married*, thought Millicent. *Has to be home when his wife wakes.*

Millicent had become all too accustomed to that routine from her own ex-husband. Hal used every trick in the book, and Millicent had always been one step behind. If she hadn't literally caught Hal with that harridan from the wig store, she would probably still be buying his cover-up stories wholesale. Millicent perceived this to be her biggest flaw; she was too gullible. How many good years of her life had been wasted waiting for Hal to sober up, as he had always promised every morning after a night of drunken chaos? Far too many. "Now, this little floozy is one you *can't* get your hands on, Hal. Whaddaya think of *that?*" she called out to the empty air.

◆

Despite the fact that Millicent hadn't retired until 5:30 AM, only allowing herself to sleep after the strange man had left Abby's house, her eyes snapped open promptly at 7:00 AM.

It was a new day.

After finishing breakfast, Millicent drove her mustard yellow, twenty-year-old Oldsmobile east to Rogers Boulevard, where the First Methodist Church was located. She hoped Reverend Smiley was in. She desperately needed advice. As last night progressed into morning, she found herself focusing on Abby's children. They were helpless little victims in this morally dehydrated situation. They needed and deserved so much more spiritually than they could possibly get from Abby, who obviously needed some redemption herself.

But Reverend Smiley had already left for a three-day seminar in Parkersburg, and Millicent was forced to accept the responsibility of dealing with this situation herself. She spent two hours in the chapel, kneeling at the altar and praying. When she left, she had no more insight than when she had come.

As Millicent guided her Oldsmobile back into her driveway, she noticed Abby was in the front yard, painting her mailbox. She did an exaggerated double-take when she saw the shiner on Abby's cheek. *Sweet Jesus, the man's hitting her!* she thought. The Rineharts' situation was far worse than Millicent had first estimated. She spent the rest of the day worrying for the safety of the children. The man was probably hitting them, too.

Dark memories of days past filled Millicent's thoughts. Hal had often come home reeking from the booze he had consumed or spilled. His temper would ignite, and Millicent could do nothing to assuage him. Conversing was like playing hopscotch on a minefield. One wrong word and POP! Black eye. POP! Busted lip. Afterward, he would nearly convulse with his obscene laughter. And then, he would head down the hall to where the children had slept.

Millicent shivered. She had never been courageous enough to follow Hal to the children's rooms. What went on in those rooms was between Hal and God.

Well, that's that, thought Millicent. Her painful journey down memory lane had delivered the one and only solution. She turned the ignition off and sat back in the driver's seat. She knew what the Lord wanted her to do.

◆

At five o'clock the next morning, Garrett Reinhart exited his house and pulled the front door closed behind him. It was a beautiful morning. Garrett had a light work schedule today and decided he would sneak back shortly after lunch to whisk Abby off for an afternoon of fun before the kids got home from school. She had been working so hard on the house, and he felt she needed a break.

Whistling softly, he twirled his key ring on his finger and went around the side of the house to the detached garage. He proceeded to the entrance on the side of the building, stopping to coil the hose, which lay twisted and sprawled on the ground like a snake. With his hands full of coiled hose as well as his briefcase, he turned around and butted the side door, which, thankfully, was slightly ajar. It swung open, and he backed into the dark garage. He couldn't access the light switch just inside until he relinquished his hold on the hose, so he carefully squatted and placed the hose on the concrete floor.

As he rose, he caught a flurry of movement from the corner of his eye. His mind only had time to register one word: Yellow. There was a flash of light on metal as the trickle of sunlight from the side door glinted against the arcing snow shovel. A sharp crack was followed by a constellation of angry shooting stars. A symphony of pain rose in crescendo. Then only merciful darkness.

As Garrett reeled with the first blow, staggering but still standing, Millicent thought it wisest to give him a second shot. She turned with the snow shovel and brought it around in a backhand motion, the flat metal surface kissing Garrett goodnight. He dropped to the floor and lay still.

Millicent's pulse was racing as she pulled the side door shut. Sweat glistened across her leathery forehead. When she saw the blood pouring from Garrett's nose and the cut on his forehead, she feared she might have killed him. She couldn't do *that*. That was the worst sin of all. With relief, she saw the rise and fall of his chest. She needed him to be unconscious for a while, though. He was much larger, younger, and stronger than she. If he were to wake, she wouldn't stand a chance against him. She had to hurry because soon the neighborhood would awaken, and Millicent would be caught. She was taking enough of a chance as it was. But there was no other way, and Millicent was sure that Jesus was watching over her, protecting her.

Millicent wiped the shovel clean and returned it to its hook on the wall. Then she retrieved the smooth, hard plastic kneepads she had brought from her own house. They had been her youngest son, Jeff's when he had played hockey. She strapped them around Garrett's knees and then crossed to the front of the garage. She lifted the wooden garage door on its tracks and returned to Garrett's unconscious body. She firmly grasped his wrists and pulled. The kneepads clacked against the pavement as he rolled onto his stomach. Then Millicent began the arduous task of pulling him forward out of the garage. She pulled the garage door closed and proceeded down the drive, dragging Garrett by his wrists. The hard plastic of the kneepads made a bone-chilling scrape against the concrete drive, but they made Garrett much easier to transport, reducing friction as Millicent tugged.

Millicent kept her head down, afraid that if she looked up, she would meet the inquisitive eyes of any one of the neighbors with whom she had shared the block for so many years. She felt even more sure the Lord was with her when she encountered no one. She had remarkable strength for a woman of her age. She pulled Garrett down his own driveway first, across the street, and up into her own drive. She continued around to the back of her house toward the weathered plank doors that slanted downward to mark the entrance to the old fruit cellar.

Millicent paused long enough to pull her key ring from her frilly yellow apron and unlock the padlock securing the doors. She then proceeded to drag Garrett into the cellar by his ankles, his head thumping heavily against each wooden step as they descended into the darkness. Once at the bottom, she dragged him to the center of the basement, against one of the metal poles which supported the ceiling. She retrieved a length of chain and a padlock from the worktable, which ran the length of the rear wall. She pulled Garrett's arms behind his back and around the pole and bound them together tightly with the chain. Once she was sure the chain was sufficiently tight, she snapped the padlock into place. She repeated the maneuver with his legs. She then strapped five pieces of furnace tape over the man's mouth.

Millicent wiped her hands against one another, then brushed the dust from her favorite dress.   She looked at Garrett, still unconscious, his head lolling against his right shoulder. "Pray for forgiveness, you bastard," she said. "As God is my witness, you'll not hurt that family again. I reckon God will see His way clear to freeing you if your repentance is sincere."

She turned and mounted the creaking stairs. Once she was back out in the sunlight, she swung the wooden doors shut. She started to return the padlock to its place when she realized she must have left it on the cellar floor.

Suddenly, Prissy was at Millicent's elbow, blithering about some television drama she had seen the previous night. Her eyes sparkled, and her rosy cheeks shined as she babbled on and on. Reluctantly, Millicent led Prissy away from the cellar door and into her kitchen. She would have to tend to the lock later.

◆

As she watched the school bus pull away from the curb, transporting her brood away as it always did at seven o'clock, Abby began a mental checklist of her tasks for the day. There was still so much to do. By the time she emerged from the shower, she had decided to go to the grocery store first. She hadn't had time to stock the kitchen fully since she and Garrett moved in, and since that first day, meals had consisted of breakfast cereal and fast food.

She dressed quickly, grabbed her purse, and headed to the garage. She opened the door on the side of the building, reached in and to the right, and flicked on the overhead light. She froze as the lights flickered on.

Garrett's car was still parked in the garage beside hers.

She took a tentative step forward and placed her hand on the hood of Garrett's car. The metal was cool to the touch. The engine hadn't run for hours. If Garrett's car had refused to start this morning, he would have simply taken her car. Yet here it was, parked beside Garrett's, just as she had left it.

Puzzled, she glanced around the garage, taking in details as quickly as possible. She didn't know what she was looking for, but something felt very wrong. Her foot slid in a very small dark, oily patch, and for a second, she thought she might fall. After regaining her balance, she glanced down and was horrified to see the trail her shoe had dragged from the oily patch was a deep, crimson red.

She jerked the cell phone from her handbag and punched in 911.

"Nine-one-one Emergency. What is the nature of your emergency?" the operator asked in a dull monotone.

Abby blurted, "This is Abby Reinhart. I'm at 4628 Wyndham Road. My husband is missing—and there's blood." She looked up, and her eye was drawn to a glint of color along the back wall of the garage. The color, bright and yellow, was inconsistent with the grimy shades of gray that tinted the rest of the wall.

The operator was saying something, but Abby was no longer listening. She was walking toward the yellow thing. She hung up the phone.

It was a swatch of cloth. Yellow and frilly. Unmistakably, Millicent Van Puce.

She pulled the rake from its hook, where it was positioned beside the snow shovel. When had Millicent been in the garage? She hadn't.

Abby ran out of the garage, her eyes darting from side to side, looking for any sign of Garrett. As she crossed the street and entered Millicent's driveway, she noticed the grass to the left of the driveway had shallow furrows in it leading into the side yard and toward the rear of the house. It was as if something with wheels had rolled through the yard.

Slowing, she crept into the yard, following the trail. Abby stayed alert and cautious, checking the house frequently to make sure Millicent wasn't watching her from the window. The trail led to a set of double cellar doors.

Abby looked up once more to verify that Millicent was nowhere in sight. Once satisfied, she gently opened the doors, careful not to make a sound, and began her descent into the dark cellar.

◆

Millicent was shaking. She tried not to, but she couldn't help it with the adrenaline coursing through her aged veins. Prissy was such a simple thing. She sat across the kitchen table, going on and on about everything and nothing, and Millicent couldn't focus on a word she said. She needed to get that padlock on the cellar door.

Just as Millicent's eyes began to cross from Prissy's incessant yammering, she saw motion over Prissy's shoulder, where a small crescent of window was visible. She leaped to her feet and crossed the room, standing far enough away so as not to be seen.

Abby Reinhart was opening the cellar door.

No! thought Millicent. *She can't see him yet! She'll just let him go! She won't understand that this is for her own good!*

Although she hadn't decided exactly what to do about Abby, much less how to go about it, she had hoped to find a way to assert her influence and lead this lost lamb back into the fold. Her little babies needed a mother. But it was too soon. Abby was still under the control of this man.

She shook with fear. Somehow, she had thought divine intervention would prevent this sort of complication. She waited for some inner voice to guide her, but her ears were filled only with the sounds of her heart pounding and pounding. Not knowing what else she could do, Millicent excused herself from Prissy and grabbed the cast iron skillet from the top of the stove as she crossed to the kitchen door.

Once outside, she could hear sirens in the distance. They were drawing steadily nearer. She quickly crossed the yard and began descending the cellar stairs. She slowed as she saw the overhead light had been turned on. One step at a time, the basement came into view. Abby stood beside her shackled spouse, her cell phone pressed to her ear. Garrett had awakened but looked disoriented. His forehead had stopped bleeding, but a dark red dried patch remained. Abby's eyes burned holes through Millicent. She had asked the 911 operator to re-route the officers to Millicent's house.

Helplessness washed over Millicent. She realized the cast iron skillet was drawn over her head, poised and ready to strike. She gasped and dropped it, sending it clunking down the remaining few stairs. She could never have used it against Abby. Could she?

The sirens were blaring just outside now. They would be here soon. Surely, they would understand she had just been trying to *protect* the young Jezebel. Surely God would see her through this. She fell to her knees and began to pray. She could hear the approaching footfalls of the officers.

Her eyes shifted to the far end of the basement, opposite from where Garrett was chained. In the dim light, the skeletal remains of Hal peered out, staring vacantly at her. Rusted chains vulgarly intertwined with bone, permanently affixing the corpse to the other support pole. Hal's alcoholism had alienated him from absolutely everyone. No one questioned a thing when Millicent spread the rumor that he had gone to Italy. God hadn't seen fit to show Hal a way to escape his eternal prison.

Millicent couldn't help but notice Hal's jaw was hanging open. Even in death, Hal's viciously cruel laughter burned Millicent's ears.

God certainly worked in mysterious ways.

Darin Miller grew up in Rosemount, a suburb of Portsmouth, Ohio. He currently resides in Grove City, Ohio. While he has worked in Information Technology for three decades, he has *not* solved a single solitary crime to date. He is the author of five volumes of the Ohio-based Dwayne Morrow Mystery series, as well as a standalone collection of short stories, *Broken Bits and Bobs: A Collection of What Ifs, What Was, and What Never Should Be*. With equal parts action, humor, suspense and mystery, the Dwayne Morrow series features characters you're sure to love—and in some cases, loathe.

Finder's Fee

Michael Whitfield

The trouble started with Slow Sam, there in my store.

Sam's real name is Samuel Conover, but nobody calls him that. He's in a wheelchair, one of those modified for high mobility, and takes offense whenever anybody calls him disabled. "Slow Sam" is more than able. Out on the block, Sam is up and down sidewalks and sometimes in the streets. Got no bumpers in his brain. Adds to his disability check by runnin' errands, 'doin' things for people' in the neighborhood.

In Sam's line of work, it pays to be an E-O-C: equal opportunity conveyor. That's how he knows so much. Sam deals with the good, the bad, and the ugly. If he don't know, it ain't been told. If he ain't heard, it must not mean to be said.

"You gonna' move today or day after tomorrow?" It was Sam to me. I was pondering my next move and had come to no decision. Truth be told, it was Sam who owned that reputation. It's how he had earned his nickname, Slow Sam, among the pawns and kings.

When I moved my black knight to reset my defenses, I heard "check" despite my earnest calculations.

I'd welcome a way out. A customer at my counter might have helped. But it was raining, and business was effectively on hold.

"Word on the street..." Slow Sam began.

Here we go, I thought to myself. 'Cause once Sam started on a topic, it could be eons before his head got back into the game.

"...Tiny Green's lookin' for something he done lost,"

That got my attention.

"Tiny? He don't lose nothin'," I said. "Only takes, including what ain't his."

"Twenty-grand," Sam answered. "Offerin' a finder's fee," he added.

"What's the fee?" I was interested and not just to delay the inevitable.

"They life. Whoever turns over Tiny's twenty grand gets to keep breathin.' No negotiation."

Damn! I said to myself. Tiny Green's deal was what you'd expect from Satan himself. In our neighborhood, Alfred "Tiny" Green was the "crown prince of terror." His boys, fallen angels run amok.

I shivered, felt that odd chill flash down my spine. Just about the only time anybody ever really feels the spine, it being part of the non-autonomous nervous system and all. But when you feel it, well, you know.

Not everyone agreed about Tiny Green, Sam included. Green was known to practice a benevolent-malevolent criminality. He sponsored little leagues and bought truckloads of fresh Thanksgiving turkeys, handing them out to single mothers and widows. Tiny was even known to show up in church: on Easter Sunday and at the funerals of his employees and associates.

"Checkmate!" Slow Sam had won another. The Bobby Fischer of the 'hood.' My losing streak continued. I couldn't catch a break and hold it without someone wanting to wrest it from my mitts.

I considered Tiny Green's message. Delivered indiscriminately, that was what Slow Sam did. The preeminent griot of the neighborhood. You want it said, employ Sam. Voice of the city. At least this part of town.

The rain slowed, I rose from another defeat and held the door as Sam rolled out of the store and opened a large umbrella rigged to his motorized chair. Under the canopy, Sam appeared to be sitting at a bistro table, oblivious to the elements and ready to do business again.

I run the carryout business established by my father. In the language of the old neighborhood, a 'corner store.' Because nearly everyone here carries a nick-name, I'm "corner store Harold."

Williams is the family name; Harold Williams the Second, mine. I'd graduated community college and was figuring on a four-year degree when Harold Williams Senior, my "Pops," took sick. I took over the store; it took my life. I never left, even when "Pop Williams" returned and was helping me more than the other way around.

When Pops passed, the business became fully mine. I'd convinced him to buy the vacant barber shop next door after the owner retired. We'd added another seven hundred fifty square feet by taking the wall down and then installing additional coolers for meat and produce.

Regrets? A few, but I'm one of a handful of African American businessmen in the neighborhood—I mean legitimate ones. And if I'd not been in this store, I'd have missed meeting Lutina, the unadulterated love of my life.

She'd come in on a very hot day wanting a soda, a bottle of Orange Crush from our new cooler. I looked into her eyes and lied, telling her that 'Crush' was my favorite, too. I lied for the purpose of romance. It's since become our signature drink, and I still stock it, mostly for her.

When Lutina left the store that day, I followed her out. I 'wet my whistle' watching that sweet African queen saunter down the sidewalk. Damn! Soda bottle bottom! She turned and smiled, and it's been on ever since.

Two kids and years later, "Lu" still has my eyes and owns my heart. She still got "back," too, but it's her sciatica, the part I can't see, that gives her trouble. My baby's a metro bus driver currently off work on disability. Waiting for a herniated disk to heal, Lu's driving Uber using her maiden name, Lutina Walker, to cover what AFLAC won't.

I'm not entirely comfortable with this covert arrangement, but ends do have to be met. Nobody gets rich running a convenience store. It helps that we inherited my parents' house. After Pops died, my mom missed him into an early grave. A splendid example of loving for a lifetime.

Lu's wages, added to profits from the store, have meant we can dream of college for Harold the Third. He's seventeen, and Lucretia, our daughter, is fifteen. My 'boo's' chronic back problems are an unanticipated setback.

The one good thing about Uber is Lu being able to stop in the store more often. She came in that day after Slow Sam and the rain, stylin' a new weave, just out of the salon chair.

"You like?" She flashed a "Price is Right" show model pose.

"Yeah, baby!" I faked my enthusiasm, an autonomic response. My cinnamon vixen underneath somebody else's hair. I mean, under that weave is a healthy head of auburn hair I do remember. Why this? And at one hundred seventy-five dollars before tipping?

Lu came close to the counter, leaning across for a peck on the lips. In doing so, she reminded me nobody buys a house for the roof. It's her 'basement' that's my 'man cave.'

I heard Lu say the hair, a curly reddish mop top was just too tempting to ignore. She needed a change. I'm back to thinking dollars. Hairdressers take in more currency under the table than anybody. No taxes, no paperwork, no worries. "None of your bid-ness!" Unlike me and the store, heavily taxed and regulated.

Lu informs me that the ladies in the salon argued about spending twenty thousand dollars if they found it. That would be Tiny Green's twenty grand. I knew they could only dream.

I got a secret. One I'm keeping from Lutina. And I've got to be very careful, I married a very smart woman.

She finishes by letting me know she might make another Uber run or two before heading home. I'm then given instructions not to be late for dinner. I watched her walk out, valuing what was mine.

Business picked up and was moderate the rest of the day. I normally do a steady business in bread and milk and frozen entrees like pizza from the freezers. Cigarettes aren't what they used to be, but I still have my regulars by the carton. Any business owner dependent on walk-ups hates to see it rain and despises snow and the bitter cold.

I had moved to coffee, put out a few tables with chairs like the one Slow Sam and I play chess at. Sometimes, it means I have company longer than I want. A few of the old-timers, retirees wanting to take in the air conditioning or feel the heat when it's cold. Shedding their cloaks of loneliness by being nosey about everything.

What I had really wanted was a liquor license. What I got was noise. "No! Hell, no! Not in any store of mine!" That had been my Pops.

And from Lutina, after he passed: "You really want to be responsible for starting children on that road, addiction to alcohol?"

And from my church friends. "Bad idea. We don't need another liquor store, not in this neighborhood!"

Okay, I'd heard it—but I didn't let it stop me from completing a liquor permit application. I still needed a sizable amount of cash for the fees. I figured I'd deal with the rest when it got approved. I mean, if Johnny Walker and Jack Daniel could escort my kids to college and open the doors to a better life, I'd stand up to the criticism, even from Lu.

I finished the day with a few regulars. The Marlboro Man, a.k.a. Teddy Robison, in for his smokes. Several customers playin' their numbers, the state-regulated lottery.

Out on the sidewalk, pulling the gate down, a patrol car rolls up. I close at seven p.m., under the protection of light. "I am Legend," too. Most goons in the neighborhood wake late to act on their damnable ideas. Looking to impose their wills on the workin' stiffs unwise in not yielding the streets.

I normally appreciate the police monitoring legitimate establishments like mine. But when I heard, "Hey Hal, got a minute," it sounded a little too much like business.

Scotty Roberts got out of the patrol car. The neighborhood beat cop. He's tall, White, and Irish. I consider Roberts good people as cops go. But his nickname, Beam Me Up Scotty, speaks to a general dislike by the local population.

Some complain that Scotty is too cozy with the bad elements on the block. "They" say "they" feed him the little fish for Scotty to pad his arrest records. A diversionary tactic, they argue. Doesn't help that Scotty never seems too interested in the likes of Tiny Green. He and the police have never come close to touching Green. Makes you wonder.

Roberts gets close and confirms what I've now heard two times over. Tiny Green is searching for his missing twenty-grand. He's promising malice over his money. If it appears that I'm nervous, well, I am. In my neighborhood, it doesn't pay to be seen talkin' to the police. With Scotty Roberts, "Good day, officer" can be too much.

"You know anything?" Roberts asks me.

"No," I answer in direct denial. "But if I hear somethin'...." I leave it at that, promising nothing.

Scotty sizes me up before saying, "There's word on the street, Harold...just a whisper." Officer Roberts has my full attention.

"The whisper is that a good Samaritan stopped to pick up a bag of trash out of the street. Tiny's twenty-grand reportedly inside, no joke. Obviously, not pre-meditated. Who knows, misfortune or fate?"

"And so...?" I interrupt, remembering Lu's warning about dinner.

"Tongues are wagging, saying the description of that Samaritan fits you."

I'm more than just a little nervous now. Enough to go quiet, mistakenly having my silence count for agreement.

"Let me help you out, Hal. I wouldn't want to see you get hurt." False concern. Scotty's sounding like Slow Sam. A messenger for Tiny Green.

I manage to say, with as much conviction as I can muster, "I don't know anything."

Scotty stares straight at me, looks long, and shrugs. "Suit yourself...in your own burial clothes. Black, gray, or blue, nothin' looks good on a dead man."

Roberts then steps off the curb and back into the squad car. He drives off, and I'm left to walk home, my normal. The mile and a half's a benefit of the business. We're not saddled with the expense of a second car. I mean, we do own one, my dad's 1984 Buick Roadmaster. I drive it only on special occasions, between tinkering with it.

I step heavily in reflection. I'd acted to give hint of nothing special about my circumstances, including when looking up to find Walter Shepherd, "Big Shep," on the path ahead, a goon of the highest order. A goon's goon gone mad. He works for Tiny Green.

He's standing in the middle of the sidewalk, pounding his big mitts like a catcher behind the plate. If I make a move to the other side of the street, I'm guilty, and the bounty on me proves credible. So, we encounter.

"Big Shep," I say. "How you doin'?"

"You, Harold. I'm doin' you."

Around here, you know fear. Sometimes a friend, more often a foe. I had learned to keep fear at a distance. "What might I do for you, Shep?"

"Not me, Harold. It's Tiny. He believes you have somethin' belongs to him." For all my self-control, Walter can read me like a first-grade primer. It's an assassin's game, sniffin' out the fear of his targets.

The nickname matches his face, long and narrow to the nose, and pointy ears. Ancient in the game, a salt-and-pepper beard kept short, adding to his canine-like appearance. Eyes dark and glowing, a tint of amber. Big Shep, a natural-born hunter.

"I do have something for Mr. Green." I try to sound respectful, business professional. Shep's big body eases a bit, still positioned to pounce. "A meeting, my store. Tomorrow night after closing."

Walter shortens the narrow space between us. His breath is hot, moist, and fetid.

"That's not the plan," he growls low so only I can hear.

"I know," I admit, summoning courage previously inaccessible to me. "But it will have to do. If Tiny, uh, Mr. Green, wants to punch my ticket."

His dark eyes lighten to recognition. Instinct gives way to thought. Big Shep then smiles, teeth white and sharp.

"Okay, Harold. You get one chance, sucker! Blow this, I bag your ass, and then call Uber!" A threat against my beloved Lutina.

Big Shep had raised the stakes. He sealed it with a soft punch to my shoulder. Laughing while walking to a car parked down the way. Getting into the front passenger's seat, the driver pulls away. He grants me a wave, dismissive, the back of his hand.

Deal or no deal, I had a suitcase to unpack. I hadn't disclosed all, it's not my way. When you run a corner store, you don't share folks' grocery lists. Although we see and hear lots like bartenders, it's not what's done.

It bothered me from the beginning not to tell Lu. I'd stopped, stooped, and pulled somebody's trash out of the street and into the store. Otherwise, I would have been scolded, she being a saint of sanitization. I was only acting as a lord of litter. Once inside, the damn thing collapsed, a cheap liner. I stock better.

Out from the trash tumbled a package wrapped in brown paper, an old-school grocery bag. Curiosity got the best of me. I opened it to find twenty-thousand dollars in two stacks of one-hundred-dollar bills bound with rubber bands. I didn't know it was Tiny Green's cash. There was a clue, but I'll tell you about that later.

The rest of my walk and into the evening, I pondered my next move. I still had one to play...carefully.

Lu's chicken noodle soup did not disappoint. Delicious as usual. The kids talked about their days. H-W-3 (his choice for a nickname), and 'Cretia (given), aspire for an M.B.A. and C.P.A., respectively. We discussed summer school and working in the store.

After dinner, they turned to homework and chores. Lu did the dishes accompanied by the *Wendy Williams Show* on her Kindle. Then on to her regular catch-up call with her sister.

I rode the sofa, dozing through an N.B.A. finals game. By the time I wandered into the bedroom, Lu was sound asleep. Soon, so was I.

The next day was strictly business. I had my plan for the meeting with Tiny Green. I'd count on God's grace.

I was due a revival after yesterday's rain. Business was good. I helped Mrs. Evers with her regular deli order: souse meat, ham salad, and pigs' knuckles. I still carry all three in homage to my pops.

I took in some supplies and joked with the Pepsi man. I listened to Grady Anderson complain about half-and-half for the coffee, wanting those expensive flavored liquid dairy creamers. I nearly sold out of chips and snacks, the next finals game being tomorrow night. Ol' Grady was boastin' on LeBron.

The lottery line at the end of the day was mostly scratch-offs. Somebody had hit at 'somebody else's' counter the day before. I looked up at six-thirty to see Big Shep entering my store.

Tiny Green's solicitor had the effect of a crow on sparrows and wrens. Customers quieted before scattering quickly. One dude got halfway in through the door, saw Big Shep, and pirouetted back out to the pavement.

Shep stood there silent, like a guard at Buckingham Palace. At precisely six fifty-nine p.m., the last customer gone, he moved to lock the door from the inside. Gravitas.

"He comin' or just you and me?" I asked. I'm permitted and keep it kept close under the counter. That morning, I had also strapped a Derringer to my ankle.

"Oh, he'll be here, 'corner store Harold,'" Shep sneered. "Bet' not disappoint him."

At seven oh-one, a Black Cadillac Escalade angles to the curb and strategically blocks my door. Two men get out, one remains on the sidewalk. Shep continues as doorman, letting the other in.

Alfred "Tiny" Green. He's barely inside, nods to Big Shep, who then sweeps the aisles of the store. Green says nothing. Just stands, looks at me, smiling. I lose sight of Shep but not the location of my Glock. Kept inside a soft canvas lunch sack under the counter, unzipped and within reach.

When Shep returns from my back room, they nod at each other. Then Green approaches me with his palm up and out.

"Cell phone." It's Big Shep's voice. I reach slowly into my pocket, producing my Samsung. Green hands the phone to Shep, who drops it. He watches it bounce, steps, and crushes it hard underfoot.

Green waves a finger over his head. Shep moves nonchalantly to join me behind the counter. He reaches for the one security camera I can afford and rips it from the wall. He follows the cables to the base unit, snatches it, and heads past Tiny to the door, both in hand. Shep goes out, leaving me and Alfred alone, facing each other.

"Let's do this quick," the melodious baritone voice of the bad man orders. He's produced his own gun deftly from a shoulder holster inside his jacket. It's up in my face too close for proper admiration.

"Your gun." Not a question, an imperative. I move slowly, pulling out the Glock and surrendering it into his free hand.

"My money." Also not a question. Again, I move, haltingly beneath the counter to produce the two stacks of bills, same packaging.

He recognizes the money, and the smile returns. Terror that he is, Tiny has an engaging smile and an athletic stature. He's dressed in dark blue sportswear, silk bottoms and top. A handsome man, genteel with fluid movements. Dude is charismatic.

Tiny counts the bills best he can without lowering the gun. Seems satisfied and begins to glide backward toward the door.

I clear my throat, saying, "Uh, Mr. Green. Please, the ticket?"

He stops suddenly. Those alluring eyes renew interest.

"I mean, I was only acting to protect your interests, staying quiet about the twenty grand."

He allows me to reach beneath the counter, the newspaper article. I lay it gently atop, its headline reading, *Police Seek Leads in Killing*. Bingo!

It all went down at the track. A man found dead in the parking lot, slumped over the steering wheel of his car. Strangulation and suspected robbery.

"It was in the bag," I say, holding up a racing ticket.

"Soccer game can wait," Green says, deciding to step forward again. His attitude has been refreshed.

"An associate?" I dare ask.

"My lady's cousin," he grants willingly, a slight shrug following. "Family and business, damn!" That last a rueful admission.

I take the chance, sliding the ticket across the counter to him. Alfred "Tiny" Green looks surprised. Smiling like the Cheshire cat, asking with some relief, "So what's this going to cost me?"

"Finder's fee," I say, meaning it. Still considering, carefully.

Tiny considers a moment before releasing one bundle of cash from his hand, laying it on my counter.

"Used to come in here as a boy." He's reminiscing. "Your father, God rest his soul, said one day I'd be a helluva' businessman."

Tiny flashes that smile one last time. He turns and heads for the door. Says over his shoulder on the way out. "Gotta' family to raise, mouths to feed, business to run."

And so do I. The bells tied to my door jingle as Alfred "Tiny" Green exits. Somewhere, according to that Christmas movie, an angel has gotten its wings. I had been waiting to exhale and did, finally. Left on my counter, interest-free financing, my own family's future.

Michael G. Whitfield holds master's degrees in journalism and education and is a contributing writer to *Reynoldsburg Magazine*. He continues to work in public schools, having written several unpublished children's books and stories. Whitfield enjoys writing fictional short stories and continues revising his cozy mystery novels featuring Morgan Stern, a spiritually conflicted insurance investigator. Whitfield continues to submit his work to writing contests and magazines while seeking a literary agent for publication.

The Attic

Storehouse of Hidden Memories

"I thought about how there are two types of secrets: the kind you *want* to keep in, and the kind you don't *dare* to let out."

— Ally Carter, *Don't Judge a Girl by Her Cover*

Vacant

Corrina Malek

A m I becoming paranoid? Their eyes seem to find me no matter where I go. It's like one of those paintings in a museum—no matter where you stand in the room, the eyes appear to follow you. I have to be careful, this much I know. I can't give them any reason to doubt me. You should be able to trust your family, and I do...it's just that I know where things like this can lead. Being in the public eye magnifies everything. Will is in his first year in his governorship, and public perception matters. Amputate the dying appendage to save the greater body.

I never thought Will would run for any sort of political office, but after taking an early retirement from corporate finance, he took an even keener interest in what was happening locally in our community. It started with a developer who wanted to buy land north of the village green. I don't recall the acreage but suffice it to say the developer's plans included a 700-unit "affordable" apartment community with very little green space. Our already crowded schools, streets, and neighborhood were on the brink of imploding.

When the news first hit the local paper, Will was furious. "Can you believe this? Look what this developer wants to do, Maggie. Just *look*." He shook the morning paper in my direction. It was the first time in twenty years we actually considered moving. The land had become a public park, and adults, kids, and dogs all enjoyed it. Will jogged there many evenings. I practiced "Yoga in the Park" every first Saturday of the month. The grounds were gorgeous—wisteria, hyacinth, and pink tulips had matured into a jaw-dropping landscape.

◆

Something about this news was a catalyst for change—it was the beginning of the end. I knew Will wouldn't be one for retirement—he could never sit still very long, and the threat of low-income housing and our decreasing home value spurred him to action. Within six months, he ran for city council and won by a landslide. Will found his passion, and two years later, he was the mayor. After four successful years with a positive budget and listening and acting upon his constituents' concerns, Will was wildly successful. His popularity soared, and it was an easy win for the Governor's office. At sixty-two, he was fully invested in another career.

Most mornings began for me with a cup of hazelnut coffee and then thirty minutes of yoga. I knew how lucky I was to have this leisure. I waited for a long while to tell my group of girlfriends that I was taking early retirement. "I'm going to start to pull back," I told them one October night when we huddled around our firepit.

"Do you mean going part-time?" Ellie asked. Ellie had four kids and spent the first half of her thirties working as a realtor. Technically, she was part-time, but anyone in real estate knows that's almost impossible. Somehow, she managed to get it all done. She went back full-time when the kids were in high school.

I shifted uncomfortably, aware of four pairs of eyes on me. "Well, no, not exactly. "I took a sip of my cabernet. "I'm...I'm going to quit, freelance maybe. Maybe Will and I will start an LLC or something." Another sip or, rather, a gulp of my wine. I felt a bit dribble in the corner of my mouth and quickly wiped it away, hoping it was too dark for anyone to notice.

I'm not sure what I expected, maybe "Good for you!" or "You're so lucky!" but instead, Samantha took off her glasses, leaning towards me, and said, "Maggie, are you okay? There's nothing going on, health-wise?" Her blue eyes assessed me in the way only a nurse can.

I let out a half guffaw. "Oh no—I'm fine! That's not it at all." I felt my face color. "Will took an early retirement from his corporate job, so I thought...I thought I would too." My grip on my wine glass was too tight. I told myself to relax my hands.

Paige and Jen looked puzzled. "What would you *do* then?" Paige asked. Paige was an attorney and Jen an executive marketing manager—free time was not a luxury they experienced. The others looked at me quizzically. I needed to change the subject: this was not the reaction I hoped for.

"I guess visit Liz and Brant more. And the LLC," I said weakly. "I think there's something there." I did not want this strange attention. My face still felt hot, and if they noticed, maybe they would think it was the fire.

They drank from their wine glasses, and seconds of silence stretched before us.

"Ellie," I said. "How is Chad doing? Can't believe he's halfway through his senior year at OU!" The change of subject worked, and once again, the lively banter started back up, much to my relief. I reminded myself that all my friends had ten-plus years of work ahead of them, and no one was anywhere near ready to retire. We all had just celebrated our fiftieth birthdays.

◆

While most days I completely embraced this new leisurely lifestyle, at times it was hard to adjust to not having to respond to emails in twenty-four hours (or even get emails) and work long hours. I still checked my emails daily, usually when drinking my coffee. There was the occasional email from Liz (Brant never emailed—just texted), and the rest of my inbox had emails from Amazon telling me my order has shipped or clothing stores with subject lines like "*Welcome! Enjoy*

20% off." I spent more time deleting emails than reading them. I didn't travel much for my Human Resources job, but there were calls at all hours, and I was expected to take them. I likened myself to a therapist, most days, listening to an endless array of problems, both work and personal, and constantly keeping my hands calmly folded, my face relaxed, and balancing genuine empathy with company policy.

I started noticing that sometimes I'd become forgetful. I chalked this up to turning fifty—the magical age when you wake up each morning with a new pain you can only attribute to living. I had needed reading glasses since my early forties, but now I was completely blind without them—even my breakfast was out of focus until I wore them. There were numerous instances when I asked Will, "Have you seen my reading glasses? I can't find them." Will would give me a crooked smile, trying to contain a laugh. "They're on your head," he pointed. My hand would fly up to my head and find a plastic pair of readers perched within my auburn curls.

Despite the yoga, my hips ached constantly, and Will and I traded daily stories of "what was hurting now." You get used to these things, but I was bothered the most by memory loss. My aunt had passed away from early-onset Alzheimer's, which she was diagnosed with at the age of forty-five. My two sisters and I rarely talked about it, but I know it was a source of concern for all of us. Will and I didn't even talk about it much—we were newly married at the time and oblivious to anything health or age-related. But we had noticed when Uncle Art had lost so much weight and began to look haggard, his cheeks hollowing out and the puffs under his eyes a constant fixture. I remembered him when I was a child, thinking he had movie star looks, with his tanned skin and bright gleaming smile. "He's worn out," Will had remarked after our last visit. I said nothing but nodded. I felt guilty that we hadn't offered to help more, but we were young and left the caretaking to the older generation.

I started to notice when I would do things like put the butter away where the dishes were or leave my keys in the bathroom. I'd walk into a room to get one thing and then find something else to do while I was there, completely forgetting why I went into the room in the first place. I told myself that this is normal, but I somehow couldn't bring myself to ask my friends if they experienced the same thing.

♦

Early in the week, I decided to go for a walk. Bursts of purple crocuses dotted my neighbors' front yards, and trees were sporting tiny green leaves, starting to unfold. The air was crisp—enough for a jacket still. It felt good to be outside. I wanted to walk more, but sometimes it felt odd—that somehow, I needed a purpose. I often remarked to Will that maybe we needed to get a dog. It would keep me company and make my walks seem like they had justification. It just seemed like everyone around me was either pushing a baby stroller, walking a dog, or holding someone's hand. I walked on anyway, casting the silly feelings aside, enjoying the symphony of bird callings and the sun on my face. My phone buzzed in my pocket. It was Liz.

"Hi, Mom!" her sing-songy voice rang.

"Hi, sweetie, how are you?"

She had called about a promotion opportunity at work and wondered if it was too soon for her to go for it. We talked for several more minutes before she brought up Jared, mentioning that it was his weekend for his daughter to stay with them.

"I've got the cutest picture of her," Liz said, and my thoughts wavered like a feather in the wind.

"Mom?"

"Yes, sweetie?"

"I said I have the cutest picture of her." Slight annoyance in her voice.

Silence again. My mind felt like a wide expanse, vacant of the memory I was searching for. My words came out softly, maybe too softly. "Who, sweetie?"

"Amelia!" Liz said urgently. "Who did you think I meant?"

I was quiet again. I said what she wanted to hear, what I knew she needed to hear. "Oh honey, I'm sorry. It was loud out here; I couldn't really hear you." Would she believe this?

Back inside my house after the call, I sat down, drinking a large glass of water. Maybe I needed to make some tea or coffee—maybe I wasn't awake enough. Yes, that was it: I was just tired.

◆

Months later, we hosted a dinner party for one of Will's old college friends, who was now also a local council member. Kirk and his wife, whose name I couldn't recall, sat on the living room couch while Will went to make drinks.

"What will you have, Kirk?" Will asked from the bar, "The usual?"

"Oh, you know us—a bit too predictable," Kirk laughed. "Make it the usual—thanks."

Will looked in my direction. "Can you give me a hand, Mags?"

"I can help," offered Kirk's wife.

"Oh no, that's okay, I've got it," I said and smiled at her. *What is her name?* I scolded myself for forgetting. *It will come to me.* I joined Will at the bar and took out two wine glasses. Will looked at me with narrowed eyes.

"Why are you getting wine glasses, Maggie?" he whispered and opened the cabinet to get the rocks glasses. *Careful now*, I told myself.

"Oh gosh, I don't know, I just reached for the wrong ones, I guess." I laughed, and finally, Will smiled a bit, his face beginning to relax.

"Yeah, scotch and soda might look a bit odd in those glasses," he joked. He looked at me a bit longer and then must have been satisfied enough to return to making the drinks.

The rest of the night seemed to be okay, but I could not remember Kirk's wife's name. I spent most of the night smiling and asking generic questions so as to not draw attention to myself or my lack of remembering. Maybe I was just tired.

◆

It was sometime later, closer to the holidays. Snow was on the ground. I woke to the smell of coffee and an unusually bright room.

"Maggie! You better get up!" Will called from the other room.

I put on my lilac robe and slippers and padded out to the kitchen. Will was dressed in khaki pants and a pressed blue shirt. His silver-gray hair, which at times could look too thick and unruly, was neatly styled and looked freshly trimmed. I squinted at this, trying to recall when he went to the barber. He re-filled his coffee cup. "Boy, you slept in! You should get moving, they're going to be here in twenty minutes."

I rubbed my eyes. "Who?"

"What?" Will asked.

"Who's going to be here?" *Oh, I shouldn't have said that*, I scolded myself.

He stared at me for what seemed like an eternity. "Liz," he said, his brown eyes softening. "Liz and Jared."

"Oh yes," I grabbed a sponge to wipe down the clean counter, avoiding his eyes. "Of course. I knew that."

Will stood there holding his coffee, motionless. Excruciating seconds passed.

"Are you all right, Maggie?"

"Yes, Will!" I said louder than I intended; it sounded harsh. "I'm just tired, that's all," I told him, my voice steady.

"Okay," he said, seemingly unconvinced. "You had me worried for a second there." He offered a small smile.

My eyes flickered around the kitchen. There was a pie covered in saran wrap. A box of stuffing mix was next to a bowl. *Oh my God, oh my God...this is Thanksgiving weekend. What happened last night? Why am I so tired? Why can't I remember? What is happening to me? I will get this together, I told myself. I cannot embarrass Will. I cannot be a reason for anything to go wrong in his career. I can handle this. I'm okay, I'm okay.*

◆

It was summer. Will was acting odd around me. At times I caught him looking at me for too long. It was just a precaution, but I made the appointment with Dr.

Kessel, the neurologist our GP recommended to me. Of course, I didn't tell Will or anyone. It was just a baseline test, I told myself—just like you do for your heart when you turn fifty.

My stomach was in knots when I arrived at his office. I was grateful to find it mostly empty—the only other person was sitting in the far corner, her head buried in her phone. Luckily, I didn't have to wait long before I was called in. Dr. Kessel was a petite man with thick tufts of salt and pepper hair. His skin looked like he spent winters in Florida. His eyes were a startling mint green, and I felt immediately scrutinized by them. I took some yoga breaths and folded my hands in my lap. *Calm. Calm. This is nothing.* After some initial questions and a family history review, Dr. Kessel told me he was going to do some testing—both physical and cognitive. The physical portion of the test was easy and just involved a bit of walking, raising my arms, and other motions.

Next came the questions. At first, they were easy.

"Okay, Maggie, I'm going to ask you some questions now," Dr. Kessel said. "Can you tell me today's date?"

"Sure," I told him. "It's August twenty-fourth, 2023."

"And where do you live?"

This seemed silly. "Warnersville, Ohio."

"Great. Now I'm going to ask you to count backward from one hundred by increments of two."

"One hundred, ninety-eight, ninety-six, ninety-four, ninety-two...should I keep going?" I smiled.

He then asked me to draw a clock and some basic shapes. I felt like I was in kindergarten and regretted making the appointment. In many ways, though, it was comforting. *I am fine*, I told myself.

"Okay, Maggie, I'm now going to tell you a name and address, and I'd like for you to repeat it back to me. Burt Jackson, 42 Lakeside Drive."

"Burt Jackson, 42 Lakeside Drive." My patience was ending. What did I pay for this appointment?

Dr. Kessel asked a series of other questions, including who was president.

"Of course—it's...oh, I can see him. He's older...he's got that crooked smile... Oh my gosh—I'm sorry..." I put my fingers to my forehead and felt the heat color my face. I could see him so clearly, but his name was escaping me. This happens to everyone, right?

"That's okay," Dr. Kessel said. "Let's go back to that name and address I mentioned before. Can you repeat it back to me?"

I was still thinking of the president. The memory was like catching a firefly. I was almost there. But now he wanted that name and address, I felt rushed. "Burt Lakeside, 22 Jackson Drive," I said and flushed again. *This was wrong, I don't think I got it right. I must be getting tired. How long have I been here?*

There were a few more questions involving math, and I didn't do much better on those. Spelling words backward, too, was challenging—I mean, who can do this? When does anyone normally do this? Dr. Kessel ended the visit by telling me that I'd receive results soon and, in the meantime, it would be good to schedule a CT exam. He was evasive about my questions, saying that "a CT exam will paint a fuller picture."

Mild cognitive impairment. Those were my results. The internet was of no help—I read articles about MCI turning to dementia in a matter of months, and other data suggested that it doesn't always lead to dementia. Dementia. Alzheimer's. No.

I didn't say anything to Will, and the omission felt like a betrayal. I wanted to confide in someone, but telling Samantha, Jen, or Ellie would be also like telling their husbands. Telling Paige would mean telling virtually everyone. My sisters came to mind, but we just hadn't talked in so long—it didn't feel like something I could just bring up. Plus, with our family history, I didn't want them to worry. Will was out of the question. I was not about to jeopardize his career. I could just envision fundraisers, reporters, and dinners where I'd be asked a question and couldn't remember. I'd look like a buffoon. Will would be embarrassed. I mean, this was probably *nothing*. It was "mild," after all. I could get more exercise, drink less wine and start eating better. Those are all the things they tell you to do. And sleep! Heavenly sleep! That was key to everything, I was sure. I was just tired.

I decided to wait a bit for the CT scan. I thought maybe after the holidays would be best. Yes, spring would be a good time. Without working, it seemed my days rolled into one another. Weekends really didn't make a difference to me, although Will had more free time then. The weather was getting really warm again—were those dandelions in the yard already? I practiced some yoga in the morning and flipped through magazines in the afternoon, and took naps. I spent time in my garden like every good retiree does. Will and I talked about upcoming trips. Maybe a cruise.

The weather turned again, and it was even more beautiful outside. I decided to go to a craft store and look at summer wreaths. Was it too early to put up a fall wreath? Maybe I could stick to daylilies or something like that. I opened up the sunroof and had the windows down—something I would rarely do—but it felt good to have the wind in my hair and feel the warmth of the sun. I'd been driving for a while, listening to a classic rock station, That's *How Strong My Love Is* filling the car. I got to a stoplight and decided I was windblown enough. Windows up. I sat at the red light and thought maybe I had taken a wrong turn. Nothing looked familiar. The light changed, and I hesitantly crept my car forward. *Where was I?* This was silly. I looked around and couldn't see any streets or buildings that I knew. *How far had I driven?* My heart started to race, and I felt the familiar pangs of panic creep in. My hands grasped the steering wheel tighter. *Where the hell was I?*

I drove on longer and realized I had to go to the bathroom. This was not good. Finally, I pulled over into something that looked like a mini-mart. I pulled my cell out of my purse and called Will.

"I'm all turned around today," I told him, my voice an octave higher than I recognized. "I need you to come get me."

"What? Maggie, are you okay? What happened? Where are you?"

"I'm not sure," I said, trying to steady my voice. "I just got turned around."

"Turned around?" Will said, "You were just going to JoAnn's. Did you go someplace else?"

"No, I don't know. No." I swallowed, feeling hot again, like a hot flash. My hands were clammy. I felt like I was sweating through my pants. "Can you just come and get me," I whispered. "I have to go to the bathroom."

"Maggie, where *are* you?" Will was clearly exasperated. "You're pulled over, I hope," he said.

"Yes—yes. I'm at a gas station. I mean a store. One of those gas station stores."

"A mini-mart? Convenience store?"

"Yes—that's it!"

"Okay, which one?"

"I...I don't know." I felt my voice shake and the tears coming.

"*Maggie, look around you.* What does the name of the store say?" More frustration. "Can you see any street signs?"

"It says United Dairy Farmers," I told him. "It's the red building."

I could hear him exhale. "Okay, UDF. Which one—the one on Claymont? Can you see any street signs?"

I looked around and could not. "No," I told him. "I can't see from here."

"Are you in the parking lot? Can you get out of the car and look around? Or better yet, just go in the store and ask the clerk for the address."

"Okay, but hold on," I told him. I got out of the car and now really had to go to the bathroom. This was bad. I walked into the store, and luckily no one was in line. I asked the young girl working what the address was and repeated it to Will.

"I'll be right there," he said. "Go back to the car."

I found my way back to the car and got it, feeling a mix of relief and foolishness.

Will arrived quickly. I opened the door and could no longer contain my tears. "Maggie," he said softly, pulling me into an embrace. We soon got into his car.

"We're just around the corner, sweetie," he said, his hand on top of mine. "We'll be home in five minutes, okay?" He was being kind, his voice gentle. He didn't ask anything more. I had to pull myself together. I didn't want him to worry.

"I'm just tired today," I told him as I blew my nose and tried to force a smile. "Just lost track of time and was tired." He nodded and patted my hand again. I had to make him believe me. My memory was still there, still within my grasp. It felt like waking up and trying to remember a dream that is just out of reach—like staring at the ocean, willing my eyes to stretch beyond the horizon. I knew something was still there, beyond this expanse, beyond this void. If I just concentrated, I could find it, I know I could. I just had to do this quietly and carefully. I held my head up, breathed calmly, and kept my hands folded across my lap.

"What would you like to do for dinner tonight?" I asked him.

Corrina Malek is the author of the novella *The Ledger* and other short stories. She has worked in the educational publishing industry for over 25 years. When she's not writing or thinking about writing, she spends time with family and rescues dogs in central Ohio.

Just a Touch

Lois Spencer

"Where's Mom?" Sherrie asked as she came into the kitchen, rubbing sleep from her eyes. Through the screen door, an early spring breeze sent a chill up her spine, prompting her to tighten the sash of her robe. At the table, her father tracked a column of figures in his ledger with a sharp yellow pencil as he keyed them into a calculator.

"Her assistant called in sick," he said, "again."

Sherrie imagined her mom tucking wild red curls into a hairnet as she stormed the kitchen at Oakwood Nursing Home, where she managed the kitchen staff and whipped up meals the residents actually ate. A year ago, Sherrie's dad had insisted that she leave her working-class kitchen job for a nice position with Shafer and Shafer, Attorneys-at-Law. Under protest, her mom had given it a try. After a week of mincing around the office in heels and dodging advances, she had resigned, sharing a piece of her mind with the two horny old men.

"Who can blame them?" Sherrie's dad had said. "They haven't had a secretary under sixty in my lifetime. You know, Joan, a woman who wanted to better herself could put up with their foibles." Her mother's response had been narrowed eyes and a swift turn on her stiletto. Before the day was over, she was lacing up her tennis shoes and hustling right back to her walk-in freezer and ovens large enough to roast a hog. Her letter to the editor did not appear in *The Palmer Pilot*.

What Sherrie had gleaned from her mother's experience was simple: In Palmer, Ohio, situated along the lovely, tree-lined Muskingum River, appearances were everything. "Don't hang your dirty laundry on the clothesline" was more than a platitude in Palmer. She guessed the rest of the world wasn't much different.

Her father snapped his ledger shut and stood up, bringing Sherrie back to the present. His trousers were creased, his white shirt starched, and a conservative tie hung loosely at his collar. Before he raised the blinds or flipped the sign in his barber shop from Closed to Open, he would lather his beard and execute a flawless straight-razor shave. Yep, Sherrie thought, appearances sure do matter.

She sat down across the table from him and reached for the box of Life cereal. She felt rather than saw her father's glance, and her shiver returned. She knew exactly where his eyes fell—on the delicate skin exposed just above the top of her robe. When the morning glances first began, she'd told herself she had to be imagining things. When they persisted for weeks, always when her mother was busy at the sink or out of the room, she had to admit that her imagination, vivid as it was, was not to blame. Such glances, even from fathers, must be one more thing a female had to live with—just like that creep David's dirty mouth on the school bus.

Most mornings, her father was the first to leave, dropping a kiss on her mother's cheek while she sipped her coffee and tousling Sherrie's bedhead if she was handy on his way to the door. "See you later" was his standard goodbye.

But this morning, he walked around the table and paused deliberately behind Sherrie's chair. This morning the hand rested for a moment on her shoulder. Then, as implausible as it seemed, the hand slid smoothly beneath chenille and muslin and cupped her breast as if it had every right to be there. Driven by an instinct she didn't know she had, Sherrie twisted from shoulder to waist, dislodging the hand. She lunged from kitchen to bathroom, slammed the door, and threw the slide-bolt.

Gripping the cold porcelain sink, she stared into the mirror at a face that couldn't be hers. Things like this didn't happen to her, to another girl, maybe, but not to her. Heavy strides crossed the kitchen, and the back door slammed, rattling dishes in the cupboard. A raspy whisper escaped her throat: "Daddy?"

She didn't know how long she stood there, still feeling the hand that could not have touched her. Gradually, though, disbelief gave way to rationalization. The hand had slipped from her shoulder unintentionally; the intimate touch couldn't have been deliberate. No wonder he'd left the kitchen the way he had. Her reaction had been over the top.

Waiting for her nerves to calm and her morning to return to normal, she washed her face and brushed her teeth. Once her hands felt steady enough to fasten a bra and button a blouse, she ventured into her bedroom. By the time she was ready for school, though, reason had returned, and the excuses conjured by denial had abandoned her. She was left with the cold realization that her father's touch had been fully intentional, maybe even calculated, and whether she lived in Palmer, New York City, or Timbuktu, that touch had crossed a line well beyond the troublesome glances.

Sherrie knew that even worse things happened to girls at the hands of their fathers—and brothers, uncles, and grandfathers. Far back in the hills, the girls at school said, it was open season on any female and even more so when she reached a certain age. Folks in and around Palmer dismissed the hill folk as an odd bunch and didn't concern themselves with what went on up in the hills. In a hurry to get out of the house, Sherrie grabbed a sweater and her books and waited for the bus beneath a pair of budding pear trees by the road. The summer before, a story her mom had told made it clear that no girl, hillbilly or not, was exempt.

Sherrie's family had bought their house the previous spring, and she and her mom had torn into refurbishing the place the minute it was theirs. Sticky with wallpaper paste from Sherrie's bedroom, they sprawled on the front porch with tall glasses of iced tea sweating in their hands. A welcome breeze stirred the stand of timothy grass across the road and eased the oppressive heat. Sherrie's mom had perfected her auditory skills early on, eavesdropping on adult tales not intended for children's ears. Sherrie knew a good one was coming when her mom began, "If walls could talk, these would have plenty to say."

In her grandparent's day, she went on, tuberculosis was common everywhere, including Palmer. Severe cases ended up in Oakwood Sanatorium, the rambling one-story building that would later become Oakwood Nursing Home. The family who had lived in their house had two daughters, a teenager, and a ten-year-old. When the mother was diagnosed with TB, the girls were left alone with their father, a mail carrier and lay minister for the Methodist church. As the months passed, people noticed the older girl's belly expanding. Speculation arose. Would the guilty boy own up to his responsibility, or would the girl's father have to get out the shotgun? When neither event came to pass, speculation turned to suspicion. Finally, a baby boy was born, bearing defects Palmer residents associated with inbreeding. Sad though it was, the infant's demise was considered a blessing. At that point in the story, Sherry's mother took a long draught of her tea. "The girl left town, and people say she never came back."

"Did the father go to prison?"

Sherrie's mom shook her head. "The women in Palmer gave him a wide berth, and the Methodists found another lay minister."

Sherrie hoped he'd been run over by a truck or attacked by one of the panthers that had roamed the countryside. But her mom wrapped up the story differently: "He's nearing a hundred and living in the men's ward at Oakwood. I puree his food, and a nurse's aide spoons it into his mouth." She caught Sherrie's expression. "Too little too late, right? Well, things were different back then."

Knowing the house had a dark past had stolen some of Sherrie's pleasure in her new bedroom, but over time, the story's impact faded. But that morning, listening to heavy wheels grinding up the grade below the house, Sherrie had to wonder. Could living in the house where that other despicable man had abused his daughter influence *her* father? Imagining her mother's no-nonsense reaction to that notion, Sherrie was struck by another puzzle. How could she ever tell her mom what had happened that morning? How could she *not* tell her?

◆

The bus door squawked open, and Sherrie climbed aboard, steeling herself for her daily assault of smut à la the charming David. A couple of stops later, a lanky boy in mud-caked boots swung onto the bus, clomped down the aisle, and dropped into the seat behind her, his opening line: "Hey, Babe. Had a dream about you last night." So it begins, she thought, staring ahead.

The bus driver, Carl, had assigned seats on the first day of school and posted "No Seating Change" above his rearview mirror. When Sherrie asked for an exception to the rule, Carl's response was, "Ignore him. He's just trying to get your goat." After the third request, Sherrie gave up.

But the morning's events and Sherrie's impossible dilemma eclipsed David's commentary. Then, incredulous, she sensed a hand snaking between the back of her seat and the metal wall, intent on invading her space. For the second time that morning, Sherrie whirled to her feet. As David struggled to extricate his hand, a fist smashed into his face, splitting his lip; blood began a steady drip onto his shirt. At least two rows of spectators had a clear view, and their shocked silence got the attention of the others. Soon, every pair of eyes on the bus watched David bleed—except his assailant's. She had resumed her seat and gritted her teeth as her hand lost its numbness and began a vicious pounding.

Instead of going to homeroom, Sherrie followed Carl and David to the high school office. Hallway traffic was heavy, and all eyes followed the parade of three. By then, Sherrie's hand throbbed in time to the pulsing beat of her arteries, and her complainant's lip had grown to twice its size. At the office door, the principal's secretary, a grandmotherly woman with the eyes of a seer, took one look at Sherrie's hand. "That needs attention, honey. I'll call your father."

Sherrie's heart skipped once, and the next beat took her breath. "Would you call my mother instead?" The unfamiliar voice coming from her parched lips reinforced the surreal quality of the morning.

"I sure will. You just sit tight."

The secretary disappeared into her separate space, and the principal clasped his hands on the desk. "What happened, Carl?" he asked.

"This girl hit him in the mouth." Translation: Any dummy could see that.

The principal turned to David. "Did anything prompt the attack?" A lift of the shoulders and a shake of the head was apparently sufficient.

The backdrop of sunlight through closed Venetian blinds polished the principal's bald head with suffused light. His eyes fell on Sherrie's swollen hand. "What do you have to say for yourself?"

Carl would never back her up, and without proof beyond a small scuff on the egregious hand, only another female would find her story credible.

"Well, missy, unless you can give a good reason for your actions, you're suspended until Monday." He pulled a notepad to the center of his desk and scribbled an excuse for David's admittance to class.

David stood and reached for the note. Despite the state of his mouth, David managed to produce a smirk, but he paid for it with a gush of tears he couldn't blink away. Instead, he sniffed back the accompanying snot and strutted out of the room. Carl, his part in the drama played out, slapped his knee with his ball cap and left as well.

Several minutes of uncomfortable silence passed while the principal filled out Sherrie's suspension papers. Finally, Mrs. Willis tapped on the door and entered simultaneously. She gave Sherrie a sympathetic pat on the shoulder and announced, "Your mother's waiting outside."

◆

"Why didn't you tell me what was happening on that bus?" Sherrie's mom demanded as she pulled away from the curb in front of the doctor's office. "I would have gone in there and had a fit."

Exactly, Sherrie thought. Every kid's nightmare was Mom making a scene at school. She adjusted the sling that held the avenging hand, thankful for two things: Nothing was broken, and the little white pills the doctor had given her had begun to calm her screaming nerve endings. Head back, she realized the pills might be doing more than relieving pain. But when she saw the neon flash of red, white, and blue on the barber's pole, the first shock of her day rushed back, dwarfing everything that had followed.

"We have to let your father know before he gets the news second-hand," her mother said as she put the car in park and ran her fingers through her hair. "Are you coming in?"

Unable to get the word out, Sherrie shook her head and watched as her mother strode, red curls bouncing in rhythm with her feet, toward the spotless glass door of the shop. Through the plate glass window, Sherrie could see the mayor seated in her father's chair, his suit jacket hanging on the valet stand. Her father especially hated interruptions when his client was a man of stature. Hearing the current news in the mayor's presence would raise his ire as fast as her earlier reaction. Her mother picked up a section of the newspaper and took a seat in deference to shop protocol.

Still fuzzy from pain meds, Sherrie's thoughts drifted back to times when her little-girl pleadings had postponed her father's evening plans. When pressed hard enough, he would read her a bedtime story, his rendition lacking the entertainment value of her mother's, but his deep voice and precise diction assured her of his presence, along with the scents of hair tonic and shaving soap he carried in from the shop.

He religiously attended her awards programs, piano and dance recitals, required functions for a father who cared about his business and his standing in the community. Family outings were rare; he stayed busy with poker nights, lodge meetings, and Jaycee events. When a wife's presence was mandated, an evening dress and a good spray of Aqua Net transformed Sherrie's mom into a lovely stranger. But once the masquerade was over, her mom always crept into Sherrie's room with whatever favors accompanied her table setting and, best of all, highlights of the evening.

Sherrie realized she had drifted off when her mother's head appeared through the open driver's side window. "I'm going to pick up a roll of gauze for your hand." With that, she trotted across the street and darted into Hart's Pharmacy a few doors down.

The courthouse clock at the end of the street struck twelve, and outside the car, life in the business district—as Palmer citizens referred to the cluster of shops, offices, and eateries—proceeded at its leisurely pace. Sherrie saw the door of the barber shop swing open. Her father covered the distance in three strides and bent to her level. Fighting the urge to shrink back, she forced her attention on the nerve twitching in his left cheek. The air had retained a chill, making the bead of sweat along his hairline as out of place as the razor nick above his upper lip. The awkward silence, she decided, was his to break.

He cleared his throat. "About this morning—you do understand that nothing really happened, certainly nothing you need to advertise. Sharing your misunderstanding of the situation would do more harm than you can possibly imagine."

His pause was her cue to respond, but she remained silent. In her left periphery, Sherrie saw her mother leave the drugstore carrying a white paper sack. Her father straightened and looked across the street.

"You know, Sherrie, how you imagine things. I suppose that's common among girls your age. But this time, your imagination could be very bad for all of us. Your little incident on the bus will make us the talk of the town." His eyes, which were yet to meet hers, fell on the bandaged hand.

When Sherrie's mother was within a few steps of the car, he forced a smile as phony as the version of events he had just handed her. As Sherrie's mother opened the driver's door, he nodded coolly in her direction, turned, and strode to the door of his shop. The back of his starched white shirt was damp and wrinkled and must have felt cold against his skin.

Why? Sherrie wondered as her mother slid behind the wheel. Why hadn't he just apologized and promised it would never happen again?

Her mother started the engine and flipped down the sun visor to block the intense midday glare. "Your father," she muttered. "I should have blurted out the whole story right in front of the mayor. 'Your little incident on the bus will make us the talk of the town.' Indeed!"

Hearing her father's words repeated, inflection and tone of voice exact replicas of the original, Sherrie would have laughed any other time. "What else did you hear?" she asked without first considering the consequences an answer might carry.

"There was something about your imagination being 'very bad for all of us.' Does he think you *imagined* that creepy kid's vulgar mouth or his filthy fingers trying to cop a feel?" Sherrie's empty stomach growled, loud enough to divert her mother's attention. Wheeling into the nearest food source, she asked, "How does a burger and shake sound?"

It was the phrase "filthy fingers" that toppled Sherrie's resistance to blurting out the morning's pivotal event. It recalled the other hand, the one she had known since she was a baby, a hand daily nourished with beard softeners and hair tonics, its blunt-cut nails spotless and devoid of unsightly cuticle tears. The hand that bore the threat and the burden she could not manage on her own.

Neon tubes on the sign in front of them connected three letters, "E-A-T," but the music streaming through the car windows was pure Beetles. As her mother nosed into the retro drive-in where girls in sweaters and bobby-sox skated back and forth with attachable trays, Sherrie put her good hand on her mother's arm. Her throat was filled with tears she determined she would not shed until she had laid everything bare.

"Mom, there's something I have to tell you."

Lois Spencer's work has appeared in *Women's Speak, Anthology of Appalachian Writers, Persimmon Tree, The Poorhouse Rag, Change Seven,* and *Northern Appalachia Review*. A collection of short stories is soon to follow her memoir, *In the Language of My Country*. Two writers' groups, Vintage Quills and Rivertown Writers, are indispensable to her staying engaged with writing.

Throwing Stones

Stephen Kraynak

Leon Kamel lived two doors down the street from me, on the first floor of the brown brick and asbestos-shingled house between the Prices and the Kazymacks. Leon had a little sister. I don't think any of the other children on our street ever knew her name. Frances was Leon's mother. His father, Abraham, had darker skin than anyone else on the street. Leon himself was somewhat dark-skinned. We thought they were Lebanese or Syrian.

The entire family did not mix well into the neighborhood. They stayed to themselves. At times I remember seeing Mrs. Kazymack talking to Leon's mother, but all of the other mothers seemed to avoid Frances Kamel. They talked about her but not to her. Frances was loud. She bragged about everything, especially Leon. She used lots of makeup, especially on her eyes, and made her eyebrows into fine dark lines. We could hear her from two houses away when she was in her front yard talking to Mrs. Kazymack.

As I remember, none of the kids on the street liked Leon. Especially Frankie Keller. Frankie, who had a short temper, made jokes about Leon and his mother, calling them "camels." I did not have a reason for disliking Leon other than that no one else seemed to like him. Not liking Leon was part of the culture of living on West 123rd Street. We used to play around Leon, ignoring him. He would play in his front yard, usually by himself, while the rest of us played together, using the street and our front yards as our common playground.

I have forgotten what started the verbal flash between Frankie and Leon early one August evening just before supper. But it soon exploded into a yelling match, a colossal magnet attracting other kids on the street. Most just came to watch for the excitement, and some took Frankie's side, yelling at Leon. Then stones were thrown from various directions. In the 1950s, before the prevalence of asphalt, many west-side Cleveland neighborhood driveways still consisted of two lanes of gravel or stones for the car tires, with a strip of grass in the middle. Stones were always available. My mother had warned me not to throw stones. Most of the time, I obeyed.

I don't know why I got involved in this dispute between Frankie and Leon. I could have stood in my front yard and watched it from a distance. Perhaps it sufficed that Frankie Keller was my friend and that I did not, or thought I did not, like Leon. I was not a skilled athlete and could not throw accurately or for any great distance. I had never developed a good throwing arm. But that summer late afternoon, I picked up a small stone from our front driveway, pulled my arm far back, yelled Leon's name, and hurled it toward Leon Kamel's front yard. I winged it as best I could in a direction away from me and toward Leon. It flew across my front yard, the Prices' front yard, and across Leon's driveway. As Leon turned to look at me, my stone hit him directly in his left eye. I saw his left eyelid immediately close and his left hand rise to cover his eye. He started to scream and ran into his house. Frankie Keller and some of our accomplices ran home as well.

I panicked. Even though I did not like Leon, he had done nothing to harm me. How could I explain what I had just done? There were many witnesses on both sides of the street. Since I knew that I was guilty, I devised an alibi. I lied. Loudly crying and covering my right eye with my hand, I ran to my own back door and into our kitchen, attesting to my mother that Leon Kamel threw a stone that hit me in my eye. My mother examined both of my eyes which probably seemed normal, except for the profusion of tears. I didn't explain about the fight between Leon and Frankie Keller or the ensuing volley of stones. I only allowed that Leon hit me in my eye with a stone—first.

To better grasp this escalating situation, the mothers on the street left their kitchens and came outside. Our next-door neighbor, Jo Randall, the old widow who lived with her older sister, Mae Lane, in the green-shingled farmhouse on the corner of Belden Avenue, stood behind the privet hedge in her front yard, silently observing. Directly across the street from Leon's house, Stella Mancini waited on her front porch watching the proceedings, drying her hands in her apron. Mrs. Kazymack leaned over the banister of her second-floor front porch. Across from our house, Grandma Fern McGlynn, the neighborhood doyenne, presided, seated, as usual, on her front porch rocker. Her adult daughter, Rita, came out to join her. Impatiently, Rita waited while her aged father, Tom, got up to give her his seat in the other rocking chair. The children had vanished from the street and sidewalks; our voices were silent as the now adult drama took center stage.

All witnessed Frances Kamel thundering toward my house as my mother stepped out onto the front porch and headed down the front walk to meet her. I stood in the living room behind the front screen door and stopped crying so I could better follow this event. Mrs. Kamel yelled at my mother about my hitting Leon in his eye with a stone. My mother defended me, saying that I said that Leon had hit me in my eye with a stone first. That was a neighborhood rule: you were allowed to hit back or fight back to defend yourself as long as you did not hit first. My mother never questioned the apparent lack of evidence in either of my eyes. No redness, no swelling, no blood. Merely because I, her son, had told her that Leon had first hit me in my eye, she went to my defense at some personal risk.

Frances Kamel, who did not have the needed information about her own son's misbehavior, turned, in seeming defeat, to walk back to her house as Dorothy Keller, Frankie's mother, approached her to inquire about the uproar. Mrs. Keller was formidable. She was tall, almost a foot taller than her husband, wide in the shoulders, with stocky arms and a large bosom, slowly pacing with the stealth of a tiger. She was a regular at the local Turner's Gym. My mother stood in our front yard to watch. I felt my lie, my attempt to protect myself, was about to result in a neighborhood disaster. Yet, I would not consider trying to stop this impending doom by admitting my guilt.

On the sidewalk in front of her own home, Frances Kamel erupted. She yelled at Dorothy Keller about Frankie and how he had hurt Leon. Dorothy Keller tried to calm her, but Mrs. Kamel continued to yell accusations at her. Mrs. Keller calmly denied knowing anything about what had just happened among the children of the neighborhood or about Frankie's participation. Then Frances Kamel dramatically raised the ante. "Liar!" she screamed at her neighbor, closely leaning toward Mrs. Keller's face. "Liar!" As the humiliating indictment spewed from Frances Kamel's mouth, the stridency with which the "l" rolled off of her tongue and the resonance of the word "liar" itself made the insult irreparably sting like a publicly witnessed slap in the face.

Dorothy Keller exploded. "Who do you think you are, calling me a liar?" she boomed in her deep guttural voice. "They chased you out of other neighborhoods. And now you're nothing but trouble here. Why don't you move? Go somewhere else! Get out! Just go!" Dorothy Keller would not tolerate Frances Kamel calling her a liar with the other mothers watching and listening from both sides of the street. Both women volleyed insults at each other, and the verbal tirade between these two neighbors continued until both of their husbands, Abraham Kamel and Frank Keller, came outside, stepped between the two women, and each physically tugged and pulled his own wife back into their respective houses. Supper on West 123rd St. was delayed that summer evening due to events unlike any we had ever witnessed.

As my mother came back toward our front door, I started to cry again. I knew that my lie had caused turmoil involving many of the families on our street. Leon Kamel was an easy target because he was disliked, as was his mother. Although I sensed that the combination of the Kamel family's being the neighborhood pariah, Frances Kamel's threats and accusations, and the street-wide spectacle offered me protection, I knew that I had physically harmed Leon and then lied to conceal my crime and protect myself. My neighborhood was roiling because I threw one little stone.

I found it impossible for a boy raised Catholic and taught about sin by nuns and priests to disregard my dilemma. I could not ignore it; I could not forget it. To ease my conscience, I rationalized that because Leon Kamel was not dead, neither the suspected damage to his eye from my rash action nor my subsequent lie met the qualifications or requirements—all of which I had memorized from the Baltimore Catechism—of a mortal sin—a sin that, if not forgiven before my death, would send my immortal soul straight to hell where it would burn in torment for all eternity, with the devil, trident in hand, standing over me laughing in scorn.

I assured myself that, upon my death, because I had not intended to hurt Leon and had not egregiously violated any of the Ten Commandments, my punishment would be that required of a mere venial sin, temporary scorching or singeing of the edges of my soul while in purgatory. I chose to ignore whether my burnt edges would still be evident after the resurrection of my body, tattling that I had not been a good enough Catholic to join the heavenly host without the warranted period of purgation. I hoped that, perhaps after my death, if anyone who remembered me went to church on All Souls Day and said the right prayers in the right order within the required time limits for the repose of my specific soul, I would be released from purgatory, thus limiting my torture to the time already served. With either sufficient purification or quick release on any November 2nd, I could then ascend to heaven and happily join the rest of my family and all of the other Catholics from West 123rd Street and St. Vincent de Paul Catholic Church.

Living with my offense and my lie was now my torment. The possibilities stormed in my mind. How could I get myself out of this mess I had made? What if Leon lost his eye? What if some other kids told what they had seen, exposing my falsehood? What if I died before going to confession? Much worse, what if I died on the way to confession by being squashed under the front tires of the No. 2 bus on Lorain Avenue, or was struck by lightning, or choked to death on a jawbreaker, or simply died in my sleep for no apparent reason before I had been able to rid my soul of these sins?

After having lived such a commendable life, after having received so many compliments for being a good student, after being liked by all of my aunts and uncles, after being praised for being a good Catholic boy—how could one little stone change it all?

To my dismay, the women on the block continued to discuss this incident, keeping it alive. When my mother went across the street to talk to Grandma McGlynn about her encounter with Frances Kamel, Fern commended her and said, "You really cooled her coffee off." Leon had no permanent injury. Without any bandage on his eye, he continued to play by himself in his front yard until his family moved from West 123rd Street

That was a summer of growth for me. I began to learn about ambiguity and to question the guilt imposed on me by my Catholic faith. I also learned that, although I was no longer a perfect little boy, I was still loveable and beloved.

Stephen C. Kraynak, a native Ohioan, wanted to be a teacher since his first day of school in Mrs. Martlock's kindergarten at McKinley School on Cleveland's west side. He taught for thirty-five years in the Columbus City Schools and loved it. Now, he wants to write his memoirs and love it.

Enticed by blue mornings and coyotes howling in moonlit washes, he and his husband, Bob Gordon, retired to the Sonoran Desert. Twice, Stephen has been a finalist in the Literary Awards Competition of the annual Tucson Festival of Books. This is his first published piece of nonfiction. He already loves it.

Secret Blood, Sacred Blood

Jyotsna Sreenivasan

Just as my tween daughter steps out the front door, I notice her pink scrunchie on the kitchen counter. I grab it and rush to her, but her key has already turned in the lock. Through the window, as she runs to meet her friend on the sidewalk, I see Athena's newly shorn hair. I'd forgotten. I slip her scrunchie over my wrist and retreat to the kitchen.

I pour myself a fresh cup of coffee, pick up my phone, and add to my grocery list: chocolate cake mix, birthday candles, maxi pads. Then I open my contacts, scroll down, hover my finger over my mother's name. Set the phone down. Take a sip of coffee. Rub the soft fabric of the scrunchie and think back to my mother's struggles when I was around Athena's age and what I never gave Mom credit for.

♦

It was a Saturday in June, soon after my eleventh birthday. We were all up early, getting ready for a two-hour drive to the Hindu temple in Pittsburgh. My parents dragged us there every couple of months because it was the closest Hindu temple to our house. I had already eaten my cereal and was about to go upstairs, shower, and put on my langa and blouse. I ducked into the half bathroom next to the kitchen, and when I pulled down my panties, I noticed it—spots of blood on my underwear.

I knew what it was. Two summers before, while on a Girl Scout camping trip, I'd shared a tent with some girls from a different troop. After our s'mores and songs around the campfire, we were packed off to "sleep." As we sat up in our sleeping bags, the other girls, who knew each other, asked me how old I was. When they found out I was only nine, they informed me they were all ten and going into fifth grade. They began whispering and giggling. One of these girls—a ghostly-pale, dark-haired girl named Lori, who had been the most talkative—looked at me and asked, "Do you know what a period is?"

Of course, I knew. "It's the thing at the end of a sentence," I said.

They all giggled. Then Lori said, "I mean, the bloody kind of period."

I was puzzled. What could possibly be bloody about a punctuation mark?

She proceeded to enlighten me. She even stood up and acted out a little scene in which a girl gets her period and tries to hold it all in until she can get to a bathroom. Lori crossed her legs, squirmed, and hopped around.

I laughed along with the others. It was a joke! No one would believe that women bleed every month, all over the world, and that it was a secret. After all, I wasn't born yesterday.

The next day, I made sure to walk next to my best friend, Caroline, as we hiked through the trees. Caroline and I were opposites in terms of looks. I was bean-pole thin and tall, a medium brown, with straight black hair past my shoulders. Caroline was short and stocky, with rosy skin and a cap of blond hair. We had been best friends forever. As we walked, I told her Lori's absurd story. But Caroline did not laugh. "It's true, Suvarna," she said. "Except you can't hold it in like pee. You have to wear a pad. Didn't your mom tell you?"

I felt ashamed and babyish. Why did I have to be stuck with an Indian mother who left me ignorant? Apparently, all the real American mothers told their daughters such important information.

So, the day I saw the blood spots on my underwear, I knew I had started my period. And I was not pleased. None of my friends had started theirs. I thought about not mentioning it to my mother, but I knew I had to. I couldn't just sit around and bleed all over the furniture. And, when I told her, I had to appear ignorant since, as far as she was concerned, I knew nothing about it.

In the kitchen, my mother was busy packing snacks for our trip. She hadn't yet put on her sari and was dressed in a pair of knit pants and blouse—her usual clothes. Her hair was still in its night braid. I could smell the coffee brewing.

"Mommy," I said.

She glanced at me while washing apples at the sink. "Aren't you dressed yet?"

"I found some blood on my underwear." I wasn't sure she heard me over the sound of the tap, but I didn't want to shout. I didn't want Daddy or my little brother to hear.

She stopped, turned the water off, and peered at me. "Come here. What did you say?"

I repeated my sentence robotically.

She dried her hands on a towel. "Show me."

We went into the bathroom. I lifted my nightgown and pulled off my panties. She inspected them, looking at the blood for far longer than I thought necessary. Was I in trouble? Would she soon start scolding me in Kannada? I never understood why she chewed me out in a language I did not know, but that was her habit. When she experienced strong emotions, she expressed them in Kannada.

Instead, she put an arm around me. "Don't be afraid," she murmured. "This is something all girls go through. It doesn't hurt, does it?"

I shook my head. I couldn't feel anything at all. That's why I'd been surprised to see the spots of blood.

"Good. I will explain tomorrow. But now, let me show you what to do."

She seemed unusually subdued as we climbed the stairs. She slid a box of pads out of the linen closet and tucked them under the sink in the upstairs bathroom. After my shower, I was to take one of the pads, peel off the adhesive strip, and attach it to my underwear. I nodded, just as taciturn as she was.

Dressed in my purple silk langa and cotton blouse, I came downstairs, holding up my long skirt so I wouldn't trip. I felt elegant despite the bulky pad between my thighs. I thought my mother would ask if I had trouble attaching the pad. But she, now dressed in a rustling silk sari and gold jewelry, with her hair in a bun, just hustled us all into the car.

During the car ride, when Daddy asked her something in Kannada, Mommy just shrugged or gave a one-syllable answer. She didn't spar or laugh with him as she usually did. She just told him the directions in English, peering at a set of hand-written instructions and at the road, making sure we weren't getting lost.

The temple was on a hill, and as Daddy drove up the curving road, as usual, he asked us to watch for the "gopuram," the tall pyramidal sculpture on top of temples. My brother, Sandeep, and I vied to spot it first. "I see it!" I screeched. The white structure was peeking out from between the green trees. "I see it!"

"Where?" Sandeep shouted. "Show me!"

My mother turned to me. "Don't shout," she said. "You are a big girl now."

"But I saw it first!" I protested.

She was already facing front again, pressing her fingertips to her temples. I thought it was unfair that she corrected me but not Sandeep. I could grimace at him, but then he'd tattle, and by the time I considered my options, we were at the top of the hill, in the parking lot.

We got out of the car. The fancy gopuram had been attached to an ordinary plain white rectangular building—an awkward juxtaposition of India and America. We swung open the heavy carved wood doors and took off our sandals in the entry hallway. I could already smell the incense. First, we stopped in the bathroom. Before I entered a stall, my mother seemed about to say something to me, but an old sari-clad lady tottered in. My mother nodded to her sheepishly and slunk into a stall.

I pulled my panties down and inspected my pad. It had some blood on it, but not much. I wasn't sure if I was supposed to change the pad. I didn't have another one. I didn't want to ask my mother. Maybe she'd scold me because I forgot to bring a spare. I just pulled up my panties and hoped for the best.

Before the pooja, as our family stood around the altar of Sri Venkateshwara, my father exchanged pleasantries with the priest, but even when the man addressed her, my mother was silent. She just nodded. During the short archana ceremony, my mother's eyes were closed, palms pressed together in front of her bowed head. She was muttering something under her breath—a prayer, I assumed. After we drank a sip of holy water poured into our palms, and after the priest had touched the heavy metal crown to each of our heads, the priest handed Sandeep and me a banana and some golden raisins as prasada—food blessed by God.

Mommy then opened her eyes and quietly reminded us to use only our right hand to eat the prasada. The priest had given her two strings of flowers. She pinned one of them above her bun. Extracting a bobby pin from her purse, she pinned the other string into my loose hair above one ear. I could feel her hands shaking and didn't understand why, but I soon forgot about this because she was instructing us to kneel and touch our foreheads to the carpet three times. Then, she led us in visiting the other shrines in the temple, where she made sure Sandeep and I dotted our foreheads with kumkum.

It was only once we got home that evening, after eating at the little Indian restaurant near the temple and after a visit to the home of family friends, that my mother asked me about my period. She sat on the edge of my bed. Her face looked tired, and she rubbed her eyes. "How do you feel?" she murmured.

"OK." I pulled the covers up to my neck.

"You put on another pad?"

I nodded.

"Tomorrow, we will talk more." And she patted my leg and left.

The next day, after breakfast, my mother led us up to her bedroom. I sat on her neatly made bed. From her dresser drawer, she took out a slim tan booklet.

"I ordered this for you some months ago," she said. "I could see that you were growing tall and developing, and I knew this would happen soon."

I was dismayed to learn that my mother had anticipated this change in my life but had said nothing. She handed me the booklet. It was called "You're Growing Up!" and had a photograph of four smiling white girls on the cover. I turned it face-down on the bedspread. I was shy to read it in front of my mother.

She still stood next to her dresser. "I want you to know more than I did," she said. "When I started my menses, my mother didn't tell me anything. I thought I had cut myself. She gave me a cloth pad and told me to go sit in one corner. That's the way it was in India when I was growing up. They didn't want to tell us anything. I was so confused and frightened. But here in America, they have information for girls. That's why I bought this for you." She was rearranging her tiny perfume bottles on top of the dresser. "After you read it, you can ask me any questions."

I jumped up from the bed. She looked so uncomfortable that I didn't want to ask her anything. I fled out the door, clutching the tan booklet. In my bedroom, I looked at the pretty white girls on the cover, made a face at them, and hid the offending document at the bottom of my underwear drawer.

♦

When I told Caroline about getting my period, she wanted to see the booklet, so I snuck it out of the house. We read it out loud to each other in her bedroom, giggling at the funny diagrams. I learned that a first period is often light and that it could take months before I had one again. So I relaxed and forgot about it. But I did decide to call my parents "Mom" and "Dad." The booklet was right. I was growing up. No more "Mommy" and "Daddy" for me.

That year, Caroline and I entered a Fourth of July window painting contest at a local strip mall. Her mother helped us fill out the application form, and we were assigned a big glass window at a furniture store. Since we were both interested in saving endangered species, we sketched out a design in which several endangered butterflies, in greatly enlarged detail, fluttered above a field of red, white, and blue flowers. We spent hours every day outlining and decorating our butterflies and flowers on the store's window.

On July 3, the last day we were allowed to work on the window, I was standing on a stepladder, reaching high to paint the name of a butterfly in blocky black letters, when I started tottering. I didn't want to fall onto our window's wet paint and ruin our hard work, so I leaned away and toppled off the ladder. The black paint can fell with me and splattered over my denim shorts and T-shirt. I screamed, first out of terror and then out of pain.

Caroline ran into the furniture store for help. Gingerly, I stood up, trying my legs. My hip was sore, and I had raw, burning scrapes down the sides of my leg and arm. I wanted to finish the window.

Caroline ran out again, with the furniture store owner following. He was a portly white man with a mustache. "You OK?" he asked me.

"Yeah," I said, trying not to limp. I didn't want him to see my scraped and bleeding skin.

He grasped the stepladder. "Seems sturdy," he said. "You just gotta move it where you want it. OK?"

"OK," I said. He went back inside. Caroline held the ladder while I painted the final butterfly names. We had just enough black paint left.

By the time Caroline's mother came to pick us up, we had finished the window. When her mother saw me, she hurried out of the car. After determining that I was fine, she put an old dog blanket on the car seat for me to sit on so I didn't get paint on the upholstery.

At home, when my mother saw me walk into the living room, where she was tending to her houseplants, she shrieked and dropped the watering can, splashing the carpet. Then she rushed towards me and gathered me into her arms. I could not make her understand that I was not badly hurt. She supported me as I climbed upstairs to the tub, where she cried as she removed my clothes, ran a tub of water, and bathed my wounds. Afterward, she bandaged my legs as best she could with gauze. We hadn't been able to remove all the paint, so I still had black splotches on my skin in places. She told me to put on my nightgown and get into bed, even though it was not even dinnertime.

When my father came home bearing the takeout pizza we often ate on Saturday evenings, my mother hovered as he, a physician, examined me, made me walk around, and asked me where it hurt.

"She is only bruised," he said. "She will be fine."

"It is all my fault!" my mother said inexplicably. She started weeping and ran out of the room.

My father called after my mother and then followed her. I was left to remain mystified.

◆

A few days later, we found out that our window won first place. The awards committee called us during dinner with the news, and as soon as my mother hung up the phone, she smiled and seemed to relax.

We were invited to an awards ceremony. An *Akron Beacon Journal* photographer took photos as Caroline and I stood on either side of our window. Fortunately, by that time, my mother had found some paint removal tips in the household hints paperback she owned, so I no longer had paint on my skin.

The morning after the ceremony, I was pinning my blue ribbon to my bulletin board, along with some Polaroid shots of the window that my dad had taken. My mother bustled into my room with a basket of clean laundry. She sat on my bed and started folding my clothes.

"Mom." I reached for a shirt. "Maybe I should start doing my own laundry. I am growing up, you know."

"Don't worry about housework." She took the shirt back. "I want you to study hard. At least I was allowed to attend college, even though I was forced to miss three days every month. I want you to be able to go as far as you can with your education."

I lounged on my bed, cradling Puff, my stuffed kitten. I'd had Puff for years, and she was no longer pink. In my mind, I always replaced her matted, dingy gray color with the soft gloss of her fur when I'd first gotten her.

My mother seemed in a talkative mood, and I always enjoyed hearing about her life in India. "Why did you have to miss three days of college every month?"

She began matching my socks. "You know my Ajji—my father's mother— lived with us when I was growing up. She was very old-fashioned. She had all sorts of rules about what a woman must not do during menses. She insisted that we sit apart during that time."

"What does that mean? Sitting apart?"

"It means the woman must sit in a corner away from everyone else for three days. We were not allowed to bathe. Many people believed that a woman's blood would spoil the water."

"What?" I held Puff near my face and pretended she was talking. "That sounds crazy!" I said in my high kitten voice. Somehow, it was easier for me to speak my mind if I said it through Puff.

My mother smiled at my antics. "It sounds crazy, but that is what many people believed. A woman should not cook because she would ruin the food. She should eat sitting in her corner. No one else should touch her. Otherwise, they would also be polluted." She began folding my T-shirts. "My mother didn't believe in sitting apart, but she wanted to respect her mother-in-law, so we had to do it. And I came to feel that I was disgusting during that time of the month. I don't want to raise you with these thoughts. But it is hard for me to give up those old beliefs. When you came into the house that day all black and bloody, I thought I had caused a tragedy to befall you!"

"But how could you have caused it?" Puff hopped up and down. "How, Mommy?" The kitten could still call her "Mommy" because she was still a little girl.

And my mother told me that she'd been feeling guilty because she'd allowed me to visit the temple on the day I started my period. "You know, in India, even now, women are not supposed to go into a temple when they are having periods," she said.

"Really?" asked Puff. I was now hiding my face behind the kitten. What my mother was saying sounded so unbelievable—as preposterous as the story Lori told about menstruation. But that story had turned out to be true.

She finished folding the clothes and stood to place them into my chest of drawers. "It is bad luck for a menstruating woman to enter a temple," she muttered, bending over a drawer. "That is what my mother believed. That is what I believed for many years. I don't even like to put these ideas into your head."

Sitting on the edge of my bed, still clutching Puff under one arm, I handed her the folded clothes. After they were all put away, she straightened up, rubbing her lower back. "When I went to college, I learned that menstruation is a natural process related to childbirth. So how could it be bad? And your father, being a doctor, also told me that menstruation is healthy, and there is nothing bad-luck about it."

I set Puff on my lap and said, in my own voice, "God gave us periods. So how could visiting God's house during that time be wrong?"

"You are right." She plucked a piece of fluff off my shirt. "I know all this logically. Still, even now, I hesitate to enter a temple or do pooja during that time of the month." She was standing with arms crossed, looking down at me seriously. "I don't want you to have such doubts. I want you to do anything you like all month long. That is why I said nothing about this tradition and just took you to the temple. But I was worried that the priest or someone else would find out and accuse us of polluting the temple."

"That's why you never asked me anything about it all day," I remembered.

"I didn't want anyone to know. Maybe they would think I was doing the wrong thing. And when you came home hurt, I thought I had caused it by refusing to follow those traditions."

I put the kitten on the bedspread, walked over to my mother, and wrapped my arms around her. I was almost as tall as she was. "Mom, I wasn't really hurt. And we won first place! So I think it was good luck that I went to the temple that day."

She held me close, rubbing my back and murmuring endearments in Kannada. Then, she stepped away, dabbing at her eyes. "Already, you are more sensible than I am." Her voice was husky. She picked up the empty laundry basket and was out the door.

I looked at my big, ruffled blue ribbon on the bulletin board. I was growing up, and my life ahead seemed as bright and happy as that ribbon. At that time, I did not understand how hard it was for my mother to break away from the harmful traditions she'd grown up with and offer me a new path she'd never had. Instead, I reveled in my mother's praise. I felt very wise.

Little did I know that every time I reached another milestone, my mother would battle with the old traditions. I could not foresee that we would argue about the clothes I wore, the boys I talked to, the opinions I held, my lack of respect for elders, and especially my refusal of an arranged marriage. More than once, she said to me, "You don't understand how much I have had to change." I didn't understand, and at that time, I didn't care. The gap between what she was willing to accept and what I wanted to do was large.

We are estranged now. She is upset because I gave birth without being married, even though I chose to live with my partner, the father of my child. During my pregnancy, my mother and I said hurtful things to each other. I accused her of being backward and ignorant. She accused me of being selfish and of causing her to be humiliated within our extended family. For years, we have both been too angry to reach out to one another.

Now, my daughter has had her first period. I did not tell Athena about the taboos my mother had to endure. Instead, I told her that in ancient India, there were matriarchal cultures for whom menstrual blood was sacred. But Athena was not interested.

I wanted to throw a party to celebrate. Athena refused. Although I've tried to be open with her, Athena is as reluctant to talk to me about her body as I was with my mother. I can see that she's experimenting with her gender identity.

Her hair is now short. I've heard friends call her "Al." She mostly wears unisex clothes, but on occasion, she chooses very feminine attire. I've tried to broach the subject with her. I've tried to indicate that I'm an accepting person. But she rebuffs me. And in truth, I fear that the "traditions" I grew up with, the patriarchal American culture I couldn't help but absorb, might get in the way as I try to help her navigate her life. Perhaps she senses my inadequacy.

Yesterday, Athena finally did agree to a birthday party. "Not a menarche party, Mom," she insisted. "I hate that word."

I'm starting to realize that no matter how hard we try as mothers, we will fail our children on some level.

I dump out my cold coffee, and then, sitting at the kitchen table, I dial my mother's number, for the first time in years, to invite her.

Jyotsna Sreenivasan was born and raised in Ohio, attended Kent State University, and currently lives in Columbus. Her parents are immigrants from India. Her new book, *These Americans*, a collection of short stories and a novella about Indian Americans, was published in 2021 by Minerva Rising Press. It is a bronze winner in the *Foreword Reviews* INDIES awards. Her novel, *And Laughter Fell From the Sky* (part of which takes place in Ohio), was published in 2012 by HarperCollins.

Jyotsna's short stories have been published in literary magazines and anthologies, including, most recently, *The Journal* from Ohio State University. She received an Individual Excellence Award from the Ohio Arts Council for 2022. For more information about Jyotsna and other writers who are children of immigrants, see www.SecondGenStories.com.

A Story You Have to Be Sober to Tell

Chase Montana

The first person I hid it from was my dad. That was who I lived with when I was fifteen, which is also how old I was when I smoked weed for the first time.

It was in the backyard of Megan's house. She was a senior, I was a freshman. I stumbled into her social circle earlier that year when I started talking to one of her friends. The friend transferred halfway through the school year, and I took her place in the group. I didn't even get high that first time, so there wasn't much to hide. In the years to come, there would be.

There are two concepts integral to adolescent psychology. The first is that teenagers crave novel experiences. Because of this, they take risks. This risk-seeking behavior is not simply because they want to try new things, it's the makeup of their brain. The logical part of the teenage brain, the prefrontal cortex, is not fully developed. Meanwhile, the limbic system, which is triggered during a stress response, becomes extra sensitive. Teenagers are wired to try new things and not always think them through, especially if those things promise an emotional rush in the short term.

The second concept integral to adolescent psychology is understanding that teenagers are consumed with their identity. This is why high school sports, which can provide a sense of belonging and camaraderie, can be such a transformative experience. Not only do team sports provide a sense of identity, but training and competing together is a bonding force. It is not uncommon to hear high school boys who once played on the football team say, "We went to war together." They may have no idea what war really means, but they understand the need to feel a part of something, particularly something that requires risk or sacrifice.

To understand why I started smoking, we can say that I wanted a new experience. We can also say that I was feeling lonely. I was lacking a sense of identity. It had been taken from me months earlier when I broke my leg playing football. The teammates who had been my friends, who I'd sat next to in class and at lunch, who I'd practiced with and walked home with after school—they had been removed from my life. That was as simple as the snapping of a bone on a Saturday in September.

I would play football again, but not for a while. First, I would learn a thing or two about getting high, and I would keep trying to learn until long after I stopped playing football again.

Given that I started smoking as a freshman in high school, I had over three years to cultivate a discreet habit. Usually, I would smoke late at night after my father and I had both gone to bed, opening up the window and the blinds just enough that the smoke could pass from my lips outside. If I looked, I might see it floating away. On the stereo, Kid Cudi sang, "I'm on a pursuit of happiness," and "the lonely stoner seems to free his mind at night." I felt risk, and I felt belonging, and all of this set me on a course that, thirteen years later, I would have to right.

◆

I also hid my smoking from my friends. I didn't know you could make friends like I made in college. I didn't know there were friends who would drink tea with you on the porch at 2 am when you couldn't sleep, friends who brought you to your knees in laughter over a plastic bag that you kept in the air like a beach ball, friends who sat in the Jeep with you as you tore across an unmarked field. In my four years of college, I formed the deepest and most intimate friendships of my life—but I wasn't always honest with them.

This dishonesty hurt me the most in my junior year. Eleven of us lived in a house with six bedrooms and two bathrooms. It was an old house that would be torn down after we moved out at the end of the year. Where the living room wall bulged and cracked behind the chimney, we painted a tree with our handprints as the leaves. The heating was so bad that a housemate sleeping on one side of the house would wake up with a bloody nose, while someone on the other side would tuck themself into a sleeping bag beneath their covers.

Though I had this novel experience that gave me a profound sense of belonging, there were still times when I felt intense depression. I felt a high level of responsibility to be the peacekeeper in the house, a role that I was familiar with from my childhood, where my parents had divorced when I was twelve, and my brother rarely spoke to any of us. On top of that, there was the pressure to perform academically, which all of us in the house felt, and which triggered its own sense of anxiety. When faced with these emotions of depression and anxiety, I turned to the coping mechanism that I had already established: smoking weed.

I spent a significant amount of that school year hiding in my room. My bedroom was on the first floor and was prone to extreme cold. The room was shaped like a trapezoid, with windows running from the floor to the ceiling on the diagonal walls. In one corner was the bed; in the other, a desk and an armchair. I was the lucky one with a single room, a perk given to me as the house's Resident Assistant. As the RA, it was up to me to enforce the University's policies, including no smoking. But our house was self-selected: we interviewed potential housemates. We kept the peace collectively. The only thing I really chose to enforce was who does the dishes.

Whether I was getting ready for class in the morning, killing time in between classes in the afternoon, or winding down at the end of the day, I found time to prop open my window, light my one-hitter, and exhale a puff of smoke. Where in high school I hid a specific behavior from a specific person, now I was hiding something more. Now I was hiding not only the act but the habit and the reasons behind it. I wanted to be a positive presence in the house, and if I wasn't feeling positive, I didn't want to be seen. There was a group of people who depended on me, which was perhaps why I felt the instinct to hide from them–as if, by making myself visible, they might see something I did not want them to see.

The music I listened to that year was notably dark. One song had the chorus, "I don't want to go outside today, I want to be left alone/I don't want to put the mask on my face, I want to be left alone." Another, which I played in moods good and bad, said, "All I ever wanted was to pick apart the day, put the pieces back together my way." What were my reasons for getting high? There was a time when I could have said, with some earnestness, that I was looking to "free my mind" or, to use another line from Kid Cudi, that I was in pursuit of happiness. But at this point, I knew that getting high did not always make me feel better. In fact, sometimes, it made me feel worse. So what was I hiding? I was hiding the behavior, I was hiding my sadness, but I was also hiding the fact that what I was doing to try and fix this sadness wasn't working. I was living with my best friends, but I couldn't be honest with them.

I made it through the school year, though I probably shouldn't have. When I returned in the fall, they moved us into a new house. This one had functioning smoke detectors and proper ventilation. It was closer to the center of campus, and inside the house, the bedrooms were closer together. All of these things made it harder to hide a smoking habit. I completely removed drug use from my life on campus. I adjusted to living with a little less discretion, feeling a little more on display. I came to embrace it, knowing that I would soon be graduating and it was probably for the best that I accept a certain kind of responsibility. The day after graduation, I began a four–day road trip to Spokane, Washington, where weed was legal.

◆

The third person I hid it from was my wife. It was not the singular act that I would hide, but the habit, the repeated use, the way it began to consume me. She knew that I liked to smoke; this was not a problem. What was a problem was the way I slowly built my life around the act. I first smoked at fifteen, I met my wife when I was sixteen, and we married when I was twenty-two, but it wasn't until I was twenty-seven that I would stop smoking. What began as a teenage experiment of enlightenment became a daily habit of isolation.

Throughout high school and college, there were friends that I would occa-sionally smoke with. But I always preferred to be alone. I always saw myself as the lonely stoner, the lonely loner. It took me several years of marriage before I realized just how harmful this mindset had become.

When you view yourself as a loner, you're saying, "I don't need anyone." If you can convince yourself that you don't need anyone, it's easy to convince yourself that no one cares about you. Once convinced of that, you quickly start to believe that it doesn't matter what you do, and that your behavior doesn't impact anyone beyond yourself.

At 15 years old, I wasn't able to go into this spiral–I was still too hungry for belonging. At 20 years old, I began to feel this spiral, but I was living in such a hypersocial environment that I was never allowed to stay there for long. By the time I was 27, and the only friend I saw with any regularity was my wife, I was living in this spiral.

It was easy to fall into such a pattern. For five years of marriage, I would get home from work first. Because I was home first, I would look for something to fill that time. Smoking was an easy way to do that. In a matter of minutes, I could free my mind and pick apart the day. I could plumb my soul for some sort of meaning. At first, getting high feels like climbing, like gaining a new perspective on your life. But when you do it every day, there is no new perspective.

Eventually, my wife would come home, and often she would ask me, "Did you smoke?" She rarely asked this question when I hadn't smoked, and she always asked it in the same tone of voice, with an emphasis on smoke. I would say, "Yes," and she would say, "I just don't want you to do it every day," and I would begin calculating, "Is two out of three days every day? Four out of five?" And in this way, each day became a question of "When can I get high?"

The rap artist Mac Miller has a song called "The Question." The question is simple, and it's the chorus of the song: "What am I doing here?" If you're listening to the song and you're not in a depressive state, maybe you hear that question with curiosity, with hope. But if you are in a depressive state and if you're struggling with an addiction, it sounds much darker. Mac Miller died of a drug overdose at age twenty-six, which is about how old I was when my drug use took its last turn for the worse.

When you're in a pattern of drug use, everything becomes a justification for using. I'm having a bad day, so I'm going to use. I'm having a good day, so I'm going to use. I only have ten minutes, so I'm going to use. I have two hours, that's plenty of time to use. This was the secret I was keeping, not just the use but the way the use had isolated me. I got sober because I ran out of justifications. I was exhausted from trying to justify behavior that I knew was bad for me, that I knew was making me lonely, that I knew was making me unable to feel a sense of belonging. I was holding onto a secret that I didn't have to. It wasn't even the kind of secret that had to be told. If I could change, there would be nothing to hide.

Chase Montana lives in Columbus, OH, with his wife, Ashley, where he teaches high school English and coaches high school girls soccer. He holds a Bachelor of Arts in English Literature from Ohio Wesleyan University. This is his first publication.

The Solarium

Stories to Tell to Friends

"I've learned that we're all entitled to have our secrets."
— Nicholas Sparks, *The Notebook*

Fifteen Minutes

Robbi Sommers Bryant

My father, Jerry Lewis, was not *the* Jerry Lewis, but he was "the *real* one*,*" he'd say, because he was born first. He always dreamed of being in a movie, playing the "kindly warden." And in his own right, he was famous, just in a different way. Like many of us, he had been waiting for *his* fifteen minutes of fame from as far back as I can remember. And I was thrilled when that moment finally arrived.

It was still dark the morning my father and I pulled into Sal's Diner—the place he went every morning for coffee, toast, and eggs over easy. Sal and the girls got there around six and always opened the doors early for my dad, even though they didn't officially serve until seven.

This was an ordinary Sunday—the day I joined my father for breakfast. Dad picked me up at 5:45, and we headed straight to Sal's. As we turned into the restaurant's driveway, my dad slowed.

"That's weird. The front lights aren't on." Dad stopped the car.

"She'll probably open any minute," I replied, cracking the window. It was fifty out, but Dad had the car heater cranked up.

"Yeah, but I'm here *every* morning, and the lights are always on. Sal should be standing at the counter." He shook his head. "Something's not right."

"She's probably running late. You always jump to conclusions."

My Dad let the car creep forward. "Wait! There's a light. See?" He pointed to the side of the restaurant. "Let's check it out." He stopped the car, climbed out, and dramatically closed the door without so much as a click.

I did the same without the fanfare.

He was already walking toward the back of the building when I heard him gasp.

Was it his heart?

"Dad, Dad!" I cried, rushing to my father.

Once I was close enough to hear, he whispered, "Ssh! It's a robbery." He pointed to a single window above our heads.

"Sure, Dad. Fine," I said, thinking Dad was up to his old tricks. Without even trying, Dad had the ability to make the smallest event into a fiasco. "Let's go eat at Bob Evans instead. They have a great breakfast."

"Everyone's arms are raised. They must be at gunpoint," Dad whispered, his voice shaky.

I stood on my tiptoes and could barely see into the building, but yes, arms were raised. I grabbed my father's hand and tugged him away from the window.

"Call 911. I'm going in," he said, pulling his hand from mine.

"Dad, no." I spit the words out of my mouth. "You're not going in."

"I've got this...." He waved his key ring in front of my face. A Swiss Army knife dangled from the ring. "It's the element of surprise. Learned that stationed in the Philippines." He pulled the blade from inside the knife and made a couple of lunges. "What are you waiting for? Call!"

"Dad, we left our cell phones at home. Remember? We're doing a day without them. I mean, what are you going to do? Hold the robber at small knife point? Seriously. Let's get out of here. We can call 911 at a phone booth. Do they still have those anywhere?"

"I'll be back," he said, turning from me.

"What do you mean, you'll be back? Where are you going?"

"To save my people," he shot back.

"*I'm* your people, Dad. *They* just make good over-easy eggs."

"Ssh. The phone booth is over there." He pointed to the other side of the restaurant. "If the damn thing even works."

And then my dad did something that floored me. He scanned the parking lot, knife still in hand, and dropped into a military dive roll. Pulling himself across the lot, he did a military crawl, disappearing into the darkness. Within minutes, he crawled back into the light.

"I need change."

"Dad, let's just get out of here." I walked toward him, digging for change in my pocket. "Mom will kill us—"

"For Christ's sake, stay down. Take cover in the shadows."

I stooped down and hurried to the phone booth. Dad, who did a military crawl behind me, came out of the shadows and tiptoed into view with his back pressed against the building's brick wall. His arms extended out and against the wall as he continued, on his toes, toward me. He quickly slid into the phone booth, picked up the receiver, and made several calls.

"I called the police and WKRC-TV," Dad said, stepping out of the booth. "The press will want a statement." He adjusted his jacket and then lunged; his knife pointed toward an imaginary enemy. "This is it! My fifteen minutes of fame. God, what will I say to the press? I'll be clever; no, alarmed."

Dad held the knife like a microphone. "Yes. World War II. Hmm? Was I afraid of the robber? No. This is what I trained to do."

"Dad!"

Dad looked at me. "Too much? Be humbler?"

"This isn't—"

"Too pushy? Ah, shit! What should I say?"

"How would I know, Dad?" I shrugged.

"*You're* the writer. Come up with a statement for me."

"Dad, I write romance."

A siren in the distance blared, getting louder by the second. "Here they come." Dad pointed to three cop cars zipping down the street. Once at the driveway, they did quick turns into the lot.

"Here they come," Dad said, combing the hair horseshoed around the back of his head.

A police officer walked over to us. "Sir. Ma'am."

"I'm the guy who called this in," my father said, pointing to the left side of the restaurant. "They're in the back."

The officer pulled his gun and headed down the driveway toward the window as a WKRC news van pulled into the lot.

"The news showed! This is going to be big." Dad adjusted his fedora several times until he was satisfied. "Okay, breathe deep. This is it. Say, 'Break a leg,'" Dad muttered.

"*Really*, Dad? If Mom finds out we didn't protect ourselves…. Like that time you didn't knock on wood and broke your nose? She's not going to be happy that we stayed in a dangerous situation," I offered.

"I'll handle that. Please, indulge me."

"Okay, Dad. Break a leg."

"Excuse me," a newswoman walked over to Dad and held her microphone in front of him. "Are you the man who called this in?"

A proud smile crossed Dad's face.

"What happened? Did you see the suspect? Did he have a gun?" the news-woman asked.

As Dad started to answer, all the restaurant lights flashed on. The officer came around from the back of the building and casually sauntered to Dad.

"Yes, Officer. Would you like a statement?" Dad asked.

"Well, sir, it's just that—"

"You gotta do whatcha gotta do. Right, Officer?" Dad flashed his Swiss Army knife and performed another lunge as he turned toward the camera. "Army Air-force. Paratrooper. WWII."

"Sir, that took a lot of guts," the police officer said.

"No man left behind. I wouldn't leave Sal and her staff—"

"No, sir, I meant World War II. Thank you for your service."

"But the robbery. Is everyone okay?" Dad glanced toward the side of the restaurant.

"Yes, sir, everyone's fine."

"Did you catch the guy?"

"No, sir. It wasn't a robbery."

"We both saw them with their arms up! Right, honey."

Everyone looked at me. "Right, Dad."

"Sir, it was an exercise class." The police officer seemed to work hard to keep the sides of his mouth from curling into a smile.

As the rusty sun reddened the morning sky, Dad turned to me and muttered, "About this...ah...adventure. Our little secret, right?"

"Our little secret, Dad."

Robbi Sommers Bryant's award-winning books include a novella, seven novels, five short-story collections, and one book of poetry. Her work has been published in magazines, including *Readers Digest*, *Redbook*, *Penthouse*, college textbooks, and many anthologies. Robbi's work was also optioned twice for television's *Movie of the Week*, and she appeared on TV's *Jane Whitney Show* to discuss her article "A Victim's Revenge."

Robbi is the past president of Redwood Writers, the largest branch of the California Writers Club. Besides writing, her professional focus is developmental editing, content editing, and copy editing. She is also a professional writing coach and professional watercolor artist. Find out more at robbibryant.com.

The Dancing Queen

Edward Gosnell

No! No! No! You have it wrong. Truly understanding what makes a woman happy is not the secret to making it work with her. Take my word for it; understanding a woman that well can only lead to big trouble. Yes, I realize that because you and your brother are now in college, you think you're too old for your grandpa to tell you anything about women. Ha! Do you seriously think I'm completely clueless about wooing the fairer sex just because I don't know much about YouTube, eBay, and all those other fancy interweb dating sites? Ha! Your old grandfather still knows a thing or two about how the game is played. But you say your dating scene is confusing, and things are changing too fast for your grandpa to understand what's up. Ha! You have no idea what real chaos is like.

Remember Children, I came of age in the Seventies, a discordant tumultuous time, when the rule-breaking counterculture craziness of the Sixties collided head-on with the rising self-satisfied Gordon Gecko materialism of the Eighties. Wretched excess was wholeheartedly embraced. Cocaine replaced pot. And up-scale fashion took an exuberant manic turn. Serious businessmen sported shaggy neo-hippy hairdos in unholy combination with elegant three-piece suits. Perfectly straight men wore poofy Liberace shirts left coyly half-buttoned to display ample tuffs of chest hair and enough gold chain to do a Serbian crime lord proud.

And "Hooray for me" became the battle cry of our generation as narcissistic hedonism became epidemic and shallowness of character was not only enthusiastically embraced but elevated to an art form. I once saw a man spend the better part of an hour expounding on his preference to be called Dan rather than Danny or Daniel, and his listeners, rather than being appalled by his clueless self-absorption, nodded in sympathetic understanding. And silly self-indulgent affectations became points of pride. It was not at all unusual for a man, who in any other era would have been unassuming and even humble, to brag with gusto about the size of the weekly dry cleaning bill for his suits.

It was, in short, the Age of Disco, that satanically decadent throbbing noise which, for a brief unsettled moment, almost displaced God-ordained Rock and Roll as America's music of choice and thereby shook the very foundation of the universe itself. And thus it came to pass that we well-meaning single men innocently plying the strobe-lit clubs of that depraved era in our search for a little romance came face to face with a new peril of unprecedented heartbreaking

"

maleficence seemingly conjured up from the very pits of hell itself by Disco's soulless rhythms—the legendary Dancing Queen.

Now you may think that your hot Goth girls like that Abby on CSI or your modern so-called Divas like that Bouncy and Fast Taylor girl are something special. Ha! They don't hold a candle to our Dancing Queens. As celebrated in song by ABBA, the Dancing Queen was the archetypical femme fatale of our era. Every town seemed to have one bent on raising havoc amongst its young male populace, and Columbus was no exception. Indeed, the acknowledged monarch of our fair city was a more virulent example than most. Born simple Patricia Jones in the small Southern Ohio city of Jackson, she moved to Columbus, graduated from beauty school, assembled a wardrobe of scandalously revealing dresses, and reinvented herself as Tish J, avant-garde hair stylist at the Rive Gauche Unisex Salon by day and reigning vamp Queen of the Discoes by night. And a whirling, twirling little tornado of trouble was she. Petite, cute, and ever so sexy with giant blue eyes, a pert perm, and a sassy smile, she relentlessly teased and tormented the gaggle of guys who swarmed around her.

But torturing men was just a hobby. Tish J truly loved and lived to dance. And she was almost as good a dancer as she thought she was. Soon after arriving in Columbus, she had begun lessons pairing with Billy Brown, a fellow beauty school student. William Anthony Brown was also from Southern Ohio, from Portsmouth, an old steel town on the Ohio River, to be precise. He was a fashionably slender, unbelievably graceful gay man who did not so much walk as seem to frictionlessly glide across a room. Like Tish J, Billy had reinvented himself upon arriving in Columbus, adopting the soubriquet, Anton. And while Tish J was a very good dancer, Anton was something more. He was a truly great dancer. They entered competitions and, within the year, came to dominate the local dance scene. When they took the floor at Jericho's, the Brown Derby, or any of the other local clubs, the other dancers moved aside and watched. They were damn good, and their moves were sexy as hell. The women watched Tish J with envy/ We straight men watched her with lust, and the gay men watched Anton with equal lust. Either would have been a notably disrupting force in the city's nightlife. Together they were a drama fest of cataclysmic proportions.

It was really a shame that Tish J and Anton were not sexually attracted to one another. That would have saved a great many people, including your old grandfather, a tremendous amount of trouble. However, I strongly suspect that if they had been romantically involved, they would have eventually ended up killing each other. While they meshed beautifully on the dance floor, they otherwise were in a continuous spat over some minor point of hair styling, some obscure question of fashion, or, most often, some perceived shortcoming in the other's dance style. Yet despite their apparent extreme distaste for one another, they spent almost every waking hour together, albeit with the apparent purpose of making each other's life a living hell.

Now any sensible person would have avoided this train wreck of a pair at all costs. But your old grandfather was twenty-five, single, and horny, which by any definition is the very opposite of sensible when it comes to dealing with women.

And as I said, Tish J was a sexy little thing with those amazingly beautiful big blue eyes. Now twenty-five can be a dangerous age indeed because you have just enough experience and confidence to get yourself into situations way over your head, which is exactly what happened to your old grandpa. In an act of supreme stupidity, I decided to put the moves on Tish J.

Getting a date with Tish J was not terribly difficult. She and Anton changed romantic partners about as often as most people change socks, and there was only one basic requirement to get that first date. You simply had to be a good-looking, sexy stud. Now I realize that you view your grandpa as this decrepit old geezer with less sex appeal than the bloated corpse of a three-day dead hippo, but believe it or not, in my salad days, I had no problem meeting that minimal standard. In short order, I had worked my magic and had a date with Tish J. And unlike most of her consorts, who she usually cut after a date or two, I began seeing her regularly, and we soon became something of an item.

Indeed, after our third week together, Tish J started introducing me as her fiancée. I can't say that I was surprised by this rather drastic assumption on her part. I knew that the woman, despite her big city façade, was from Jackson, Ohio, after all, and things had happened that, to a small-town girl, implied eventual marriage. However, I still found her pronouncement more than a little disconcerting and certainly premature. But it will give you some idea of the power of those wonderful blue eyes that I did not sprint for the door the first time she trotted out that unsettling term. It was then that your poor old grandfather, to his surprise, realized that he was firmly ensnared in her wicked web.

Now you may wonder, Dear Children, how your old grandpa was, if anything, a little too successful in his pursuit of Tish J, whereas most of her other suitors almost immediately flamed out. Was it because we shared common interests and were truly meant for each other? Were we perhaps at heart, even soul mates? To which I would answer with a simple, "Hell no!" Aside from our pure lust for one another, we had absolutely nothing in common. She spent most of her time pattering on about cutting hair and the latest dance moves, topics which had next to no interest to me. And I don't believe that she ever asked a single question about what I did or liked. It was my job just to be the sexy stud that I was and simply adore her, which was not all that difficult given those beautiful blue eyes and the lust in my heart. And yes, I agree, Dear Children, lust is not something to build a lasting relationship on. But human nature being what it is, pure lust can keep a relationship burning bright for a lot longer than you can probably imagine, and if truth be told, being twenty-five, I was only thinking from night to night anyway.

At any rate, returning to the question of why I was successful in my pursuit whereas the others were not, your old grandfather had a couple of advantages over the common herd of her admirers. Being from Chillicothe in Southern Ohio myself, I had more insight than most as to what made her tick, and I also quickly realized that the key to successfully dating Tish J was to get past Anton. He and Tish J had this weird love-hate thing going on, and although there was no sexual attraction between them, both were insanely jealous of one another's romantic partners. Thus, they constantly did their best to subvert each other's relationships. Anton was particularly adroit at this game. He was a true master in the arts of the catty comment and pointed sarcasm, and he took great relish in slicing and dicing Tish J's relationships to shreds with his cutting remarks. But I understood his sense of humor, unlike Tish J's previous boyfriends. I found his conversation extremely funny, which to a large extent, mollified him as time went on. As a matter of form, he continued to throw out a barbed comment about me on occasion to irk Tish J, but you could tell that his heart wasn't really in it, and Anton and I began to get along quite well.

Nonetheless, even with Anton neutralized, dating Tish J was still not exactly a cakewalk. As I said, she was amazingly sexy and often quite charming, but she was also very moody with an explosive temper and was almost unbelievably jealous and vain. Just glancing at another woman was enough to set her off, and God help the man who made what could be construed as even the least disparaging remarks about her person or talents. Being involved with Tish J was much like living on the edge of a volcano, but your old grandfather quickly learned to dodge the fire and brimstone she occasionally tossed his way. And for a while, things went swimmingly.

We even adopted cute nicknames for each other. I called her "Blue" because of her big blue eyes, of course, and she called me "Wheaties." "Why Wheaties?" you ask. Well, if you must know, it was because she thought I looked like the picture of Bruce Jenner on the Wheaties Box. And don't think I didn't notice those smirks. You have to remember everybody thought Jenner was quite the stud back in those days, being an Olympic gold medalist and all. That nickname was quite a compliment back then. Anyway, as I was saying, everything was going really well, and things had gotten so serious that I took her down to Chillicothe for a day to meet the family. The reviews were mixed. My brother was absolutely taken with her. And my father flashed me a giant clandestine grin and a big thumbs up. However, my mom and sisters kept giving me furtive looks, which could only be construed as, "Are you out of your fricking mind?"

As we entered into our eighth week together, my relationship with Tish J settled into something of a routine. On Sunday and Tuesday nights, we would hang out together. On Monday, Wednesday, Thursday, Friday, and Saturday nights, we would join Anton and his boyfriend de jour at one of the clubs. We always took a table right next to the dance floor, and the surrounding tables would quickly fill with Tish J and Anton's admirers, who would send over drinks and stumble over each other to jump across to our table to light their cigarettes.

Anton tended to treat his entourage with thinly veiled contempt, like some medieval lord forced to sully his person by actually having to interact with his peasants. But his haughty demeanor only seemed to increase their adoration. I felt particularly sorry for one poor soul named Jimmy Smucker. He was almost the polar opposite of Anton. He was clumsy, a tad overweight, a bit sloppy, and incredibly clueless about fashion. He wore a short sleeve shirt with his three-piece suit, and his partly unbuttoned shirt revealed a white tee shirt under his gold chain, for God's sake. Anton continually mocked him and treated him like dirt, but Jimmy just smiled back with a worshipful look in his big brown cow eyes. It was just pitiful.

Tish J was gentler in her approach. She spent much of the evening shamelessly flirting with her admirers, benignly acknowledging their lame attempts of gallantry with a smile or a wink and sometimes even remembering their names. Sadly, these small attentions were enough to keep her worshipers coming back night after night. As Tish J's consort, her crowd eyed me with jealous respect. I, after all, was "The Fiancée" and was actually living their fantasy. As a result, I too soon took on the role of a minor nightlife celebrity, basking in the reflected glory of Columbus's reigning Dancing Queen. And while not treating the lesser mortals surrounding our table quite like dirt, I perhaps came off as a bit full of myself. Actually, in retrospect, to be perfectly honest, I was a complete dick. But I was soon to get my comeuppance.

My downfall began innocently enough. Our merry band was at Jericho's for our usual Friday night conclave. Tish J had actually deigned to dance with one of her admirers while Anton and I watched from our table. The song, as I recall, was Jungle Boogie, a rather boisterous tune with a bit more bounce than the usual disco fare by a band called Kool and the Gang, and Tish J was really getting down with the song. She had a big joyful smile and improvised this neat little hop step to match the beat. She looked happier than at any time since I had known her. I leaned over to Anton and whispered how cute she looked, how I loved her little hop, and how it reminded me of a square dance step.

Now, Dear Children, I am sure that you remember the sinister smile that would cross the face of a Disney villain when they were about to commit some particularly heinous act, like when Scar was about to let Mufasa fall to his death. That was exactly the smile that appeared on Anton's face as he rose from the table and made his way across the floor to Tish J. As he bent down and whispered in her ear, I saw the joyful smile drain from her face, and she looked toward me with a quizzical expression like she could not quite comprehend what he was saying. But as he continued to whisper, her expression began to turn decidedly darker, and she shot me an angry withering look that spelled big, big trouble and came stomping toward me across the dance floor. It may have been some odd play of the strobe lights, but I would swear that I saw puffs of black smoke coming out of her ears. When she finally reached our table, she stopped and, leaning forward with the tip of her index finger planted firmly on the end of my nose, menacingly asked, "Did you say that I looked like I was *square dancing*?"

I rather feebly replied, "Well, not exactly," which I quickly discovered was not the correct answer. An extremely robust denial sworn by all I held holy avowing that I could never have entertained such a blasphemous thought was probably the only viable response, although even that probably would not have sufficed. I, of course, had always known that Tish J had a bad temper. But as she loosened her wrath upon me in full-fledged fury, it exceeded anything I could have possibly imagined. She exploded with a torrent of obscenities that would have made a drill sergeant blush and did so with a cadence and creativity that were truly impressive. For example, she somehow managed to use the f-word not just as a verb, noun, adjective, adverb, and gerund but also as a participle, preposition, and conjunction. It was a virtuoso verbal performance that could be justifiably described as the Gettysburg Address of profanity, and it was all directed at me. I suppose I should have been honored by the effort, but somehow was not. Finally, as Kool and the Gang shouted out the last chorus of "Get down, get down" to Jungle Boogie, Tish J finished her rant by saying, "I never want to see your ugly (insert a long string of very vile obscenities here) face again," took my drink, a Harvey Wallbanger as I recall, from the table, threw it in my face, and then turned abruptly and walked away. Completely rattled, I could only think to yell after her, "But what about our engagement?" She turned, shot me a hate-filled look that would have halted a Mongol horde, and then giving me the finger with each hand, proceeded to pump them up and down with a vigor that seemed to leave little doubt that our engagement was well beyond over.

Now keep in mind, since Tish J had been screeching at the top of her lungs like a demented banshee, I was not her sole audience. Everyone else in the club was gapping at us in slack-jawed wonderment. And her worshiping entourage of worshipers really enjoyed the show. As she turned for a final time to walk away, I became aware of their smirks and muffled giggles. It was easy enough to read their thoughts, "Neener, neener, neener, suck it, you smug a-hole, you're no longer 'The Fiancée.'" Completely humiliated, I slunk from the club.

I freely admit that I was truly heartsick for a day or so. But by the end of the second day away from those intoxicating blue eyes, I began to realize that not being engaged to Tish J had its upside. I was, after all, no longer in danger of marrying the woman. And after a few more days passed, I actually began to enjoy my freedom. I, of course, had to avoid the prime nightspots where Tish J, Anton, and their crowd hung out. However, being exiled to the second-tier establishments was a small price to pay to avoid any awkward encounter with Tish J or to endure the gloating looks of her entourage. Moreover, while the women were perhaps not as glamorous as those in the fancier clubs, they were just as good-looking, and some of them could even carry on a conversation that did not involve fashion or dance steps. I even found a couple of places that still played rock music instead of the dreaded disco. All in all, life was good. But I was soon to learn that my tribulations with Tish J had yet to run their course.

It was at about 3:00 a.m., a month or so after the Great Breakup. I had just fallen asleep, having spent a pleasant evening at King Tut's, a relatively low-end disco joint up on Morse Road, when my phone rang. I woke up in one of those fogs where you are not quite sure where you are and knocked over the lamp as I pawed around for the phone. It was Tish J. At the time, I had no idea what was going on. However, I have since been able to piece together the general scenario, which went down something like this:

Tish J returns from a date in a sour mood and stomps her little foot. "How dare he say that Mona has prettier eyebrows than me. The nerve of that man! I'll show him. I'll marry Wheaties." Eventually, she dialed my number.

My phone, "Ring! Ring! Ring! Ring! Ring! Ring! Ring!"

Me, in a state of semi-conscienceless, having finally found my phone, "Ullo, whosh dish?"

Tish J, "It's me, sweetie."

Me, now suddenly wide awake, "Tish?"

"Yes, darling. I've decided our wedding should be in May."

Me, "What??"

Tish J, "I just talked to your father. He's ever so excited, and I could hear your mother screeching with joy in the background."

Me, "What???"

Tish J, "I was first thinking that St. John's Arena would be perfect for the wedding but then decided I should invite some more of my old boyfriends and admirers, so I think Ohio Stadium would be a better fit."

Me, "What????"

Tish J, "Anyway, we can discuss the details after work. Stop by and see me then. Kiss, kiss, bye, bye, love you, Wheaties." And she hangs up.

Me, "What?????"

I had every intention of putting Tish J in her place and telling her I wanted nothing more to do with her when I dropped by her apartment that afternoon. But when she opened the door, gave me one of her amazing smiles, and flashed those big blue eyes at me, I completely caved. The next thing I knew, we were seriously planning our upcoming nuptials as I silently cursed myself for being such a sorry, whipped wuss. It was those damn giant blue eyes. The only redeeming part of this whole sad episode was my anticipation of seeing the look on the faces of her entourage when we entered Jericho's arm-in-arm that evening. Well, to be honest, that was not the only redeeming part. We got a bit frisky about fifteen minutes after discussing our wedding.

Anyway, as I had hoped when we came through the door of the club that evening, the looks of dismay on the faces of her worshipers were a delight to behold. They, of course, pretended to be happy to see me and groveled in a most satisfactory manner. Just to rub it in, I made it a point to engage Tish J in several rather indecent public displays of affection over the next half hour while we waited for Anton and his date to arrive. As you would expect, Anton already knew about our reconciliation and impending marriage. Tish had naturally called and told him her plans at 3:00 a.m. before she had bothered to call and tell me.

Surprisingly, Anton actually looked happy to see me and was quite friendly. After a little small talk, he and Tish J got up to dance. As he rose, he gave me another Disney villain smile which I found a little disconcerting. However, I was soon caught up in just watching them dance. They performed together even better than I had remembered and were indeed a pleasure to behold. Their routine was almost flawless as they spun and twirled around the floor. But then Tish J made a slight misstep, and I heard Anton say, "Well, do-si-do," which, as he obviously intended, reminded Tish J why we had broken up and rekindled her wrath. She turned toward me, gave me a very dark frown, and started marching in my direction with a killer look in her eyes. This time I did not wait at the table. I was drinking a Kahlua, cream, and coke, which I knew would make a sticky mess if thrown in my face. I got up, cut for the door, and did not look back.

Two days later, I was nursing my PTSD (post-Tish J stress disorder) at the Serene Lounge on High Street just south of the OSU campus with a couple of my graduate school buddies when your sainted grandmother and a gang of her inebriated sorority sisters came bounding in. I was smitten on sight and immediately introduced myself. Oh, your grandmother told you we met at an ice cream social at the Campus Christian Center? Yes, yes, of course, that must be right. I am sure my memory of her standing on a table at the Serene doing the bump with Cathy Bosman is a false one. What was the bump? It was a dance where you put your hands in the air and spun around, periodically bumping your butts together in time to the music. Yes, I agree it sounds really stupid, and it was. But for some reason, in those primitive times, it was an almost mandatory ritual among groups of drunken women out for a night on the town. At any rate, your grandmother and I went out the following night and soon started dating regularly. And I never ventured into the dreaded disco scene again.

Whatever happened to Tish J and Anton? Well. I couldn't have answered that question until about a year ago. Then one Sunday last winter, I was sitting in the living room with your grandmother and leafing through the travel section of the Dispatch when a quarter-page advertisement for a rustic bed and breakfast named "The Two Bears' House" caught my eye. According to the ad, it was located just a few miles west of Portsmouth near the entrance to Scioto State Park. The ad pictured the two proprietors standing arm in arm on the front porch of their establishment. One in his pressed denim jeans and designer flannel shirt, looking every bit as rustic as an L.L. Bean manikin, was a bearded Anton who did not resemble a bear. He looked more like a large self-satisfied tabby cat. His partner, however, was decidedly bear-like. He looked like a giant unkempt grizzly in a pair of bib overalls. It was Jimmy Smucker. And he was staring down at Anton with that same look of adoration in his big brown cow eyes as he had those many years before, and it was still every bit as pitiful, which made me laugh. Your grandma wanted to know what was so funny, and I told her I knew these guys, Anton and Jimmy, from the disco days. They were now hooked up and had a rustic bed and breakfast place in Southern Ohio. As I started to elaborate on why I found this funny, your grandma cut me off and asked, "Anton, wasn't he Little Miss Blue Eyes' buddy?" The woman has a memory like an elephant. I hadn't mentioned Anton in forty years.

Now I need to interject a particularly important piece of grandfatherly advice at this point. If you should ever be ranting for two hours about how awful your old girlfriend was to your new girlfriend, and she asks you why you didn't break up with her sooner, be very careful what you say. Having seriously thought about this for the last four decades, I believe the correct answer is, "Because I hadn't met you yet, and I had no idea what true love was like." I know for a fact that the wrong answer is, "Because she had these amazing deep blue eyes." And this is probably an especially bad answer if your new girlfriend's eyes are sort of a watery brown, something like your grandmother's. Now your new girlfriend will perhaps raise her eyebrows when you make this remark, and she might even reply with a mildly annoyed "hmmp," but she will probably let things slide at the time since you just started dating. However, mark my words, she will not forget what you said, and you will soon rue the day you said it. From then on, every time you appear to be winning an argument, you can expect her to end things with the phrase, "Well, I suppose you'd rather be with Little Miss Blue Eyes," as she storms out of the room. There is no viable comeback to this statement. Even if your logic is rock solid and you occupy the indisputable moral high ground, you have lost the argument. But we are, of course, just talking hypotheticals here.

At any rate, returning to my story, your grandmother took the ad from me and got out her laptop. As you know, I have as little to do with computers as possible, but because of all of those years crushing candy and playing Farmville, your grandma is quite the computer wizard. She found a computer address in the ad and then got on this really amazing computer thing called Facebook, did her computer magic, and in a matter of minutes, broke out in laughter. "Well, well, well, it looks like Little Miss Blue Eyes turned into quite the little porker," she said.

I went over and looked at her computer screen and saw an older, rather matronly version of my old flame. However, while she definitely had a well-fed look to her, I thought calling her a little porker was a bit over the top, especially when certain grandmothers, who shall remain nameless, are not exactly as trim as they used to be. But this thought I kept to myself as I replied, "Yep, that's Tish J,"

Your grandmother didn't take long to trace Tish J's history since I last saw her. That Facebook thing is wonderful. Apparently, Tish returned to Jackson shortly after our breakup for her five-year class reunion and, using her big city wiles, managed to nab Danny O'Malley, Jackson's most eligible bachelor. Old Tish J did herself proud. The O'Malleys are as close to royalty as you can get in Southeastern Ohio. Among their many interests, they have Hyundai dealerships in both Jackson and Gallipolis and the O'Malley Beverage Company, the nation's third-largest distributor of Blatz beer. But they are probably most famous as the owners of the iconic Southeastern Ohio restaurant chain O'Malley's Taco Hut and Dairy Dream, home of Mama O'Malley's world-famous Hawaiian Pizza. Every town in that quarter of the state with a population over 500 has at least one of these restaurants. I believe that there are as many as 12 of them altogether.

It was obvious from Tish J's Face Booklet that she had leveraged her position as wife of the O'Malley heir to become the society queen of Jackson. The list of her community positions and honors seemed endless. She was president of the Jackson Country Club and the chairperson of the O'Malley United Charities. There were pictures of her presenting O'Malley Perfect Attendance Awards to school children and O'Malley Trophies of Excellence to the fruit and vegetable exhibitors at the county fair. She had been grand marshal for the O'Malley Apple Festival Parade for the last ten years and was honorary president of the O'Malley Animal and Children's Shelter. She had been Jackson County Woman of the Year five times and had even been honored by the governor of Ohio for her community service. But one office seemed especially important to her. There was even a video about it on her Face Booklet. The video showed a very happy Patty Jones O'Malley with the same joyful smile and doing the very same hop step as she had dancing to Jungle Boogie those many years ago, except this time she was dancing as the team captain of the Jackson County Do-Si-Dos in the Ohio Square Dance Championship Finals. Ha! And you think your old grandpa doesn't understand women. I nailed it! I recognized exactly what would make Tish J happy, and you see how that turned out. Understanding her desires is obviously not the secret to making it work with a woman.

Well, then, what is? How can you ask that? Seriously, have you learned nothing from what I have been saying? As my rather long-winded dissertation should make perfectly clear, the secret to making it work with a woman comes down to just two simple words "complete honesty." Avoid that, and you might have a fighting chance.

Seventy-six and proud of it, Edward Gosnell was born in Chillicothe, Ohio, and graduated from Chillicothe High School in 1965. He is a graduate of the Ohio State University, where he majored in geography and marketing.

He has been married to his wife, Judy, for forty-four years. They have two children and two granddaughters. Edward is also the caretaker of two cats. One is sweet, but the other all too often races across his computer keyboard while he is trying to type.

Catacombs

Bill Vernon

Four weeks of stress preceded our Ford Cortina's chugging arrival in Rome. There, caught in what resembled a stampede of hyper-ventilating cattle, circling in rush-hour traffic on the 4-lane ring road, the *Grande Raccordo Anulare*, I blew a gasket, parked in a wide spot on the right curb, ordered my brother-in-law Jerome out, and screamed that this time I was going to kick his ass. What caused this outburst was the fact that I could not read the map, drive at the same time, and handle his refusal to navigate me to the campsite. Only the pleas of his wife Carol and his sister, my wife Lily, and my guilt at losing control saved him.

Thus began our visit to The Eternal City.

We came like Visigoths to sack Rome, but exhaustion prevailed. The next day, it made us break routine and enter air-conditioned comfort in an idling Greyhound-like bus. Beyond its tinted windows were a sweltering late afternoon, tooting and scurrying tiny cars and motor scooters, gassy exhausts, swarming crowds, and dust and dirt that had failed to cake on our skin.

I said, "God, this feels so good," and my three companions giggled, collapsing as I'd done on a softly cushioned seat, letting the sudden coolness and good fortune wash over us.

We talked loudly in pleasure while our hosts gathered their quota of riders. This unplanned excursion was weird, but our desire for a little pampering told us it was risk-free—an opportunity made in heaven.

I was self-conscious, though. We were dressed roughly: in shorts, light, loose shirts, sandals, and floppy hats except mine, a Cincinnati Reds baseball cap. I also suspected that we smelled after a month of spotty bathing. My wife Lily, seated beside me, had no offensive odor, nor did Jerome and Carol, just across the aisle, so I hoped my aroma was likewise faint.

Lily said, "I can't believe that people from the States are selling something here?"

I shook my head. "And only to Americans. They picked us out of all the others."

199

My wife smiled. "Maybe they heard us talking."

I laughed. "Or saw how we're dressed."

"I wonder what they're selling."

"It doesn't matter. We'll just listen to their spiel, tell them no, and leave."

When our bus finally rumbled away from The Colosseum, I closed my eyes and considered our luck: a free air-conditioned tour of the city, free admission to the catacombs, then a free dinner inside an air-conditioned hotel. All for listening to their "short sales pitch." After we declined to buy whatever that involved, we'd return to reality—our night-cooled tent, our rubber air mattresses—and sleep as best we could.

This was a vacation away from our vacation. *Carpe diem*. We were recently married teachers just starting out in the profession, educating ourselves and having fun. Our tent was waiting, but we were still curious and nearly on budget doing Arthur Frommer's *Europe on 5 Dollars a Day*.

As the motor's drone, the driver's voice describing Rome's wonders, and 30-some days of tiresome travel lulled me toward sleep, Lily squeezed my hand and said, "I'm enjoying this."

♦

Forty-five minutes later, nearly down the steep stairway into the under-world, she said, "I don't like this." She was so close that her knees jabbed my back with each step.

I said, "Relax. And please don't push me like that. It knocks me off balance."

I was already anxious. My shoulders brushed the wood scaffolding in the long shaft, the lights flickered, and in the horizontal tunnel, weak bulbs strung widely apart on black wires allowed shadows to swallow big areas. I could see the shape of the person ahead and little else.

Doubts were swarming me. There were many catacombs around Rome, but I didn't know exactly where ours was or its name. The bus had parked at a large building, and I'd guessed that we were at a convent when a nun appeared, our new leader. I couldn't hear her introduction, but she clearly roared her last comment: "Hold onto the railing going down and do not touch the remains. The Church considers them sacred." Then her black-and-white habit disappeared below us.

Thankfully, the level tunnel floor was wider than the stairs, yet that fact also made me imagine why: to provide room to turn bodies 90 degrees and push the stiff cadavers into the rectangular holes scraped from the walls?

Remains, she'd said. The holes we were passing looked empty. Which was good. I suddenly realized that I didn't want to encounter a corpse. Had bodies rotted down here? Or were the bones brought here afterward? If our nun had explained, I hadn't heard her. Of course, the burials occurred over centuries....

Our line of living people abruptly paused, letting Jerome turn to me and say, "Smell it?" He chuckled. "It's death warmed over."

Hoping to keep his humor from further upsetting Lily, I said quickly, "It smells like that big church in London."

"Yeah, right, Westminster Abbey. People were buried in it too."

Lily said nothing, so maybe she hadn't heard. I didn't try to identify the smell clearly.

As we wormed farther into the earth, gray objects appeared in the holes alongside us. I couldn't be sure what they were because the light bulbs on the ceiling barely touched the cavities.

The second time our string of people paused, the lights flickered, then went off entirely. My wife grabbed my arm, knocking me forward. I reached out for the tunnel wall. My fingers, though, touched only air, then curled down into a hollow. A burial hole? I quickly withdrew my hand and took my wife's.

Lily leaned totally against me. "I really don't like this. I mean, I hate it!"

Hearing fear in her voice, I disguised my feelings. "Hang in there. It's not so bad."

When the lights came back on minutes later, Jerome laughed and said in what sounded like a shout, "*Sacra Ossis!*" We'd put up with his loud voice in our tent and car. Now here too. He taught Latin, which I'd studied in high school myself, so I knew he was saying holy bones. But his happy tone was odd.

I looked over his shoulder. He was pointing at a skull. It was facing us from the edge of a hole in the wall, and it looked as if it were smiling. Maybe his two years of study in a Jesuit seminary had taught him to accept death more nonchalantly than I could.

The lights went off again.

"Oh God," Lily said, squeezing my arm tightly. "I've got claustrophobia."

"It's okay." I wrapped an arm around her shoulders. We waited quietly. Patiently. The lights, however, did not come back on as they had before.

Lily muttered a Hail Mary. Then said loudly, "Please put the lights on."

Other people were mumbling. Someone yelled, "What's going on?"

"Please turn on the lights."

Lily yelled, "Yes. Turn them on."

There were other shouts of agreement.

Voices crying in the darkness. Wasn't that a biblical phrase?

Jerome, though, laughed loudly while rearing back so that his head bumped mine. "Sorry," he said, but he'd also irritated Carol. She said loudly, "Jerome, stop it!" His response was to laugh again. He actually seemed to be enjoying this.

I hoped the two would not start bickering. Anger surged through me, then prickling fear and contrition. No lights on cell phones back then. We were in the dark ages, 1971.

Seconds later, a small light went on, and I felt hope. It flashed back and forth, approaching us. A stirring of voices and movement came too. The nun, a flashlight in hand, was asking to be let through, squeezing past people, assuring them that everything was fine.

Lily didn't move aside. She blocked the nun's way and said, "You're not leaving us."

Not clearly a threat, an order, or a question, her statement implied all three.

The nun's lips moved in a vague, ghostly manner: "A fuse burned out. It happens. So I have to go topside where they are to replace it. The lights will be back on momentarily."

Lily said, "I need to go with you. I'm sick. I may throw up."

"A few more minutes, please. I'll be right back. Don't worry. You're safe here."

And she whisked herself past us, her black habit flying up like the wings of a bat, striking my bare legs and an arm. I leaned away from her and bumped into a wall I couldn't see.

Lily said, "I'm going to follow her," and stepped apart.

"Wait, Honey." I grabbed her arm and looked for the nun. The walls seemed to have absorbed her light. There was nothing to see, only blackness.

A few feet away, somebody yelped. There were stomping sounds. "Something ran over my feet. I think it was a rat." Somebody else said, "Settle down." Another voice: "Where is that woman?" Another, "How long will this take?"

Lily spit a word in my ear, "Vermin," and her hand shook in mine.

I shivered but said calmly, "No one can see anything. Control yourself."

Somebody lit a match farther up the tunnel. When it went out, a cigarette lighter rasped, and a flame danced for a few seconds. I saw a cigarette's end burning pink, then red, off and on like a traffic signal. The smell of burning tobacco reached me, and I welcomed its familiar odor.

I also guessed that the smoke was following the nun. A draft was flowing back to where we'd come in, back to the entrance, the opening to the outside. I felt the urge to follow the smoke. When someone said, "Let's get out of here," I was about to agree.

But Jerome said, "Listen, everyone. Remain calm. The sister will be back shortly. The lights will return."

The voice of reason. From him, no less. I was surprised. I was also the oldest of our group by two years.

I said loudly enough for everyone to hear, "Yes, give her a chance to change the fuse."

There was a storm of other comments.

I grew afraid to move. We could get lost. The darkness was so thick and the lights so dim we could have passed side tunnels without realizing it. It was very stupid to come here. What if the walls collapsed? How sturdy could they be? Shouldn't they have buttressing of some sort? We could be buried, suffocated here. Panic threatened to overwhelm me.

How long we stayed in the dark is questionable. It seemed a long time. Fifteen minutes? Half an hour? Admittedly, it could have been only a few minutes. My sense of time was off.

All in our party started moving simultaneously, presumably toward the entrance. Maybe holding hands or belts or whatever was available ahead and behind, as I did. Of course, I couldn't look and see. How far we actually went was questionable.

When the lights came on and the nun appeared, we told her in no uncertain terms that we wanted to leave. Without argument, she turned, led us out, then bid farewell to each of us at the bus, repeatedly apologizing for the lights' failure.

She was expecting donations? Anger made me reserve the right to give none. Surely our hosts were paying her religious order for the catacombs tour, such as it was. But they'd probably picked the least developed catacomb they could get for the lowest cost.

What kind of hosts would send potential clients into a cut-rate, dangerous catacomb, whatever its name was? I expected nothing better from whatever else they had prepared for us.

Breathing the relatively fresh air of Rome, observing the dusk studded with lights and the breadth of the sky darkening above us brought a relief greater than I'd felt when first accepting the invitation to dinner and a cool bus. This was Deliverance. The catacomb had taken us down into ourselves. The depths had tested our spirit. We'd encountered fear and doubt and sensed our vulnerability. I may have even prayed. I had fervently hoped for escape.

Lily said she was certainly glad that was over. Jerome said he needed a drink. Carol said, "There'll be wine with dinner, Dear. The man who invited us said so."

Who were our inviters? What were they selling? On the bus to yet another destination, I had the uneasy sense of being manipulated, of naively entering a situation that could have grave consequences. Had we willingly stepped into a trap?

◆

Ten minutes later, I found out they'd planned the evening much more thoroughly. The hotel had spotless, aromatic restrooms adjacent to our spacious first-floor meeting room. Using the facilities, awaiting our turn at the shiny porcelain furnishings, we men were in a jovial mood.

One said, "What're they gonna do now, poison us?"

Another said, "I saw a pile of brochures that looked like they're selling real estate."

That idea evoked laughter, too, including from me. Outlandish! Crazy, if true. I had no interest in buying Italian property. Did we look rich? We had no money to invest.

Two men in suits near the restroom exits directed us into the dining area. "Please, find your name on a table and sit there. Your meal is ready to be served."

They had more than that ready. First, they divided us by couples. Each was seated side by side at one of nine cozy, disconnected rectangular tables facing a movie screen onto which a slide projector threw bright pictures of tropical scenery. Facing the pair at each table, another chair was for a salesman.

Ours was Gary, in his 20s, about our age. He shook our hands, freed a chair for my wife, pushed it beneath her as she sat, verified our names on his clipboard's list, gave us menus, explained the entrees, poured water, offered wine, poured that for us, and smiled. "I'm glad you joined us for dinner."

Gary reminded me of our friends and relatives back home: white, lean, clean cut, affable, in a casual brown suit without a tie, top button open on something like a green polo shirt under the nicely pressed coat—a salesman who resembled us hiding beneath the grime.

I drank my wine glass dry, and he refilled it.

I said, "Thank you, Gary. Now, what're you guys selling? I heard it was real estate."

He laughed. "Frank, my boss, will briefly describe our program when we're all seated. Where are you folks from?"

Smooth and evasive. He was maneuvering, setting us up. I said, "Your air-conditioned ride was nice, but the catacomb tour scared us. The lights went out and stayed off so long we felt trapped and nearly panicked."

He frowned. "I didn't know that. Frank will be disappointed."

My wife said, "We're from Ohio." We chit-chatted like that until the presentation began.

Frank, middle-aged, suave in suit and tie, welcomed us all and finally announced what they were selling: Land in Florida.

It was such a cliché even back then, I almost laughed aloud.

Frank went on smoothly. Our food was coming, but first, this idea to consider while we ate: a small investment blossoming into a flower of plenty in just a few years. Florida was the fastest-growing area in North America. Investments in it had quadrupled in worth in the last five years, as had the population. An investment could be small enough to be unnoticed yet bloom into a beautiful pile. It could be done in installments.

Five minutes maybe, and he stopped. We ate, and it was good. I drank a bit more wine, and it was good. We chatted with Gary into dessert.

That's when he shifted our talk onto the properties for sale, our needs, desires, and financial capabilities. Gary asked, and my wife answered. I tried to figure out the game: keep us talking, agreeing where possible, leading us toward the question of specific cost and property for sale. Lily asked for details, and Gary provided them printed on glossy flyers with pictures and maps. He pointed out the location of the pictures in the state, enthusing about the possibilities for expanding our financial security.

None of our group had left the room. The same presentation seemed to be going on at every table. Two salesmen were standing, bending across their table, pointing at something their "guests" appeared to be reading. I heard my wife saying yes, something was possible, startling me. Was she falling for this sales pitch or just continuing to be nice?

"Excuse me, Gary," I said. "I don't want to waste your time and energy any further. We aren't going to buy into this scheme. We don't have the money or the inclination. I'm sorry, but that's the truth."

The least I could do was save us from the falseness. We had agreed to listen to the company's presentation in exchange for the tour, meal, and cool air. Our commitment was complete. We still had to get back to our parked car and drive to our campgrounds.

Lily said, "Why don't you let Gary go on? Don't be so negative."

I shook my head. "Look, you and I have already agreed not to fall for what-ever this scheme was. It's not Gary's fault. I'm not blaming him, but let's be honest here, okay?"

Gary said, "Bill, I wouldn't call it a scheme."

I said, "Well, frankly, maybe you'd buy land without seeing it, but we wouldn't."

There were further remarks about how we could visit Florida and see the property in person. On the flyers we'd received, Gary did indicate phone numbers, names, and addresses related to his company. I felt the pressure he was putting on us but resisted politely, and he gradually accepted our rejection.

When two other couples left the room, I excused myself, went to our com-panions' table, and asked if they were ready to leave.

"Not yet," Jerome said and turned back to the salesman who was showing him what looked like a schedule of payments.

Carol said to me, "I think he's going to sign up."

"Really?" I said to him, "All you've seen are pictures, Jerome. Come on."

"Please, sir," their salesman said to me. "We're in a serious discussion here."

I said, "Are either of you considering Carol? She's not interested, are you?"

She shook her head. "No."

Jerome said to her, "We haven't even discussed this."

"Dear, you know we have student loans to pay off. We already have debts."

I said, "You've only heard stories, Jerome, and you haven't been there and seen the land. How do you know it'll go up in value? Or even that you can build on it? Don't get drawn into a debt you'll regret. Give yourself time to think about a deal like this."

The salesman stood and faced me. "Sir, please, you're creating a scene."

I looked around. People at the two nearest tables were watching us, but the others continued with their own business. Frank, over at the slide projector, was watching us.

Carol said, "Well, I don't want to do it."

I shook my head. "Boy, oh boy. Okay, we're leaving. We'll wait for you two in the hotel lobby. Of course, do what you want?"

Awkwardly, Lily and I sat in the lobby for twenty minutes. We checked the map, orienting ourselves, finding the way to where I'd parked our Ford rental car, British variety.

The day had worn me down, and the people working there kept eyeing us. The hotel was, after all, a business, and our image might discourage those who considered staying there.

When Carol and Jerome emerged from the meeting room, they were quiet but anxious to get back to our tent.

Walking dark streets to the car, I said, "Did you buy something? Did you do it?"

Carol said, "No, we decided not to."

Jerome said, "I just played along to see what they'd say. I wasn't serious, you know?"

Their faces flashed in the passing car lights. Maybe he was joking, but he'd seemed serious talking to his salesman. Maybe he was embarrassed and didn't want to admit the truth.

Walking along in the cradle of Western civilization, the home of our religion, here, far from our homes, I was aware that American capitalism had reached out and tried to pick our pockets, tried to sell us a bill of goods.

Somehow that seemed appropriate.

Writing connects the dots for Bill Vernon. Draws lines between his inner and outer life. Explores the old and the new. Discovers shapes and colors them with vignettes of his college teaching, Marine Corps enlistment, outdoor activities, international folk dancing, places, and people. His novel *Old Town* is a murder mystery with a historical slant. Recently published shorter things include nonfiction at *Agape Review*, *Smoky Blue Literary & Arts*, *Still Points Arts Quarterly*, and fiction at *Synkroniciti Magazine*, *Superpresent*, and *New Feathers Anthology*.

The Woodshed

Things That Are Not Wholly Normal

"Sometimes, the biggest secrets you can only tell a stranger."
— Michelle Hodkin, *The Evolution of Mara Dyer*

Being Normal

Steven Kenneth Smith

*B*oy, *that's one hot chick.*

Jimmy Stephenson looked up in surprise at the grown-up sitting beside him on the bus. Earl Burg. The man hadn't said anything out loud; it was just Jimmy's talent for picking up thoughts.

Nice tits and a big round—

As usual, once Jimmy became aware that he was picking up someone's thoughts, he quit being able to do so, especially when those thoughts disturbed him. He looked toward the front of the bus, where a young woman in black tights and a blue tank top stood in the aisle. She'd gotten up so the lady in the window seat could get out. Her back was to him, so he couldn't get her name. He turned back to his comic book and shifted away from the guy beside him as far as the seat would allow. Jimmy wasn't quite sure what he'd meant by "hot chick," but it didn't sound nice.

A short time later, the bus stopped again, and the woman stood and made her way to the door. Jimmy glimpsed her face as she left and caught her name: Julia Davenport. It was another aspect of his talent. He knew peoples' names when he saw their faces. That part seemed to work always whether he was stressed or not.

Mr. Burg gave an appreciative nod. "Nice," he said. Jimmy didn't need his talent to pick that up. He'd said it softly but aloud.

Jimmy's seatmate was respectably dressed, and a brown leather briefcase rested on his lap. He'd taken the seat at the stop after Jimmy had boarded the bus. Jimmy guessed he was about as old as his father. Mr. Burg returned to reading a magazine now that the woman wasn't there to ogle.

The next stop was one earlier than the closest one to Jimmy's home. He got off anyway, so he wouldn't have to sit next to that guy any longer. It was only another fifteen minutes to walk home from there. He stuffed his comic book into his backpack and slipped the straps over his shoulders for the walk home.

The air was warm for mid-September, and the trees had only a bare hint of color starting to show. The sun warmed his back under his windbreaker as he walked along the nearly empty residential sidewalks. The library books in his pack weighed it down, though the thought of the novels inside made him eager to get home. Although only eleven, he read on a level that put comic books beneath him. He identified with Peter Parker, though, due to Spiderman's "Spidey sense," so he kept up with that one.

Jimmy's father, Allen Stephenson, was stirring a pot on the stove when Jimmy came home. The aroma of spaghetti sauce with ground beef filled the house, and Jimmy's mouth watered. His father turned toward the kitchen door when Jimmy came in. *Where the hell have you been?* Jimmy heard him think. Out loud, his dad said, "You're a little late getting back. Did something happen?"

"I walked home from the stop at Market Street instead of getting off at the regular stop. The man sitting by me on the bus made me feel weird."

If he touched Jimmy, I'll kill the bastard—Allen thought, and then Jimmy's talent cut off. Allen put the spoon down on a spoon rest. "Are you okay? Did he do anything to you?"

"He didn't touch me. He said some nasty things about a lady."

Jimmy's father pursed his lips. "I'm sorry you had to hear that. It's a shame that some people can't be respectful. Get cleaned up for dinner. Your mom should be home soon." He turned back to the pot on the stove.

Jimmy ran upstairs and dropped his book bag on his bed. In the bathroom, he wet his hands, made a brief swipe over a bar of soap, rinsed, and then dried his hands on the towel hanging by the sink, leaving a dark stain behind.

Back in his room, he emptied the book bag and spread the books on the bed. A worn copy of *Have Spacesuit, Will Travel*, by Robert Heinlein, caught his eye. The cover showed a man in a 1950s guess at what a spacesuit would look like who was taking a purposeful step forward, a grim expression on his face. Jimmy pushed the other books aside and stretched out on the bed to read.

◆

By the time he was seven, Jimmy had realized he was different from others, that other people—*normal* people—couldn't pick up the thoughts of the ones nearby. He'd earned a black eye on the playground for being right about what some older kid had thought but had not said out loud once. Usually, though, he'd earned ridicule before he'd learned to keep quiet about his talent by being unable to perform on demand.

It wasn't often even a useful talent. It was often upsetting to know someone's unfiltered opinion or desire, like with that man on the bus, Earl Burg. It didn't even help him with examinations in school. Usually, his talent left him under the stress of taking tests, but on the occasions where it didn't, he found his answers were more reliable than those of the ones around him. He was a better student than most of them.

It did at least give him the right code word to deflect his father's anger at the thought that someone on the bus might have "touched" him. Of course, if he hadn't known Mr. Burg's nasty thoughts, he wouldn't have felt weird in the first place, wouldn't have gotten off the bus early, and his dad wouldn't have wondered why he was late. More and more, Jimmy found himself wishing he didn't have this talent.

◆

A week passed without any particular incidents. The fifth grade was almost a month underway, and his best friend, Erik, sat beside him on the city bus coming home from the library on a Tuesday afternoon. They had books open in their laps—science fiction, of course—reading as the bus made its way. A good time for them was when they each read separate books together, then swapped them and discussed their merits. Lately, Jimmy was reading a lot of old science fiction from the fifties, sixties, and seventies. It was fun to see where the predictions were right and where the authors had missed their guesses.

As Jimmy sat there reading, his talent kicked in. *First, Eddie grabs him and pulls him out of sight. Then I push his head back and cut his throat. We'll take his wallet so it looks—*

Jimmy gasped and dropped his book. His seat was on the inside, and the book landed on the floor in the aisle. The man sitting on the inside seat across the aisle picked it up and held it out toward him. He gave Jimmy a smile.

Jimmy stared at him wide-eyed. Herman Myers. His name was Herman Joseph Myers, a tall, thin man wearing a dark blue sweatshirt and light gray slacks. His straight black hair was trimmed short and combed neatly to the side, parted on his left. He'd seen this guy on the bus before on his way home from the library, but he'd never previously picked up any thoughts from him. After a pause long enough that Herman's smile wavered and he gave his head a questioning tilt, Jimmy took the book from him, his hand shaking.

Jimmy gulped. "Th—thanks."

"No problem." He went back to reading a sports magazine.

Jimmy closed the book. Erik looked over at him. "Are you okay? You didn't finish that one already, did you?"

"No. No, I'm not finished. I just—uh—I just don't feel like reading right now."

Erik furrowed his brows. "Who are you, and what have you done with Jimmy?" It was a stock phrase for Erik lately. He'd heard it on a TV show somewhere and used it on every occasion he could fit it in.

"I just don't want to read right now."

"Why not?"

"I just don't. Leave me alone, okay?"

Erik stared at him for a second, and his eyebrows lifted. "Okay. Sorry." He turned back to his book.

Jimmy put his head down. When he tired of that, he tried looking past Erik out the window. He looked at the backs of the heads of the people seated ahead of him. Anywhere but toward Mr. Herman Meyers.

Mr. Myers still sat there when the bus stopped at Jimmy and Erik's street. Jimmy slid past him, keeping as far away as possible, but the man didn't look up. Jimmy hurried out of the bus and jumped from the top step to the sidewalk. Maybe the guy was going over a story in his head. Maybe he's an author who writes crime stories. Maybe he was remembering a movie or something. None of those possibilities seemed believable. Herman Joseph Meyers and someone named Eddie planned to murder someone. He was sure of it.

"You want to come to my house and play video games?" Erik said. "I got Minecraft."

Jimmy gave his head a quick shake and turned to Erik as if surprised he was still there. "Uh—no. I got to get home."

"You can call your dad from my place. C'mon, it'll be fun."

"I got homework."

Erik tilted his head. "Who are you and—"

"—and what did you do with Jimmy," Jimmy finished for him. "Yeah, I know. I don't want to play video games right now. I gotta get home." He ran off, leaving Erik standing with his mouth open.

♦

Jimmy ran straight to his room when he got home. His dad called, "Jimmy—" as he thundered up the stairs, but Jimmy slammed the door before he heard the rest of his father's sentence. He threw himself on the bed and pulled the pillow over his head.

A short time later, he heard the door open but didn't look up. After a second, his dad sat on the bed next to him. "Jimmy, what's the matter?"

"I don't want to talk about it right now."

His father laid a hand on Jimmy's shoulder. "Did someone hurt you? 'Cause if so, I need to know about it."

Jimmy kept his head buried under the pillow, even though it made it a little hard to breathe. "No one hurt me. I don't want to talk."

Jimmy's father sat there for another few seconds, then removed his hand and stood. "We're here if you decide to talk. We want to help you, and we need to know if something's wrong."

"Nothing's wrong."

That's obviously not true. "Well, your mom's taking a deposition tonight, and she's going to be home late. How about you and I go out for some pizza after a while when you're feeling better?"

Jimmy paused a second or two. "I guess."

"Okay. Come downstairs when you're ready." A moment later, the door opened and then clicked shut again.

Jimmy waited for another minute, then peeked out from under the pillow. His father was gone. Rolling over, he sat up and clutched the pillow to his belly. There was a tight knot in his chest when he remembered Herman Meyers' thoughts. He'd been so matter-of-fact about it, like killing someone was something he did every day. Jimmy felt he should do something, but he didn't know what. No one would believe him, and he didn't know where or when the murder was going to occur.

Then it hit him like a blow to the gut. He'd picked up his father's thought, "That's obviously not true," despite being upset. His heartbeats sounded loud in his ears. He'd recently started Boy Scouts, and two points of the scout law, "A scout is brave" and "A scout is helpful," came to his mind. Jimmy gritted his teeth and took a deep breath.

He often saw that guy on the bus on his way home from the library. If he could get past his block on his talent again while near him, he might be able to get enough information to warn the intended victim somehow.

Jimmy swung himself out of bed and tossed the pillow in the general direction of the headboard. "Dad, I'm ready," he called as he came out of his room.

When Jimmy and his dad got back from the Pizza Palace, Jimmy's mom, Rachel, was already home. She greeted them at the door and gave Jimmy a hug, then kissed her husband.

His dad rubbed her back. "How'd it go?"

"Not bad. I can't get specific."

"Yeah, I know."

Jimmy hung his jacket on the coat tree by the door. "Are you defending a criminal?"

His mom turned to him. "I'm representing a defendant. He's not a criminal unless he's convicted."

"What did he do?" Jimmy asked.

"I can't get into that. Do you have homework?"

"A little math."

"Well, get it done. Your dad or I will check it afterward. We have some ice cream in the freezer for when you're finished."

◆

Later, as Jimmy sat at the kitchen table and his mom looked over his homework, Jimmy asked, "If you knew someone was planning to do something bad, what would you do?"

Rachel looked up from the paper at Jimmy, silent for a few seconds. Then she said, "It's almost never possible to know something like that for certain. If I really thought someone intended to commit a crime, I guess I'd have to do something, but it'd depend on the specific situation."

"What if you knew someone planned to kill somebody?"

She furrowed her brows. "I can't imagine a situation where a client would tell me that, even if that's what they intended."

"What if they're not a client? What if you happened to hear them talking about it, and you thought they really meant it?"

Rachel put Jimmy's paper down on the table. "I guess, in that case, I'd have to go to the police with what I knew." She raised an eyebrow. "What's this about?"

Jimmy shrugged. "I'm just wondering."

She furrowed her brows, lips pursed. "Jimmy, despite what you might see on television, we almost never know the facts—all the facts—about a case. But even when I'm as sure as I can be that my client is guilty, I have to represent him to the best of my ability. That's what a public defender does. That's how our system works."

Jimmy nodded. "I know that I guess. But what if you *knew* that someone intended to kill someone else in the future?"

"We can never know for certain what someone intends to do, and an intention is not a crime. It's only a crime if they do it."

Jimmy nodded. He heard his mom thinking that there were many caveats and exceptions to that statement but that she didn't want to complicate the conversation with them. He'd have to look up the word "caveat" when he got a chance. "All right, thanks. Is my math okay?"

◆

The next day after school, Jimmy went to the library again and took the bus home. Herman Myers was there, sitting near the middle of the bus. Swallowing hard, Jimmy sat just behind him next to a lady with graying, dark brown hair— Ethel Williams—who had a magazine out. He took a book from his backpack and set the pack down at his feet.

For a minute or two, Jimmy just sat with the book closed on his lap, concentrating on the back of Mr. Meyer's head, but nothing came through.

"Aren't you going to read your book?" the woman beside him said.

Jimmy turned to her, startled out of his concentration.

"*Citizen of the Galaxy*," Mrs. Williams said, pointing to Jimmy's book. "You took it out of your bag, but then you didn't open it." She leaned toward him as if sharing a secret. "I read that one when I was young. I'm surprised young folks are still reading it."

"I've been reading a lot of old science fiction lately," Jimmy said. "Stuff from the nineteen fifties through the seventies."

"I used to read a lot of Sci-Fi myself, Clarke, Asimov, Heinlein, and such, but lately, my taste in reading material has been more toward crime stories and murder mysteries."

My killing Joe Blenford will always remain a mystery. It's perfect.

Jimmy took a sharp breath and stared at the back of Mr. Meyer's head.

Mrs. Williams' eyebrows raised. "Is something wrong? You've gone all wide-eyed."

"No—ah—nothing. It's nothing. Excuse me a second." He picked up his backpack and pulled out a pencil. On the back of the library checkout receipt for his book, he wrote, "Joe Blenford," and stuck the note back inside. Jimmy closed the book, but after a few seconds, he sensed that the woman was about to speak to him again. To discourage that, he opened the book and tried to read.

Reading wasn't successful. He stared at the words on the page but couldn't concentrate on them at all. Finally, the bus came to a halt at the bus stop just before his, at Market Street. Close enough. He didn't want to share the bus with that man anymore. As he stood and opened his backpack to put the book inside, someone coming down the aisle bumped into him, and Jimmy dropped the book in the aisle. It landed on its spine and fell open where he'd stuck the receipt. Herman Meyers bent to pick up the book and handed it to Jimmy with a smile.

"Making a habit of this, aren't we?" he said. Then he noticed the name Jimmy had written on the slip, and the smile evaporated. He stared into Jimmy's face, his eyes hard.

Jimmy grabbed the book and hurried out, leaping to the sidewalk from the top step of the bus. With his hands full, holding the book and backpack, he almost fell but caught himself in time. Still gripping the book, he slipped on the backpack and ran down the sidewalk along Market Street instead of heading directly to his house. He looked back to check if Herman Meyers had gotten off too, and he was relieved to see he hadn't.

Halfway down the block, Jimmy staggered to a stop. He leaned over a boxwood shrub and threw up. That man—that murderer—had been so casual about it. He'd felt satisfied—proud even—of his ability to do a job well. Jimmy hadn't detected whether the murder had already occurred or not, though. He turned the man's phrase over in his head: "My killing Joe Blenford will always remain a mystery." It could mean either one, that he had done it, or that he intended to do it.

He looked at the book still clutched in his left hand. There was a slimy smear of green vomit on the plastic-coated dust cover. He wiped it off on his trousers, knowing his dad would be mad about that, but the reflex to protect a library book took over. Then it occurred to him that Mr. Meyers had thought, "It's perfect," not, "It was perfect," after his expression of pride. That indicated the murder hadn't occurred yet. Maybe.

He wiped his mouth on his coat sleeve. He needed to get home before it got too late, or his dad would question him. He started off again, and by the time he'd reached the end of the hedge in that yard, he was running.

♦

Jimmy avoided his father until he'd gotten the book cleaned up a little better and changed his pants. In the family room, he sat at the computer and googled "Joe Blenford" and his city's name, but nothing that looked very useful came up. Too many names, and he knew nothing to narrow down the search. There was no obituary, and no article about a murder, anyway. He scrolled down a couple of pages and was about to give up when he saw an article about a "J. Allen Blenford," who was prosecuting the leader of a small-time organized crime gang.

He tried reading through the article. There was a lot of legal jargon, but the gist was clear. Someone named Jonathan Gibson was in jail for conspiracy to commit murder, and Mr. Blenford was in charge of the prosecution. Gibson had escaped conviction on several other charges before, but according to the article from the local newspaper, the case against him was pretty strong this time.

He tried googling Herman Meyers too, but nothing came up. He did another search on "J. Allen Blenford" and skimmed some of the sites. One of them confirmed that the "J" stood for "Joseph."

"Hi, Jimmy. What are you reading?"

Jimmy jumped at his mom's voice and knocked the mouse off the desk. He spun the chair around. "Uh—nothing. Just looking around."

His mother picked up the mouse and clicked the "back" button on the browser page a couple of times, leaning down and reaching over Jimmy's shoulder. She furrowed her brows. "Why are you reading about Al Blenford? And who's Herman Meyers?"

"You know Joe Blenford?" Jimmy blurted.

"Of course. He's the city's Chief Prosecutor. I work with people from his office all the time." Her eyes narrowed. "How'd you know his first name is Joseph? He always goes by his middle name. I didn't know it myself until a couple of months ago."

Jimmy looked down at the floor. "I overheard someone," he mumbled.

His mom straightened back up. "Who'd you overhear? Where?"

Jimmy squirmed in his seat and looked out the window. "It was on the bus."

She took Jimmy's chin and turned his face toward hers. "Look at me, Jimmy. I don't want you bothering people from the prosecutor's office. I especially don't want you trying to contact any of them. It could look like I'm trying to improperly influence the prosecution about my cases. You could get me into big trouble." *Theoretically, but not likely,* Jimmy heard her think. She released his chin. "Do you understand me?"

"Yes, ma'am."

"Who'd you overhear?"

Jimmy gulped. "It was Herman Meyers."

"Who's he?"

"Some guy I saw on the bus." Jimmy's lip quivered, and a tear formed at the corner of his left eye, threatening to drop off.

Rachel squatted to put her face more on Jimmy's level. "How do you know that man? How old is he, and where's he from?"

"I see—see him on the bus. He's old. Probably forty or more. I don't know where he's from." Jimmy wiped his eyes with his sleeve.

"How do you know his name?" Rachel asked.

Jimmy shrugged. "I heard him say it."

He looked up to the right. He's lying. "Are you sure that's how you know it?"

Jimmy concentrated on looking directly into his mother's face. "Yes."

She pursed her lips. "How did Mr. Blenford come up?"

Jimmy erupted into tears. "Mr. Meyers said he was going to kill him!" He lurched forward and wrapped his arms around his mother. Off balance for a moment, she teetered back, but she caught herself and stood again, pulling Jimmy's arms away.

"Jimmy, that's a very serious accusation. You can't just go around saying things like that."

"It's true! He said someone named Eddie was going to pull him out of sight and that he was going to push his head back and cut his throat."

"Why would he say something like that on a bus when someone might hear him? This just doesn't sound believable."

Jimmy wiped his eyes. "He didn't know I could hear him."

"Still, he wouldn't say something like that out loud."

Jimmy stood silent, sniffling, trying to figure out what to do. Finally, he said, "He didn't say it out loud."

His mom shook her head. "I can't believe he'd even whisper something like that on a bus."

"He didn't whisper it either. Sometimes—sometimes, I can hear things that people are thinking."

"Oh, Jimmy, this is no time for make-believe. You've got to drop this."

"It's real. I swear. I heard him think that just like I heard you think that I was lying because I looked up to my right, and earlier when you thought, 'Theoretically, but not likely,' when you said you could get into trouble if I contacted Mr. Blenford."

She opened her mouth as if to speak, then closed it. Her eyes widened. "What am I thinking now?"

Jimmy looked down and wiped his eyes again. "I don't know. It doesn't work all the time."

Yeah. I thought so.

Jimmy's head snapped back up. "There! You thought, 'Yeah. I thought so.'"

Rachel jerked her head back, and her brows shot up. She ran her fingers through her hair. "Try it again."

Jimmy closed his eyes. There was nothing for a few seconds. Then he got it. He parroted what he heard from his mother's thoughts: "Course of human events it becomes necessary for one people to—"

His mom took a sharp breath. "That's enough." She stepped to the couch and dropped into it, then looked up at Jimmy, who'd followed her to the couch but hadn't sat. "How long have you been able to do this?"

"Forever. But it doesn't work all the time."

Jimmy's father came to the doorway. "Dinner's about done. Jimmy, could you set...." His voice trailed off as he saw the expressions on Rachel's and Jimmy's faces. Rachel stared at him with wide eyes, and Jimmy stood with his eyes downcast, his hands hanging at his sides.

"What's wrong?"

"Jimmy, go up to your room for a few minutes. Your dad and I need to talk."

Jimmy went to the door of his room in the upstairs hallway, opened it, and then closed it again, still standing in the hall. He sneaked back to the top of the stairs and crouched low by the wall, trying to hear. He couldn't make out anything at first, then his father said, "That's ridiculous!" and his mother replied,

"I know, but how do you explain—" Then she lowered her voice to the point that Jimmy couldn't hear.

Jimmy sat back against the wall, pulled his knees up to his chest, and closed his eyes. He concentrated for a good thirty seconds, but he got nothing. Too far away. Or he was too upset. He ran fingers through his hair, then finger-combed it flat again.

His mom believed him, but he wasn't sure she would convince his dad unless they got him to "perform" for him too. A tear ran down his cheek, and he wiped it off on his shoulder. Whispering, so his parents couldn't hear him, he said, "I never asked for this. I wish I were normal."

Jimmy just picked at his food at dinner, even though it was one of his favorites, broiled chicken with potatoes and glazed carrots. No one spoke much, but Jimmy caught his father staring at him a few times. He hadn't been able to catch any of his dad's thoughts when they asked him to try earlier, though. Finally, he asked to be excused with about half his dinner left on the plate.

Back in his room, he opened his math book, but it was hard to concentrate on the assignment, a sheet of stacks of four five-digit numbers he had to add. He plowed his way into the assignment, though he didn't see the point of it. It was the same skill as adding two or three three-digit numbers, just more tedious. Besides, if he needed to add four five-digit numbers, he'd use a calculator or a spreadsheet. At least concentrating on the problems kept him from thinking about Herman Meyers.

As he leaned over the paper on his desk, adding the numbers, his talent kicked in. *I'm going to see if I can get Jimmy tested.* It was his mom.

His dad's thoughts followed. *Okay, I guess that can't hurt.*

Jimmy sat upright. This was different. They were talking to each other, not just thinking the words. He didn't remember his talent doing that before. He sat still, concentrating, but he got nothing else. He didn't know what she meant by "tested," but he didn't like the sound of it.

After a minute or so of trying, he sighed and turned back to his math worksheet. Midway through the next problem, he detected his mom thinking. *I just don't know what I'm going to do about Al Blenford.*

The pencil dropped onto the desk as Jimmy sprang upright in the chair. This time she'd just thought it. He couldn't say why he knew that. He just knew. He looked at the worksheet, and his eyes widened. He picked up the pencil and re-started the problem. *What if they want to take Jimmy away?* His dad this time, and it was a non-spoken thought.

Jimmy took in a sharp breath. Take him away? The pencil fell to the floor. His heart raced. The scene in his mind was from the old movie *ET, the Extraterrestrial,* where the scientists had captured ET and conducted tests on him. He needed to leave. Tonight. His stomach hurt.

His scout backpack sat at the bottom of his closet, and his sleeping bag was on the upper shelf. He had to move his desk chair to the closet to reach it. It and the pack were new, birthday gifts after he'd graduated from Cub Scouts a few months ago. There was room in the pack for a few extra clothes stuffed in along the side by the sleeping bag.

He checked his clock radio. Too early, only 7:48. He'd have to wait until his parents were asleep, and that might not be until eleven o'clock or later. He moved the backpack into the closet again and put the chair back by the desk. He set the alarm for midnight.

The arithmetic worksheet still lay on the desk, about half done. His mom or dad would be up after a while to check it, so he found his pencil and continued working. It was slow going, what with the buzz of his parent's thoughts in his head and, once, those of a neighbor—Andrew Mason—whom he saw through the window walking a dog along the sidewalk while ruminating about having to fire someone.

◆

The walk to the city center where the courthouse stood was long and creepy after midnight. He tried to stay out of view of cars he saw as much as possible as he went. A small park stood across the street from the courthouse. Using his flashlight as little as possible, he worked his way underneath a spruce tree whose lower limbs rested on the ground. It was hard to work out his sleeping bag and crawl inside, wiggling between the branches, but finally, he was in. Dreamless sleep came quickly to him.

Birdsong woke Jimmy the next morning before sunrise. It had been an uncomfortable night, and sleep was fitful, curled between the low branches of the spruce tree. Some scratchy pine needles had made it inside his sleeping bag. He thought for a second that his parents would be mad about that, then he realized they'd have something a lot more serious to be angry about if they found him.

Clouds covered the sky, but it wasn't terribly cold. The sidewalk nearby was almost deserted. Trying to make as little noise as possible, he wiggled out of the sleeping bag and managed to stuff it into his backpack. The dark green cloth of the pack camouflaged well under the pine boughs. He pulled some branches into position to conceal it further and left his improvised campsite, careful to remain unseen in the dim, pre-dawn light as he emerged, carrying the book he'd brought with him. His stomach growled, but he hadn't packed any food. He only had a few dollars, and that wouldn't buy much. Nothing nearby was open where he could buy something to eat anyway.

The courthouse was a massive structure, built more than a century ago of local stone, with ornate architectural details and arched windows. Jimmy sat on a bench directly across the street from the main entrance. He held the book in his lap, unopened for the moment, and observed the few people walking along the sidewalks nearby. As he looked into their faces, he caught their names, but only occasionally was he able to "hear" what they were thinking. His plan, to the extent that he had one, was to watch for Mr. Blenford and then try to warn him. How he would do that in such a way that Mr. Blenford might take him seriously, he still hadn't figured out.

He'd been there about an hour, and the clouds had begun to break up, showing patches of blue in the east, when he looked down the block across the street and saw Herman Meyers approach. Jimmy stood, careful not to attract attention, and moved behind an arborvitae standing like a bushy green exclamation point beside the bench. Trying to remain concealed by the tree as much as possible, Jimmy watched him as he passed the courthouse and stopped at a newsstand on the next block up, which stood beside an alley.

Mr. Meyers unlocked the side door to the newsstand and then appeared inside as he opened up the bifold shutters covering the front of the structure. A moment later, he set a bundle of papers on the counter and put them into a rack. Then he pulled up another bundle.

As Jimmy watched, another man approached the newsstand from the opposite direction and stopped. Jimmy concentrated on his face, and after a couple of seconds, he got his name: Edward Baker. He took in a sharp breath. Eddie.

Eddie and Herman talked for a moment, then Eddie went around the newsstand toward the alley and disappeared from view. Herman put another bundle of papers on the counter.

Jimmy backed around the arborvitae toward the bench, concentrating on keeping concealed from Herman Meyer's view.

"A little late for you to be out here on a school day, isn't it?"

Jimmy jumped and spun around. A police officer stood behind him, hands on his hips. He was a young man, probably in his early or mid-twenties—Devon McAllister. A fringe of closely cropped kinky black hair showed under his cap above his ears, and his face was a medium milk-chocolate brown, pocked here and there on the cheeks by the marks of ingrown hairs.

"Uh—yes, sir." Jimmy gulped and thought fast. "School's out today. Teacher's meeting. I'm waiting for the library to open at nine o'clock." He held up his book.

Officer McAllister nodded. *Sir. That's a good sign.* "What's your name?"

"Jimmy Russell," he said, selecting a last name from the main character of *Have Spacesuit, Will Travel.*

"Got any identification?"

"No, sir."

"Where are your parents?"

"They're—uh—at work. Mom works at Julie Anne's." He gave the name of a woman's clothing shop nearby that his mom had occasionally dragged him to when he was younger before he was old enough for her to drop him off at the library while she shopped. He held his breath.

Officer McAllister nodded. Jimmy heard him think. *Damn, schools don't care about the problems they cause for folks with these odd days off. This kid looks okay, anyhow.* "Okay. I'll be around by the courthouse. Call out if anyone bothers you. Hope you enjoy your day off school."

"Thank you, Officer." After Officer McAllister left, Jimmy let out the breath he'd been holding. He retook a seat on the bench, positioning himself so that the arborvitae blocked Herman's view of him. The sun cleared the top of the library to his right, and he opened the book but didn't read it. With quick looks up as people came by and then back to his book, he continued to watch for Mr. Blenford as the morning advanced.

It was almost nine o'clock before Jimmy saw him. Joseph Allen Blenford was a medium-tall, slightly heavyset man starting to go bald, carrying a briefcase. He wore a dark grey business suit and a light blue shirt with a dark tie. Jimmy stood and hurried to the crosswalk, realizing a little late that he wouldn't make it across the street in time before Mr. Blenford went inside. His stomach knotted.

However, as Jimmy waited for the light, Mr. Blenford passed the courthouse and continued up the street. A couple of other people joined Jimmy, waiting for the crosswalk, a white-haired woman with a cane—Gloria Steinburg—and a girl of about 13 years old who appeared to be with the old lady—Tamara Steinburg.

Jimmy considered crossing against the light, but the traffic was too heavy, and Officer McAllister was watching him. He tried to focus on "hearing" Mr. Blenford, but he got nothing.

Mr. Blenford continued walking ahead, and finally, Jimmy realized where he was going. He was heading toward the newsstand. A chill went through him. This was it.

He looked at the woman beside him, and a desperate plan took shape in his mind. As his mouth went dry, Jimmy looked up and down the street and saw a break in the traffic. Taking a deep breath, he grabbed the woman's purse and darted forward. Mrs. Steinburg screamed. Officer McAllister yelled, "Hey, kid, stop!" Jimmy ignored him and kept running. He dropped the purse and his book.

Mr. Blenford was at the newsstand now. As he ran, Jimmy saw Eddie's arm shoot out from behind the stand and grab Mr. Blenford's upper arm. The briefcase fell to the ground. Mr. Blenford and Eddie disappeared into the alley. There was one brief cry of surprise which Eddie quickly muffled. Then a giant hand clamped onto Jimmy's shoulder and jerked him to a halt just before reaching the newsstand.

"What do you think you're—" the police officer started to say, but Jimmy shouted, cutting him off.

"They're killing Mr. Blenford! They're in the alley killing him!"

"What the hell?"

Jimmy stomped on Officer McAllister's foot, twisted away from him, and ran. He didn't get far, but far enough. He made it past the newsstand to the alley's entrance before the officer caught him again, knocking him to the ground this time. Jimmy banged his head when he fell.

"You're in a lot of trouble, kid," he said as he restrained Jimmy.

Through a haze of pain, Jimmy cried, "Look in the alley! Look in the alley!"

Officer McAllister turned to look. Herman was running toward the other end of the alley. Eddie held Mr. Blenford from behind, standing in a doorway, wrapping him in a bear hug. He pushed Mr. Blenford to the pavement and started after Herman. Before he'd made his second step, Mr. Blenford grabbed Eddie's foot from where he lay on the cobblestones and tripped him.

Officer McAllister drew his gun. "Halt! Police!" he shouted. Herman kept going. He turned the corner behind the building and disappeared from view. Officer McAllister keyed his radio and called for backup, giving a brief description of the suspect.

Eddie appeared to have had the wind knocked out of him when he fell. Officer McAllister snapped handcuffs on him behind his back.

"Thanks for stopping him, Mr. Blenford," the officer said, "but you shouldn't have done that."

"I know. Let the police do what the police do." Mr. Blenford dusted himself off. "It was a long time ago, but I spent a few years on the force myself before I went to law school." He pointed to a knife lying on the ground across the alley. "That should have my assailant's fingerprints on it."

The officer nodded.

Mr. Blenford straightened his tie. "How'd you know to come this way?"

"I was chasing that kid. Seems he knew something was going on." They turned toward Jimmy. He sat there on the sidewalk in front of the alley and looked toward them with blank eyes, unseeing. Then he slumped to the ground.

◆

Jimmy woke up in stages over a couple of minutes. His head hurt, and his throat felt as if he'd tried to swallow razor blades. Beeps sounded in the background, and occasional voices faded in and out, along with the sound of footsteps on linoleum. The white blur above him slowly came into focus to reveal white ceiling tiles and a fluorescent light fixture, currently unlit. He groaned and raised a hand to his head. A thick dressing covered his skull above his left ear, and a tube ran into his arm, leading to a bag suspended from a pole beside him.

His mom appeared, bending over him. "Jimmy, can you hear me?"

Jimmy blinked. "Mom?" The word came out like a hoarse croak.

His dad appeared beside her. His mom pressed the call button by the bed. When it answered, she said, "He's waking up."

Jimmy scanned the room. The walls were painted sky blue, and yellow curtains covered the window. A white blanket covered him, and the bed had side rails around it, like a crib. A television hung on the wall in front of him, but it was off.

Leaning over the bed rails, his dad took Jimmy's hand and squeezed it. "Jimmy, do you know us?"

Jimmy stared at him for a moment. He furrowed his brows, but it hurt to do so. "Yes. Mom and Dad."

His dad closed his eyes and lifted his face heavenward. "Oh, thank God." Rachel hugged him, her eyes moist.

A woman in scrubs patterned with pictures of puppy dogs and kittens in lab coats with stethoscopes and such entered the room. Her name was—. Jimmy blinked. His eyes went wide. He didn't know her name!

"He recognized us," his mom said to the nurse as she entered.

The nurse nodded briefly toward her, then turned to Jimmy. "Hi, Jimmy," she said. "I'm Janel. I'm a nurse, and I need to check you out."

He let her work on him, cooperating with her requests as much as possible. She gave him a cup of ice water with a bent straw and raised the head of the bed for him, showing him the controls as she did so. The cold water soothed his throat.

She stood beside the bed and patted his shoulder. "You had a hard blow to your head, Jimmy. There was some bleeding inside, and they had to do an operation to relieve the pressure. Some things might be hard to do for a while, or you might not remember some things that you think you should know. We're all going to help you get better, though, okay? Try not to get frustrated if it takes a while. Your doctor will be in later, and he'll have more information. Right now, you just need to take it easy."

Jimmy nodded. He tried to "hear" Janel's thoughts, but nothing came, neither with her nor his parents. He took a sip of water. "Mr. Blenford?"

His mom nodded. "He's okay. He was here earlier but had to go before you woke up. You saved his life. Do you not remember that?"

He shook his head.

"That's not uncommon with concussions," Janel said. "There's often some amnesia for a period before the injury.

"Herman Meyers?" Jimmy croaked.

They turned back to him. His dad tilted his head. "Who?"

"The killers." He lifted his head to see his father better.

His mom nodded again. "They have two suspects in custody. One of them they caught at the scene, and another, as he tried to get away. A car hit him while he backed out of a parking spot without looking. Al Blenford made a positive ID on both of them."

Jimmy heaved a sigh, dropped his head back on the pillow, and then moaned as his head hit it.

"I can get you some medicine for the pain," the nurse said. "Would you like that?"

Jimmy nodded, wincing.

"It'll make him a little groggy," she said to Jimmy's parents. "I'll be right back."

♦

Jimmy spent two weeks in the hospital and went for physical therapy three times a week after that. At first, his right side was a little weak, but that improved quickly. His memory seemed mostly intact up to a minute or so before he hit his head.

Regardless of how he tried, he couldn't hear anyone's thoughts, and he no longer knew people's names when he saw them. He even tried working math problems to see if that cleared his mind to enable him to hear thoughts again.

It didn't.

♦

One afternoon about six weeks afterward, Rachel was driving him back from PT. It was coming up on Thanksgiving, and she had taken some time off work before the holiday.

Jimmy had just graduated to needing to go only once a week, and physically, he was about back to normal. He rode shotgun, looking out the side window at the holiday decorations starting to go up. A book rested in his lap, but he'd finished reading it while waiting for PT to start.

Keeping her eyes on the road, his mom said, "Have you got back any of your ability?"

She hadn't mentioned it since only a few days after "The Incident," but Jimmy knew at once what she meant by "ability."

He shook his head. "No. Not since then."

She spared him a glance and sighed, then looked back to the road. "I'm sorry, Jimmy."

"Thanks. I'm sorta surprised I miss it. I always used to say I wished I couldn't do it." He shrugged. "I guess I got my wish. I'm normal now."

His mom was silent for a few seconds. "You were normal before," she said, "because being able to do that was normal for you. And you're normal now, too. Except that no one's really normal. We're all unique." She gave a little laugh. "I guess it's normal to be unique."

Jimmy furrowed his brows. "If I was normal before, and now I'm different, how could I still be normal?"

His mom pursed her lips as she concentrated on merging onto the freeway. Then she said, "When I was little, we used to have picnics at my Grandma Johnson's house every Fourth of July. My cousins and my brother, and I would play hide and seek after dinner before the fireworks started. I had a place where I used to hide in one of the upper bedrooms, in the press."

Jimmy tilted his head. "The press?"

"Really old houses—Grandma's was built in 1840—sometimes had what they called a 'clothes press' instead of a full-sized closet in the rooms. It was like a shallow closet with only room for some hooks on the back wall to hold a few things inside instead of a rod to hang a lot of them. People didn't tend to have as many clothes back then. It was only a few inches deep between the door and the outside wall.

"Anyway, I'd hide there, squeezing between the walls to the left of the door so that someone opening the door and just peeking inside wouldn't see me." She smiled. "I won the game a couple of years using that place.

"Then, when I was twelve or thirteen, I went to hide there, and I didn't fit. I couldn't wedge myself inside in time, and Robert—your uncle Bob—caught me." She paused as a semi-truck passed them. "I'd changed," she continued afterward, "and could no longer do something I used to be able to do. But I was still normal."

"That's different." Jimmy shook his head. "You were just growing up."

"How do you know that's different?"

"What?"

"My Grandma Johnson used to say, 'Everything happens for a reason.' Maybe you had your ability for a reason, and the reason was so you could save Al Blenford's life. And put away two very bad people for a long, long time." She shook her head. "Most of us don't get the chance to do that kind of good deed. Maybe you lost your ability, not because you hit your head, but because you'd done what you were meant to do with it and didn't need it anymore."

For several seconds Jimmy sat still, his eyebrows pressed together, thinking. "I don't know."

His mom nodded. "We never will."

Steven Kenneth Smith is a fiction writer, poet, musician, and retired engineer currently living in Newark, Ohio. His poetry has appeared in many journals and anthologies, and he has short fiction published in both English and Esperanto. He enjoys backpacking and is a former regional champion on the Mountain Dulcimer, and has been a performer at the Ohio Renaissance Festival since 1992.

Who Wants Pie?

Sandy Kachurek

I blame it on the moon.

I don't think I could have made a worse move during my mother's funeral wake than quietly mentioning to my cousin that I'd been interested in FamilyPie. Com and its "Discover Your Roots" program. Carlotta Benzzetti, two years older and 100 decibels louder than I could ever be, announced it to the packed room of cousins, aunts, uncles, and my father.

I might blame it on the wine, too.

"Do it, Angela!" Big Mouth Cousin shouted. "I got my results last month." She waved her cell phone at me, showing off the company's pie graph logo. "I'm part Sami. You know, Laplanders. Reindeer herders. Can you believe it? An Italian and a Lapp?" She knuckled my shoulder, and I grabbed it in pain. "You've never been like any of us, Angie. Let's see who you really are!"

The room gasped. Who I was and where I came from was one of the biggest not-kept secrets in the family. At twenty, I never attained the rich brown hair and dark eyes with an Italian sun-drenched complexion nor the agrarian build of every other Benzzetti. My hair was a thin halo of white wisps floating atop pale ashy skin. No amount of makeup and lipstick could make my skinny, waif-like body look like anything but a bad, starving actor.

Right now, this body wanted to slide under the table. Sure, I'd been craving a search for my true ancestry, but not publicly and not around my father.

All heads turned from us to Dad, who put down his forkful of spaghetti, stood, leaned his hands flat on the table, and bore his limpid brown eyes into mine from two tables away. I giggled, trying to deflect the tension and growing humiliation. "It's not a big deal, Dad."

"Big deal?" He ignored the loved ones, who only moments ago had paid verbal tribute to my mother. Her love for nature led Dad and me to reserve this picnic pavilion along Luna Lake at sunset, her favorite time. It'd been a long, bittersweet day, a day suddenly gone completely sour. "A government scam to gain ammunition to destroy our privacy? I'll not have it! I am your father. Your mother is...was...your mother. You're a Benzzetti, and that's final!" The lawn chair quaked as he dropped back down into it.

I pulled out my inhaler and breathed in my mother's homemade mixture of patchouli and sage. When I could look at my family again, I mumbled my apologies. They patted me on the back, excusing Dad's actions due to Mother's death.

The ride home in the late autumn night was silent. I didn't know how to deal with this angry kind of father. Maybe it was grief. But maybe it was fear that I'd discover something he and Mom had been hiding. The clear sky full of stars and almost a full moon gave me the confidence to talk.

"Dad, I'm sorry."

"This nonsense about searching for your ancestry will stop." He drove up the last hill and turned into our driveway. "You bring it up again, and you're out the door."

"You're not serious?"

"Darn right, I am. Your mother and I have loved you since the day you were put in our arms. You've always been different, but that's part of why we love you. If you can't accept that without insisting on searching for your 'true' roots, then that's it. You can pack your bags and leave. I'm done with you."

Dad's threat hit home.

I wasn't the easiest kid to raise. I missed a lot of school until the principal insisted on a medical excuse. My mom was into herbs and home remedies, not doctors. My parents decided to home-school me. Later I took online classes. Now I do data entry from home.

I'd be lost without my dad.

After a few months, we were back to our normal selves in a reconstructed life without Mom. The other Benzzettis didn't feel the need to check on us anymore. We both enjoyed watching television and discussing books. A retired truck driver, Dad puttered around on our fifteen acres while I cooked, cleaned, and stayed inside until evening. Our nearest neighbor once called us the Addams family because we tended to be nocturnal. My fault. The sun hated me. I'd burn walking to the mailbox, even when slathered in potent SPF lotions. I grew up loving picnics in the moonlight. Even now, a night sky had me stretched out on my lounge chair, counting comets.

◆

Then it was spring when trees budded with promise. Beautiful trees. Family trees.

FamilyPie.Com dropped its price from one thousand to fifty dollars.

I wasn't going to tell a soul.

I hit "Send."

The package arrived within a week. The tube of my saliva was in the mail the next day.

I waited. And waited. Three weeks became four became six. Dad was right. It was a rip-off. Not that I'd ever tell him. Take it as a sign, I told myself. I'm a Benzzetti, albeit an odd one. After week eight, I forgot all about it.

I was by myself one afternoon when they came to the door.

Two women in Air Force uniforms.

"Angela Celestina Benzzetti?"

They extended their hands.

"Lieutenant Colonel Casey."

"Major Minerva."

The Colonel nodded toward a black sedan with black windows and a government license plate idling at the end of the driveway. "We'd like you to come with us."

Major Minerva removed a pair of mirrored racing glasses that reflected my image in rainbows. She wore a lot of make-up. Too much, I thought. Black liner and heavy mascara encased her unnaturally green eyes, thanks to contacts. Her cheeks and lips were far too red, her complexion far too peachy tan. Was she a real officer or a bad stage actor, too?

She handed me a clipboard of paperwork. It looked official, and I pretended to read it, but my heart beat so badly that I could only see my name in big, bold blue letters at the top. I had a feeling they weren't here to tell me I'd won the lottery.

I almost forgot what she'd asked of me. "Can't you just tell me what you want?"

"No, not here." They turned their heads as if checking for cameras.

I looked around for cameras, too, though at this isolated end of the township, nobody invested in surveillance technology any more than they invested in street lighting. A good dog handled security. I wished I had a dog.

"You want to come in?" I panted. Maybe I could stall them until Dad got back from the grocery. He'd know what to do. I dug in my pocket for my inhaler, but it wasn't there.

Colonel Casey said, "No, we must talk at the base. It shouldn't take long." She tried a smile, but it didn't convince me. Muscles in her arms rippled underneath her uniform jacket. I was defenseless.

"I can't breathe. I need my inhaler. It's just over there." I pointed to the kitchen table as if to assure them that I wouldn't sneak out the back. They stepped inside the door. I inhaled deeply the soothing patchouli and sage, which also gave me a moment to think. Regular breathing returned. Normal heartbeats did not.

"The base? I don't go out much to get into trouble. Is it my father? Is he hurt?"

Major Minerva touched my arm. "Neither you nor your father are in trouble. We have some questions to ask you. We cannot ask them here."

Her voice was soft, whispery. Amidst the absurdity of her facial getup, she sounded familiar—a far-off, maybe in my dreams familiar.

I couldn't think straight anymore and was helpless to do anything but obey. They were quietly patient while I put together some personal things in my messenger bag, like my cell phone and laptop, only to have it locked in the car trunk.

"We'll give it back to you later." They opened the door for me.

"What base?" I slid into the back seat. No one answered. Each officer took a seat by the window, wedging me in between them. Only when the car pulled away did I realize someone else was with us. But who, I couldn't say. A thick black wall divided the front and back seats. Only a dim running light on the floor at my feet gave any glow in the otherwise dark car.

The longer we traveled, the sicker I felt. I wasn't a hacker. I hadn't stumbled onto secret websites. Maybe Dad was in trouble. A retired truck driver? Nothing top secret there.

I squirmed. The muscle-bound Colonel stared straight ahead as if the most interesting part of the drive was the solid black glass in front of her. Major Minerva reached out her hand as if to touch my arm but drew it back. The hand didn't match the overdone colors of her face. Her hands were pale white.

I stared at my own ashy hands, trembling in my lap. Dad was going to disown me for sure when he found out about this. Whatever it was.

And then I got it.

Disown me.

FamilyPie.Com.

Dad was right again. I was on someone's list. My next breath was a struggle. They let me keep my inhaler, thank goodness.

Major Minerva on my right whispered. "It's okay. Close your eyes. Focus on breathing slowly."

Her lips were a voracious red, which spoiled any kindness in her smile. I again tried to place where I'd heard her before but failed. She smelled like patchouli.

Colonel Casey never moved except to flex her right hand. Her trigger hand.

I'd bitten off most of the nail on my left thumb and moved on to my pinkie when the car paused, slowly moved down an incline, and stopped. The engine died.

We sat in silence.

I wished I'd worn more deodorant.

Colonel Casey's door opened. We all slid out to where a third female officer waited, one with regular flesh tones and subtle makeup. We stood in an underground parking garage filled with black cars and bare lightbulbs. It was useless to ask, so I guessed we'd arrived at "the base." I shoved my hands in my jeans and played with my inhaler, trying not to conjure up every movie where bad things happened in underground garages.

We walked down a series of sterile hallways. Nothing adorned the walls. The ceiling was a continuous line of dim squares of light. The sound of shoes on tile echoed as we marched to an elevator, silently rode to the ninth floor, and marched to a solid wooden door no different from all the others we'd passed.

The conference room was windowless and gray, with a table big enough for twelve. Two female officers and one male officer sat on one side, looking as normal as one would expect of an interrogation, including a lack of expression. I was told to sit on the opposite side. My two escorts sat on each side of me. The third from the garage left the room, shutting the door with a straightforward click of the lock. I was doomed.

Major Minerva was to my left. She handed me a small packet of tissues. "Use these when you feel faint." Only her voice convinced me she was concerned for my welfare.

To preserve some kind of dignity, I sat as rigid as they, but my mind went flying into scary territory, one with body disfiguration and insane experimentation. One of the female officers facing me looked like Major Minerva with overdone cosmetics. What was hidden under that makeup? I wilted and fumbled to open the plastic pack of tissues and caught a whiff of patchouli. Major Minerva nodded. Who was this woman?

A female officer whose name tag said, "Major General Loudon," slid a white notebook at me.

"Tell us about this." Her finger reluctantly left the edge of the binder as I peered at the cover.

Case #509104793056RTV

ANGELINA CELESTINA BENZZETTI

Welcome to Your Servings of FAMILY PIE!

I slumped in my seat. Dad was going to kill me. My life, as different as it was from the rest of the family, would never be the same.

"I don't know," I stuttered. "I wanted to know about my ancestry. I'm so different from my cousin Carlotta, Uncle Vito, and the others. So I filled out the forms. Sent in the saliva. I didn't do anything anybody else wouldn't have done.

It was legal. I paid the fee. My cousin said it was fun. My dad.... It's not his fault. He said no, or he'd throw me out."

I was babbling. I started to cry.

They let me go for a couple of minutes. If these officers were robots, I wouldn't have been surprised. Or maybe they enjoyed bringing in twenty-year-old civilian women and making baseless accusations to see them break down.

The patchouli-scented tissues helped, and I didn't need my inhaler. When I regained some sense of myself, I opened the book. Inside was the cover page welcoming me to FamilyPie. It included the right to privacy and stated that the company wasn't an expert. The results were for entertainment purposes only. Nothing revealed about my ancestry would be admissible evidence in any court. Their website said the same.

As scared as I was to sit at a table in an inescapable place with five military officers bearing down on me, waiting for me to do something, confess to something, to worry about what my dad was going to do to me if I did get out of here alive, I was curious.

All along, I only wanted to know where I came from. No matter how much they insisted otherwise, my parents never convinced me I was family. In every Benzzetti photo and video, I stood out like a mascot in costume. Yes, my parents loved me, and I was grateful because a lot of kids didn't have the super family I had. But I felt more connected to Major Minerva and her naive over-application of makeup than I did my parents.

God, I was going to hell for ungrateful daughters. Not a reassuring thought, considering my chances of dying today were pretty high.

Here in this cheap, white plastic ring binder was the answer for better or worse. Whether I was freed or imprisoned for life, I was going to get my answer.

I flipped the page and got nothing. Nothing.

Gone were the fear and disappointment. I moved into indignation. I slapped the book shut and slid it back to General Loudon.

"Did my dad put you up to this? Did he tell you to scare me to death so I wouldn't go searching for my ancestry? Did he?"

Unmoved, General Loudon asked, "Did you receive the results of your ancestral search from this company FamilyPie?"

"No."

"Are you sure?" said another emotionless officer at the table.

I'd had enough. Either they were to tell me what was going on, or I was going out the door. If they didn't attack me first.

I stood with my hands flat on the table. Neither of the officers at my side moved to stop me, not even the trigger-finger Colonel Casey.

"Who the hell do you think you are? No, no results. I get the mail every day. It never came. I got ripped off."

"She's telling the truth," Major Minerva said to the table.

Her artificially green eyes apologized to me.

I raised my voice to a level that would have made my cousin Carlotta proud. "Of course, I'm telling the truth. I want to know why I'm here, or I'm calling my lawyer." Not that I had a lawyer, but if Dad couldn't help me, I'd find one.

Major General Loudon told me to sit down. "We intercepted your ancestry results from the FamilyPie Company. We are within our rights to do so as a matter of national security. Our concern is whether you received the results, too. We apologize for keeping you here, but we must fully understand what we are dealing with."

"And exactly what do you fully understand now that you forced me to come here?"

The Major General nodded to the uniformed women and man. "Before we answer that, let's take you to a sitting room where you can relax." At that, they all stood up. Major Minerva nodded as I looked at her as if seeking reassurance. I picked up the binder.

"Leave it," someone said.

I dropped it with a muffled bang.

The lounge was minus everything: no televisions, clocks, coffee makers, power outlets, or windows. What was left was a tiny bathroom and a variety of chairs, sofas, and coffee tables with magazines about food and fashion. I fell asleep worrying about Dad, about my job, about my personal family pie.

I awoke to three officers escorting my dad into the room. I wept when I saw him. He saw my hesitation to move toward him and came up to embrace me.

"Angela, it's okay." We said nothing more.

The officers left except for Major Minerva. She stood against the closed door, her unnaturally red lips signaling danger.

Dad sat across from me at an oblong coffee table with magazines between us.

"I'm sorry," he said.

My mouth was open to say the same. "You, Dad? I'm the one who did the very thing you told me not to do."

I played with a food magazine, lining its bottom edge to match the table-top's edge, working on where to begin my apology. "Out of This World Summer

Salads," it said on the cover. I looked at it as if it was the most important thing in the world.

"You were right, Dad. The whole ancestry thing is a rip-off, the government's attempt to gain access into our privacy." I glared at Major Minerva. "I don't care anymore who I look or don't look like. I love my family. I love being a Benzzetti."

Dad leaned over and took my hand, his strong hands shaking a little. "Listen to me." He glanced once over his shoulder at Major Minerva, whose scarlet lips parted in a smile. He faced me again, his discomfort an unusual stance for him.

"I've been here at the base with these fine...military folks...for a few hours now and have been guided on how best to tell you our family history. I'd be the first to say that it sounded like the biggest hooey this side of the Mississippi, but I know better now. The officers, like the Major here, filled in the gaps of what I thought only your mother and I knew." His hands trembled. "It's true. You're not a Benzzetti. We don't know who or what you are."

I gasped, but he hushed me as I started to speak.

"You see, I was there on the hilltop when you first arrived. Your mom, too."

"You don't have to, Dad," I couldn't help saying, though quite rattled about this "hilltop." "I'm okay not knowing." Dad patted my arm and took a deep breath.

"Twenty years ago, there was a total lunar eclipse. Your mom and I stood atop the tallest hill on our property, along with a couple hundred other folks. Some invited. Some not. We'd been partying long before the eclipse began. Many were passed out on the ground."

I began nibbling at the fingernail on my pinkie.

"Your mom and I wanted to watch the whole convergence by ourselves. We edged away from the crowd and walked over to Plum Creek Meadow."

I knew the area well. My mom had her favorite spot on an old tree stump in the middle of wild grasses and flowers. Plum Creek gurgled nearby. But the memory made me feel edgy, not nostalgic. This family story was what I'd been pining for, yet I was uncertain now. Who would I be afterward?

Dad cleared his throat. "The eclipse is almost at its darkest when something floats down from the sky and drifts toward us. I don't know what it is. A hallucination? A play of light? Someone from the group screwing around with us? We don't recognize it, but we know it's real."

"No." I stood up, clinging to the arm of the sofa. "Air. I need air."

I gasped at Minerva. "My inhaler's empty. My bag. My bag is in your car." My lungs wheezed hard against my ribs. I shrugged off Dad's attempts to hold me.

"I've got you." Major Minerva steered me toward a smaller sofa and got me to sit. "Breathe into my hands," she said.

I rasped, "What the hell?" I almost apologized for being rude, but I was desperate for air and would have breathed into a trash can if it promised relief.

Her hands smelled of patchouli and something else exotic. I inhaled deeply, closed my eyes, and wished I was home.

I didn't get my wish, but soon I felt better. Much better.

The officer took her hands away and resumed her position at the door. "Sir, your daughter needs to hear the rest of her story. Ms. Benzzetti. Angela, you need to listen."

Dad moved beside me and put his arms around my shoulders, and continued talking as he once did when he read me bedtime stories as a child.

"The figure isn't human. It's a bluish-gray floating mist sort of shaped human but with no distinguishable legs or arms. It's carrying something like a football in front of it. A small dense gray cloud of a football. I smell incense, woody incense."

He squeezed me and kissed the top of my head. "Your mom and I are scared. I'm wishing I had a beer bottle to throw at it, but we have nothing. It stops within reaching distance of us."

I looked up at him. Now eager.

"It speaks. A very breathy English. We barely hear her, let alone understand what she says."

"Her?"

Dad nodded.

"She says, 'Give her earth home' and extends the cloud football at us. 'Tell Jerry. I miss him. He not come back to moon.'"

"The moon? You two on acid?"

"I know it sounds crazy. Your mom says, 'Jerry Adams? The Apollo astronaut who spent three days on the moon?'"

"'Jerry,' says the mist."

"I tell the moon creature that Jerry Adams had recently died. And I swear I wasn't on drugs, but the news seemed to break her heart. Not that we were certain she had one."

Dad almost smiled. "The eclipse is on its way out when the creature extends the bundle to us. 'Please,' she says. 'Please.'"

"I feel bad for it and think, what the heck. The misty creature hasn't killed us yet. The ground hasn't swallowed us up. And this may still be a prank. I reach out my hands."

Dad looked at me like I was the most important thing in the world.

"It feels like a bundle of bubbles. Light and formless. Then the creature blows on it, and the bubbles dissipate. The bundle is suddenly heavier and begins to cry."

"What was it?" I now knew but had to ask.

"It was you."

♦

I heard Dad softly calling my name.

I awoke to the same bland room of couches and chairs. Dad was busying himself, pouring me a glass of water from a pitcher on a tray.

"Mom and I were going to tell you, but we were afraid. Like now. You fainted a lot as a child. We worried you might have died from the truth."

I stared at the ceiling, digesting what I'd heard. I wanted to say it was nonsense. My dad's grief for my mother making him crazy. But my heart was forcing me to admit how right it felt.

Dad handed me my inhaler. It smelled of patchouli. It smelled of the woman with the face most likely as pale as mine under all her makeup. I looked at the door.

"Where is she? Major Minerva."

"Gone. She'll be back to walk us to the car. She and the others are part of a special task force. As you might guess, many of them aren't from around here. They're aliens, all right. The best kind."

A fainting spell threatened at the word "aliens," but I resolved to remain conscious. "We get to go home?"

"We're invited to come back when the news of who you are settles in and 'becomes a normal part of your life' is how they expressed it."

"We have a choice?"

"No, I don't think so." Dad chuckled. "Honestly? I wish I'd met them years ago."

The escort to the car was the same as before: no talking, the echoing of shoes in empty hallways, the dark ride home, except Dad and I were the only ones in the back seat.

Major Minerva opened the door, apparently having driven up front. She wore sunglasses that wrapped around her head and mirrored the earth and sky around her. Her face and hands, exposed under the sunshine, were a mottle of gray and white.

Her bold red lips said, "Take care of yourself." She handed me a familiar three-ringed notebook and messenger bag. "I look forward to seeing you soon."

I headed for the house with the sound of her voice echoing in my heart and my father's story of a wispy figure who had handed him a baby-me with her own pale skin. Could Minerva be my family?

We both savored our experiences by not saying anything more in our normal quiet way. When the day turned into evening, my father went to his study, probably relieved to go back to mundane crossword puzzles and TV quiz shows. I escaped to my room and welcomed the sunset.

With moonlight pouring over my desk, I opened the notebook.

The title said, "Here is Your Family Pie, Angela Celestina Benzzetti!"

Except it wasn't a pie.

It was a map of the Moon, mottled in grays and whites and blues.

Highlighted in yellow, just to the left of the famous spot marked Sea of Tranquility, was a crater named Jerry Adams. Like every junior high student taking science, I learned about one of the most famous and bravest astronauts. They called him "Tough Guy" Adams for enduring over eight hours in one moonwalk. Tapes only covered six hours of his exploratory walk, a gap he laughingly brushed aside, explaining he'd done nothing more than gather rocks and admire the moonscape. Surveillance wasn't as sophisticated then.

When I was done poring over each page two or three times, I closed my family pie notebook and propped it up on the top of my bookshelf. According to what the "special task force" told my dad and me, the average American would never get the whole story about "Tough Guy" Adams. Adams had done quite a lot during those missing two hours.

And now, when I struggle to breathe or grumble at my pale ashy skin, I know what to do.

I blame it on the moon.

Sandy Kachurek is the author of biographies of George W. Bush and Francisco Pizzaro. She's the director of Into the Springs Writers' Workshop in Yellow Springs, Ohio, and volunteers to help nonprofits advertise their good work on social media.

Last of My Kind

Maureen McGuirk

y dog Lucy hates me. Well, that's a little harsh. She just gets confused. At least, that's what my neighbor tells me.

Whenever I open the screen door to retrieve the mail in the afternoon, Lucy bursts past me across the street to the home of my neighbor Gabbi. I'm so used to the occurrence that I don't even watch to see if she makes it. I hear her bark and jump up—most likely into Gabbi's arms.

I squint as I step onto my porch. I haven't been outside all week and am debating whether to go out ever again. There doesn't seem to be much point other than to unburden the mailman, Bobby, who I avoid for...alternative reasons. I open the slot of my mailbox and filter through the pile of ads for ways to cure my adult acne and coupons for the latest devices to enhance the quality of my life—I still can't get my printer to work.

There's a postcard with the Great Wall of China on the front. I turned the card and read the message: *Wish you were here!* Another one. The fourth in two months from Imogene.

She sometimes includes pictures, but not today. Just as well.

I flip through the remainder of the pile, most of which have my mother's name. I do my best to ignore them until the last envelope catches my eye—*The Institute of Biological Studies*. Reluctantly, I rip the seal and skim over the words:

Dear Ms. Bishop,

We were recently made aware of the sudden passing of your mother, Renee Bishop, and wanted to send our deepest condolences. She, like your late father, was a major backer of introducing human cloning into society. The Bishop family's support is one of the many reasons human cloning has been considered a success.

With your parents' departure, you are now the sole controller of your DNA samples, so graciously provided by your parents during our trial period. We hope you will reconsider your current membership and make your DNA continually available, even after your death. This will ensure that further generations of human cloning will continue to flourish. The Institute hopes that the future will be painted with familiar faces.

Sincerely,
Rebecca B. Turner
President, Institute of Biological Studies

Condolences, my ass.

I crinkle the letter in my fist. They've been waiting for my mother to die. Now all they have to do is convince me.

I turn to go inside when I'm startled by a familiar greeting. My shoulders jolt as I twist back to see Gabbi holding Lucy.

"I didn't mean to scare you," she reassures while bouncing Lucy up and down in her arms as if she were a two-year-old child. Her leg takes claim on the first step of my porch.

I feel nauseous. Lucy doesn't help by panting stupidly in her arms. I open my screen door and wave Lucy in. She hesitates before hopping out of Gabbi's arms and into the house. I want to follow, but Gabbi takes my hand before my legs can move.

"Oh, don't you hate these ads?" she whines, noticing the mail in my hand. "I get them all the time. I hate distracting gadgets."

"Yeah, same."

"Did you happen to get my card?" Her voice dips while her lips meet in a sudden embrace.

"I did. Thanks.... I should've said that sooner."

"No, it's fine. It can be such a tough time—losing people."

My eyes dance between Gabbi's forehead, the ground, the distance between our houses—anything to keep from looking at her. It's something I've never gotten used to despite her living across the street since we were young. Her eyes, teeth, the size of her nose, the sound of her voice, even the way she tucks strands of her auburn hair behind her pierced ears—they're all mine.

"It's fine, Gabbi." I interrupt her babbling and take my arm back. "I appreciate the card and your sympathy, but I have some things to do."

"Oh, of course, sorry." She takes her leg off the step in an attempt to leave. "It's just...I can't help but feel I've lost my mother—"

"Well, you haven't!"

My volume seems to frighten her as she retreats. I feel bad about this, but not enough.

I tuck my hair behind my ear and clear my throat: "Sorry, Gabbi. I have to…" I nudge my head in the direction of my house and disappear inside.

♦

Lucy sleeps by the fireplace in our living room—*my* living room. It's strange to think this house belongs to me now. Only me.

I walk past and into the hallway, Imogene's postcard in hand. The answering machine blinks a red "2". I hit *play* as I continue down the hall. The walls appear to be some sort of shrine, but they're no different from any other family hallway. Walls of faces—all mine.

The first message plays in the background. It's for a new security system I've been selected to receive for free, cameras and all.

I stop at the portrait of Imogene. Her wide smile dominates the space as though her very image wants to bust through the frame.

Moving past four other portraits, I continue down the hall to a large cabinet handed down from my grandmother. The latch opens and pulls forward a drawer of files—five files with names. I placed the postcard in one marked "Imogene Clyde" and put it back between two others. My fingers can't help but flip through them: Louise Fletcher—Margo Lowell—Tess Cooper—Gabbi Randall.

"Gabbi…" My head shakes as I flip through her file. Photos from grade school, report cards, health records. A photo taken on her fifth birthday. My parents held it at the house and took a picture of us smashing chocolate crème cake into our mouths. They thought it was cute—not the mess, mind you.

The second message plays in the background. At first, there's nothing. It must be a hang-up. Then, a voice—my voice. Well, not mine.

"I need to talk to you. It's Margo."

A loud *click*, and the machine beeps.

The photo slips from my hand and back into Gabbi's folder as my cellphone rings from the kitchen. It's Wednesday, and I know who it is before the name flashes across the screen. I answer before it flips to voicemail.

"Yes, Owen, I'm still home."

"How long is this going to go on?"

"I'm not going out there."

"You're grieving. It's normal to feel this way."

"There's nothing normal about me."

He's silent for a moment before I hear him breathe out. "This again."

"Yes, *this* again. These *things* who won't leave me alone."

"I'll be there soon."

I hang up, and in the same fluidity, I slide into my living room, wrapping myself in the plush blanket my mother bought me on my last birthday. I bring it closer and breathe in. The fragrance of plum and musk invites her back into the room, and it's like she is here with me. If I could, I'd smother myself with this blanket.

Lucy snores from her pillow on the floor, and I turn on the TV to block it out.

MISSING.

My face glares back at me from the floor-based TV across my living room. Adrenaline pumps directly into my heart. Honestly, who expects to see themselves like that? But it's not me.

MARGO LOWELL.

Her auburn hair is shaved on one side—much different than the portrait hanging in my hallway. She looks pissed in the photograph, and I can't blame her.

Oh, my God...

According to the report, she's been missing for two days and was last seen outside her apartment in the city.

"Two days?" I utter out loud. "That can't be right."

My head turns, staring at the machine where Margo's voice is recorded. I get up and head into the room, pushing the button as though it is attached to a bomb.

"One old message," the male voice inside the box tells me.

"I need to talk to you. It's Margo." She doesn't sound worried or stressed. Not frantic either.

Frozen in thought, I'm startled as my doorbell rings, followed by a loud knock. I notice a figure who resembles Owen in the window, so I open the door a crack.

"No sun, no sand..."

"No way we're escaping," his voice comes through.

I unlatch the second lock and open the door to his dark features. His feet find their way up the three steps leading into my kitchen. The bags in his hands containing food and the shampoo I'm sure I need find a home as he flops them on the table and takes off his jacket.

"Do you always answer the door with that dumb poem of yours, or am I special?" he knowingly asks. His head dips into the living room, looking for the source of the voices.

"It's not dumb," I fire back as I finger through the various chips, sandwich meats, and fruit he's bought for me. "That's one of my favorites and highly useful for us, don't you think?"

I can feel his eyes roll.

"For you, maybe. I enjoy seeing men with my face. I like getting my mail delivered by Bobby, even if it bothers you."

"It's odd, that's all. I do my best not to run into him. It's like *you're* delivering my mail."

"But I'm not. Bobby's a completely different guy. A great guy, and seeing him is a highlight of my day. And I love getting legal advice from Caleb, and my teeth cleaned by Joshua, and...well, not Joshua so much—he's a bit of a talker, and it's difficult to answer." Owen laughs as he walks into the next room.

I don't expect him to ever agree with me. It would take something drastic for him to understand the danger. Something like—

"Did you see this?" I grab my remote and turn up the volume as Margo's image covers the screen.

Owen stares for a bit, his expression a mix of confusion and amusement. "Wow. She looks—"

"Different, yes."

"I don't think I've had the pleasure of meeting Margo. I would've remembered."

"She's never been involved in my life—I've appreciated that. She, out of all of them, understood I wanted space." I push past him to get closer to the television. "But this. I mean—look," I emphatically point, "two days she's been missing. Two whole days. And *nothing.* Not a sound."

"So?"

"So, you know how they are! Those crones at the Institute never hesitate to notify us whenever our clones have so much as a paper cut. I got phone calls for each of Tess's babies, and when Imogene broke her arm on Mt. Rainier, they mailed me her fucking x-rays and entire medical chart!"

"What are you suggesting? You think the Institute is responsible?"

"I'm just saying it's odd."

Lucy's head perks from sleep, and stares in the direction of the front door. The rap of knuckles is familiar, and my fingers run through my hair in frustration.

"And that..." I gesture as Lucy sits attentively at the door. It opens at my pull to Gabbi, huddled at the screen.

"Have you heard?"

"If it's about Margo, then—"

"It's just awful...awful." Gabbi opens my screen and bursts past me into my living room. "Do you think something horrid happened?" Her nose sniffs, but I don't notice much fluid.

"It's probably nothing, Gabbi."

"You're right. What did the Institute tell you?" Gabbi watches my face for any hint of information.

The house phone rings, and all of us turn toward the sound. I leave Gabbi in more obliging hands and answer the phone. The voice on the other end causes my breath to slow.

"Margo?"

Both Owen and Gabbi glance over at me.

"No, it's Louise. You talking to Margo now? You never talk to me! I've been trying to get ahold of you ever since your mother died, and all I get is that damn—"

I pull the receiver away from my ear as her tirade continues. My lips utter a quick goodbye before I hang up. Out of all of them, I dislike conversing with Louise the most.

"Was that—who was that?" Gabbi asks.

"Louise. She doesn't know about Margo." I flop down on a chair and rest my head on the kitchen table. "I wish I knew what she wanted to tell me."

"Margo called?"

"Left a message. I should check my machine more often."

"Don't blame yourself. It was probably nothing—maybe she needed money or something." Gabbi folds her arms into her chest. She thinks I'm not paying attention as she peeks down my hallway.

"Margo wouldn't call me for money. She didn't even call when my mom died."

"How selfish..." Gabbi snaps.

Owen opens my front door. "Gabbi, you should go home. We'll call if we hear anything."

Gabbi looks at me as if she wants me to rebut his offer, but frankly, I can't wait for her to leave. An ache takes form above my right brow as I gaze at her.

"Well, be sure you do," she coos and then exits.

"God, she's annoying." I stand up, pulling my hair behind my ears.

"She's not so bad. Didn't you two play together all the time?"

"I was a kid. I had no choice."

Owen takes two bags still on the table and puts their items away. "You should call the Institute and ask if they've heard any news," he suggests while placing bread on the counter.

"They're not going to tell me anything. All they've ever wanted from me—" My speech halts as my hand grasps my mouth. "Oh my God...."

"What?"

"They did this. It has to be them."

"What? Why?"

"They want me to update my membership. It's all they ever talk about. And I always blow them off. And what if—what if they did something to Margo to make me change my mind?"

Owen stares at me, mouth ajar. "That makes no sense. Their business thrives on clones. Hell, I ordered ten more to be released last week. Why would they kill one?"

"Ten more, Owen? Christ..."

"It's inevitable! We are the future—you, me, and hundreds of other donors out there! Our faces will be on the planet until life ends. Doesn't that excite you? Our essence, our faces, will be immortal. We'll never have to know true loneliness ever again."

The room is quiet after his outburst. I don't know how to reply, so I don't. Instead, I pass him and return to the living room. It's the top of the hour, and Margo's face returns on my screen. I stare at it for a moment before blinking. It's the first time I haven't thought of it as being my face. It's not me. It's another person entirely. And she's missing.

I've become a pro at keeping my emotions in for so long that it's surprising to feel myself slipping, stumbling over words to hold on.

"I can handle being alone. I've handled it. Some days are difficult." I turn away from the TV and move towards the hallway. "Change is hard, but...when nothing changes...that's when things are at their most bleak." I walk down it. I can feel Owen following me. I turn to face him. My eyes, against my will, water and redden. It's from the shock. The realization of what this all is really about: "She loved me," I whisper.

Owen's silent but nods the way a friend should at such a statement. It's a matter of certainty. But he doesn't truly understand my epiphany.

"My father had me cloned for technological reasons, but my mother...she loved me so much...she wanted more of me." My lips quiver as I release the pent-up emotion. I wipe away as much as I can. My voice shakes. "No one's ever going to love me like that again."

I take hold of the wall for balance. Owen comes toward me, takes my other arm, but I don't allow him. Instead, I walk farther down the hall—a funhouse of mirrored portraits laughing at my absurdity.

"And all the while, I'm the disappointment. All their letters, pictures, updates—reminders of things I would never do; I'm not a mother or the best neighbor or an adventurer..."

Their portraits halt my speech, judging me. I look back to Owen's sunken face. I can tell he's not so sure of his stance any longer. "This isn't living..." I tell him. "These women aren't me. And when I'm gone, I'll be *gone*. No number of replicas will change that."

I curl up on my couch, sipping tea and watching some sitcom. Owen told me to take a break from the news before he left. My mother's blanket nestles over my body, and I bring it up to my nose to smell her fragrance once more. Will I ever get over the loss of her?

A laugh from the TV catches my attention, and I do my best to get lost in the humor. As I snuggle in, words scroll across the screen—more on Margo's disappearance. No new information.

"Yeah, I bet," I utter.

The Institute will bury this, just like they did with Margo, and then they'll call, asking me to issue another clone to replace her. That's where it will—

I sit up and stare at the screen.

How did she know?

Jumping to my feet, I grab a pair of shoes and my sweater. I look over to Lucy, sleeping on her pillow. "Lucy! Lucy, come!"

The dog graces me with rare recognition before returning to sleep.

The door opens, and I step outside. "Stupid dog."

Gabbi's house is barely lit. She usually doesn't stay up very late, mostly to get in her morning jog. As I make my way to her side door, I notice her garden in the back; she's extremely proud of it. The ground is rich with dark, churned soil. Wet soil, yet it hasn't rained for days.

A porch light flicks on, and I see her figure staring at me from her side door.

"Gabbi, sorry, I know it's late—"

"Why are you in my yard?" Her words direct themselves to me, but her eyes remain on her garden.

"I shouldn't be here, but there's something I need to ask you."

"So ask."

Her tone is one I've never heard from her before. I walk up towards her and gesture to her house. "Inside."

◆

I try to remember the last time I was inside Gabbi's house but can't, probably before high school when her parents still owned it. Every surface is remarkably clean, except for the dishwasher hanging open. I know it must bug her for me to witness as she pushes past me to close it.

"I hope everything's all right. They didn't find Margo in some ditch, did they?"

"I don't think they will find Margo. Will they, Gabbi?"

Her lips open, but nothing comes out at first, so she tries again. "I don't know. I hope someone will find her. What if someone's looking to harm all of us?"

I circle about the room. The porcelain knickknacks on her top shelf have an odd layer of dust. I can sense Gabbi fidgeting and decide to let her for a bit.

"Didn't your mom collect these?" I ask.

"Yes."

"I thought you hated them."

"I do..." Gabbi turns away from me. "I'd really like to get to bed soon. You know I look forward to my run."

"It's Margo," I say.

Gabbi turns back to face me. "Did you find her or not?" she asks, exasperated.

"How did you know she was missing?"

Her eyes are foggy, and her nose crinkles in annoyance. "I...they—the Institute called. Told me."

I step closer to her. "No. Try again."

"I'm telling the truth."

"Louise didn't know about Margo when she called. If they would've called you, they would've called her too. And for that matter, they sure as *hell* would've called me. Now try again, Gabbi."

"No, you're right. I...saw it on the news. That must be it."

"You don't own a TV," I say, pointing into her living room. "You 'hate distracting gadgets,' right?"

"I'd really like to go to bed now." Gabbi opens her side door expectantly.

The air seems thinner, and I take a deeper breath than normal. My balance improves as my butt leans on her table. "Where's Margo? Tell me where she is, and I'll leave."

The door shuts, and Gabbi pulls her hair behind her ears. The sound of the lock clicking startles me, and my once firm stance now begins to retreat.

"Why all of a sudden do you care about Margo? You didn't want anything to do with any of us only twelve hours ago. And now you want to play the concerned sister?"

"I never wished harm on any of you. I just wanted you to leave me alone."

Gabbi disappears into the hallway, and I scamper to the side door only to feel her hand on my arm, pulling me back into the room. I steady myself. My eyes scan the room for any weapon. They stop on her other hand—the one holding a gun.

"Margo was going to tell you awful...awful things about me." A slight laugh escapes her. "Like she was so perfect, right? Right?"

"Right. She wasn't perfect."

"No, but she thought she was. She thought she was *special*. I mean, look at the mess she made of her hair! Not to mention the mess she made of her life— selling drugs, AA dropout. She was only going to hurt us. Our brand."

"Brand? I'm not some *brand*."

The hand with the gun inserts itself into the conversation, and my hands ascend in submission.

"Gabbi, calm down."

It's fear that binds the two of us. I feel closer to Gabbi as she circles me. She's tired and upset, and she resembles me more than ever.

"Gabbi, please." My arm juts out in front of my body. I try to touch her, but I can't reach.

"You know what memories stick out in my mind? The ones I've been playing over and over and over in my head since I was six?"

My head shakes.

"Your mother...calling me 'sweetie,' making me a Birthday cake, tucking me in during one of our sleepovers. You remember? She treated me like I was a human being—her own daughter, not some mere *copy*."

Gabbi steps closer to me, raising the gun. My system splits into wanting to fight or remaining frozen.

"We were never good enough for you—I was never good enough to *be* you, right?"

"Gabbi, stop," I plead, but her feet continue their march toward me.

I have no choice. My hand lunges for the gun, pulling it up in the air. We dance about the room—gripping and grunting. The gun fires a shot into her ceiling. My head turns into hers. It's odd, like being pressed against a mirror.

"Gabbi, they'll put you away. They'll stop producing any more of me. It's over!"

I attempt to pull her down, but she only struggles more. My body starts to tire, and I'm not sure how much longer I can go on.

◆

The police have only just put up their yellow tape in the last half hour. It took them that long to respond to my call. I thought by now, with all the advancements in the world, police officers would respond faster than a turtle. No matter.

I take a sip of my tea and sneak another glance outside my front door as a car pulls into my driveway. I must admit, the sight of Ms. Turner exiting the back of the vehicle catches me off guard. I cough to relieve the tea going down my windpipe as she waves, her eyes glancing back at the disturbing scene of flashing lights in the darkness.

I open the screen and slip out onto the porch. "You must have heard. It's all so—"

"Terrifying. Uh," Ms. Turner shakes her head as she takes another glance at the scene across the street. "I can't tell you how sorry I am that this has happened, Ms. Bishop. We at the Institute take pride in our monitoring of clones. We should have seen this—"

"Oh, don't blame yourself. Gabbi hid her psychosis well, I guess."

We both turn as one of Ms. Turner's men interrupts with papers. EMTs emerge from the house, wheeling a bagged body to their van.

Ms. Turner signs and then hands the pen to me. "Only protocol. You've lost two clones. This acknowledges you've been made aware of the situation."

"Two clones?" I ask a little too calmly.

"Don't tell...you didn't hear about Margo?"

"I heard she was missing. Wait, no. They didn't find her?" My hand points across the street as Ms. Turner nods.

"Her body was found buried in Gabbi's garden. We'll do a thorough investigation, of course, but we think Gabbi must have had some sort of psychotic break, killed Margo, couldn't live with the deed, and then killed herself."

"My God..." I utter, bringing my outstretched hand to my face. I turn to see Lucy staring at me from inside, her tail wagging the moment she realizes I've noticed her. "It's all my fault."

"No. You couldn't have known Gabbi was so...unhinged."

"But I should have. I should have been more involved in her life—in all their lives. I haven't been a very good sister to them, have I?"

Ms. Turner touches my shoulder. I can tell she's trying to be persuasive in her comfort. I can't help but admire her technique. "You've never taken to the idea, have you, Ms. Bishop?"

"It's taken me some time. Too much time, obviously. My unwillingness to change has cost us two people."

"The Institute doesn't blame you for this."

"But I blame me. And I want to make it right." I glance over as another body bag is wheeled out from behind the house. "Ms. Turner, I'm willing to reconsider my membership."

Her expression changes to cautious delight. "Really? You're sure?"

My breathing changes, if only for the way she's looking at me, as though she's trying to decipher if I'm a fraud. "Yes. I owe it to those women. To the future, wherever it takes us."

Lucy jumps up onto the screen and barks. Welcoming the distraction, I open it. The dog hustles past the two of us and over to the action across the street.

"Oh, do you want my men to fetch her?" Ms. Turner asks.

"No, I've got it. Lucy! Lucy, come!"

There's a halt from the dog. She tears through the commotion around her and scampers back to our side of the street. I can't help but laugh as she hops into my arms. She's been so loyal as if she's always known where she truly belongs. I bounce her up and down, her panting a sign of her contentment.

Any question on Ms. Turner's face vanishes and is replaced with naïve satisfaction. "She really loves you."

"She always has," I reply with a smile.

I find it's best to always end with the truth.

Maureen McGuirk earned her Bachelor of Fine Arts degree in writing for film and television from the University of the Arts in Philadelphia. Her short story "Miss Fortunate" was published in *Quiet Shorts*, a Seattle-based arts journal. Her one-act play "A Private Conversation" earned an honorable mention in the New Works of Merit Playwriting Contest in 2016 and was published in *Two Sisters Writing & Publishing Second Annual Anthology* in 2019. Recently, her short story "Rule 49" was included in B-Cubed Press's anthology *Alternative Deathiness*. She lives in Cleveland, Ohio.

Salted Away

Craig Webb

"**I**'ve come from the salt mine," said the important-looking fellow led into my office by the department secretary.

"That's just great," I said. "Welcome to mine." I'd been struggling all week with the destruction caused by ISIS to the Assyrian World Heritage site of Nimrud and was in no mood for visitors. A modern political movement at war with ancient history made me want to strangle somebody.

"I'm from a real salt mine, Professor Stern. We've found something that might interest you." To a classical archeologist like me, the idea that something of value could ever be found in Northeast Ohio was preposterous on the face of it. There was nothing remotely associated with my archaic period of expertise located closer than Mesoamerica (although I dabbled in excavations at the Serpent Mound in Southern Ohio for the benefit of my Cleveland State University students). Still, something of potential interest found *under* Lake Erie was sufficiently bizarre to merit attention.

Of course, I was aware salt is taken from man-made caverns far below Lake Erie. No doubt, tours were available during my childhood years. Nowadays, the over-litigious nature of society renders such excursions impossible, although television crews are periodically allowed below for public relations purposes. You can Google some impressive subterranean vistas on the Internet.

◆

Arriving at the mine headquarters, I was reminded of the starkly utilitarian appearance of industrial Cleveland. This forgotten realm of muddy roadways, weedy fields, and jumbled structures appeared more like inhabited machinery than architecture. It was a neighborhood solely constructed for trucks and trains, with miniature mountain ranges of raw materials drawn up from the depths below and piled several stories high all over the southern half of so-called Whiskey Island.

Richard Ivers, the superintendent of the facility and my uninvited visitor at Cleveland State met me at the door. There were a number of safety procedures to review and a battery of liability waivers to sign before going below. A sternly worded contract of absolute secrecy gave me pause to consider the true nature of my visit.

"This is a three hundred million dollar operation," Superintendent Ivers said. "We don't want trouble over anyone's academic hysteria...."

Suitably sworn and intrigued, I was led to the elevators. I envisioned some sort of gigantic, slanting tunnel into the underworld, but access consisted of only two vertical shafts. One for elevators delivering workers and machinery to and from the depths below, and the other for conveyer belts belching up salt from the mine.

♦

Our descent was 1,800 feet of semi-dark clattering, with rough stone walls rising slowly past dirty, screen-reinforced windows. Ivers and I wore hard hats and reflective vests, and each carried a large battery-powered hand lamp, plastic bottle of water, and emergency cylinder of oxygen said to last one hour.

"If they can't dig you out by then, you're probably dead already," explained my stoic companion. This was the first time Ivers brought up the prospect of mortality. An immediate vision of being crushed under tons of salt somewhat tempered my former enthusiasm.

At the bottom of the shaft, we stepped out into a small island of light spilling from the elevator cabin, surrounded by a dry, surprisingly warm realm of absolute darkness.

"The salt sucks all the moisture out of the air and radiates a certain amount of chemical heat," Ivers said.

"Why so dark?" I asked, expecting at least minimal illumination in the vast system of passageways.

"There's over four square miles of cavern down here, Professor. It's too expensive to light anywhere we're not actually working."

We boarded a modified electric golf cart carrying a smattering of tools and started down the mammoth corridors, only partially illuminated by our headlights. I felt like we were traversing nocturnal desert ruins with fifty-foot halite walls of rock salt on every side and sand-like layers of loose salt under our tires. Only when using my hand lamp could I glimpse the continuous overhead ceiling of rocky, machine-carved salt forming our oppressive sky.

The corridor was cross-cut at regular intervals by similar corridors going in perpendicular directions. My hand lamp revealed that these were themselves intersected by numerous corridors parallel to our own. The entire cavern system must be a gargantuan grid-work of mined passageways interspersed by solid floor-to-ceiling blocks of salt crystal—a hidden cathedral of darkness beneath my everyday world. *I imagine Hades himself would find it spacious.*

"Why leave so much salt behind?" I said.

"To hold the roof up. There's at least 1,500 feet of solid rock and clay above the salt layer and millions of tons of Lake Erie water above that. At least a quarter of the entire area must remain as salt pillars. The spacing is critical to bear the load."

"Has the lake ever broken through?"

"Not here. There was a collapse under Lake Michigan. They blamed it on an earthquake, but the seismic shocks may have been caused by catastrophic roof failure."

"Would we all drown?" I asked, now imagining a second mode of personal annihilation.

"Not unless we were directly under the breach," Ivers said. "It would take days to fill the entire cavern. You're not going to drown, Professor. You're more likely to get lost down here in the dark and die of dehydration." That completed a trifecta of lethality I'd never considered previously. *Who calls archeology boring when faced with so many potential dangers by simply leaving the office?*

◆

Deeper into the mine, we began to run into traffic. Enormous front-end loaders roared down corridors bringing newly crushed salt to the conveyors. They were lowered into the mine in pieces and assembled below. Anything that broke down and could not be repaired on-site was left behind. Elephantine graveyards of discarded machinery sat rusting away in played-out sections of this vast salt maze. Someday, I imagined, future archeologists will consider this forgotten horde a gold mine of ancient technology.

After an hour of driving, we arrived at a corridor blocked off by drilling equipment and caution tape. Ivers got out and cleared a passage for us to drive through.

"Remember Samuel," he said. "Nobody hears anything about what you find here except me—absolutely nobody!" By this time, I had imagined a thousand improbable discoveries that might lay ahead, from lost anchors to a marooned time machine. After his morbid disclosures and reinforced warning, I pictured mass graves of miners or sailors from some forgotten past.

The corridor continued for about 300 feet until we came to a partially excavated dead end. Ivers parked our cart and shut off the headlights, submerging us in utter darkness. He searched with his hand lamp until he found a gas-powered generator atop a leftover ridge of loose salt. Starting it, the hollowed-out area beyond the salt ridge became illuminated by work lights. A palpable feeling of awe and dread swept over me as I wondered what lay beyond. Ivers laughed from atop the ridge at my obvious hesitation.

"Come on, Professor," he said. "History isn't going to write itself." Suitably chastised, I clawed my way up to where he stood.

At first, I saw nothing but a jumble of rock salt boulders strewn against the irregular corridor end. If there was some fossil or archeological pattern I was supposed to find, it was not immediately apparent.

I looked toward Ivers for clarification, but he simply indicated I should go closer. As I struggled down the other side of the tumbled salt ridge, a strange anomaly came into view. Amid all those jagged, machine-scarred surfaces, a smooth area of less crystalline whiteness embedded in the wall came into focus. It rose three to four feet from the floor and appeared to be an exposed segment of a curve, like a portion of a column or the edge of a raised dais.

I knelt beside it at an angle not blocking the work lights and rubbed the exposed surface with my hand. The distinctive feel, so reminiscent of other antiquities I've encountered, was unmistakable.

"This isn't salt, is it?" I said.

"Marble," he answered. "I chipped off a piece to test it. But it's not uncommon to hit upon impurities down here, outcroppings of stone, even fossilized coral reefs. This salt was deposited at the bottom of an inland sea."

"It seems man-made—carved and smoothed by someone," I said.

Now Richard Ivers paused. He stared up toward the rugged ceiling for a moment, exhaled a long sigh, and then walked down the salt ridge toward me.

"That's what I thought," he said. "I was hoping to be wrong." He sat down beside me and placed his hand on the smooth surface. "Are you sure this can't be some kind of natural formation? I mean, who could have done this? Please don't tell me I've found Atlantis in the middle of Lake Erie."

"I honestly do not know," I said. "How old are these salt strata?"

"Fifty million years, more or less."

"Fifty million! Then nobody did this. Nobody human anyway."

"Damn it!" he swore, jumping up and heaving a chunk of salt explosively against the corridor wall. "You said it was man-made. Try to make sense, will you!"

"Well," I sputtered. "I mean, it *looks* manufactured...or carved, at least. That's not to say humans had to make it. Evolutionary science would say there were no humans 50 million years ago, especially in North America. There were other creatures, of course, dinosaurs and so on, but we've never discovered any other creature known to create or modify objects like humans do."

"So, Professor Samuel Stern," he bellowed. "This thing—this thing right in front of our eyes can't exist? You and I are imagining the whole God-damn thing?"

"Hold on," I said. "There must be some explanation. For instance, look at these salt walls around us." We both turned our hand lamps on the surrounding walls. "See these horizontal striations. See the layers and the slightly different colors of the salt."

"Yes, We know all about that," he said. "Laid down over millions of years as conditions changed year by year until the ancient sea dried up. The whole salt deposit looks like this."

"Not quite true. Look at the salt wall over our, um…artifact, shall we say. Notice how the horizontal striations are gone. The colors are all mixed up, possibly even vertically oriented. Someone, conceivably much later in time, could have excavated a hole in the salt, placed the artifact here, and covered it up again."

"Yes!" he said. "I can see that. The…artifact could be from any time after the sea dried up, lost or hidden in the lake, then forgotten. But who would do that?"

"We still don't know," I said. "But it's a workable hypothesis. We'll remove the salt around it and examine it more closely. There may be markings to provide the answer."

Ivers agreed to assign a trusted group of miners to the project. They would have to work slowly, as heavy machinery and explosives were inappropriate. There would need to be supportive scaffolding erected around the artifact to stabilize the ceiling if, indeed, it had been previously excavated.

I calculated the probable diameter of the artifact to be 20 feet if it were, in fact, circular, and Ivers estimated the work would be completed in three days. We both left the mine with high expectations of momentous discovery. *All former shadows of doom completely fled my mind under the white-hot light of true discovery!*

◆

The next time I visited the location, I found the work of Ivers' men impressive, but the artifact itself far less so. The barrier ridge of salt rubble was gone, and our workspace was well-lit and spacious. The floor-to-ceiling scaffolding looked sturdy as it ringed the exposed artifact at a respectful distance allowing unimpeded access from any angle.

The artifact, however, appeared disappointingly utilitarian—like a huge vertical drainpipe with a cap. The top rose just over three feet above the salt floor, presenting a slightly domed circular appearance. The entire thing was approximately twenty feet in diameter, as expected, and the depth to which it might extend below the cavern floor was unknown.

"Not much to it," said Ivers as we stood together assessing the situation.

"Could it be part of the municipal water system?" I asked. "It looks vaguely industrial."

"This area of the mine is way out beyond the intake crib for Cleveland's water supply."

"Maybe a piling for some never-completed pier or lighthouse?"

"Not according to anything we can find in city records," Ivers said. "Even in the 1800s, they would have built a cofferdam, pumped the water out, and poured concrete. Nobody uses carved marble unless it's meant to be seen."

I walked down to run my hands over the newly exposed top and found the surface rough and gritty. This was not the smooth marble of the original surface.

"This still feels like salt."

"It is. The guys were using power tools and didn't want to scar it by cutting in too close."

"Then let's get some hand tools and really get a look at it," I shouted!

◆

Our handwork made all the difference. The sides still presented a smooth curve of polished stone, but the top rim was heavily carved with shallow, inset markings visible from both the side and the top. The domed cap proved even more elaborate, with two dramatic arched ridges perforated at regular intervals and meeting in the center to divide the circular whole into four distinct segments.

Inside these segments, a rich pictographic style took over, presenting a possible storyline or sequence of events that thrilled us with every scrape of chisel and sweep of cleaning brush. Ivers photographed everything, and I made detailed drawings and rubbings of every inch of the carved surface. I imagined the happy years I would spend researching their origin and meaning.

The rim markings were clearly some unknown form of writing composed entirely of intersecting circles, dots, and spirals. Better still, these seemed to repeat the same complex phrase or word multiple times, so its entirety could be perceived at any angle from top or side. Whatever this word or phrase meant, it was obviously important, although, of course, absolutely meaningless to us.

The pictographs were even more cryptic, consisting of three types of symbols superimposed upon wavy backgrounds of deeper incisions. The three symbols were small ovals with four declining curved lines (possibly representing individuals but appearing more jellyfish or mushroom than human), rectangular boxes of various sizes (possibly dwellings), and a cloud–like mass or growth appearing to increase in size from segment to segment (to which we could assign no meaning whatsoever).

In the two opposing crescent segments, the oval figures and box combinations increased in number and complexity within close association with the cloud. The two smaller triangular segments showed the ovals and boxes decreasing with the cloud's expansion.

◆

Much later, as I went over the day's momentous findings in my office, a feature of the rim markings struck me. The repetitive dots, while making up a small portion of the whole, were always displayed in varied groupings of five. This feature triggered an ominous flash of recall. I had seen or read about this repetition of dots somewhere before...with some context of fear or menace.

I ran computer checks on all known archaic writing systems and found nothing. I scrolled through my pictures of Nimrud, thinking there was some ISIS connection or even some reference to the ancient cities of Ur, Babylon, or Assyria. Finally, I tried a broad Google search, which kicked up an obscure reference to a deceased author of fantastically grotesque fiction, a Mr. H. P. Lovecraft.

Yes, I thought. *I used to read this guy in high school.* I remembered some absurd tale of Antarctic exploration and frozen plant beings still lurking in my subconscious containing this five-dot symbolism. I laughed aloud at the unlikely coincidence, deciding to reread this fanciful story when I found the time.

◆

I was called back to the mine two days later without making any progress in identifying the source of the artifact. Superintendent Ivers introduced me to a young intern named Henry Danforth working with his engineering department. Henry had designed the scaffolding surrounding our artifact and, during his daily inspections, discovered something important.

"This will knock your socks off," Henry said.

Danforth, Ivers, and I descended into the mine, drove to the well-guarded corridor, and approached the artifact. The young man took a small rock hammer and asked Ivers to kill the noisy generator powering the work lights. In the resultant silence, illuminated by our hand lamps, we watched him tap the side of the artifact. It gave forth a solid sound, which was repeated as he tapped the upper rim—being careful to avoid marring the carved markings. Then he carefully tapped the top of the artifact on one of the arched ridges. The sound produced was startlingly different. As Ivers and I drew closer, Henry tried several other top locations to similar effect.

"It's definitely hollow," he said. "And I think I know how to open it up." In retrospect, we should have postponed this irreversible step—but I am an archeologist. We always brave the desert or the jungle. We always open the tomb. The unknown is just that addictive.

◆

While Ivers and I were fascinated by exotic markings, Danforth focused on the artifact's construction. He probed everywhere he guessed the salt coating might hide a seam or joint.

Based on his careful observations, he felt the pictographic top rotated out of the thicker, marking-covered rim. He thought the key was the arched ridges and the small stone wedges he discovered locking this cover plate where each ridge met the rim.

We quickly organized the necessary equipment to test his theory. Five hours later, we had a small mobile crane ready to hoist the lid by chains hooked into the perforations on the two arched ridges (which now seemed obviously positioned for just such a purpose). Henry worked at the supposed wedges with his pocketknife, a pair of locking pliers, and a can of WD-40 spray lubricant.

Amazingly the four wedges came out with minimal effort. Danforth signaled for the crane operator to exert a small amount of lift and began knocking sequentially on the four ridge endings with a rubber, auto-body mallet. When minor rotation was detected, Ivers assigned three more workers with mallets to assist in the careful hammering at all four ridge ends.

Slowly and with generous amounts of lubricant, the top plate rotated free. Danforth gave the signal to raise it. A moment later, we were all hit with the most terrible, wretched stench anyone had ever experienced.

Our entire workforce retreated down the mine corridor as far as the caution tape barrier, with a good deal of vomiting along the way. Electric ventilator fans were brought in to help circulate air, but fifty steps down the corridor were as close as anyone could withstand. Ivers felt there was danger of an explosion or possible health risk. It would take days to have the air tested. He decided we'd have to shut down the investigation until then, but his young engineer was too impatient for such bureaucratic temerity.

"Look," Danforth said, flicking on his plastic cigarette lighter. "Not flammable, see. The crane's engine would have set it off by now if it were. I vote we see what's in that damn thing today!"

"I could fire you for that," Ivers yelled. "Who said you get a vote? What if it's poison gas?"

"Nobody's skin is burning. Nobody passed out," Danforth argued. "Sure, it smells like holy hell, and the air is hard to breathe, but that's why we carry oxygen down here."

"All right, smart guy," Ivers finally said. "You can take a look—if you can get anyone else to go with you."

The rest of the crew stepped away from the young, firebrand engineer with screwed-up faces of revulsion and distrust. It looked like the Superintendent would have his delay until I raised my hand. I feared we might have already triggered some primeval burial curse or even worse—so why worry about an ancient stink bomb?

Danforth and I improvised gas masks by stuffing our noses with Kleenex and using our oxygen tanks to avoid breathing the putrid air. It wasn't perfect, but it cut the smell enough to let oxygen and curiosity energize our work.

At the rim of the artifact, we shone our hand lamps down into a dozen feet of empty stone cylinder and onto a glistening gelatinous pool of inky-black goo.

"Damn," the young man said. "What the hell died in here?"

"Only one way to find out," I said, and we began to improvise the means to gather a specimen. Carrying only one hour of oxygen each, a degree of caution had to be forfeited. The pictographic lid was lowered to the floor, and the chains dangling from the crane's cable were fashioned into a sling. Only Danforth knew how to operate the crane. Therefore, I reluctantly volunteered to enter the ominous stone vessel.

Carrying an emptied glass bottle and screw-on lid from some miner's lunch, I arranged myself on the chain sling and was lowered into the cylinder. Since there were only two of us, and Danforth had to stay with the crane that made excessive engine noise, we devised a system of hand lamp signals in the darkened workspace.

The darkness of the cavern above and the glistening pool of blackness below made for a nervous descent. I had no desire to touch the inky substance with so much as my shoe. It took a delicate maneuver to get close enough to scoop some into the jar. Even more so when I discovered the pool's surface was congealed into a rubbery pulp. I had to utilize my own pocket knife to slice out a viscous sliver and skewer it into the jar.

In doing so, my hand lamp slipped from my lap and landed on the gelatinous black surface. It seemed to trigger a slow, sinuous ripple moving out to the surrounding cylinder edge in a disturbingly animate manner. I snatched the lamp from the opaque surface, terrified of losing my means to signal for an escape, and flashed it desperately above for Danforth's attention. Mercifully, he responded and raised me above the glistening, dark mass as it continued a languorous undulation seemingly quite out of proportion to the disturbance I'd created.

◆

Back at Cleveland State, I commandeered a biology lab and prepared a smear of my carbonaceous specimen on a microscope slide. Under high magnification, I observed that the substance seemed to be an agglutination of iridescent black bubbles. So small a sample did not give out the unbearable stench of the entire mass but was still distastefully pungent.

I used a drop of sterile liquid to prepare the slide and found it absorbed into the substance quickly. This lubrication appeared to create cellular movement as the bubbles expanded before my eyes. Had I not been positive the specimen had endured ages of internment, I would have sworn it was still alive.

Obviously, as an archeologist, I was far outside my field of training. I would ask a biology professor or a petroleum engineer to examine this unknown substance in the morning. I sterilized the slide with some alcohol and prepared to lock up.

Turning to collect my bottle, I was startled to see the specimen, initially the size and shape of a large garden slug, now completely filling the sealed container and churning inside like a liquid swarm of coal-black maggots. Afraid to touch it, I watched the bottle burst and gelatinous ooze spread over the metal lab counter.

Only then did I remember the ultimate horror revealed in that obscure Lovecraft fiction, *"The thing that should not be"* that bubbled up from some volcanic abyss to swallow and absorb all life before it—the fetid, murderous effervescence he called a *Shoggoth*.

I poured the bottle of alcohol over the expanding black slime. When it caused no effect, I ignited the volatile fluid with a Bunsen burner. Still, the flaming, viscous jelly grew and cast out slithering appendages of ooze as if searching to gain the floor.

Fearing I had made matters worse by introducing a fire hazard, I grabbed the large CO2 fire extinguisher from the lab wall and smothered the protoplasmic abomination with clouds of freezing vapor. The flames extinguished, and better yet, the creeping black mass retracted and diminished into an inert blob. I emptied the extinguisher on the damned thing, scooped it into a lockable metal container with the help of a lab tray, and stashed it in a cryogenic freezer where I prayed it would remain harmless, barring a lengthy power failure.

Afterward, I was so overcome with fear and adrenaline that I slumped to the floor and lay there panting like a winded sprinter until my heart slowed to a bearable rhythm. Then I remembered the salt mine, where the cylinder was still open, and the great bulk of the creature lay totally unfettered!

I shot to my feet, almost fainting again from the shocking realization of the danger I helped release! Immediately I called Superintendent Ivers at the mine headquarters to warn against approaching the artifact for any reason except to replace the lid.

"I'm way ahead of you," he said. "We're going to dig this putrid thing up and haul it out of the mine entirely. Danforth is down inside now, probing how deep that black shit goes...."

◆

By the time I arrived at the worksite, the worst had already happened, or so we thought. Poor Henry Danforth harnessed safely to a wooden platform attached to the crane's cables, had been carefully lowered into the mouth of the cylinder carrying a ten-foot length of steel rebar.

The acrid stench of the black mass had dissipated sufficiently for Henry and the rest of the workers to breathe through simple painting masks. However, the result was still exceedingly unpleasant. As his crewmates watched from the rim, Danforth began to thrust his steel rod into the placid, opaque mass of goo. What happened next was still under debate.

"It sucked him down!" one worker said. "Took the rebar and all."

"No," said another. "It came up and grabbed him. A big black claw of liquid fingers came up from all around the edges and closed over him like a fist!"

Whatever happened, it was clear Danforth had not fallen—since he was tightly harnessed as per OSHA regulations about the waist and shoulders. His complete disappearance suggested (however horribly) that he was torn apart in the process. One terrifying scream was uttered, and then nothing except the agitated sloshing of the black slime pool. Sending a second man down to try a rescue was out of the question.

Huddling with the grief-stricken mine superintendent and workers, I described my experience in the lab and my admittedly outlandish appraisal of our danger. Their reaction was both alarmed and incredulous.

"You're talking science fiction!" Ivers shouted. "I've lost a good man to something, but not some made-up monster from a ghost story!"

I explained that the "fictional" sometimes manifests in real life. If something is conceivable by man (Lovecraft certainly pulled this creature from his own troubled psyche), then it may actually exist. Before getting into examples of Jules Verne's Nautilus and Star Trek's communicators, the creature proved my point.

Danforth's platform, still dangling below, abruptly took a tremendous hit and splintered apart. Something began pulling on the chains with such force that the tip of the crane's boom slammed down to the rim of the stone cylinder lifting the back tires of the crane off the floor—displaying the awesome power and weight of whatever was climbing up.

To witness such a thing is to lose forever that part of your rational mind defining what is possible and what is not. What bubbled, crawled, or slithered out of that damned hole was glistening black madness. To say we were all *"like deer in the headlights"* is to imagine the laws of time and physics were still in play and not decimated by the horror oozing up over the cylinder, crane, and scaffolding like a slow-motion eruption of iridescent evil.

We staggered backward, unable to take our eyes off the abomination's advance. And it had eyes on us too—hundreds of them extending out on pustule stalks of ooze to peer at us with greenish glowing intensity. Mouths it had also, opening up in disgusting volume and all uttering forth the single fatal scream copied from poor Danforth. Chaos and unstoppable doom had broken loose, and we would all soon be trapped deep underground with it...in the dark.

Helpless and hopeless as we were, the Earth itself and the unknown ancients who buried the artifact came to our rescue. This squirming, slithering fountain of living glop had a weakness, a weakness that lay all around us. Wherever it flopped onto the loose salt of the cavern floor, a sizzling steam arose. Salt dissolved the creature at the slightest touch like a common garden slug, and except for the stone cylinder, crane, and scaffolding, salt was all there was in these caverns.

Everything that bubbled forth dissolved on contact with the floor, walls, or ceiling. The scream—the only voice the creature possessed, echoed throughout the cavern as it gained some primitive understanding of its captive fate.

Slowly it began to diminish, dissolving into a putrid, oily stain and retreating to its sanctuary of stone. We began using shovels and even our hands to throw more salt upon it. Ivers ordered men with front-end loaders to bury the damn thing in a white crystalline avalanche.

Eventually, I convinced him against totally destroying the creature. Who knows what could be learned from such an implausible beast? Instead, we resealed the artifact, buried it under loose salt, and closed off that corridor. I had a frozen specimen at the university and all the photographs and drawings needed to document this astounding encounter.

I began this adventure enraged over a present-day attack on ancient history. Now I understand that ancient history could return that aggression to our present day. If a Shoggoth still survived, what about its original captors? Did they intend to punish it or preserve it for some future purpose? And how, in God's name, did Lovecraft guess their existence? Of all the questions remaining, the unknown phrase on the cylinder rim still haunts me nightly. Perhaps I will understand its message someday. But for now, I translate it as—*Danger: Do not open!*

Craig A. Webb is a retired highway worker from Cleveland, Ohio with a BA in theater from Cleveland State University. He's performed with Shakespeare troupes, circuses and theaters. He writes plays, fiction and fictionalized autobiography. His novel *Varoom: The Passion of E.Z. Cash* and story collection *The Shadow Over Cleveland: Thirteen Lovecrafted Tales*, are available from lulu.com.

Fates Entwined

Jerry Roth

On the wind were whispers of her name, and they insinuated her demise. From an ethereal plane, a soul traveled to a human shell without knowing its fate. Children, with their resilience and adaptability, became something too easy to throw away.

Naming a child before *the turning* was forbidden, considered almost reckless. But as her child ventured into the light for the first time, the mother had a name already chosen. Was she spitting into the face of God? No one knew but her that the girl even had a name. She listened to the child's quiet breaths and realized they shared the same air, giving her the courage to keep saying her name in her mind until the mantra filled her up like a cup. It poured out over the sides.

"Anam," she whispered in defiance of the Gods.

The caretaker, wise in the ways of childbirth, summoned the spirit to the body of the newborn. Her grasp was the way a piglet came into the world. Harsh and precise rather than handling something fragile. It wasn't human yet, after all. Everyone in the room felt the heavy burden weigh them down, suffocating their chest with the suggestion of what might come next for the child. The caretaker snatched the child's tiny legs, with both fitting inside her palm easily. Yanking upward, she peered toward the privates to discover what the mother already knew instinctually.

"It's a girl," Salvi, the caretaker, said.

"Open her eyes," a voice demanded from a distance.

There were tools for that as well that made an appearance from a leather bag. Violence gleamed off the silver device and promised pain as it headed toward the infant. A scream welled inside the new mother, but before outrage slunk from her opening, Salvi's dexterous hands examined the child's eyes.

The thin, smooth surface of the instrument slid between and under the tiny eyelids and spread out to either side. Skin widened like canvas stretched by the wind. Even though *the turning* wasn't likely to happen so soon, anticipation stopped the breathing of everyone who witnessed the familiar first duty of the caretaker.

"They are normal," Salvi announced to no one in particular. The room expelled air in unison. The turning coming on at birth was rare, but it happened from time to time. Salvi's clinical attention to an infant was warm compared to a discovery of a child found amid turning.

"Anam," the mother whispered. There was a clicking of bone rubbing against bone when Salvi snapped her head her way. The mother closed her mouth tight.

◆

Life teetered on the edge of a razor and cut deep in every prolonged moment. Selma counted the precious days left with Anam. The girl's eyes never changed to a shimmer, but that didn't mean her child was safe from danger. Most babies that began *the turn* did so during the fourth week of life. One week away.

It was decided long before that day that men had no place in the birthing process. A belief Selma held firm until she had to face it alone. Although she didn't have her husband to reassure her during her darkest moments of doubt, she had an army of women in the infirmary to reach out to if that was what she wanted. She didn't. Throughout her three weeks of observation, many floated in and out of her room like a feather in a breeze. They examined Anam and prepared the way for Salvi's daily visit.

The women had been where she lay, awaiting the fate of their own children. With the shimmer reaching ninety–five percent of the population, it was safe to say none of her attendees had offspring that lived—revealed in the eyes. They yearned to be close to Anam. Selma saw their hunger and imagined they knew all too well what was coming for the small thing. When the chatter in the hallway quieted, Selma prepared herself for the night visit from the clairvoyant.

"Good evening," Salvi said before emptying her medical satchel next to the cradle of the baby. That was all she would say day after day.

"You were chosen as a caretaker because you can see the future," Selma said with a voice that trembled with each word. Caught up in the rhythm of her examination, Salvi ignored the new mother's comment. "Why all this pretense? If you know my baby's fate, why not plunge the dagger into my heart now? This waiting is agonizing."

As Salvi reached the point in her assessment that confirmed if the child's eyes possessed the shimmer, her arms stiffened like the hardest woods. An unthinkable thing transpired. Salvi turned to Selma and leveled her gaze at the frightened mother.

"So many without the gift of clairvoyance beg to know their future. And very few can live with the knowledge of an unchangeable destiny. Do you believe you are so different?"

Selma nodded when the words failed her but pushed the feeling of cotton from her throat and spoke.

"No woman's spared from this horror. One is the minimum pregnancy. All for the good of the world," she said with bile coating each syllable.

Salvi set off a laugh that began low in her belly, then finished in her nostrils. "Have you ever seen a child turn?" Selma shook her head. "But you've heard the stories?"

"A day or so after the shimmer takes hold, the baby crawls. First toward the scent of its father and then drawn to the heat of any living creature." Salvi nodded her head for the mother to continue. "And then it eats," Selma said, turning her head from Anam.

"And why does it seek the father first?"

"The father's hormones. His testosterone. Everyone knows that."

"You're right, though. The infirmary chooses caretakers because we see the future. A curse I've endured well before the turning began. But my usefulness is in seeing the surrounding signs that others cannot."

"What signs?"

The same breeze that carried Salvi into the infirmary room floated her back toward the baby.

"Your daughter, Anam, has a mark." A shade drained from Selma's complexion. "You think you're the first woman to name their child against the infirmary's wishes?"

The threat of danger propelled Selma off her bed and onto her feet. Salvi placed her palms out to calm the mother.

"It's normal and expected. I deal in superstition for a living. So, I understand." Selma loosened her body from whatever she intended to do. "You gave your child a name to make her real in hopes it will tether her to this existence." Salvi gave her a knowing smile. "If you would have been so bold as to invite your husband or other family members into your scheme, we within the infirmary would have been called upon to act."

"Act?"

Salvi nodded and waved her hand toward herself like a siren beckoning a captain to the rocks.

"Here is the omen the infirmary awaited so long." In the absence of gentleness, the caretaker turned the girl's foot over to expose two red birthmarks.

"What does it mean? They are just birthmarks. Nothing more," Selma said. Salvi saw the mother dig nails into her palms.

"Naevus is what we call the birthmarks. The superstitious among us thought they showed up on a child when the mother resisted a hunger craving in pregnancy. We now know better."

"What's the meaning?" Salvi ignored the question and returned her view to the birthmark.

"This large circle represents our sun." The older woman traced the shape with her finger. "The smaller but equally important circle is where we live. Earth. When I took measurements, they were identical compared to our celestial bodies."

"And the meaning?" Selma asked in a shrill voice.

"Anam, your daughter, will be the last child shunned for her affliction."

"The last?" Selma fell back with only her bed, sparing her from tumbling to the hard floor below. "Then you've seen her future. Will you take her to the basement of this facility like the rest?"

"No visions of her. It is this naevus that's invaded my dreams."

"But you said Anam was the last. She will show the shimmer?"

"I'm sorry. It's her destiny," Salvi said and headed for the door.

"It's a birthmark," Selma shouted at the caretaker's back. "You're wrong about Anam. A witch is all you are!" she screamed toward the empty doorway. "Nothing you say is true!"

◆

A sound disturbed the quiet of the house and everything within. It was a hammering that stirred Samael from his slumber. For one moment, the noise was alive in his head, where consciousness pulled in all stimuli to assemble delicate dreamscapes. As the throbbing sound penetrated his sleep, it stripped his dreams of their fragile nature.

The incessant thump became a pounding that lifted Samael into a sitting position on his bed. The vibration drew him off the bed and onto his feet. An invisible string coaxed him toward the door. The night remained in the throes of darkness, and his wife had another week left at the infirmary. Nothing good would come from a knock at his door, and no visitor brought good news at such a mischievous hour.

With a hand curled around the handle, Samael was content to let the pounding on the other side go on for an eternity until he heard a cry for help. A faint squeal passed through the wooden layer of protection. The cry was from no man. When anxious hands opened the door, Selma cowered in the cold air.

"What are you—" Her dark form, wrapped in several layers of clothes, thundered into the cavernous home.

"Start a fire," she said and moved further into the center of the home. "Now, Samael."

He bustled to the fireplace and finally listened as well as heard her plea. As he shoved small pieces of wood into the opening, he saw his wife as she sat on a couch closest to him. Adding more kindling to his growing pile, he stole a glance her way and guessed she had three blankets arranged across her body to give her the appearance of someone three times her size.

His construction of the wooden pyramid within the fireplace was perfect because the wood went up the instant a matchstick kissed it. Sitting back on his haunches, Samael marveled at his newborn fire, then turned to his wife.

"Why are you here? Is it over already? Did the infirmary take away the child?"

Selma tilted her head toward Samael, squinted her eyes, and seemed to study him as if he never spoke a word. "Is it gone?" he asked with more force than he intended. Selma jerked back against the couch as if the question had weight beyond its meaning. Samael turned back to the flames and watched them dance when an answer never came.

"It's for the best, you know," he whispered to the undulating blaze. "It's as dangerous to have a child that's normal as it is to have one with the shimmer. Friends and family are always waiting for it to turn. No matter the age." When he turned back to her, the animation of the fireplace transfixed her. "Our debt is paid in full. We're free now. This is a good thing. Our burden has lifted."

A small tear glistened from the fiery light and fell down her cheek. Selma shifted her face from the warm burning logs to Samael. Unwrapping the blankets in a spiral motion, she let the fabric fall to the couch, revealing a baby.

Samael's eyes went wide. He pushed himself across the floor as if a monster were in pursuit. A nearby chair halted his escape.

"What is that?" he asked with words soaked in agitation.

"This is Anam. Your daughter."

"Anam?" Samael heard the fire crackle louder when he craned his neck to glimpse the tiny bundle in the arms of his wife. "How did she not turn like all the others?" he asked while steadying himself on two feet for a better vantage of the child.

"She belongs to us," Selma said and positioned Anam toward her husband. The girl opened her eyes, and they shone as bright as the sun. "Shimmer and all."

Samael clawed at his mouth to stifle a scream and stepped back from the fiery eyes of his offspring.

"For three weeks, I sat next to Anam, thinking her a demon, despising my choice to have a child at all. Longing for the caretaker to be wrong, or worse, a sham. And as her eyes turned, I realized we didn't choose our children. They've chosen us."

Samael edged closer, dropped his hands, and attempted to touch Anam on the forehead before withdrawing his touch just as quickly. His expression softened.

"You must be thirsty. I know I am," Samael said and headed for the kitchen.

The air in the room returned, if only for a fleeting moment. Anam had a golden glow because of the light of the fire, matching her phosphorescent eyes.

Samael's hands shook when he handed Selma a glass. She smiled for the first time since she had arrived back home.

"These aren't the features of an animal or a vicious creature. They were wrong, Samael."

Looking into his daughter's eyes and hearing the crackling wood caused him to shrink back inside himself. He took a swig of his drink to hide his sight from the mother and child.

When Selma kissed the cheek of Anam, who had fallen to sleep, a knock at the door started her. Her attention swayed toward the entrance, but she saw that Samael never turned.

"What did you do?"

Bringing the cup back to his mouth, he drank deeply.

"The target of a turning child is the father," he said, looking into his cup. "No one is safe, but a father is the genuine target for a child in The Shimmer." Samael backed away toward the door and saw terror in his wife's expression.

"Don't do it. Please," she said as he opened the door.

Salvi and three attendees rushed inside. Their movements were swift, en-circling her with the precision of a military operation.

"It's time to go, Selma," Salvi said and pulled mother and child to a standing position in front of the couch.

"You're taking me too?"

"Your actions have led us to this decision."

Selma glanced at her husband, who had already tilted his head in the floor's direction.

"You've killed us both," she shouted to Samael. Hands grew stronger as they moved her to the door. "Not a word falls from your mouth as they take me?"

Samael looked at his wife and shook his head as they escorted them out of the house forever.

◆

A cloud of death followed Selma from her home back to the infirmary. There was no cushy room at the top of the building that awaited her. She clung tight to Anam.

"Will it be a quick death for her and me?" When Salvi didn't answer, Selma glided her head upward to the top floor of the infirmary. Light filtered out of the only lit level like a lighthouse from a gothic novel. Shadows of dark forms passed back and forth in front of the windows. "The poor mothers. They have no way of escaping their fate. No more than I did."

The attendees, along with Salvi, marched the mother and child to the back of the infirmary. When they could walk no further, stopped by a storm shelter built into the ground, Salvi turned.

"Your action brought you here. But we are nothing if not forgiving." Hope. The saddest of all emotions transformed the mother's face. "Anam will be taken down into that basement," Salvi gestured toward the door cut into the earth. "If it's your desire to leave here now and return to your husband. You will not share your daughter's fate."

The wind whipped across the steel doors as Selma stared down at the baby in her arms. The girl dozed in and out of sleep with fluttering eyes that flickered like the embers of a fire.

"This child's fate was sealed when I gave birth to her," Selma said as the caretaker nodded. "I knew our destiny when I stole her from the infirmary. Fates entwined."

Salvi gestured to an attendee, and the steel doors opened to the blackness below. The scraping sound of their feet on worn cement steps reverberated as they descended further into the murk.

"I don't want to do this anymore," she said and felt hands grasp her arms to guide her direction further down. When she reached the bottom of the stairs, she realized she had closed her eyes. They'd been shut the entire expedition into the earth.

"You may open them now," Salvi said in a whisper.

When Selma obeyed, she saw fireflies dancing all around her. The tiny points of light jostled in the blackness with no discernible reason for their movements. As her senses adjusted to her surroundings, the sounds came to life to break all reason.

The fireflies were glimmering eyes. No different from Anam.

"Illuminate," Salvi spoke to a nearby attendee, and the room went from black to a dim light. "This is the most they can tolerate."

Children by the hundreds bustled around the lowest level of the infirmary.

"They weren't killed?" Selma asked and watched kids of all ages scurry around her.

"Of course not. But that was their fate many years ago. Until we intervened. There are thousands of infirmaries like this across the world."

"Why are we told they are being slaughtered?" Selma asked.

"Fathers, mostly but not all, shun their offspring who turned." Salvi bent down and picked up a little boy. "When children began to take on the shimmer, the public got scared. Politicians instilled fear in the heart of parents. A path to the unthinkable was set in motion. That's when the infirmary was born."

"You wanted to save them."

"Men were already outside of the birthing process. So, it seemed logical to take it a step further. Then give them what they want. A feeling of safety. If they thought those that turned were being destroyed, they wouldn't take it upon themselves to make it happen. As humans, we all prefer to look the other way."

"They don't attack the fathers or us?"

Salvi laughed and placed the boy back into a group of other children. "Ridiculous."

"Then what are they?" Selma asked.

Salvi moved toward the mother and child and lifted Anam's foot to reveal the birthmark. "The future. It's true that I can see the coming, but caretakers don't see the future of people. We see the Earth's destiny. Your daughter's birthmark was the omen we'd been expecting."

"What does it mean?"

"Nature doesn't make mistakes. These children, as awful as they may seem to the world out there, serve a purpose. Bright light hurts their eyes. Their gift is sight. Perfectly in the dark. By itself, the change in humanity seems random and without meaning. But that isn't the case."

"How is Anam's birthmark of the sun and moon an omen?" Selma asked while staring into the baby's blazing eyes.

"The birthmark is the sign of a cataclysm. An event will cause the Earth to spiral away from our sun. These cursed children we safeguard will inherit a dark world, and in turn, they will safeguard us."

"So why did you save me?' Selma asked with tears sliding down the curve of her face.

"No matter what the world said your child would be, you resisted. You showed sympathy. Humanity."

Selma stood in silence and watched the children play. Flames cascaded in the air with every skip and jumped from the small forms. She looked down at her daughter and the birthmark that told of a new world and wept for the old one.

Jerry Roth is an award-winning author with works that include the psychological thriller *On the Tip of Her Tongue* and his short story collection *Throwing Shadows*. Although his writing career began as a screenwriter, he transitioned into a traditionally published author with his first novel *Bottom Feeders*.

As an Ohio writer, Jerry includes memorable locations of Ohio towns and cities in his stories to highlight the places that influenced him. The author currently lives in a converted 1908 Catholic church in Ohio.

Such Secrets as Starfish Keep

Steve Kaczmarek

Ohio, 1957 or thereabouts.

It's just lying there like a rain-soaked brown rag draped over muddy sandstones. I count four—no, five—limp, tapering protuberances that could be arms. Stubby triangles. The mottled skin shines, and if I didn't know any better, I'd think it was some impossible starfish, twice as big and hundreds of miles from the nearest ocean. Now, what would a starfish be doing tucked in among the mayapples and ostrich ferns in a lonely patch of woods?

Hirsch, ever the intellectual, is poking at it with a stick. The thing quivers like jellied pig's feet but otherwise doesn't stir. With each jab, it makes a little wet sucking noise against the stone.

"This sure is strange," he says. "Looks kinda like a starfish."

"If you say so."

"What do you think, Jake?"

"I think maybe you should stop poking at it."

"Hmm," Hirsch says, still poking.

He has one hand in his pocket and the stance of a bored suburban dad checking the grill marks under everyone's Porterhouse. Overhanging cypress fronds dapple late-afternoon sunlight across his pale skin and Clark Kent specs.

"Maybe some kids dropped it here," he decides. "You know, brought it back from a beach vacation like those people who flush baby alligators down the toilet."

"Why throw it in the woods?"

He thinks on it.

"Probably too big to flush. What do you think we should do?"

Hirsch wears corporal stripes while I have lowly mosquito wings, but he doesn't care much about military niceties like rank or duty. He might look like an engineer, but that's all appearances. He's even lazier than I am, and as we stand here in these hot, loamy woods, I know he's scheming about how to do the least

275

amount of work in this situation, starting with getting me to make the decision for him. Of course, leaving the starfish where it's at and driving away would be simplest. Let it be somebody else's problem. But the starfish is an intangible oddity even Hirsch can't ignore, something the U.S. government no doubt would want. That makes it what the Army calls a priority.

That's all on one side of the scale.

On the other are mounds of paperwork and hours of debriefings. Oh, man, explaining to Colonel Kelleher what we were doing in the woods in the first place. And that doesn't count packing the starfish up and getting it into the truck. All thankless work that could be avoided.

Because of my silence, the gears jangle up in that crew-cutted melon atop Hirsch's sloping shoulders. There's no sound except for our breathing and the little sucking noises each time Hirsch pokes the starfish.

Well, there's no escaping the reality of the situation, and Hirsch knows it. He whips his half-smoked Marlboro into the dirt.

"Aw, sonofabitch!" he declares.

◆

I find a cardboard box in the back of the truck.

The starfish is bigger than a Packard hubcap, and there's no rigidity to it at all. I'm worried I'll tear it in half trying to pick it up, not that I'm touching the thing with my bare hands. No, sir.

Instead, I slide one of the box flaps under the base of the rock, figuring I can kind of nudge everything with my boot.

"Hurry up, Jake," Hirsch says from the truck, not surprisingly having nothing to do with the actual effort. Rank, even meager, doth hath its privileges. "I'm hungry."

Food is the last thing on my mind. Ever since I laid eyes on this thing, I've felt queasy. I think I'm getting a little headache, too, maybe from a combination of dehydration and Hirsch's double slap of Old Spice.

I nudge.

The starfish folds onto itself like an insolent crepe.

I give the rock a swift kick, and with the *vbrrrttt* of a Band-Aid peeling off skin, the thing pulls free and plops into the box.

As we're barreling down the dirt road, Hirsch says, "Maybe we should have left it alone. I mean, it could be dangerous, you know. It could even be from outer space. Now that I think about it, we could have marked the spot and told someone to pick it up. Did you even consider that, Jake? Huh?"

Real leadership material Hirsch is, figuring all this out after the fact and looking to blame me somehow.

No matter. I saw *This Island Earth* at a matinee last Saturday. There was a flying saucer, a bug-eyed mutant, and Faith Domergue's big, gravity-defying jugs, but nothing that looked like the starfish. If it's from outer space, it's from some mundane corner where they lay around and do as little as possible. Hirsch would love it there. Come to think of it, so would I.

"Take a nap," I tell him.

He mulls it over and then pulls his cap down close to his eyes. In a few moments, he's snoring.

Yes, Hirsch is most definitely budding officer material in this peacetime Army of ours. If the Russians ever parachute into Washington or the Red Chinese charge screaming over the Rockies, it's heartening to know the Hirsches are here to lead us to victory.

◆

At Camp Perry, little Doc Garland shines a penlight in my eyes. He tells me to follow the brightness. It leaves annoying brown spots on my retinas each time he takes it away.

"Come on already, doc," I tell him, holding up my hands. "I'm fine. Besides, neither of us even touched the thing."

Garland is as animated as a mad scientist, flitting about in his white lab coat. When they'd brought the starfish in, he'd blurted, "Remarkable! Truly remarkable!" before doing a cursory physical examination of Hirsch and me from the other side of a hanging sheet of transparent plastic. Then an orderly in some kind of white anti-contamination suit came over to take our blood and temperature before another scanned us with a Geiger counter and tweezered soil samples from our boots.

"Well?" Colonel Kelleher says impatiently from behind Garland.

Kelleher is tall and lean, with the demeanor of a Halloween skeleton that keeps forgetting the holiday is for kids. Back when the Germans tried their best to kill him at Bastogne with snow and panzers, his steely hair must have been as black as his eyebrows, mustache, and heart.

"Oh, they're fine," Garland notes. Compared to the starfish, our status is no more urgent than potato salad left too long in the sun. "But this. Just remarkable, sir, just remarkable!"

He waves some gizmo over the starfish gleefully. It beeps and crackles.

"That thing's not alive, is it?" Hirsch says.

Garland winks at him.

"Wouldn't that be something? I have no idea. There's no pulse, no respiration, no body temperature. If it's from another world, its physiology could be completely alien. For instance, it could be in a state of advanced hibernation."

"Or decomposition," Kelleher grunts.

Captain Dunn, always looking a little worried, leans over to him. "Washington is flying their top men here in the morning, sir. Meanwhile, we've got the woods cordoned off."

"Morning? Guess that New Mexico debacle in '47 didn't teach them anything. Weather balloon, my ass."

"Yes, sir. What should we do with these men?"

Kelleher sizes us up with his small, hard eyes, his long face taut as a drumhead.

"What were you two idiots doing in the middle of the woods, miles from your post?"

"Taking a shortcut to this base, sir," Hirsch says without missing a beat.

That part is true. What Hirsch leaves out is that we can also get a smoke break in along the way and still catch dinner before the mess hall closes. In fact, we were lighting up when I spotted the starfish. If I hadn't been glancing down at the right moment, I might even have pissed on it.

Kelleher has our number. I can tell he misses a time when a field commander could solve problems with summary execution.

"That so?"

"It cuts ten minutes off the drive, sir," Hirsch offers.

"In a hurry to get to the chow line, were you?"

"Supply run, sir. Sergeant McCaffrey wanted us back as soon as possible."

I figure what's coming next is a reminder about protocol, how our duty post—the reserve fuel depot and motor pool—requires we follow a strict route to and from the base. That means main roads and regular hours. Instead, he grumbles to Dunn, "Peacetime Army. Keep these heroes under observation for the night. Then put them back on duty." His voice goes mocking. "After all, Sergeant McCaffrey wants them back as soon as possible."

Kelleher stalks out, and Dunn shakes his head sympathetically. If the colonel is the bad parent, he's the good one.

"Seems I recall that shortcut saves twenty minutes, not ten, boys."

Hirsch and I look at each other.

"Peacetime Army, sir," Hirsch says.

I shrug. "What are you going to do?"

◆

Hospital beds await us in one of the other rooms. Hirsch is snoring as soon as that melon hits the chlorine-scented pillow. I can't blame him. In the Army, you learn to sleep when and where you can, whether that's a doorway or a bump in the road. But I lie there, staring at the dimpled institutional ceiling tiles. After all the poking and prodding, it finally hits me that we might have discovered something from outer space. I mean, that would be the greatest scientific discovery since splitting the atom. Of course, we've seen where that got us.

A cheerful voice says, "Hey, buddy, you awake?"

I get up on my elbows. The room is dark, but I can still make things out. I see a wooden desk against one wall and a green office chair next to a clothes locker.

No people.

"Who is it?" I say.

"Come on, pal, help a guy out."

The voice is fast, upbeat, jovial. It sounds young, but I can't tell where it's coming from. My bare gunboats hit the cold floor and feel for my sandals. I pull the door and find the examination room dimly lit and deserted.

"Where are you?"

"Over here, friend," the voice tells me.

I start for the row of filing cabinets.

"Nope. Cold. Colder." I turn to the examination tables. "Okay, you're getting warmer. Warmer."

Before I know it, I'm standing in front of the big glass tank the starfish is in. It's lying there like a used shower cap someone tossed at the trash can.

"Red hot, partner!"

"You've got to be shitting me," tumbles out of my mouth.

"Relax, chum. Take some deep breaths. Smoke if you got 'em! I know this might be hard to believe, but it's all really happening, mate."

"How...how are you talking?"

"Telepathy, brother. That means I'm talking in your mind, but you hear me like it's through your ears."

I have to sit down. I roll a stool over, the wheels rumbling against the checkerboard linoleum.

"There you go. Take a load off, fella."

A million questions flood through my mind, and yet somehow, I can't speak. I'm numb and tingling at the same time. My heart is leaping. I must be going into shock.

I finally manage to say, "Just call me Jake."

"Okay, Jake, here's the situation. Some guys in black hats and sunglasses are coming to put me in a jar and take me away for dissection. Or worse. Now, I don't mind playing dead for a while, but I'd rather not make it official if you know what I mean."

Crazy as it sounds, I'm calming down more with each word.

"I need you to get me back to the woods. You can do that, can't you? You see, Jake, my ship is there, and, well, it's time for me to leave. You're the only one who can help me now. What do you say? Be a stand-up guy? Help a friend out?"

As he speaks, I find my mind becoming pliable, like taffy being pulled into a gooey, obedient string.

I know the guards posted down the hall outside have locked and loaded M–3s, along with a .45 holstered to each of their webbed belts. I'm not getting past them. That means I have to find another way out.

And that means I need Hirsch's help.

When I wake him, he's less than enthusiastic, even less when I explain the situation.

"You asshole, I'm not spending the next 20 years in Leavenworth for this."

Hirsch rolls over to sleep again.

I grab his nose. He sputters and sits up.

"Have you lost your mind?"

"Probably."

"Then what gives?"

I show him the plastic medical bag the starfish is now in.

"I'm helping out a friend."

"Hey, thanks, Jake," the starfish says cheerfully.

Hirsch's eyes widen.

"How'd you do that?"

"Do what?"

"Throw your voice. Who are you, Edgar Bergen?"

The starfish sticks up for me.

"Aw, give him a break, Hirschy. He would for you."

"The name's Hirsch," Hirsch says to the bag before catching himself. "What am I doing?"

"Look, I'll prove it," I say, setting the bag down gently and fetching a glass of water from the nightstand. "Okay, watch this."

I drink, and as if on cue, the starfish starts singing "Only You (and You Alone)."

Hirsch's jaw drops.

There's an overhead air duct, but it's far too narrow for me to get through. Besides, the grate is screwed down tight and painted over. The window opens, but we're four stories up, and there's no spout to shimmy down. That means using the sheets as a makeshift rope. With nothing substantial to fasten them to, Hirsch will have to help lower us down.

"How are you going to get off base?" he says while we tie things together. "You think about that?"

"I'm working on it."

Hirsch's suspicious eyes go flat behind those glasses. He gets a conspiratorial look.

"If he's from another planet, how do we know he's not some kind of invader? Maybe we're helping him escape so he can come back and vaporize everything."

"Aw, I wouldn't do that, Kemosabe," the starfish says.

"Like he'd tell us, Jake," Hirsch points out. He says a little louder to the bag, "Like you'd tell us."

I'm too busy gauging the makeshift rope to worry about it.

It's after 10:30 p.m. when I start Batmanning down the side of the building, boot heels scratching against the brick, the bag tied around my neck and slung over one shoulder. The starfish, heavy against me, feels like a child clinging to its father.

"You okay in there?" I whisper.

"A-OK, Jake."

My arms and legs are burning when I finally touch ground. I look up. Hirsch's face shines with sweat. He still looks dubious but does a half-assed salute before yanking the sheets back up.

Big as an airport, Camp Perry never sleeps. You can still see the lights miles out on Lake Erie, like a little city. Thankfully, it's quietest at night, which is to say, not as loud. I stay close to the building shadows as I sneak past the barracks and over to the firing range. I'm not driving off base without a pass, but if I can get to the far end of the range, there're some places where I can hop the barbed wire fence. I follow the scent of soapy milfoil and dank pond weeds from the beach. In deeper summer, this place reeks like a water buffalo's ass, complete with biting flies.

The unlit firing range is alive with lightning bugs and twinkling stars right here on Earth. It mesmerizes me, a wondrous mirror to the celestial sway above.

"Looks like the night sky, doesn't it, Jake?"

I stop.

"What is it, Jake? You got something in your boot?"

"Are you reading my mind? I mean, you can talk by thinking. Can you hear my thoughts, too?"

He chuckles appreciatively.

"Read your mind? Nah, Jake, that's science fiction. My ability goes one direction."

If he could read my mind, would he admit it?

"Trust me, muchacho," he assures me.

I start walking again.

"Say, Jake, can I make an observation?"

"You giving me a choice?"

"For someone who's discovered that there's life on other planets, you're taking all this quite well. I mean, you don't even have any questions for me."

"Like what kind of questions?"

"Oh, where I'm from. What I'm doing here."

"Okay. Where are you from? What are you doing here?"

"Sorry, but I can't tell you, Jake. You understand."

I stop again.

"You being a wise guy?"

"Aw, come on, Jake, quit clowning around. We've got a lot of distance to cover before daybreak."

We reach the chain-link fence with three parallel lines of barbed wire capping it. Everything looks formidable, but it's not really. The barbed wire is a reverse awning—after all, the goal is to keep intruders out more than soldiers in. There are gaps if you look hard enough. Truth is, the threat of federal prosecution keeps people away, so this is for show. On the other side are woods and then intermittent fields and roads and houses beyond that. If I had a heavy tarp, I'd just throw it over everything. Instead, I climb carefully.

The fence shimmies with each step, and I grip harder, the links biting into my fingers. Suddenly, I don't feel so assured. What if I hook myself or the starfish on the fence? It could all be over in one painful, humiliating moment.

"Why are we stopping, Jake?" the starfish says.

"I'm getting my bearings."

"I see. Remember what the wise man says: Hesitation is but the skinned knee of the soul."

"What does that mean?"

"It means quit overthinking and just get your ass over the fence, Jake," he explains pleasantly.

At the top, I carefully place my hands between the barbs, test my weight against my footing, and pull myself up, making certain not to snag the bag. I cartwheel over and drop to the other side.

"You okay?"

"That was fun, Jake!"

It kind of was. Who'd have thought simply getting here from there could do it?

With open ground before me, I sprint for the trees. There's enough moonlight to see a bit of trail that I know. I'm huffing thick night air, my sinuses running in the humidity. I feel like I'm going to blow my lungs all over myself. Hirsch's concerns cross my mind. For a moment, I want to hotfoot back. What am I doing? Have I lost my mind? It's not too late. All Hirsch needs to do is lower that makeshift rope.

As if to make up my mind for me, a break appears through the patches of silver maple.

I hold my breath.

"What do you see, Jake?"

A tiny white house beckons, along with a rusty blue Ford truck in ruts that are the driveway.

"A miracle if I can find keys."

The lights in the house are on, and I hear a Tigers' ballgame on a radio. Bottom of the eighth, the announcer calls. This is going to take finesse. While I walk, I want to put the starfish down, but if I can get the truck started, there won't be much time to—

Something dark and powerful pads around the truck. It barks.

I freeze.

"That sounds distinctly unpleasant, Jake."

The muscular cur pulls its mouth back. Rows of threatening white teeth glisten like a leering movie vampire's.

I'm painfully aware I'm unarmed.

No way I can outrun the dog. If I so much as unclench my sphincter, it'll lunge. My best hope is that it's on a short chain.

Cold sweat drips down my back.

Suddenly, the porch light erupts to life, silhouetting a giant of a man.

"What's going on out here? Jake?"

I'm so startled by the man's sudden appearance—*how does he know my name?*—that I don't realize at first he's talking to the fucking dog.

 Then his posture changes, leaning out as though straining to see and hear.

"Who is that? You best not be fooling with my truck." When I say nothing, he whistles, then commands, "Jake!"

The growling dog starts closes the distance, each step heavy and deliberate.

"Okay, okay," I say.

I feel the man studying me.

"Who are you?"

"I'm from Camp Perry."

"Camp Perry? Well, what are you doing here?"

"I'm unarmed," I assure him, my trembling hands up. "I'm not trying to cause trouble."

He steps down from his porch, the wood groaning, and I see he's in Bermuda shorts, a white tank top, and an untucked Madras shirt. He sports a tan fedora with a paisley band. And he's Black.

♦

The inside of his house smells foreign to me. I can't explain exactly why. It simply does. The tiny living room is full of old furniture. We sit in shopworn chairs centered around a Philco radio that looks like a battered, walnut-colored cathedral. From it, Van Patrick and Dizzy Trout preach at the Church of Nine Innings, accompanied by overmodulated AM squeaks and hisses.

"You a deserter?" he says, handing me a Faygo orange, his fingers like kielbasas.

"Not exactly."

My heart is pounding. I don't know what this guy wants, and we're wasting time. He stares at the bag with the starfish.

"Whatcha got there? Looks like you've been fishing, but I don't know what that is."

"I'm not sure either," I tell him.

He's curious, his broad, mustachioed face placid but brown eyes deep in thought. He looks like he wants to reach past me and open the bag with the starfish—and he's big enough I couldn't stop him with a howitzer.

Instead, he takes off his hat and rubs his shiny bald head.

"Best clean that before it starts to turn."

"Good advice," I say, hoping he can't see me shaking.

He'd introduced himself as Hannibal, a Red Ball Express driver who now hauls furniture and does odd jobs for a living. There's a photo of him on the mantle with a bunch of other Black GIs in front of a white-starred Jimmy. It feels hotter in here now. He drinks from his sweaty Faygo bottle and studies me with an old combat soldier's gaze while his dog watches like a gargoyle from the other side of the screen door.

"You fixin' to steal my truck?"

Cautiously, I say, "Borrow, maybe."

"Borrow." Hannibal mulls that over. He regards me, and his face goes all thoughtful again. Meanwhile, the ancient grandfather clock in the corner swings its shiny Edgar Allan Poe pendulum with purpose. I have to sit there and take it. Tick fucking tock. Finally, he rises to his towering frame like something out of Greek mythology.

"Where you going?" I say, my heart thumping a mile a minute. For all I know, he could have a scattergun behind the canary yellow archway to the kitchen.

He finishes his pop and gestures for my empty bottle.

"To get the keys. And I need that bottle for the deposit if you don't mind."

◆

"Why are you letting me borrow your truck?" I say while it idles like a sputtering calliope.

Hannibal has his hands in his pockets. Jake sits calm as a puppy next to him.

"Mister, I been on the wrong side of trouble before. Seems like there's no escaping it in this life. But trouble like yours? I figure a man going up against the Army is a special kind of desperate."

"I could have murdered somebody."

For the first time, he smiles. It's an easy, knowing smile.

"You didn't murder nobody."

"Don't be so sure."

"I'm sure. Anyway, try not to wreck her. This truck is my life. Well, and ol' Jake here. Both of us need it back when you're done."

He rubs the dog's ears. The cur could be smiling, too.

As we rumble down the road, the starfish in his bag on the passenger seat, he finally speaks again.

"Some adventure, huh, Jake?"

"Yeah," I say, still thinking about Hannibal helping me for no other reason than I needed it.

"Funny how you can't always tell about people. Makes you think, doesn't it?"

"What would you know about it?"

"Not much. But it makes you think."

"Look, I'm trying to drive here. You got a point?"

"Only that life's funny that way, huh?"

"Yeah, a real vaudeville show."

The truck cuts at least an hour off our trip, both from its speed and because we can take the roads instead of rambling through woods and fields in the dark. Hopefully, no one is looking for us yet. But getting to the starfish's ship is going to be tough. After all, the woods there are probably crawling with scientists and military personnel by now. It dawns on me. I don't even know what the ship looks like.

"What do you think it looks like, Jake?" the starfish says when I ask.

"I dunno. A flying saucer? Big and round and shiny like a fishing sinker. Isn't that what you guys use?"

"Where'd you learn that?"

"I saw *The Day the Earth Stood Still* a few years ago. That guy came in a flying saucer. *The Thing from Another World. Invaders from Mars.* They all use them."

I realize I've seen a lot of those kind of movies. I don't know what that says about me, but maybe that's why I'm not so worked up about the starfish. He's nothing like they predicted. No long antennae or a head like a green, bug-eyed speed bag. He's as threatening as a Kewpie doll.

He asks me to explain the first one to him. When I'm done, he chuckles.

"Now, what's so funny?"

"It's not a comedy?"

I'm surprised. How on earth could he have gotten comedy out of the story of an alien—played by regal Michael Rennie, of all people—with the power to destroy the planet but who instead comes to love us enough to want to save humanity?

"The hubris, Jake. Humans think intelligent life must look like them: two arms, two legs, and a face. Or, for that matter, it must look like you. That's not even true on this planet. Most humans live in Asia. So, even if a visitor was humanoid, why would it look like a European and not, say, a Chinese or Indian? Or even an Arab or Tutsi?"

"I'd never thought of it that way."

"That's okay, Amigo, you've never had to. It explains some things, though."

My eyes narrow.

"What things?"

"Your undeserved fear of Hannibal, for one."

When I say he doesn't know what he's talking about, he explains, "Your basal heart rate rose from fifty-eight beats per minute to nearly ninety. Even extrapolating from the initial surprise, it remained high for the duration of our stay. You perspired profusely, and your hands were shaking. This is a human fear response."

How does he know all that?

"I wasn't afraid of him."

"Aw, Jake. You're a modestly intelligent human specimen with some common deficiencies. But intellectual dishonesty isn't one."

That assessment so bothers me. I skid the truck to the berm and stop.

"He was a big guy, a stranger. With a big, mean dog who's got teeth like railroad spikes. If I was scared—and I'm not saying I was—I had good reasons."

"You were afraid because he's Black and you're White."

"That's not true."

"Does your culture not have a history of unequal treatment based on skin color? Am I incorrect that you even have discriminatory laws to this effect? You fear all the colors that aren't your own, and even many people that are your color, but Black seems to terrify you the most."

"All humans are afraid of others."

"Don't change the subject, Jake. We're talking about you."

"Now, see here—"

"*Jake,*" he says like a father who knows better.

I realize my hands are gripping the steering wheel as if it's a ledge fifteen stories up. I'm probably leaving imprints in the hard rubber.

"Look," I say, breathing deeply to calm down. "I'm not a bigot."

"If you say so, Jake."

"I'm not some clown in a sheet who burns crosses on lawns or makes people sit in the back of the bus. I mean, some of my best friends are—"

"Of course they are," he says cheerfully.

I fume, sitting there listening to crickets, watching flashes in the distance from an electrical storm over Lake Erie. Then it dawns on me. I smile.

"If I were a bigot, why would I be driving this truck? Why would I want to have anything to do with it or with Hannibal? For that matter, if I was so afraid, why would I be helping you?"

At this, the starfish is silent for what seems a long time. Then, he says, "Well, that just proves my point, doesn't it, Jake?"

"What do you mean?" I demand.

"I came here in a spaceship from an entirely different world. You don't even know my name. But you're still more afraid of Hannibal than me simply because your complexions are different."

By the time I pull back onto the road, I'm more or less calm again. There's no point in arguing with, what, an aquarium exhibit from the Crab Nebula. But to change the subject, I do ask him his name.

With sunshine in his voice, he says, "It's a series of singsong notes and low-pitch warbling you couldn't do if you tried. Sorry, Jake."

"Wait a minute. You can't even talk. How could making sounds be an issue?"

After a pause, he says, "How about calling me Allen?"

I give him a look.

"As in Allen the alien? Why not Adrian? At least it rhymes."

He chuckles.

"See, that's why I like you. You're quick on the uptake. Okay, call me Ed."

"Ed."

"Yes. You know, E D."

It feels like another joke, but I don't get it. He's amused with himself, though.

"Why not, Ed, you chuckling sonofabitch."

When we get to the woods, that part of the road is sealed off with a candy-cane-striped sawhorse barrier. The two guards standing watch don't look happy. I don't blame them. Even from the safety of a bend in the road, I can see lights moving in the trees behind them. They're searching but haven't found anything yet.

"What's your ship look like again?"

"You wouldn't believe me if I told you, Jake."

"Yeah, that figures."

The truck is parked a few hundred feet behind us. It's about half that distance to where the guards are. I don't know how I can get past them. I'll make too much noise going through the woods, stomping around on cracking twigs, assuming I don't trip and fall ass over teakettle like Jerry Lewis in the darkness.

"It's okay, Jake. I'll have to get there on my own."

"What?" I whisper. "I didn't say anything."

"I read your thoughts."

The back of my neck goes hot.

"You said you couldn't do that."

"I'm a big stinker, Jake. But I couldn't let you know. Human paranoia is too easily provoked as it is."

"You understand how creepy that is?"

"See what I mean?"

I rub my tired face, feeling suddenly naked, not sure what to do or think now. I smell the sweaty damp of everything on my hand while I try not to think of choking Ed—if he had a neck—for treating me like a chump.

But then he already knows all that, doesn't he?

"Relax. I didn't find anything in there I haven't before. If it's any consolation, the rooms of your cerebral house are a lot tidier than most. Tell you what, I'll switch it off. Like putting earmuffs on my brain."

"You can do that?"

"Would I lie, Jake?"

I rub my face again.

He has me set the bag down gently. I open it, and with surprising dexterity, he slides out. In the moonlight, his skin looks shiny and wet.

"Boy, that air feels good. Hot in there."

"You're not going to grow into something monstrous or anything, are you, Ed? Try to take over the world?"

"You mean like this?"

With a sudden gesture, he rears up on two arms. Or legs. It happens so fast that my mind can't comprehend it at first. I jump. He folds back down.

"Gotcha! I'm fooling with you, Jake."

My heart is up in my throat.

"Are you nuts? I might have screamed."

"Nah, you're a good egg."

"Yeah, well, I've about had it. Look, it's time you told me what all this is about."

If he had a mouth, Ed would be smiling.

"What's anything about, Jake? Life is an adventure. The rest is what we impose on chaos to make sense and get through it. So, I'm on an adventure. As are you. Our adventure together. What's truly important is not what life is about but what we plan to do with it."

He waits as though I'm supposed to gush with sudden enlightenment. Instead, I say, "That's it? That's the best you can do?"

He scratches—well, I can't really say his head—himself in thought.

"Gee, I don't know. I mean, shouldn't that be enough? Oh, wait. Let's try this: *Klaatu barada nikto!*"

"I thought you didn't see the movie."

He chuckles.

"I watched it in your head, Jake. Funny, funny stuff."

In the distance, I hear men moving around in the brambles. They might be closer now. Ed notices, too. His posture goes alert.

"Okay, I don't mean to rush, but I really have to leave now. You understand, right? A thousand pardons. Thanks, and see you around, kiddo."

With that hasty, unceremonious goodbye, he sidles off into the dense brush. I follow him with my eyes but lose him in the shadows. A part of me feels empty and conflicted, as though I'm sending a tagalong brother to camp for the summer while I'm left behind. The rest thinks that if I get this truck back to Hannibal and then can get up to my hospital room before dawn, maybe no one besides Hirsch will even know I helped Ed.

I start to head back when suddenly the forest comes alive with white floodlights. I spin around to see soldiers bearing down on Ed, weapons drawn, faces grimly determined. Colonel Kelleher leads them.

"All right," he barks, "that's far enough."

Ed looks to be getting into something. I can't quite tell what from here, but maybe it's the sandstone I found him on. Only it has a hatch now.

Of course, stupid!

The Army doesn't want Ed. They want his ship and everything that makes it go. The hardware. But they couldn't figure out where it was because it doesn't look like a spaceship. All this, including our escape, was a scheme to recover it.

Wait—think this through, man. In the confusion, I can easily get back to the truck and hightail it out of there. Act like all this never happened. No. Once they have the ship, Ed is expendable. What would Colonel Kelleher care if they took the starfish back in a couple of jars instead of one?

Before I know it, I find myself racing to Ed, thinking of nothing but his safety.

"Ed!"

That thing they say about time slowing down in a crisis is true. My arms and legs pump furiously, the flesh coiling and expanding with each labored step. Everything is unnaturally real—shapes, colors, sounds all alive with brilliance. One soldier has the olive pocket flap below the white strip with his name unfastened. Lewandowski. Another yells at me, but the sound gets caught in his throat. Colonel Kelleher—his blue eyes nearly violet in the light—spots me, and his mouth curls to give an order he's been waiting a decade to say again.

Their M-1s level on me, each man zeroing in on my body's center mass, lining up the kill shot.

"Fire!" Kelleher says.

Hammer clicks ping my ears. Discharging cartridges explode with fire and force. Bullets fly straight and true.

And then everything actually does slow down until still.

Except Ed. He waves a little arm.

"Hey, buddy. You okay over there?"

I can move. Carefully, I step toward him. Inches from me, bullets hang sparkling in the air like deadly Christmas ornaments. Dozens of men stand as waxworks in a museum of war.

"You can stop time?" I manage to say.

Ed gestures with two arms like, Jake, how could you ask?

"I would have said something, but I didn't want you to think I was showing off."

I look down into the ship, cool, conditioned air brushing my face. There's a lighted room at the end of the hatchway. Things hum and pulse with purpose.

"Of course, your spaceship wouldn't look like a spaceship, either."

"Ah, you're getting it, Jake. Okay, now that we have some time, let's try all that goodbye, lessons learned stuff again. I'll let you in on something. A lot of things don't look like what you'd expect. Take me, for instance. From your point of view, I don't make any sense, biologically and otherwise. That's okay. I'm here, right? That's all the sense I have to make. I'll tell you something else. I'm not alone."

I look around.

"There are others like you?"

"On Earth? No. But the universe is a big place. Just because a living creature was here when you were born doesn't mean it's from here originally. Next time you're on a hike and, say, a curious dragonfly hovers at your nose or a meditative skink looks you over from a fallen tree, consider maybe it's you who's being studied and not the other way around."

He's half in the hatchway.

"This time, I'm leaving for real, Jake."

"You're forgetting about those jokers," I say, gesturing to the troops.

"No worries. Gather the bullets and toss them into the underbrush where they won't hurt anybody. When I unfreeze everything, I'll wipe their memories accordingly. They'll think they're on a night training exercise, you with them."

"Hirsch?"

"Already taken care of. Also, the good doctor and the men from Washington, who right about now are wondering why they're loitering around the men's room in a Louisville Greyhound station."

"Are you going to wipe my memory, too?"

"No, Jake. My gift—my gift in genuine friendship—will be for you to remember all of this as it happened. Me, the escape, Hannibal, four-legged Jake, and finally, that you're not alone, here or in the universe. But the rest of the human race isn't quite ready for all that yet, so it'll have to be our big shooshie."

"Big shooshie?"

"As in shoosh. Secret, Jake. Even starfish have them."

"Big shooshie. You came up with that?"

"Catchy, right? Remember, I've been studying your kind. I'm hep! Feel free to use that, buddy." When he sees I'm unimpressed, he says, "Not poetic enough for you? Okay, how about 'In matters vital and true, we come together, man and not man, to pledge such secrets as starfish keep?'"

"Oh, brother."

"Too long-hair?"

I put aside his torturing of the language. Standing there in these steamy woods surrounded by frozen time, reeling from the implications of his almost limitless power, all I can think is that I don't really know anything about Ed, who I'm about to send off to his next adventure. The weight of it all, lost on me in all the excitement, crashes down.

"You can do so much."

"And more."

"It's incredible. But you must help humanity end wars, cure diseases."

"I'm not a cosmic Ed Norton, Jake, here to unstop your terrestrial toilet. You have to learn to fix your own problems, beginning with the ones you cause in the first place."

"A few years ago, I fought in Korea. That taught me some problems you can't fix yourself."

"Getting to know each other better is a start."

"Not when someone's trying to kill you."

He seems older when he says. "If you want to understand someone else, Jake, romp around in their shoes for a bit. Breathe their air and get a look at things from their perspective. See your world as an adventurer, not a conqueror, and, when the time comes, other worlds, too. Someday, your kind will point to one of those twinkling dots in the night sky and sally forth to parse the stars. Perhaps even your progeny will make that trip. Wouldn't that be something, Jake? Wouldn't that be something to strive for? There's a whole universe out there and more— space, time, other dimensions. A lot will surprise you, a lot will scare you, and a lot will make you shake your head—that is what you call that funny-looking thing on your shoulders, right? But a lot will give you great joy, great wonder, and every once in a while, great understanding."

He climbs down, then stops.

"One last thing. Despite it all, you're nobler than you give yourself credit for."

"I'm not so sure anymore."

"You helped me, didn't you?"

"Did you make me, like you have those G-men from Washington stumbling around?"

"Let's say I nudged you. You did the rest. You helped me, despite your latent bigotry and misguided sense of superiority over your fellow human beings."

"Hey!"

"I mean it. Stop looking down on Black people. And Yellow people. And Red and Brown people. And—well, you get the point. Stop thinking you're doing all you can in this regard when you're not, my friend. Do that, and you will have ascended the evolutionary ladder. If you don't understand, consider my example. I don't think I'm better than you, merely different, and I could transform this lonely little planet into a fulminated asteroid belt if I wanted to. So, noble as you can be, promise me you'll do better?"

How he says it—no jokes, no lightness, just utter sincerity—convinces me enough that all I can do is nod.

"That's my boy. Now, I really do have to go."

This I'll believe when I see it.

He gives a salute and shuts the hatch. Soon I hear a low thrum, and the earth quivers and then glows. I smell ozone, heavy and metallic. I stagger back, feeling the power surging beneath my feet, heat against my skin. With a wrenching sound, the ship breaks free, shaking loose muck, bathing me in light, an alien, space-faring rock twice bigger than a Patton tank that floats effortlessly skyward.

When it gets to the tree line, I hear him in my head.

"Okay, I really mean it this time."

I knew it.

I wait for another big speech. Instead, I hear but a few words, his voice close and quiet and not a little wistful.

"Take care of yourself, son."

His ship hangs there for a moment and then streaks away.

Everything unfreezes. The men find themselves with rifles aimed but not knowing why. Colonel Kelleher's face drains from a fierce snarl to fierce irritation. He sees me standing in the middle of the road without combat gear or a weapon, looking, I imagine, as though I've had a spiritual awakening the likes of which can never fully be explained.

"Fucking peacetime Army," is all he says.

A few days later, Hirsch and I are back in the very same woods, enjoying our smokes. He's studying the fresh crater into which loose earth has settled—I swear, it still feels warm—one hand in his pocket, the sunlight glinting off his glasses. He's bored and taking a drag on his cigarette.

"What do you think did all that?"

In a half-trance since that night, I let slip, "Maybe it was a spaceship,"

I bite my lip. How could I be so foolish? Ed wanted me to keep it all a secret.

Does Hirsch remember Ed?

His mood changes and his mouth turns down. He looks as though a memory is slogging through silt to catch up to him.

"Like a flying saucer?" he says, rubbing his chin. "Flying saucer. Flying saucer."

I laugh it off.

"Aw, forget about it, Hirsch. Think too much, and you're going to strain your brain."

Suddenly, his eyes widen with recognition. My heart sinks.

"Jake!"

"Yeah?"

"What day is it?"

That catches me off guard. I have to think, too. Time as I knew it doesn't seem to matter anymore.

"Wednesday. No, Thursday."

"Shit! What are we standing around here for? It's Salisbury steak night. Come on—the mess hall closes in half an hour."

I pat him on the shoulder before he double-times it back to the truck.

"Sure thing," I say, the tension draining.

Behind the wheel, though, I have to sit for a moment. Camp Perry is over that rise and across those sunburnt fields. In between is Hannibal's place, where I left his truck with a tank of gas and a juicy T-bone for the other Jake. In this spot, the air is still but cool, and with the moss and ferns reaching for the sun through the growing late afternoon mist, it could be a million years ago. Something might even be spying on me from under the brush, watching with curious, other-worldly eyes.

Through treetops, the sky is so blue and clear I can see beyond.

"You all right?" Hirsch says.

Am I?

Perhaps even my progeny, Ed had offered. Wouldn't that be something to strive for?

I'm better than all right, I decide. More grounded than ever but hardly earthbound anymore.

Hirsch joins me in looking out the windshield.

"Think there's anything up there?"

"I hope so."

In a rare moment that doesn't involve sleep or his stomach, he says, "Know what, Jake? Me, too. Only don't tell anybody. I wouldn't want people thinking I'm a nut."

"It'll be our big shooshie."

"Big what?"

I can't help but smile while starting the engine.

"Such secrets as..." I start to say. Then, watching Hirsch look hungry and bewildered but mostly hungry, I tell him, "Come on, buddy, let's go get you some chow."

Stephen Kyo Kaczmarek is a writer and educator in Lewis Center, Ohio. Much of his writing has been for nonprofits, education, and business and industry, and he also co-authored the textbook *Business Communication: Building Critical Skills*. More recently, he began submitting fiction to publications. Steve's work in multiple genres is available at *Every Day Fiction*, *Five South Journal*, *Outcasts: An Anthology*, *The Columbus Dispatch*, *The Ohioana Quarterly*, *The Worlds Within*, and more.